Love, Jake

An Outer Banks of North Carolina Novel

J. Willis Sanders

ISBN-13: 978-1-954763-15-9 (paperback)
ISBN-13: 978-1-954763-16-6 (hardcover)

BUGGS ISLAND BOOKS

Printed in the United States of America

Cover by MiblArt

Amazon Reviews of *The Diary of Carlo Cipriani*

"This is the story of a shipwreck. No, a survival story. Actually, it's a history lesson worked in to the tale of Carlo's life after a shipwreck told as entries in a diary to Carlo's daughter. Wait, it's also a love story from earlier in his life, and again now. An impressive work of fiction."

"Many twists and turns, lots of tragedy but always hope. At several points you are not sure what is real and what is the narrator's madness due to his loneliness. A very satisfying resolution answers all our questions."

"This is fascinating tale of survival, both of shipwrecked sailors and of how wild horses came to live on the Outer Banks. I enjoyed the characters and the character development, as well."

Amazon reviews of *If the Sunrise Forgets Tomorrow*

"What a captivating book. I read it in 2 sittings because we just couldn't put it down. Brought tears to my eyes!"

"To be honest, I wasn't certain I would enjoy this book. I've read other books at in the Outer Banks and a lot of them seem to be sloppily written and just capitalizing on the setting to prey on die-hard OBX readers. I was pleasantly surprised to find it very well written and descriptive. It was easy to visualize the island, the characters, and the story as it all unfolded."

"This book was captivating and it was difficult for me to put it down. If you like a touch of history and have a love for Ocracoke, this is a great book to read. It was very descriptive and made me feel like I was there. Virginia and Ruby are typical sisters who are loving each other one minute and the next they are disagreeing. I enjoyed the strength they displayed as they overcame many obstacles. A Great Read!"

Novels By J. Willis Sanders

The Eliza Gray Series
The Colors of Eliza Gray
The Colors of Denver Andrews
The Colors of Tess Gray

The Outer Banks of North Carolina Series
The Diary of Carlo Cipriani
If the Sunrise Forgets Tomorrow
Love, Jake

Writing as J.D. James: the Reid Stone Series
Reid Stone: Hard as Stone

Readers: Please enjoy the first chapter of *The Coincidence of Hope* after the book club questions in the back of this book, coming in the spring of 2022.

Author's Note

This is the third in a series of three novels that take place on the Outer Banks of North Carolina. Those who know this amazing place understand how it begs us to return every so often, like the tide tugs at our hearts and souls.

The first novel, *The Diary of Carlo Cipriani,* starts in 1521, and is a fictional account of how the wild Spanish Mustangs arrived north of Corolla. There's much more, of course, but why spoil a good story?

The second novel, *If the Sunrise Forgets Tomorrow,* occurs in the early days of World War II, when German U-boats were sinking ships off America's eastern coast at will. It takes place on magical Ocracoke Island, where four British seamen were buried after a U-boat torpedoed their ship. Although serious, this novel contains two of my favorite characters: twin eighteen-year-old sisters who made me both laugh and cry, sometimes within paragraphs of each other.

This novel, *Love, Jake,* takes place at Nags Head. It is decidedly contemporary, with a character who experiences problems that few were aware of in the distant past. It also contains romantic heat not found in the first two, described tastefully instead of graphically.

Each has a certain flavor. Each has a specific voice. Each should appeal to lovers of the area in different ways. And who knows? More books about this unique place may emerge from my imagination yet.

Please enjoy, J.W.S.

*Dedicated to those who know mental illness,
with its intricacies, its frailties, and its strengths.
It is not something to fear.
It is something to understand.*

Love, Jake

Chapter 1

It doesn't take much for a person to question their sanity, and sometimes it's completely justified.

I got married yesterday to a woman I love more than I ever thought possible. For our honeymoon, Andy and I drove to South Nag's Head, North Carolina. The sand and the shells, the salt air, the October sun glistening on the surf, the gulls crying and wheeling overhead—absolutely nothing compares for us.

We unpacked at our oceanfront rental, went out for seafood, and came back to make love late into the night. To start the next morning, I planned to make breakfast while she slept.

Instead, I woke to an empty bed, threw on shorts and a T-shirt, and went all over the house calling her name. Giving that up, in case she was on the beach looking at the sunrise, I went to the living room window facing the Atlantic, and that's how I ended up where I am now.

On the slight rise above the dying waves, where they transform to foam and hiss their final breaths, I'm sitting in the sand, soaking wet and shivering. My elbows are on my knees. My forehead rests in my hands. Vomit drips from my chin.

Yes, I'm justified in questioning my sanity. Look away, look at something else. Anything else.

On the eastern horizon, all crimson and shimmering and gorgeous above the ocean's aquamarine swells, the sun frees itself from the grip of the Atlantic.

Now—now I can look again.

Beside me, wearing a one-piece swimsuit in cobalt blue, Andy lies in the sand. Wet hair hangs in slitted eyes. Sand coats red-painted toenails. One hand lies limp at her side, the skin as pale as a nearby seashell.

No, I can't— This can't— Is this real? Did this really happen?

The surf rises and falls, whispers and calms, similar to the white lace on her nightgown last night, delicate and feminine, a deep V diving to her heart.

Yes, it happened. It really did just happen.

I carried her from the surf and tried mouth-to-mouth resuscitation and chest compressions. I turned her over and tried to drain the water from her lungs. I tried everything I could think of until I pulled her into my lap and cried myself sick.

What was she thinking? It's the second week of October, too cold to swim during the day, much less at sunrise. At least I saw her blonde hair before the suck and pull of the undertow took her away.

Footsteps shuffle sand beside me. "My Lord," a gravelly voice says. Walking a golden retriever, the elderly gentleman stops and takes a phone from his pocket to call 911. His voice breaks, he says to hurry. The retriever whines. Its nose, wet and cold, nudges my arm. Catching a whiff of wet dog smell, I look into brown eyes filled with canine empathy. The dog whines again, long and high at first, ending soft and low in his throat.

Sunrise beachcombers gather around us in a fragmented circle. "Is she dead? What happened, did she drown? He must be her husband, did he get sick? Yes, he's her husband, I talked to them on the beach yesterday. They just got married and came here for their honeymoon." A woman quietly weeps. A blinking man shakes his head mournfully. Someone covers my shoulders with a towel.

A siren's scream halts the murmurs. A vehicle engine rumbles near, a door slams, and a different voice speaks to me. I only know the words are questions because of the upward lilt of the inquiring tone at the end of each sentence. Another siren comes, whooping and dying. Paramedics administer CPR, check blood pressure, place a stethoscope into the hollow between Andy's breasts. Electricity from defibrillator paddles arch her upward. Water seeps from the corner of her mouth. The stethoscope returns, then the paddles. She arches upward again and again. Water gushes. Blue eyes half-open, unfocused and dull, will never see me again. The stethoscope returns. The paramedic listens, listens, listens. "I'm sorry, sir, she's gone." I roll to my knees and heave and cry again, until I'm out of both tears and bile.

They load her onto a gurney. Take her away. Someone lifts me by the arm and leads me to a vehicle. My vision blurs. My hearing fades until only heartbeats thud within my brain. Grief has driven a wedge into my senses; the world around me is awash with loss.

What does it mean to love so much? "Soulmate" doesn't do my emotions justice. White lace and kisses and caresses and *I love you, Jake,* are all gone forever, including the intimate promise of a future with the one person who knew me better than I know myself, cut fresh and bloody from my heart.

This is going to kill me. I know it is. I *know* it is.

I smell vanilla. My sight clears. My heartbeat abandons me.

The vehicle door opens. I drop to the rear seat. Someone reaches around me to click my seatbelt. A brunette ponytail withdraws from the door and it slams. Another door slams. Air from a vent, stale and warm, blows into my face. We bounce over vehicle tracks left in the sand. Tires sing on pavement.

To my amazement, I find more tears.

Not to my amazement, I want to join Andy.

Chapter 2

My father-in-law drives my Toyota Camry toward Oregon Inlet. I'm holding a cremation urn and trying not to cry.

It's a week later, Mid-October and the wind is up. Marsh on either side of the road gives way to head-high scrub brush and stunted pines. Everything shakes and shudders.

I shudder too—a human marsh on the verge of being ripped from the mud by the hurricane of Andy's death.

Stan looks my way. We haven't spoken since leaving Manteo, ten minutes ago. The person he pays to watch his wife couldn't make it. A neighbor is with her and he's worried. I see it in the slump of his shoulders, the twitch of his lower lip. A graying mustache hides the upper. Crow's feet splay from his eyes. Fisherman's eyes.

In my lap, the ceramic urn is cold against my palms.

Pelicans chevron the sky, blue as Andy's eyes. Gulls sweep toward the Atlantic. Clouds, dark and scattered, scud across the southern horizon.

Stan's suspicion fills the silence. Neither he nor Marie, my mother-in-law, attended the wedding a week ago. I never met Marie. She shuns the outside world and fears visitors. Andy never said why and Stan refuses to talk about it. Secrets lie in the eyes of hurricanes. The hurricane hunter aircraft flies in and

5

flies out. Both trips will scar it, along with those inside trying to discover the mystery of massive storm's origin and how long it will survive.

We pass Bodie Island Lighthouse on our right. It resembles a stack of black and white doughnuts, wide at the bottom, narrowing as it rises. The bottom doughnut is white, followed by alternating doughnuts on the way up, totaling five. Above the walkway, painted a shiny black, glass panes reflect a burst of sunlight. We continue. The burst dies.

On the left, the brush and pines end and huge sand dunes begin. One resembles a cliff, except sea oats whirl and stutter on its crest.

I imagine the rustle of Stan's unsaid questions: Did Andy have bank accounts? Did Andy have life insurance? Did Andy leave a note? Did Andy commit suicide?

Then the worst: what did you do to make her do that?

In a nearly three-mile-long ribbon of curving concrete, the new Marc Basnight Bridge rises over Oregon Inlet. Stan takes a right and parks at the fishing center. Rows of charter fishing vessels—bows sleek and sharp, sterns wide and stable, outrigger poles extended upward from their sides—wait at piers. Named *Fishin' Fool, Gal-O-Mine, Wave Runner, West Wind, Lisa J, Rock Solid, Fintastic, Fishin' Frenzy,* and more, they range in color from burgundy, lime green, robin's egg blue, pumpkin orange, aquamarine, to straight white and black. Beside the tackle shop, a mount of a world record Blue Marlin—nearly fourteen feet long, weighing 1,142 pounds—crowds a display case. Capable of reaching speeds over sixty miles an hour, these seaborne bullets of the deep are gorgeous, with spearpoint noses, silver sided bellies, navy blue backs, and forked tails shaped like slender scythes in black. Females grow up to four times as large as males. Tall tales say they've driven those spearpoint noses through men's chests.

I'm not surprised.

We get out. Stan gives me the keys and I lock the doors. A gust of wind shoves me aside. Stan goes to his boat, *Hope,* and climbs in. I follow, put the urn in the cabin, and help untie ropes from cleats. Oil swirls sickening rainbows in black water. In hints of silver, pinfish swim near the stern. The engine roars. *Hope* leaves her berth.

To our left, more marsh is licked by the wind. I close the cabin door and sit across from Stan. He's put the urn on the console between us.

A hard chop marks the sound with whitecapped waves not tall enough to wet the windshield. We enter Oregon Inlet Channel proper. I dread what will happen when we clear all land at the inlet itself, when we're open to the gusts that *Hope's* weather radio static says are reaching gale strength, including small craft warnings.

Stan spreads his thighs against the sides of the chair and shoves his back against the seat, bracing himself. I take the urn and do the same.

It's fitting how Stan named his daughter Andrea Doria Miller, after the liner that went down in 1956, three years after her maiden voyage. Andy did the same thing almost three years after I met her.

She's still cold against my palms.

Hope takes a violent hitch to the right; water sprays my window. In the distance to my left, the wind flattens hundreds of yards of marsh. We've cleared all land and are nearing Marc Basnight bridge, including the skeletal remains of the Herbert C. Bonner Bridge. Opened in 1963 to connect the northern Outer Banks to Hatteras Island, the Bonner Bridge closed in 2019, a derelict skeleton of concrete and steel, its pillars weakened and scoured by sand and tides rushing through the inlet.

Stan steers us into the wind. The rumble of the engine beneath my feet rises a notch. The pillars of both bridges rear before us: needles to thread, a gauntlet to run. Red, green, yellow and every color between, paint from countless charter boat strikes, as well as the boats of family fisherfolk, mar concrete with evidence of taught nerves, monetary loss, and livelihoods ruined.

The bow rears up and slams down. The urn's ceramic lid rattles and Stan curses. I hold the lid and he looks my way. "Andy's libel to take us down with her, Jake."

We clear the bridges. In the distance, enormous waves rise, curl, and crash, marking the bar. We're fools for doing this today. Weather forecasts say it's now or wait another week.

Spray coats the windshield with froth. Stan turns the wipers on. Despite the closed door and windows, diesel exhaust and the brine of the Atlantic combines with the faint aroma of pipe tobacco on Stan's coat and ball cap. The bow rears and slams again. Between the violent motion, the combined smells, my breakfast of eggs, bacon, toast and coffee at a restaurant across from Jennette's Pier, including my fragile emotional state, nausea shoves its sickening finger down the back of my throat. I swallow; it doesn't ease.

My parents first brought my sister and I to the Outer Banks. I was thirteen and she was ten. From Corolla to Ocracoke, fishing, history, wild Spanish Mustangs, great seafood, Atlantic Ocean sunrises, Albemarle and Pamlico Sound sunsets, I've loved the area ever since.

Andy graduated as a MRI tech, having previously graduated as an ultrasound and x-ray tech, and was working in Raleigh. I floundered in college but graduated with an English degree.

Teaching appealed to me until my first year with junior high students. It takes a certain amount of teaching at home for a kid to behave in class; many got none. When I complained to a friend, he suggested selling MRI equipment. I met Andy on a sales visit, and our running joke while we dated was how we both were transparent. We were twenty-eight but felt like thirty-eight. Old souls and all that. Late night talks about life and death. Weekend trips to Nags Head. Concerning her sunrise swim and her resulting death, I have a feeling her transparency was opaque. None of it makes sense. I doubt it ever will.

Tears blur my vision. The bow skews sideways. Spray fills the air and slaps the windshield. The bow straightens. We wallow in the tide.

Stan works the seatbelt around his middle. "Buckle up, Jake. Ain't never seen it this bad."

I do as he says.

The bar looms. We hit the first wave; the bow rises and slams. I have no idea how much stress fiberglass and wood can take before it splinters and sinks.

"Stan?"

"Yeah?"

"Where's the lifejackets?"

"Look yonder." He points left and then right, toward our windows.

I look. "What about it?"

"Look ahead and behind us."

I look. "And?"

He taps a gauge. "This nor'easter's got the water temperature down to sixty. Damn cold for October."

"And?"

"See any boats anywhere?"

"No."

9

"Whatdaya think that means? No, I'll tell ya what that means. We put on lifejackets. The hull cracks. We take on water. Cain't call the Coast Guard 'cause I ain't got the money to fix my broke two-way radio, same with the wore out bilge pump. We panic an' bail and piss our pants. We sink. The outgoin' tide snatches us a mile or more out to sea. Ain't a single soul 'round to hear us screamin'. Longest we'll last is two hours, not a minute more. Andy meets us at the pearly gates. Gulls eat our eyeballs. Hammerheads take our legs. Our bodies rot. We tip over. The ligaments in our necks give way an' our skulls sink to the bottom. Come spring, somebody surf fishin' finds what's left floatin' by, maybe ribs and a backbone. Or someone on a pier see's us. Or one of the charters trolls past us. Point is, the ID tags on my life jackets will tell the tale, and anyone who cares will know what happened, and we'll get a land burial and that's that. Personally, if and when we sink, anyone who cares will know we're dead, and I'd rather spare them the view of my ribs an' backbone. You get what I'm sayin'?"

"Thanks for your positive outlook."

The bow rises, the bow slams. A pipe rolls off the dash and clatters to the deck. Blackened bits of tobacco scatter. The window on my side cracks.

"My outlook fits the situation, Jake. Stick your feet in my boots anytime, you'll see what positive is."

We're halfway across the bar. The wind eases. The waves calm. My insides unclench.

Stan blows a kiss upward. "Andy's watchin' out for us."

"I could use some watching out, Stan."

He looks my way. His crow's feet crinkle, the closest I've ever seen him smile.

We hear and feel and see the rush and froth and suck and pull and rise rise rise of a building wave. The bow reaches forty-five degrees. I shove my shoes against the seat's footrest. We hang in mid-air. Stan curses. My guts rise to my throat. We hang hang hang and slam into the trough. I whiplash forward, the urn safe in my grip. The seatbelt cuts my middle. My neck cracks. Pain fires through nerves. Synapses tell me my neck isn't broken. The bilge pump alarm screams. We clear the bar.

Stan unclicks his seat belt. "Take the wheel, Jake. Want that life jacket?"

I set the urn on the console and trade seats. A streak of heat across my middle says I'll be sore from the seatbelt cutting me. From the base of my neck to my left shoulder blade, a stab of pain demands ibuprofen.

Stan raises a section of deck and sticks his head in. The scream stops. He replaces the section and stands. "Loose wire. Old girl's tougher'n I deserve."

We trade seats; the calm remains. Inlet clear, Stan steers us northeast. Clumped and scattered on the beach to our left, sea oats fade to suggestions of wispy brown. Between us and the beach, an oblong of thrashing water marks fish gorging on breakfast. A single pelican javelins into the mass, rises to tilt its skin-basket beak upward in a swallow, then climbs into the sky on broad wings to begin the process again.

Hope passes the first beach houses in South Nags Head. I don't look because I don't want to see the one where Andy died, but I remember how some of the shingles on the house beside it were loose from Hurricane Dorian a month ago.

We approach The Outer Banks Fishing Pier. Aged pilings of black and silver rails of treated pine snake towards us. Just above the waves, barnacles encrust the pilings. Three people fish on the end, two toward the middle, all hard core in this wind. Sunlight catches the lines just so, illuminating bellied filaments. Rods are flung outward. Bottom rigs plunge. Rods are whipped underhand. Pencil lures zig and zig in hopes of attracting Spanish Mackerel or Bluefish. Like everything on the Outer Banks, if you visit it enough, sight isn't necessary to see.

We pass more houses. Beachcombers wearing jackets seek shells and solace. Up ahead, the huge pier house and three wind turbines, each mounted on ninety-foot-tall metal poles in equal distances along the decking, announce Jennette's Pier and its modern concrete structure. I slice my hand across my throat, and Stan throttles *Hope* down. The aquamarine swells magically glass over.

"Andy's watching over us, Stan."

"Wouldn't be surprised, Jake. Wouldn't be surprised at all."

We go to the stern. Sunlight dapples the water. A pair of gulls hover. Orange beaks turn our way. Black eyes wait for a thrown tidbit: bread, bait, anything. We wait; they leave.

I remove the urn's lid and open the folded plastic bag. Andy's ashes, gray and crumbled, accuse me of not loving her enough.

"Why'd she want this, Jake? I don't —" Stan's voice breaks. I assume he means cremation and scattered ashes a mile offshore.

"You know how she loved the area. She wanted to be part of it when the time came."

"Never told me that. When she tell you?"

"When we met."

"Cain't understand it, not for the life of me. Had everything to live for. Smarter'n me, not that I'm smart. Kinda reminded me of that woman in that movie. All blonde hair and blue-eyed."

"What movie?"

"'Bout them orphans. Boy never got adopted. Learned how to doctor. Fell in love with that woman. Somethin' 'bout cider."

"*The Cider House Rules*. You mean Charlize Theron."

"That's it. Andy coulda been her twin." Stan faces me. "Did you love her?"

I see Andy on the beach. Waves of blonde hair mimic the sunrise shading the ocean golden. Hourglass figure in cutoff jeans. A bikini top and bare shoulders, freckled by long walks on the sand beneath summer sunshine. A smile seared into my memory until I join her in death. Of all the seconds and minutes and years of my life, the first weekend we came here is the best.

"I loved her, Stan." I look into his eyes that I can't see behind. "I still do."

"You ready to get this over with?"

"Did you tell Marie?"

"You know how scared we were when that bilge alarm went off?"

"I was more scared when the bow stood almost straight up and the sky filled the windshield."

"I'm more scared than that to tell Marie."

"Mind if I ask why?"

"She'll say, 'why that's so sad, but who's Andy?'" He touches the ashes. "I love you, baby girl. Me an' your mama'll be on directly." He removes his fingertip. "Think you'll ever remarry, Jake? Some say it's a fine thing."

"I haven't thought about it."

"You're not bad lookin'. Little flab 'round the middle. Might stand losin' thirty pounds. Kind pasty faced. Might wanna grow a beard to bring your chin out a little more. Let that brown hair grow instead of cuttin' it so close. What are you? Six foot?"

I tip the urn toward him. "You do the first handful. You loved her a long time before I did."

Stan fills his palm and closes it. His knees thud to the deck. His shoulder's heave. Sobs shake his huge frame.

I'm beyond crying now. I gutted myself with tears when I found Andy. Still, like when Stan and I were on the way to

13

Oregon Inlet in my Camry, emotion has a way of letting you know who's boss.

I rub his shoulder. He places a hand on the stern, works his way to his feet.

In a gray cloud, Andy fills the air.

I do the same with another handful. Then we take turns until she joins the molecular structure of the Atlantic.

Chapter 3

*H*ope clears the Basnight and Bonner bridges. During our return, those scudding clouds to the south congeal to form a gray mass overhead. Rain dots the windshield. The wind picks up. Invisible threshing machines cut and swirl the marsh.

Stan points. Beside my Camry, a Dare County Sheriff's vehicle waits. The frame height indicates four-wheel drive, necessary for duties like driving onto the beach to investigate the mystery of a newlywed husband's drowned wife.

We dock and tie ropes to cleats. The vehicle, the same silver Ford Explorer that took me from the beach a week ago, rocks from a wind gust. The door opens. Sheriff Scott climbs out. Dark brown slacks. Tan long-sleeved shirt. Dark brown tie that matches the slacks. Sliver badge on the left breast pocket. Brunette hair in a ponytail, which might reach below her shoulder blades untied. Like me she's thirty pounds overweight. Most men think visually when they meet a woman. I didn't think at all when she drove out onto the beach after I found Andy, but I'm thinking visually now. Sheriff Scott overdoes eye shadow, eye liner, lipstick, and blush on her round face. Her nose is straight and her lips are defined and full. Much as I hate to admit it, beauty hides in there somewhere.

She places her hand on the Glock bulging in its belt holster. Garish red polish on manicured nails assaults my eyes. A huge diamond accompanies the wedding band on her ring finger. I didn't notice this stuff before. Husband must be well off.

Rain dapples spit-shined shoes walking my way. "Mr. Smith, I need to ask you a few questions."

I played acoustic guitar in my younger days; do it enough you get an ear for tone. Sheriff Scott's voice is a wound E string: dull and lifeless, tarnished and in need of a change.

Stan climbs to the dock. "This gonna take long?"

"I prefer to question Mr. Smith in my office."

I give Stan the Camry's keys. "Sheriff Scott can run me over when she's done."

Stan's eyes dart from the sheriff to me. "Be careful what ya say. For what it's worth, I don't think you had anything to do with Andy's death any more'n I did."

"Just doing my job, Mr. Miller." Sheriff Scott and I get in the Explorer. Highway 12 takes us north.

At the intersection where a driver decides to enter Nags Head or take a left, we take the left to the causeway. The sound reaches endlessly on both sides of us, the perfect place to watch a sunset. Seafood restaurants line the road. A few rental jet skis and kayaks bob in the gray water to tempt late season vacationers.

The Explorer's tires thump over the first bridge, a short span named after Melvin R. Daniels. Walkways where people can fish line the sides. Dad and I did that way back when. The next bridge, similar to Basnight Bridge's arching span, takes us over the Albemarle Sound to Roanoke Island, home of the town of Manteo, the Lost Colony, and more history than you can shake a surf rod at.

The bridge touches land again. To the right is Pirate's Cove Marina. Charter vessels similar to those at the Oregon Inlet Fishing Center line piers. About halfway along the row, a huge yacht, mahogany trim gleaming in the drizzle, waits for the rich person owning her. Nice wild hair to consider but I'm too frugal to consider. Sixty-footers like her have all the amenities: kitchen, washer, dryer, king beds, walk in shower for two. Probably stocked and fueled for a month's cruise. The name, *Out for Fun*, sprawls across the stern. Lots of money on the Outer Banks. Some say too much, some say not enough. It's nothing like when Orville and Wilbur Wright made history with the first powered flight on December 17, 1903.

Names and history have always intrigued me. Either that or this stuff fills my head because I don't know why Sheriff Scott wants to ask me any more questions after we ran the question gamut for most of the past week.

She takes a right at the next set of lights, waits for traffic, takes the next left, and parks in a spot beside the Dare County Sheriff's Department's sprawling two-story brick complex. White pillars line the entrance.

Inside, her dress shoes click on white linoleum; my boat shoes do not. The top of her head comes to my eyes. Hers are green, intense, and brilliant. She stops at a door. "Restroom? This will take a while."

"Couldn't hurt. Got a coffee maker? A sandwich? I haven't eaten lunch."

She points a red fingernail. "Restroom's around the corner. I'll scrounge something up."

Done in the restroom, I return to smell coffee dribbling into a carafe and potato chips and some kind of sandwich on a table beside a chair in front of her desk. She places a digital recorder between us. "You okay with chicken salad on whole wheat? It's part of my lunch."

"It's fine."

The dribble stops. "Cream? Sugar?"

"Black."

She fills mugs and sits. "I called your attorney to find out where you were."

"Lucky you."

"Antagonism won't make this easier."

"You're not the person suspected of killing his wife on the morning after their wedding." I sip coffee, stronger than I like. She takes a bite of sandwich and washes it down with coffee, frowns, then adds Splenda and french vanilla creamer from a dorm-sized fridge behind her.

On a shelf behind her is a photograph of her and her husband. He's taller than me. Wears a three-piece suit, a bleached smile, and is cutting a yellow ribbon strung across an entrance to a community called Four Winds, according to the sign beside it. High-dollar people smiling high-dollar smiles surround them. Sheriff Scott's smile is non-existent. She wears a low-cut dress. Ample cleavage, not too much. The dress is red to match her lipstick and nails. His arm is around her waist. Hers is not around his. The dress ends at her knees. Andy said I have bullfrog calves. Said she didn't want me to father her kids because other kids would call them bullfrog. Sheriff Scott's calves shimmer in tan panty hose.

No photos of children. No photos of parents. Curious.

I use the silence to eat, drink coffee, and crunch salty chips.

To the right against a wall, on a table twin to mine, is a photo of what must be Sheriff Scott as a teenager. She's forty pounds lighter, no makeup, wears a track uniform. I'd never recognize her if I couldn't see them side by side. Another is there with her riding a four-wheel ATV, like lifeguards do on beaches up and down the east coast. Mud coats the ATV and her. She's tanned and smiles hugely. The husband has sucked the life out of her. Made her smile nonexistent. Made her cover herself with makeup. Money never makes anyone happy; it just makes them *think* they're happy. Then they wake up one day to realize nothing's worth a damn without love.

On a triangle shaped table tucked in a corner, a skull grins, teeth white and gleaming.

I nod toward it. "Someone you tortured?"

Sheriff Scott leans my way to press the recorder button. I catch a whiff of perfume. Her green eyes fix me in place. "Do you want an attorney present?"

"Do I need one?"

"Making sure."

"That's not an answer."

"I'll answer your question with a statement. I contacted the couple who stayed in the rental beside you on the same week you and your wife stayed. They say you and your wife were arguing loud enough to be heard."

"We only stayed one night. That happens to honeymoons when a spouse dies."

"Why were you arguing?"

"You know my attorney's in Raleigh."

"It's a simple question."

I shut off the recorder. "Why's your marriage on the proverbial rocks?"

"What makes you say that?"

This surprises me. I expected red cheeks and *that has nothing to do with you.* "That photo on the shelf behind you makes me say that. Everyone's smiling but you."

"One day of marriage doesn't make an expert."

"I loved Andy since the day I met her. Marriage is nothing without love. Or compromise. Or recognizing moods. Or giving space. Or—"

"Do you want to finish this or not?"

I eat more sandwich; the whole wheat is drying out. I drink more coffee; it's getting cool. She ignores her lunch. Finally, although I didn't expect it, either embarrassment or anger shades a splotch of cheek red, where it isn't covered with makeup.

A red nail hovers over the recorder. "No more personal comments."

"Eat your lunch."

"I'm not hungry." Without pressing the record button, she leans back in the chair. "Take your time. While you do, I'll refresh your memory concerning the events in question. "Last Saturday morning—"

"You don't have this written down?"

"All I've done since last Saturday is work on this case."

"You don't want to misspeak without evidence. Dare County can afford a lawsuit from all the tourist income. The press will crucify you out of a job."

"Because I'm a woman."

"Defensiveness is unbecoming, regardless of sex."

"Do you like it?"

I just said defensiveness is—"

"I meant sex. My marriage is, as you said, on the proverbial rocks. After my questions, I'll tell you to stay in town until further notice. We can meet for drinks and sex."

"Just like that?"

"Unless you want to skip the drinks."

"Refresh my memory. I plan to head to Raleigh regardless."

"Last Saturday morning, after I got the call, I found you sitting by your wife's body on the rise above the surf. Paramedics came and pronounced her dead from drowning. You didn't seem the least bit upset."

"I did my crying after I pulled her from the surf. If you remember correctly, I did the same in your vehicle. I also left a pool of puke between my legs."

"Your wife left her sandals on the sand fence at the end of the deck. A single set of footprints left the steps of your rental and went straight to the ocean. Did your wife usually take sunrise swims in October? The water's not at all warm then."

"She only swam when the water was warm. You forgot my footprints beside hers. They were farther apart than hers. As in running in panic."

"Her biceps were bruised. They matched your grip pattern. Care to tell my about that argument now?"

"She drinks—drank too much. I grabbed her to make my point. I wish I hadn't."

"How much did she drink?"

"Never drunk. She kept a wine glass nearby at home. Did I tell you we lived together six months?"

"Yes. Did she drink away from home? Bars? Restaurants?"

"The same."

"And you never saw her drunk?"

"No."

"Then why argue about it?"

"My dad died from cirrhosis five years ago. Things like that affect a person." I refill my mug and take half her sandwich. She probably doesn't like me asserting myself, but I don't care what she likes or doesn't like. The whole wheat is almost toast. Coffee's still strong.

"Did she go to bars much?"

"She went with girlfriends after work on occasion. She never got a DUI."

"Maybe she slept her way out of a ticket."

Anger floods me with an Atlantic sized temptation to wring Sheriff Scotts flabby neck. Then I realize I have a card to play.

"Says the sheriff who propositioned the guy she suspects of murdering his wife."

"You control your anger well. Maybe I'm wrong about you."

"I tend to get upset instead of mad. Sure, I got mad about Andy's drinking to the point of grabbing and yelling. I was mad about the drinking, not mad at her."

"The night before she died, you ate at one of the seafood places on the causeway. The greeter was out of town but came back today. She remembered you. Said your wife got loud there too."

"Andy was ..."

"What?"

"Prone to the rare outburst."

"As in?"

"She has—had a thing about lights. She clapped her hands and said the restaurant's chandelier was a portal to another galaxy. Since I was driving, she had more than her usual glass or two of wine. That had to have been it. That also led to the argument."

"You understand why I want you to stay until further notice?"

I'm tempted to tell Sheriff Scott I'll stay so she can screw me when she pleases but don't. She's the last woman on the entire Outer Banks—hell, in Dare County—I'd ever sleep with.

"I can't afford to stay."

"Did Andy overspend?"

"She'd go on sprees."

"Unexplained sprees?"

"Yes."

"Did that have anything to do with your current financial crisis?"

"I'm not in a crisis. I just need to get back to work."

"Expensive wedding?"

"Just Andy and me at the courthouse in Raleigh."

"No parents?"

"They were busy."

"No friends?"

"Some."

"I still need you to stay. Hey, maybe Andy left you a huge life insurance check. You can stay as long as you like then."

"Not that I'm aware of." I'm sure the life insurance comment is an opening to more questions about money. Sheriff Scott's been filleting me like a fisherman fillets a flounder. She warms her coffee, foregoing Splenda or french vanilla, and sips.

"Did you have joint checking and savings accounts?"

"No."

"How much in her savings?"

"I never asked."

"Checking."

"I never asked."

"A private wife. Was she prone to affairs?"

"We know you are."

"You'd have been my first, Mr. Smith. Mind if I call you Jonathan? What's the J in your middle name stand for?"

In my pocket, my cell vibrates. "This is my attorney. I'm taking it outside. Attorney-client conversations are privileged." She waves me away. I go out and close the door behind me.

"What is it, Mac?"

"Is that she-devil sheriff grilling you, Jake?"

"Like a well-done steak. Wants me to stay but I need to get back to work."

"You didn't tell me about arguing with Andy the night before she died."

"I didn't tell you about the greeter at the restaurant saying Andy got loud there either. She tell you that too?"

23

"Yeah. Look, I've known you since your dad died and your mom remarried. Are you being straight with me about Andy?"

"Absolutely. I'll never find another woman to love like I loved her."

"You holding up okay?"

Mac means mentally. Our conversation after Sheriff Scott's first interrogation ended with me bawling all over again.

"The initial shock is wearing off. For the life of me I can't figure out what happened."

"I'm sure it was an accident. I can't see Andy committing suicide, not with how you two were together that last dinner we had. All that kissing and smiling and holding hands means a lot."

"I hear you. Still, I need to know what happened. Did you call just to check on me and the sheriff?"

"Sorry, I forgot. I got in touch with Andy's attorney. He says she bought a life insurance policy with you as beneficiary a year ago. If sheriff she-devil rules Andy's death an accident, you're going to have enough funds to ignore work for a very long time."

"How long a time?"

"If invested intelligently, the rest of your life."

My knees sag. I thump against the wall. "Give me a minute, okay?"

"Sure."

I take several deep breaths. Andy's thoughtfulness is either a gift or a curse. A gift if the sheriff doesn't find out. A curse in the form of a motive if she does.

"Ok, Mac. How much?"

"Three million dollars."

Chapter 4

The phone slips from my fingers and clatters to the white linoleum. I grab it and stand. "C'mon, Mac. A life insurance policy worth three-million-dollars?"

"More proof she loved you, Jake."

The aroma of coffee makes me turn. Sheriff Scott, who just heard the perfect motive for murder, stands in the doorway.

"Got to go, Mac. Call you later."

"Well, well, Jonathan. Your case just got a lot more interesting." Sheriff Scott returns to the desk chair. "Close the door and sit."

I do both. "That doesn't mean a damn thing. All your evidence is circumstantial. Married couples argue and accidents happen. No district attorney in his right mind will charge me with murder."

"Her."

"Her what?"

"*Her* right mind. Our DA's a woman."

"Unlike you, is she happily married? I can call a string of witnesses that'll vouch for how much Andy and I loved each other."

"You sound so romantic."

"I am—was—hope to be again one day."

"Life can throw us the worst curve balls, can't it?"

"Do you know how unprofessional you are?"

"It's been building for a long time."

"Where does my case stand?"

"My husband has made a fool of me on too many occasions. Since my team couldn't find a suicide note, I don't intend to prosecute an accidental drowning as murder and be made a fool of again, but in public. Besides, the autopsy report showed no drugs, no skin under her nails from a fight, and you don't have any wounds."

I close my eyes at the thought of a scalpel slicing a Y incision into Andy's chest, across her breasts and down the gentle rise of her stomach, leaving a bloodless line in her soft skin where I kissed and trailed my tongue only a week ago. The thought of a surgical saw whining its way into her skull, hair and bone burning, filling the air with that horrible smell, her brain taken out and studied, the grayness of the shining globe that defined Andy as Andy, along with her heart, to be removed and sliced and examined and everything stuffed back into her pale body, to be taken to the funeral home, to be placed in a cardboard box and reduced to bits of ash and bone, to be ground into spreadable grit after, which is now embedded under my fingernails, is almost unbearable.

"You didn't have to mention the autopsy."

"You know what?" Sheriff Scott asks the ceiling. "If I had anywhere close to that kind of money, I know exactly what I'd do. Hell, if I could get out of this crap marriage, I'd do it anyway."

"Go to school to be a coroner?"

"Not even close, Jonathan. I happen to be a month pregnant, so those dreams are long gone. What are your dreams now? Other than finding another woman to love?"

"I like my job. I'm going back to work."

"Do you like surf fishing? Could do that all you want."

"I love this area. I'll be back."

Sheriff Scott raises her coffee mug and tips it toward me. "It's a date. I'll bring the chicken salad on whole wheat and the coffee and the chips."

I leave her office and call Stan to pick me up. To hell with getting sheriff she-devil to drive me anywhere.

Stan answers. "Jake, I just got a call from some guy who claims he's Andy's attorney. He said if her death is determined to be an accident, I'll get a life insurance check for three million dollars."

Andy's attorney must've held that information back from Mac. "How do you feel about that?"

"How do you feel about it? He said you'll get one too."

"Floored covers it."

"Me too. I mean, I hate to get money because Andy died, but I sure can use it."

"I understand, Stan. You can replace your two-way radio and bilge pump. You can even retire if you want."

"What I can do is afford better help for Marie. Can't stand much time with her. What're you gonna do now?"

"Unless a wild hair hits me, I'll keep working. I like my job and I've got friends there."

"You won't be friends if you tell them about that three million dollars."

"I'll keep that to myself." I tell Stan I need a ride. He says he's on the way.

* * *

I take Stan to his place and wish him well, drive back to Nags Head and pay the two-dollar fee to walk Jennette's Pier. On a metal pole outside the double doors, a huge pair of metal-bodied binoculars say to look down the beach for the house Andy rented for our honeymoon. I don't. This feeling congeals in the back of my throat. It's not nausea, not fear, but the realization that a glimpse of that house will send me into the same crying jag I experienced when I found Andy face down in the surf. Sobbing and vomiting simultaneously over a death you can't get over is a sure way to insanity.

I wonder if her sandals still hang on the sand fence at the base of the deck. The only thing I can think is she hung them there before she went swimming.

But did she go swimming? Was it an accident or not? Did Marie pass on whatever issues she has—they must be mental issues—to Andy?

Stupid questions. Andy was perfect in every way.

My boat shoes slap the pier's decking. The wind turbines whir above me, rhythm rising and falling like a Monk's chant: *ohmm, ohmm, ohmm.* I palm the first aluminum pole—cold, hollow, and thrumming—resonating my own heart.

A pyramid sinker and twin baited hooks on a bottom rig slings back, someone about to cast. A pinfish flops beneath a bench. A brazen gull snakes its neck out, snatches it and swallows it whole. Its neck bulges and convulses, the squirming meal trying to escape the inevitable.

I pass the second and third turbines. Andy's calm is fading. Swells gather and roll. On the older wooden piers, a person can feel the ocean's rise and fall beneath their feet in the sway of the gray planks, curled and cracking.

The inevitable seizes me. I leave the pier and drive the Camry to South Nags Head to find the rental named Endless Love.

I was touched when Andy surprised me by driving there after the wedding reception. Such a name must mean she loved me like I loved her.

After dinner, I went to the deck overlooking the beach. She came out in a lace nightgown, white and sheer. Starlight illuminated those blue eyes, the rise and fall of her breasts, lips shaded red, blonde hair down her back, thick and heavy. Ocean mist carried her perfume like nothing ever invented, shimmered on our naked bodies like nothing ever imagined.

Exhausted, we collapsed on the sofa. Andy drank more. We argued. I grabbed her arms. I apologized. We went to bed and made love again.

For the last time.

No cars fill Endless Love's driveway. I park, go underneath the stilted structure, see the pink sandals on the fence.

And everything goes black.

Is it possible to vomit and cry while unconscious? I wake to my cheek in sandy puke and tears crusted in my eyes.

The sun is setting in the west, maybe an hour to go. Pink shimmers of ribboned clouds streak the horizon. I stay long enough to bury the sandals beneath the fence and tell Andy goodbye.

A quick shower and change of clothes in my hotel room later, I drive to one of the causeway restaurants. Not the one Andy and I went to. The greeter takes me to a table overlooking the sound and gives me a menu. I order a craft beer from the waiter, along with broiled flounder, shrimp, and scallops, a salad with vinaigrette to start. I'm a seafood fanatic, nausea be damned.

A young couple paddles kayaks beside the endless marsh. Gulls sit on pier pilings that support nothing. In the distance, as if it's growing from the marsh, a lone house—ramshackle gray—makes a memory for someone's past. It was there when I was a boy. How can something last so long in a place of nor'easters, hurricanes, floods, and gale-force winds that rise on a whim?

My beer comes. I gulp half the bitter coldness. My food comes. I pick at it and the salad. The waiter brings a Styrofoam carton. I put a credit card on the table, and my cell buzzes in my pocket. Great, it's my mother.

"How is everything, Jonathan? Are you doing all right?"

Mom's always proper. No *how's it goin'? You doin' all right?* for her, even though she's from North Carolina

"I'm getting a bite, Mom. You?"

"I want to make sure you aren't angry with me for not coming down for the— What do you call going out on a boat and spreading ashes?"

"I'm not angry. How's things in Maryland? Michael trying some new sensational case?"

"He just finished one. I mustn't talk about it, so he says. Are you going back to Raleigh soon?"

"In the morning. I'll have tomorrow to recuperate for work Monday."

"Jonathan?"

"Yes, Mom."

"You mustn't blame yourself. Something wasn't right about Andy."

"The police ruled it an accident."

"Of course they did. Are your finances in order? You know, with you missing work for a week."

"Everything's fine."

"I only want you to be happy. You know that, Jonathan, I'm sure."

"I know, Mom. Look, I'm tired and—"

"I won't hold you up. I only wanted to make sure you aren't angry."

"Not at all, goodnight."

Mom watches a lot of those PBS shows, what Andy called British soap operas. She thinks because she married a high-end Baltimore attorney, I'm entitled to a better wife than she thought Andy was. I finish the last swallow of lukewarm beer and put the bottle down hard enough to catch the attention of a woman a few tables away. No, Mom, Andy was perfect. You'd do well to remember that.

On my way to the door, I hear an acoustic guitar, the tap of drums, a saxophone's voice, melodic and thick, and the heavy *dum, dum, dum* of an electric bass running a minor scale. A band is setting up in the lounge. I take a booth. A waitress takes my order of a local favorite, a High Tide. Mixed with vodka, rum, gin, cranberry juice, and a splash or orange juice, it's not something to drink and then go swimming. What the hell, I'll have one or two and make the short drive to my room without a problem.

In the corner by the bar, a huge bouncer, tattoos on his arms like sleeves, black goatee decorating his chin, biceps bulging, scans the building crowd. This guy lifts weights seriously. I look away before he decides to lift me.

The drink comes. The band starts an Eagle's cover: *Lyin' Eyes*. The drink goes down as smooth as any drink I've ever had. The second loosens my brain enough to make me wonder if I missed any clues to Andy's death. The third makes me slouch in the booth. The fourth hazes the lights in and out. Like my wife, I'm sucked inside a portal to another galaxy and really don't give a damn. The lights darken. Passing out? Who cares? That bouncer can dump me in the shrubs. I'll stumble to the Camry when I wake up and drive to the hotel to sleep off the hangover.

Chapter 5

My head's been run over by jet ski. A low rumble reverberates between my ears. My mouth is filled with glue, eyelids too, which I refuse to open for fear my skull will split and empty the alcohol-congealed mush in my head onto my pillow. Dingy light shines through curtains and my eyelids, so I made it back to my room and don't remember how. The bed rises and falls, then yaws sideways. Maybe Stan threw me onboard *Hope* and plans to dump me out with Andy. At the moment it'd be a relief.

I roll over, clamp my eyes tighter.

Thinking back to the previous week, I've hardly slept. Dreams and nightmares, or a combination of the two, woke me with the sun. This twilight moment is when we drift between waking and reality, where we almost touch what we desire most of all.

Andy's hair is heavy in my hands. It tended toward coarse instead of silky, waves instead of straight. Humid summer afternoons made it frizz. We spent a weekend in Clarksville, Virginia, at Occoneechee State Park our first summer, in a log cabin on Kerr Lake, what the locals call Buggs Island Lake. Boats motored by. A pair of ospreys glided overhead, white underbodies darkening to black wingtips. Fire glowed in the fireplace regardless of the ninety-degree heat. We took turns dripping sweat on each other, bodies slick, heaving. Afterward she told me I was filled with too much love for one woman. I told her she was all the woman I could ever want.

Her whispers come, warm breath in my ear: *I'm a star, I'm a meteor, I'm destined to burn out long before you will. Thank you, Jake, for guiding me through the galaxy, but I'll leave one bright morning, with a red sunrise calling.*

Slap-slap.

I wake but keep my eyes closed. Just freaking great, alcohol poisoning is making me dream a fish is slapping my face.

The sun brightens the curtains. Midday at least, but the bed still yaws and the rumble still purrs between my ears.

Slap-slap.

"I've seen drunk but not this drunk. It's a wonder since I'm a sheriff."

Unbelievable. The waitress phoned Sheriff Scott, who threw me in jail so I wouldn't drive. I open my eyes. Leaning over me, hair down around her shoulders, she wears a white cable-knit sweater, faded jeans, and no makeup. The sweater sags at her neck. No bra either.

"Not your regular work attire." I sit up and see I'm not on a jail cell cot nor in a jail cell. I'm somehow in a king-sized bed. I slide my legs around. No pants. "What the—"

"You peed yourself, your pants are in the dryer. My husband's underwear fits fine." She goes to the other side of the room, takes a chair from a mahogany roll-top desk, and sits. "Questions?"

I realize I still hear that low rumble between my ears. Then I realize the bed still yaws. Then I realize we're on some kind of huge boat. The aroma of bacon and coffee comes from somewhere.

"Questions? You got it. Where are—"

She holds up a hand, no red nail polish. "We're on my husband's yacht."

I hold my throbbing head in my hands. "Any chance it's called *Out for Fun?*"

"Saw it at Pirate's Cove yesterday, huh?"

"This is kidnapping."

"You didn't object."

"People passed out *can't* object."

"Aren't you curious about where we are?"

"Are we the only people here?"

"Got my baby on autopilot. GPS, you know."

"Where's your husband?"

"I assume he's with one of his girlfriends in Europe."

"That's too vague."

"To clarify, he's in Europe on a business trip. As far as I know, he has more than one girlfriend with him." Sheriff Scott spreads her somewhat bat-wingy arms. "I take my baby out now and then. We need a vacation to get our heads on straight."

"We? What do you mean we?"

"I took a leave of absence from work. Your Camry's in the impound lot. I finished the paperwork clearing you, you can pick it up when we get back. I dropped your hotel room key card in the mail. Your luggage should be in the unclaimed bin at your hotel. The bouncer at the restaurant—we dated way back—called and said you were in no shape to drive. I knew why because of the hell you're going through and decided we needed a vacation. He could've carried two of you. He left before you peed yourself. You're about the same size as my husband." She waved a hand toward a mahogany door. "Plenty of clothes in the closet. Your penis is above average in size."

It's rare I'm completely speechless. I am.

"Hungry?"

"Where are we?"

She points again. "If you pull the curtains on the window, you'll barely make out the black and white candy stripes of the Cape Hatteras Lighthouse. When I go on vacation, I go on vacation."

"Are you completely insane?"

"Until we get to the Florida Keys I will be."

"You just proved my point." I get up. "Where's my phone?"

"In a safe on the bridge." She stands. "Let's keep this strictly plutonic, Jonathan. I'm not looking for love nor sex, but if sex happens, I won't be upset." She offers her hand. "Remember the original *Star Trek*? The one where the Scottish guy kept the Enterprise going when Captain Kirk demanded, 'more power, Scotty, I need more power?'"

"It's a bit far back, why?"

"For the duration of our trip, please call me Scotty. Sheriff Scott will absolutely not do now that I've seen your penis." She offers me her hand. "No handshake? Fine." She leaves for a mahogany door. "Follow me if you want your pants instead of my husband's."

I go to the window. The Cape Hatteras Lighthouse, too far to swim to, is a black and white pinprick on the horizon. Walking around the room I see no weapons. Dumb move, I couldn't kill her if I wanted to. Well, I could knock her out and tie her up and pilot *Out for Fun* back to Pirate's Cove.

But.

She's right, I *do* need a vacation. Since the Florida Keys is far enough away from South Nags Head, Endless Love, and blacking out from the nightmare of Andy's death as I can hope to get, and as *quickly* as I can hope to get, why not?

I follow bacon and coffee smell, stop at a door and look in. Yep, huge double shower. I look in a door across from it.

Another king bed, this one undisturbed. Her uniform lies across it but no Glock. Like I'd shoot her if it were there. In the closet hangs more jeans, three sweaters, several flannel shirts, a few nice blouses, and a navy-blue robe of shimmery silk. Given the thirty pounds of bulk around my middle, I'm not one to fat-shame. Still, I know what I find attractive in a woman. That robe won't do a thing for flabby Scotty, even braless.

I find her in the galley at a stove—might as well get nautical—barefooted without red nail polish. It's like she has a complete makeover in mind. Yep, her hair, the color of dark chocolate, is halfway down her back.

"I heard those big feet thumping, Jonathan. Mugs in the cabinet by the stove. Fill us some."

I do so. "We're really going to the Florida Keys?"

"Why not?"

"Why there?"

"Most romantic place I know of. I have some friends who run a bar there. Haven't seen them in ages."

"You do realize we're still in hurricane season."

"My romantic comment doesn't shake you but hurricanes do?"

"You're in no shape to rape me."

She squeezes her waist above the jeans. "Don't like my muffin top?"

I take my coffee to a table by a window. "How are we staying on course?"

"Radar and an alarm system and the GPS I told you about." She plates eggs over-easy, bacon, whole wheat toast, and sits across from me. Those green eyes fix me in place. "Do you not find me the least bit attractive? I was something else as a teenager. How old do you think I am?"

"As your hostage, I'd rather not say."

"Life with the hubs has made twenty-eight look like forty."

"Won't you need a doctor for your pregnancy?"

"It's only a month, too early for morning sickness."

"Yet."

"I'm too tough for morning sickness." She takes eggs, crunches bacon, sips black coffee. Complete makeover, no doubt about it, including coffee without cream or sweetener.

"Look, Sheriff, this is interesting, but I need to—"

"Go back to work, I know. Why worry about it with three million dollars coming your way?"

"I've got a life, friends."

"Don't you consider me, Engineer Scotty, a friend? I'll never let you down like your other friends will."

"Friends don't kidnap friends."

"That's what makes me the best friend you'll ever have. Admit it, you're a walking train wreck bent on suicide over your wife."

I crunch bacon, sip coffee.

"Until I met you," she says, "I was considering an abortion."

"After offering sex, why not go ahead with it?"

"I like the idea of creating a new life. Don't you realize that's what I'm trying to do for us with our vacation?"

"How long?"

"The hubs is leaving Europe in a few days and flying to Australia. All in all he'll be gone at least a month."

"You want us to ride around in this boat for a month?"

"Along with stops for fuel, shopping trips, and experiencing different, as the hubs says, cuisine. Do you dance?"

"Plutonic dancing, you mean."

"Of course. Or until I work my muffin top flat, my flabby neck firm, and my bat-wings—you've already called them that in your head—flightless. Then, who knows?"

Scotty—might as well call her that—bites toast. No Jake for her—no way, no how. Jake belongs to Andy and always will. All Scotty gets is Jonathan.

Breakfast done, she suggests I shower. I get up. "You made me forget my pants, where's the dryer?"

With a fingertip, she scores a mark in midair. "Score one for Scotty for making you forget your pants. I'll get them while you shower. Soap, shampoo, and linens are in the closet in the bathroom. Use all the hot water you want. Hubs put a huge potable water tank on my baby for showers for two. I demanded a huge fuel tank to lessen stops."

I start toward the door.

"Jonathan."

"Yeah?"

"You mentioned liking your job yesterday." Scotty takes a phone from her pocket and offers it to me. "As a token of my trust, call your boss and your attorney and let them know you'll be out of town for the near future."

I take the phone. "What if I dial 911?"

"Go ahead."

My index finger hovers over the nine.

"Problem, Jonathan? More problems than me seeing that above average penis of yours?"

I make the calls. "In spite of this terrible pun, why does it seem you have my number?"

"We're creatures of the heart."

I can't believe I agree with her but I do. "And our hearts have been broken."

"Exactly. Get that shower while I check our course. Then I'll show you how the bridge operates so I can take a nap. I've been up all night, evidenced by my uniform you saw on my bed and how far south we are."

"How did you know I looked in your bedroom?"

Scotty softly smiles. "Got your number, remember? Did you like the shower too, when you looked?"

"I'll let you know when I'm done." I give Scotty my phone. "Put that somewhere safe. I don't plan to use it again anytime soon."

* * *

Hot water does wonders for a sore neck, even when that sore neck is from *Hope* slamming down at the bar yesterday. Clean hair and skin create a brighter outlook. No red streak marks my stomach from the seatbelt Stan made me buckle. I wrap a towel around my waist and get out. Scotty comes in, puts the blue robe and my pants on the commode.

"I was planning to top off the tanks in Savannah. NOAA reports say Tropical Storm Nestor is headed this way from the Gulf Coast. We'll play it safe and weather it in the harbor. Should pass fairly quickly."

"Dorian did a number on Ocracoke with all that flooding." I towel my hair. "Nice shower."

She goes to the glass door. "Good."

"As in?"

She pulls the sweater over her head. Jeans and panties drop. She gets in the shower. The clear glass door leaves nothing to the imagination.

"Really? You just waltz in here and undress?"

"Body odor's not my thing, and I'll nap better clean."

"You could've waited until I was gone."

"You're a grown man, stop being a prude."

"I wanted to shave."

The water sprays. "Who's stopping you? Ever thought of a beard?"

"No."

"Longer hair? Some guy's hair curls when it grows. Why aren't you turning around or leaving?"

I go to the sink. Behind the mirror, a razor's in the cabinet.

"Shave cream's in the cabinet under the sink, Jonathan."

Despite the steam fogging the shower door, I catch glimpses of skin and curves. Naked Scotty's more rounded than dressed Scotty. Whiskerless, I open the cabinet door to return the razor.

"Did you dull it much?" she says.

"It's fine."

"Give me that and the shave cream. I'm getting bristly."

Eyes averted, I do as I'm told. I don't ask where she's bristly.

"Get the dishes. I'll show you the bridge when I'm done."

I dress and head to the kitchen, where smooth skin and curves won't distract me. Even overweight, Scotty's got my number worse than Andy ever did.

With the sink filled enough for our few dishes, I squirt soap, wash, rinse, and dry. A ship's horn, low and deep, bellows. A freighter passes a mile to the left.

Scotty's bare feet patter behind me. She goes through the door to where I assume the bridge is located. The blue robe clinging to curves does more for her than I thought it would. Her hair, wet and shining down her back, doesn't hurt.

I set the last mug in the strainer. She returns, sits at the table, crosses her legs. The robe opens to reveal thighs and calves gleaming with lotion that smells like vanilla. Her complexion is pink, her eyelashes dark, her brows plucked to a perfect arch. She smiles softly again.

"You're handling this better than I thought you would."

She's either talking about the kidnapping or her blatant attempts to seduce me. "How long until Savannah?"

"We're running fifteen knots. Twenty-four hours or so, depending on wind and currents. I'm glad we outran that nor'easter in Nags Head."

I go to the shoreside window. Cape Hatteras is long gone. "Should we have sex and get it over with?"

"Not romantic enough. I expect you to fall in love with me before we get back to Manteo."

"And do what? Take you away from your rich husband and give you a life of happiness?"

"Stranger things have happened."

"I'm damaged goods."

"So am I, which we've already established."

"You expect me to raise your husband's kid too?"

"You will if you're half the man I think you are."

"Wrong tense. It's 'would', not 'will.'"

"Stranger things." Getting up, she yawns. The robe closes and those legs vanish. "Let's check out the bridge before I collapse."

Her rear shimmies beneath blue silk. We enter a room with a slanted windshield. Three wipers wait for rain. Gauges line more mahogany panels, a stainless-steel wheel in the center.

She runs fingertips along gauges. "These are labeled, I assume you can read. The GPS screen is taking a nap like I need to do. The radar and fume detectors are audible alarms."

"Where's the engine?"

"In the stern, away from the bedrooms. These yachts are modern and safe, but not foolproof."

"You mean fire?"

"The reason for the fume detector. A ventilation system keeps the engine room clear. If it didn't ..."

"Fire?"

"Try explosion. That's why the engine room is away from the bedrooms. Depending on the size and strength of the explosion, a person might get out or might not." She hovers a fingertip above a button marked Test. "Want to hear it?"

"Go ahead."

She presses the button. A dozen demons from hell electronically screech in my ears. She lifts her finger. "That'll wake the dead, won't it?"

I finger my ringing ears. "And deafen a person. Life jackets?"

"You might not have noticed. The beds have compartments beneath them for lifejackets."

"Where's the generator for the electricity?"

"In a walled-off room next to the engine. All the rooms have smoke detectors. Fire onboard is bad news. Grab a life jacket and go to the bow and let me deal with it."

"I know how to operate a fire extinguisher."

"I know my baby like the back of my hand."

"But I can—"

"The odds are so small as to be nonexistent. Still, you need to know what to do if it happens. Like I said, let me deal with it." She pats the back of one of the two leather upholstered chairs by the instruments and wheel. "Have a sit and get used to her. She's as sweet as butter pecan ice cream."

I sit. "Your favorite?"

Scotty pokes her belly. "My downfall, as well as a hubs that made me stop caring if my ass got fat or not." She waves a hand to a dorm sized fridge at the far wall beneath a window. "Coronas in there if you feel like a *cerveza*. Plenty of bottled water too, which I added because of the baby."

"Have you ever piloted this thing alone? What about a watch?"

"Never alone. Solo sailors stay awake in busy shipping lanes. It's two of us but I trust our GPS and radar. The alarm's in my room. I get up every thirty minutes to take a look. We'll move closer to shore and anchor when we sleep later, but I'd like to make Savannah before that tropical storm hits."

Scotty shimmies away. Her voice, still low like a worn E string, has a youthful lilt to it, along with a soft North Carolina drawl. Being away from Manteo agrees with her.

To be honest, it agrees with me too. Be that as it may, I'm sure Andy will forgive me for not thinking about her since I passed out in that restaurant.

Chapter 6

By the time we cruise into Savannah Harbor, torn fringes of gray cloud hang low on the southwest horizon, and gusts of wind make Scotty fight the wheel. We bump into place at the diesel nozzle and take fuel; the dial on the pump spins far longer than on my Camry. Scotty pays with what's probably an unlimited American Express card. The hubs must make a killing in real estate. She docks *Out for Fun* at one of the last open slips. Lots of boaters have the same idea about the storm. Lucky for us there's only one other yacht as large as ours.

Despite Scotty's frumpy appearance and off-putting attitude, the fact that she has the guts to be a sheriff and pilot this yacht in the open waters of the Atlantic raises my approval of her a notch above kidnapper and seductress. I can see, in another life, us being friends, talking, confiding, maybe even about spousal issues.

Andy was a clinger, didn't do anything around the house other than what she called lady stuff: dishes, cleaning, vacuuming, cooking. I didn't mind but I like the idea of a woman who's willing to go out of her comfort level, like with changing oil in a car, cutting grass or, at the least, climbing on top for sex. When I met Andy, I never thought another woman would interest me. If Scotty and I were single and didn't carry so much emotional baggage, who knows.

When I dress, the hub's jeans and a shirt fit fine but not his shoes. Good thing my boat shoes are fairly new. Thinking Scotty and I could make a couple is pretty dumb. For all I know, she could be planning to blow herself up on the yacht to escape her cheating husband. Then again, since she's pregnant, I can't see it. She actually seems like she'd make a good mom.

I thought I'd make a good dad before Andy died. We talked about it off and on, but she wanted to give us a year or two by ourselves first, which I admired. Living together six months is nothing like being married. Married carries a permanence about it, a commitment more than saying *hey, let's shack up.*

I find Scotty on the bridge. She wears tan slacks, a red blouse, a string of pearls with matching earrings. No wedding paraphernalia decorates her ring finger. The dark chocolate hair is brushed shiny and soft. A hint of mascara pops green eyes. For a frump she looks great. Sandals reveal green toenail polish. She walks toward me. The girls shimmy, no bra. My pervert eyes have a mind of their own. I wait to see what she says.

"It's sprinkling and getting cool. Might need jackets and an umbrella."

The yacht shudders; I nod. "The wind usually calms after sunset."

"Not with a tropical storm on the way." She opens yet another mahogany cabinet. Navy blue windbreakers on and umbrella open, we leave the docks. Lamps on poles mounted to the docks sway circles of yellow light around us. We head for a street where similar umbrellaed and jacketed people go into bars and restaurants. Quite the crowd the storm has kicked up. Scotty passes the first restaurants and bars. She walks like a woman on a mission: wide stride, sandals plopping in sidewalk puddles. I work to keep up.

"What's wrong with those other places?"

"Hubs and I visited them."

"Meaning?"

"Do I have to tell you I don't want to be seen with you?"

"Because you're going back to him and be the happy little family."

"Shut up the first chance you get, Jonathan."

She turns a corner and speeds toward a sign swinging in the wind over a recessed doorway, dark instead of lit.

"Doesn't look particularly safe, Sheriff. Got your Glock on you?"

"I can handle it."

It's not bad inside. One wall lined with booths. Several tables, cozy and round, scattered about. Scotty grabs my hand. "Let's get that corner booth, Gilligan." She tosses the collapsed umbrella on one side, hips me into the other, and drops beside me. "Drink? Food? Kiss?"

"You look very classy, Mrs. Thurston Howell the Third."

"We've watched too many Gilligan's Island reruns, Gilligan."

"I prefer Captain Kirk."

"He slept around too much. I like sex—haven't had it for fun in years—but I wouldn't sleep with just anyone."

Two women enter and go to the bar. Both look college age. Minutes later two men come in. Tattoos. Cigarette stink. Beefy types that probably mechanic around the docks. One nods our way; a tight grin separates his goatee and mustache. I face Scotty. "You've got an admirer."

"Not my type. Here comes a waitress."

Scotty orders a burger all the way, fried mushrooms, and iced tea with lemon. I order a cheeseburger with lettuce, tomato, mayo, and pickles, fries on the side, and a Corona. The waitress leaves. Scotty pats my shoulder. "Let's pretend we're married."

"And?"

"We'll be me and the hubs—no sex."

"Not my kind of marriage. When did yours go bad?"

The goateed beefcake comes over. "What's the chance me an' your wife could dance?"

I face Scotty. "You hear music? I don't hear music."

"Not a note, dear."

Beefcake stalks back to the bar. A minute passes. He strikes up a conversation with the two women. His fellow beefcake joins the trio.

Giggles bubble from Scotty. "I didn't take you for the aggressive type. Protecting my honor?"

"Didn't you have sheriff training?"

"All in all, Dare County's pretty quiet." She bumps my hip with hers. "I do kidnap the occasional drunk now and then."

"I was asking about you and the hubs."

"Lots of tide under that bridge, Jonathan. I'd rather not drown."

Our meals arrive, fries and mushrooms crispy brown. My mouth waters. Scotty peppers her burger liberally. I ketchup my fries, not so liberally. We eat and drink. I order another Corona. We continue the cycle. I need to loosen my belt and pee.

"I'm heading to the restroom, Sheriff. Be right back."

"I'm good." Scotty takes the credit card from her jeans pocket and waves the waitress down.

Beefcake comes out the restroom door as I go on. I say nothing.

It's the weirdest thing, when you think you gotta go and can't go. I finally do, zip, and wash my hands. The door flies in and slams the wall. Jackets and umbrella under one arm, Scotty grabs my arm. "Time to go."

47

"Why's your forehead bloody?"

She pulls me out. Beefcake's on his back in the bar floor, hand over his nose, blood in his goatee. His neck is scarlet. The friend is kneeling beside him; the waitress rounds the bar with a wadded dishcloth. I assume it holds ice. Scotty drags me to the door. "She called 911, run."

Stinging rain pelts us. We splash in the street, breathing hard. Siren's scream behind us. We run harder. My heart thrums in my temples. I have *got* to lose some weight.

Our feet thud on the wooden docks. A wall of wind-driven rain flails us. We climb aboard *Out for Fun* and fall into the two leather bridge chairs. Scotty's soaked. The red blouse clings to distraction. The diluted splotch of blood on her forehead stains her cheeks red. Either that or the run is making her flush.

We heave breaths, which gradually slow, which allows her to smile.

"Damn, Jonathan, that was fun."

At least she didn't call me Gilligan. "What happ—"

"I'm interrupting you. Do you mind me interrupting you? Heaven knows the hubs interrupted me enough over the years."

I go to bathroom for a wet washcloth and wipe her forehead. That hint of mascara streaks. Those green eyes glow. "You're insane."

"Beats dull any day of the week." She touches her forehead. "I will *not* look my best with a bruise in the morning."

I fold the washcloth and hang it over the wheel. The dock lights shudder yellow into the window. I flip the lights and turn the thermostat up. "It's getting cool."

She puts the jackets and umbrella away and takes a Corona from the fridge, opens it with the opener affixed to the side and gives it to me. "No sirens, we made our getaway." She goes back to the fridge for a water.

I tap the plastic bottle with the glass one and swallow. "Do I get to know what happened now?"

She returns to the chair. "As soon as the waitress brought my credit card back, that butthead pressed the point of dancing with me. I thought, what the heck, one dance and we'll go." She swallows water. "He leaned in for a kiss. I leaned back and told him he had to pucker better than that if he expected to take me away from you." She grins, giggles, and shakes her head. "He puckered and I grabbed his collar. If he hasn't been head butted before, he has now. I heard the bones crunch."

The Corona goes down cold. "They teach you that in sheriff school?"

"That was me using my brain on the fly. I bet he won't ask anyone to dance without touching his nose for a long time to come."

In one long pull, Scotty empties the bottle. Green eyes blink, blink again. Her face screws up. The bottle slips from her fingers; the crinkly plastic clatters to the deck. Her chin lowers. Sobs shake her shoulders.

I don't know why she's crying or what to do. I caught Andy crying a few times. One was about 3 a.m. on a winter night. When I asked what was wrong, she wouldn't even look at me.

"You okay, Skipper?"

Scotty fingers dripping hair behind her ears. "The hubs and I used to have fun like that. Well, not fun like what just happened, but you know what I mean."

"Andy and I did too."

"I don't want to talk about him. Do you want to talk about her?"

"Not really."

Rain clatters against the windshield. *Out for Fun* bumps the dock.

It's the strangest thing. I couldn't stand her when we met and now I want to take her to bed. No, not for sex but just to hold.

I go to the bathroom for towels for our dripping hair and give her one. She doesn't look up. "Isn't it funny how the years go by? One minute we're kids, the next minute we're in high school, having dreams of true love and finding a job where we can make a difference. Next thing you know, life is a huge wave that slaps you down from the back and scrubs you into the sand. The worst part is, and this is the killer, you never see it coming."

I give my hair a few rubs, hang the towel around my neck, and take her towel. "Can't have you catching cold and leaving me to pilot us to Florida."

Rubbing gently, I dry her hair. It smells of rain and wind. I work individual lengths, squeezing and kneading the water out. She swivels the chair—hair hangs in her eyes. I catch a whiff of vanilla lotion. Her forehead lowers to my chest. She wraps her arms around my waist and sobs again.

What can a man do but comfort a woman in pain? I hold her until her cry is done. Move her hair aside. Wipe tears with the towel. Kiss her forehead. Those green eyes promise spring mown yards and summer swims in the surf at South Nags Head. I wonder how it'd feel to have her astride me, looking down, dark chocolate strands covering her breasts but not quite, the exquisite rhythm of those heavy hips, eyes closed, small moans escaping those lips, full and parted enough to see her teeth, white but a little crooked on the bottom.

I hate how I keep comparing Scotty to Andy but I can't help it. Andy kissed hard, like she wanted to suck my soul from my lungs. Her tongue never failed to dart, a dagger between my lips.

Scotty kisses great, full lips defined to where I feel the edges. Her tongue is a campfire cooked marshmallow: hot and silky, soft and liquid. Hot air pulses from her nostrils to my cheek: a freight train climbing a grade. She takes my hand and places it to her breast. The train chugs harder. She squeezes my hand within hers. The steam engine of her heart thrums beneath my hand.

Maybe it's the situation of her assaulting the beefcake and running from the law. Maybe it's the rain slashing the windshield. Maybe it's the howl of the wind careening like wraiths seeking a victim in Savannah Harbor.

I have never felt like this before, including with Andy.

Sure, I dated in high school and college. Experiments with sex in dorms, stoned on marijuana once, I now prefer a clear mind. Well, as clear as it can be with the dull buzz of those Coronas sloshing in my skull.

Scotty's lips leave mine. "I shouldn't have done that."

I am completely stunned. Never, ever have I wanted a woman this much.

"Are you mad?" Her voice is soft. I don't feel her breath on my cheek and wish I did.

"Just disappointed."

"The day before yesterday you were spreading your wife's ashes. I hope you want me for me instead of what you had with her."

"I—" Flashlights pierce the night, shining amongst the docks. Intoxicated boat owners seeking beds.

Scotty turns. A beam slices through the bridge window. "Take your shirt off."

"What—"

51

"Cops." She kills the lights; we unbutton. She throws her blouse beneath the window. "Do the same so they can't recognize us from the waitress's description." I do as she asks, and she presses against my chest. Despite the dire situation—and her trying to act like we've been at foreplay for a while and are about to make love—she kisses me as only she can.

The beam plays across the room. Her breasts warm my chest. Her tongue is absolutely amazing. She writhes against me, licks my neck. "Uh-huh," she murmurs, "definitely larger than average."

The light leaves. Scotty gets our shirts and hands me mine. "Get dressed, Gilligan. Mrs. Howell can't take any more of that."

"You're kidding."

"Nope."

"Do I get to know why?"

"Brush your teeth and dry your hair. I'll do the same and bring you some of the hub's PJs."

"Your kisses say we sleep naked."

She slips the blouse on, leaves it unbuttoned. "I'll tell you why when we're in bed."

"You're carrying this foreplay thing way too far. I mean, I'm as ready as ready can be."

"I'm *not* ready, that's the point. I told you before the cops came how I shouldn't have kissed you. Do like I say and I'll tell you why."

"You're serious?"

Scotty nods and I put my shirt on. It's not like I have a choice.

Chapter 7

Scotty comes to my room. Red plaid flannel PJs assault my sense of romance. "C'mon, Mrs. Howell, you can do better than that."

She throws the hub's PJs, white cotton with narrow vertical stripes, at me. "Tops and bottoms. On. Now."

I do as she demands, get in bed and raise the covers for her. She kills the light and snuggles into my shoulder. "You're sweet when you want to be."

"You're a terror when you want to be. You really heard the guy's nose crunch?"

"Maybe I imagined it when it caved in and blood went everywhere. Sorry about getting you turned on with no follow up."

"Plenty of time left in our trip."

"Which leads to why I'd rather not."

I let the silence bloom between us. After all her flirting and nakedness, including rubbing against me nude, she's either the most confident woman in the world or the most complicated. I opt for both.

She surprises me by not continuing.

The rain still clatters against *Out for Fun*, the gusts less so. The lights outside spill yellow into the room.

"Jonathan?"

"Hmm?"

"I've never been as scared as I am now."

"A kiss would fix that."

"Believe me, I want to."

"And?"

"Lust is what made me marry the hubs. I didn't think long term. I didn't think kids. I didn't think about myself and what I needed in a husband. Spouses should be best friends."

I kiss her hair. "Best friends with amazing benefits."

"Did you have that with Andy? When I saw you beside her on the beach, the first thing I thought was how much you must love her."

"Our relationship was interesting. There were times I couldn't read her. She'd go on shopping jags, buying useless stuff and clothes she didn't need. She'd go out with girlfriends after work and come home all hyped up."

"Drugs?"

"It was more in her eyes than anything. She was more ... I guess it was like when a light bulb flares before it goes out."

"That's strange."

"I plan to ask around when I get back to Raleigh. None of it makes any sense. It's like she existed on a different plane than me at times."

Scotty goes quiet, then: "Any chance she was having an affair?"

"Never crossed my mind."

"You know people do that."

"Because of your husband."

"He's just a jerk, Andy doesn't sound like a jerk. Knowing you like I do, you wouldn't marry a jerk."

"What if I proposed to you, Sheriff? You're pretty close to being a jerk."

"You forgot about why I don't want to make love to you."

"You said lust made you marry your husband. That means you based your relationship on sex instead of love, and your lust for me is an issue you don't want to repeat." I laugh. "If it's any consolation, my lust throbbed as hard as ever when we were kissing."

"I have no doubt we'd be amazing." Scotty yawns. "I want to stock the kitchen in the morning. You need anything? Most everything is overpriced in the Keys."

"Swim trunks. Your hub's clothes are a tad tight."

"If we keep eating like we did tonight, we'll outgrow everything on board. I don't like being overweight. Maybe I'll do something about it after I have the baby." Scotty kisses my cheek and rolls over. "Goodnight, wanna-be lover. You're entirely too good for me."

* * *

I hate sleeping hot. Worse, I hate waking hot and sweaty. I fan the covers and see Scotty hates sleeping hot too. She's completely nude, offensive flannels on the foot of the bed. I fan the covers again; she stirs not a jot. Drop my PJs and nudge her awake with my larger than average penis made larger because I need to pee or not? The choice is clear: get out of bed and jerk the covers off.

She groans. "And I said you were sweet."

"You said when I wanted to be." I jiggle a plump cheek. "I don't want to be."

She slaps my hand. "Coffee. Pancakes. Sausage."

"What happened to losing weight?"

"I'm eating for two, remember?"

55

I pull the covers back over her goose-bumped behind. "And here I am, hoping for breakfast in bed by the woman who likes my larger than average penis."

"I bet you don't know what to do with it."

"You'll find out on our honeymoon."

Scotty rolls over to face the wall. "Please don't go there. I'll go home after our jaunt to the Keys and play the good little wifey. You'll go back to Raleigh to work and I'll never see you again."

"What happened to pretending we're married?"

"I was stupid to suggest it. We've got almost a month left, don't ruin it."

I kneel on the bed, brush her hair away from her eyes. "I didn't mean anything by it. The best thing that happened to me since Andy died is this trip."

Her eyes close. A tear squeezes from the corner of one.

At a complete loss, I dress and go to the kitchen. The least I can do is prove how good a cook I am. When we go shopping, I'll suggest one of those portable propane grills for those isolated islands we'll visit in the Keys. T-bones, center-cut pork chops, salmon fillets, chicken breasts, shrimp—all are great seared to perfection on a grill. Add Coronas and bottled water, tossed salads and whatever else Scotty likes, including a campfire as the sun sets, I can't think of a better way to spend our remaining time together.

She comes in. Jeans and a sweater and a bra, no jiggling. "Haven't you started cooking yet? I want to shop and head south."

I find sausage in the fridge. "Mind making the coffee and mixing the pancake batter?"

"She grabs the sausage from my hand. "I'll do it."

"I want to help, I like to cook."

"You would."

"What's that supposed to mean?"

"Make the coffee."

"Will we spend time on some of those small Keys islands? The isolated ones?"

"I shouldn't have taken my flannels off or took a shower in front of you. All you want me for now is sex on an isolated island."

"I just thought we could pick up one of those portable propane grills for steaks and chicken. Maybe shrimp and salmon too. Whatever."

"I'd like that coffee anytime now."

"Where is it?"

She takes a can from a cabinet and slams it on the counter. "Men." At the counter, she saws the roll of sausage violently with a serrated knife.

Still at a complete loss, I luck up on a set of measuring spoons in a drawer, measure coffee into the machine, and fill it with water. "I wish you'd tell me what's wrong. A month's a long time to be around someone in a mood."

She stops sawing, raises a hand to cover her eyes. "I don't want to go back to the hubs but I have to."

"I have no control over what you do."

She lowers her hand. "I wish things were different."

"In what way?"

"You'll think I'm crazy."

"Try me."

"I'd like to spend about six months with you."

This admission clears things up. She likes me enough to want to see if we could be a couple. A serious couple. As in a real marriage couple. I'd like that too, but see no need in admitting it. She's got a baby to think about and a husband who might be a good dad and change his ways. I shouldn't get in the way of either one. "You could take me back."

"I need this, Jonathan. I've been putting money away for a while now. A little here. A little there. If I ever get the nerve to leave the hubs, I can start over."

"Is it fair to take his child away?"

"Is it fair how he treats his wife?"

"You kidnapped me, remember? I didn't beg you to do this."

"I can't help how I feel. I want to finish the month and see how it goes."

I go to her, lift her chin. "I like you a lot and it has nothing to do with wanting to make love to you. I'm not one of those guys who thinks about his own pleasure and not the woman's."

"You *would* be one of those guys."

"That's the second time you said that, Scotty. What the hell's going on with you?"

She goes to the window. "I told you I'm afraid."

I say nothing. The only thing I can think is she has serious feelings for me now and is afraid I don't have them for her. I do like her. I like her more than I thought I would in so short a time after losing Andy. She's funny and intelligent and classy and attractive, despite her weight. No challenge scares her either, like head butting that guy and telling me she'll handle any emergency with the yacht. The combination is amazing, especially because I wasn't attracted to her when we met. This verifies I have above average feelings for her.

I sit at the table. "Can we talk this out so we can go shopping and head south?"

She goes back to sawing sausage. "What's there to talk about?"

"You already said you're going back home when the month is over. That means I'm going back home too. I propose we treat what's happening between us like adults and not let it override the reality of the situation."

She turns. "Meaning what exactly?"

"I realize you need to get back home for your pregnancy. I also realize you may decide to leave your husband one day. I have money, you have money. Let our time left show us if we have what it takes to at least consider if we can make it work. If, at the end of the month, we find out we're not compatible, no harm, no foul. We return to our lives and that's that."

"And if we think we're compatible?"

"You leave your husband and we make a life together."

"He'll fight for the baby. That's how he is."

"No court will take a baby from the mom without good reason. At worst I'll move to Nags Head and he'll get every other weekend and alternate holidays. Judges award that all the time."

"I still think he'll fight."

"Does he have friends in court?"

"Just the ones involved when he makes real estate deals. Actually, being sheriff, I have more contacts."

"There you go. Can we give my plan a try and see what happens?"

"I don't want to get hurt."

"You think I do? I just had the hurt of a lifetime when I lost Andy."

"Can we not have sex until we know what we'll do?"

"That'll make it even more amazing, won't it?"

She comes over, pecks my cheek, and returns to the sausage. "Don't tempt me before breakfast."

Chapter 8

Sausage, pancakes, and coffee disposed of, Scotty goes to her room to call a cab. At the bow, I take in the briny air, the morning chill, the clearing sky, the low line of black cloudbank marking Tropical Storm Nestor's retreat northeast. More sailors emerge from boats. Some survey tangled ropes dangling from masts. Some hose bits of debris from nearby trees from decks. Some shake their heads in amazement because they have little to no damage.

Out for Fun came through like a trooper.

I find myself wanting to go to Scotty and tell her again how much this trip means to me. When Stan took me to Oregon Inlet, I couldn't take pleasure in the simple sight of pelicans cutting the sky with wide wings and huge bodies, those intrepid beaks leading the way as they chevroned across the blanket of blue overhead. I couldn't take pleasure in a flock of gulls careening against the wind in their eternal struggle to survive along the Outer Banks. I couldn't take pleasure in the gentle rise and fall of Stan's vessel before the wall of wind off the Atlantic slammed us sideways. I couldn't take pleasure in the simple act of breakfast with a woman I cared about, all while remembering the rise and fall of Andy's body against me as we made love the night before she died.

Scotty's boat shoes plod behind me. Hands slip around my waist and meet at my middle. "Bite of sausage for your thoughts."

"I'm glad we talked."

"Ready to go?"

I tug the windbreaker sleeve on her arm. "I need a jacket."

"It's across my shoulder."

I start to turn within her arms. She holds me tight. "The hubs called."

"Great. Perfect. Amazing. Did you tell him you've sailed off to the Keys with your boyfriend?"

"Let's see if I can get his voice just right." Clearing her throat, Scotty lowers her tone a notch. "Just don't wreck my boat."

"Touching."

"Well, he did say he made an appointment with an OB/GYN for when I get back."

"To make sure his progeny will continue his lineage, no doubt."

"I think she's a girl." Scotty's arms loosen. I turn.

"Any reason why?"

"I want another brunette hellion like me around to make his life miserable."

I palm her cheek, kiss her forehead. "How's that hard head this morning, hellion?"

"Fine as fine can be."

I stay there, letting the loose wisps of her bangs brush my cheeks. She's wearing a ponytail. Strands of hair hang from her temples. She smells like vanilla. I'd kiss her but the thought of marshmallows is now an aphrodisiac.

"Now, Jonathan, if we stay like this any longer, you'll ge*
bulge in your jeans before we go shopping."

"Good point, Skipper."

The cab arrives. Scotty tells the driver an address that I don't hear. The day is perfect. She's strong beyond strong. I trust her completely.

At a grocery store, she tells the cabby to wait. We buy two carts of groceries, including everything on my list, two containers of butter pecan ice cream, a case of Coronas and more water for her, saying how she likes beer but her baby girl's health is more important.

The cabby opens the trunk. Scotty's already told me she has a portable propane grill and enough small propane canisters to sear a side of beef aboard *Out for Fun*. The cabby closes the trunk. She climbs in back. Down from the grocery, a storefront catches my eye. I tell her to wait, run inside, and come back with a guitar case that holds a classical guitar, strung with nylon strings. She appraises me with a single arched eyebrow. I get in the cab and put the case between us.

She leans forward to look around the guitar. "You're a musician too? Be still my beating heart."

Those tendrils of hair hang along her cheek. The slightest shade of pink lipstick tints those full lips. I don't care about the slight waddle hanging from her neck or the fullness that gives her a somewhat jowly appearance. Those intense green eyes draw me in, a tide beneath the Basnight bridge, churning, rushing, swirling.

I lean toward her and whisper: "I could eat you alive."

"With butter pecan ice cream on top?"

"Oh, yeah. Add whipped cream, cherries, a T-bone steak, I'd be good to go."

"No salad? I need to think about my baby girl."

"All the salad you want, Scotty. Acres of lettuce. Fields of tomatoes. Rows of cucumbers. Any and everything and as much as you want."

She reaches over the guitar case and rubs my thigh. "Cucumbers sound interesting."

Heartbeats pound my eardrums. The tingle of adrenaline zips along my shoulders. "I'm gonna have a hard time hiding my cucumber when we get out for our groceries, Skipper."

"Mm-hm, my ice cream's melting as we speak." She sits back and allows the silence to churn our imaginations.

Outside Savannah Harbor, Scotty sets course and speed. We fill the fridge. I check the propane grill and wash the grate. She goes through her clothes to decide what needs washing after hanging in the closet since the last time she and the hubs took *Out for Fun* out for fun, which, she says, was a month ago, when she got pregnant. She also tells me it happened in her bedroom so I won't feel weird by sleeping in the same bed where they last had sex.

She retires to the bridge with a paperback. I retire to my room with my guitar.

When I played in my younger years, it's a wonder I never thought about how a guitar resembles a woman. Luthiers design and make them in various shapes and sizes. The most obvious difference is the bout size, both above and below the waist, similar to the hourglass shape of a woman. My classical guitar resembles Scotty: bottom bout slightly larger than the upper. The neck is a bit wider than most guitars for fingerstyle playing, the nylon strings softer and more supple than metal strings. She's throaty and full toned, mature and serious, but she can be playful when strummed delicately, like running fingertips gently along the sensitive contours of rounded breasts, the dip of a feminine waist, and the flare of voluptuous hips. If strummed with a firm hand, the player can lower their cheek to the sound hole and feel the satisfied breath of her.

I tune the guitar and take it to the bridge, sit in the other chair and play some nondescript tune floating in my brain. Scotty's green eyes peek above the paperback. "Aren't *you* the artist?"

I allow the notes to flare, petals on a rose shimmering with dew, then soften them to a whisper. "I try to be."

"Are you that good in the sack?"

I fingerpick an A minor scale that resolves to C. "Better."

"We'll see, Jonathan, we'll see."

I case the guitar in my room and return to the chair. "Who are these friends of yours we're going to visit?"

"I was thinking you shouldn't go. The hubs might see them again one day and you'll come up in the conversation."

"Does your 'was' mean you changed your mind?"

"I think of them more as family than friends. After a few late-night talks, when the hubs fell asleep in a booth from too many Long Island Iced Teas, they understood how miserable I am. They'll keep you a secret if I ask."

"What are they like?"

"As in?"

"Born there? Young or old? The standard descriptions, Sheriff."

"Mary Lou's a southerner transplanted from Georgia. Has a redneck drawl you wouldn't believe. Sammy's from Louisiana, just as Cajun as Cajun can be. Listening to them talk is hilarious. The best thing is they know it and don't mind."

"I admire that in a person. Too many people get their panties in the proverbial wad over nothing these days. Any kids?"

"They met in their early forties and got married. Adopted a beagle the first year, a five-year old named Elizabeth the second. Then they bought the bar and moved into the apartment overhead."

"They took on the responsibility of a kid in their forties?" I manage to keep my skepticism from raising my voice.

"That's them in a seashell. Lizzie's cute as a clam. All brunette curls and sassy like Mary Lou."

"I understand the water in the Keys is shallow in spots. Can we dock within walking distance?"

"It's right on the water. They've got a pier but the water's not deep enough for us. The hubs keeps an inflatable dinghy to paddle there and to any islands with the same water depth problem." Scotty returns to the paperback.

I put on a windbreaker and go out on the bow to lean within the V at the railing. Now I know how those actors felt in the movie *Titanic.* They knew they were headed on the trip of a lifetime but didn't know how it would end. Unlucky for them, it ended with one dying and, like me losing Andy, one losing the love of a lifetime.

I definitely like Scotty but can't say if I'm ready for love so soon, not to mention the added responsibility of raising another man's child. Sure, I want kids, despite Andy's joking insistence we not have any because they'd inherit my frog leg calves.

I look down. A pair of bottlenose dolphins, gray bodies beneath the crystalline green surface, ride the bulge of our bow wave. Dorsal fins scythe water. Boomerang shaped tails beat franticly. I can't help wondering what life has in store for me. Like the dolphins, will I find someone to share the sea of existence with like I intended with Andy? As unlikely as that is with Scotty, given her circumstances, is that someone her? Especially since she keeps referring to the hubs, jerk that he is, as someone she refuses to leave?

The thought leaves me intensely sad, and I'm not sure why when it shouldn't. Regardless of how I loved Andy, I'm not sure if I'm one of those people who believes in soulmates. It's a matter of finding someone who has similar desires, not only in life but in love. Humor—Scotty has that in abundance—is important too, as well as the attitude of gratitude to enjoy the simple pleasure of doing absolutely nothing together. Sure, Andy gifted me amazingly with the three-million-dollar life insurance check, but money's not everything. With the right person, I could live modestly and be completely happy.

I go to the bridge and nuzzle Scotty's neck; the smell and taste of vanilla flavored skin is intoxicating. "How goes it, Skipper?"

"Distracting, that's how it goes."

"Any stops before the Keys?"

"Miami to top off the diesel tanks. We'll cruise the Keys until we need to restock the fridge."

"Your logistical proficiency turns me on."

"My mama didn't raise no fools."

"You realize I don't know anything about your parents?"

"Like I know nothing about yours."

"Conversation starters while we lollygag on those isolated islands."

"Good idea." Scotty reaches behind the chair and pats my behind. "Parent talk to keep our minds off the fact that we want to bang each other silly."

I turn the chair to see the paperback. A half-dressed woman and man grace the cover. "I pictured you for detective novels instead of romance."

"I'm picking up tips for when I bang your fat behind into the sand on one of those isolated islands."

"We're overweight, not fat."

"I'll have to do something about that one day."

"Me too. I'd like to live to the ripe old age of reasonable instead of kicking off from a stroke or a heart attack."

"Exactly." Scotty returns to the paperback.

At the bow again, I lean against the rail, grateful for the sunscreen I slathered on after stocking the fridge. It's getting warmer now that we're further south, sun beating down from a cloudless sky.

The dolphins still dart. One's dorsal is notched on the leading edge.

They leave us when we refuel at Miami, rejoin us on the open sea. Freighters, cruise ships, and Coast Guard vessels pass but the dolphins stay: a pair of seaborne lovers waiting to discover if mine and Scotty's story will become theirs.

Chapter 9

W ho doesn't know about the Florida Keys?
Compared to Scotty, I know squat. To relish the last leg of our journey, she slows *Out for Fun* to a crawl.

Between meaningless chitchat about meaningless subjects, then lunch and supper followed by another night of cuddling in my bed, then breakfast on the bow, including a complete rundown of the bridge controls afterward, an hour of afternoon sunning, ended by a storm that spiraled a waterspout into the Atlantic, which fizzled and cleared to leave us with the bloodiest sunset known to humanity, all accompanied by warming breezes, the constant aroma of salt that flavors the increasingly humid air, and the apprehension of knowing we have a lessening number of days like these and nights like those and the desire to make love when we're not sure if it's a good idea or not, this veritable fount of Floridian knowledge fills me in while we pass the first Keys, starting with North Key Largo, Key Largo, Tavernier, and Islamorada. Sammy and Mary Lou's bar, Island Hopper, is located in Key West, the final tropical island in the chain.

Starting at its northern tip, the Florida Keys stretches south-southwest and then west to form a chain of sandy isles decorated with swaying coconut palms. Sun worshippers wear bikinis, one-piece swimsuits, and swim trunks, usually floral and colorful. On the occasional yacht or sailing vessel we pass, they wear nothing but smiles we can't see. Plenty of fishing vessels of all shapes and sizes, from those similar to Stan's, to single-outboard boats with platforms on the bows for fly fishing, frequent the Keys. They hunt bonefish, whose scales resemble chain mail on knights of old; silvery tarpon, known to reach eight feet in length and 280 pounds, whose prominent lower jaws make them appear to have an extreme underbite; and permit, flat sided and blunt faced, resembling pompano caught in the surf on the Outer Banks. Pompano are rarely more than a handful; permit can reach four feet in length and weigh up to eighty pounds. Many a fly fisherman has lost a full reel of line to each of these species of fish, fraying nerves, causing cursing and, at the end of the day, expensive bar bills.

Passing the islands and the Overseas Highway, the four-lane asphalt road that spans 106.5 miles long—one section is seven miles long and is called the Seven Mile Highway—one never thinks the Keys hosts a population of around 77,000. Coral reefs abound. Seas vary from aquamarine to dark blue to emerald green and every shade between. Celebrated author Earnest Hemingway's home is located on Key West; it's now a museum. There's also a Naval Air Station close enough to Key West for sonic booms to unnerve residents when they least expect it, because they don't always hear them coming.

When it comes to the Florida Keys, Scotty is most definitely a fount of Floridian knowledge.

We arrive at Key West late one night; a crescent moon glows orange over the horizon. Anchor dropped, bathroom duties done, we collapse in my bed. Scotty wears a sleep shirt. Spaghetti strapped, low cut, green to match her eyes, no bra to match my libido, it barely covers her ice-blue panties. I wear a pair of the hub's boxers when I want to wear nothing. In the engine room, the generator thrums and the air conditioner purrs. It's just cool enough for a sheet. I leave the bedside lamp on and crawl in beside Scotty. Goose bumps dot her arms.

"Need a snuggle, Skipper?"

"Where were you when I met the hubs? You're the sweetest thing since butter pecan ice cream."

Leaning on one elbow, I place my hand on her tummy. "Is this baby bump or ice cream?"

"A bit of both, I imagine."

How I never noticed her long lashes, I have no idea. Her tummy is warm. Her chest rises and falls. If the sheet wasn't covering her breasts, she'd slap me for not looking her in the eye. A second passes. Her nostrils flare, her lips purse and relax, her respiration rate nudges upward a notch.

"Jonathan?"

"Hmm?"

"You and I both know you shouldn't look at me like that."

"Because you still think I want you for sex instead of you."

"We only met a few days ago."

"Not true. I officially met you in your official capacity on the most terrible day of my life. That makes ten days, right? Time kinda flies out here."

"You have no idea."

The night is still. Beneath us, *Out for Fun* creaks. An outboard motor buzzes within hearing distance, probably some late-night bar goer on the way to their vessel.

I rub a slow circle on Scotty's tummy. She places her hand on mine to stop me. Like Yoda from *Star Wars* might say in his squeaky voice, *deterred, I am not.*

The kiss begins soft and smooth. The intention to make it firm fades. I slip my hand from beneath Scotty's hand and slide it downward. Her pupils expand. She doesn't stop my hand. My head is beside hers on the pillow, my lips next to the curve of her ear. A gold hoop decorates the lobe. The aroma of tropical sunshine resides in those dark chocolate strands, hint of vanilla along her neck.

Every summer, as sure as the tides rise and fall and the seasons come and go, tropical waves form off the west coast of Africa. If conditions are favorable, they become tropical depressions and then tropical storms on their westward journey across the Atlantic. If conditions are favorable for hurricanes — warm ocean surfaces and no wind shear — hurricanes form. Hurricanes are Mother Nature's release. Feeding on heat and moisture, they churn and rotate. Eyewalls cycle; they strengthen and weaken, tighten and relax. Waves build. Winds nearing 200 miles an hour moan across the open seas as she reaches maximum strength.

Scotty is all those things and more. Her moans reach category five. Her breath hisses through clenched teeth. She's a huge wave rising from the depths, crashing and writhing, feeding on heat and moisture, eye wall tightening, relaxing, tightening.

As quickly as the storm began, Hurricane Scotty calms. The wind of her breath gradually slows to a soft tropical breeze. The wave of her warm body rolls against me, cloud of dark hair on my chest. The storm passes. We sleep in each other's arms.

For no explicit reason, I wake around 1 a.m. Lying next to Scotty, I look back at mine and Andy's time together and ask her to forgive me.

And for her blessing.

I can't explain it at all and I don't care at all.

I'm as happy as I've ever been.

Possibly, remotely, genuinely, I'm even happier.

Chapter 10

In the morning, as a reward for last night, Hurricane Scotty bans me from the kitchen while she makes breakfast. We wear shorts, sandals, non-descriptive T-shirts of thin material— she wears a bra since we're going ashore— and we bear the heat outside as best we can. Thank whoever invented air conditioners. Who could sleep otherwise?

At the bow, I find my dolphin friends blowing spray and playing. Apparently they think their faith in Scotty and I is justified. I'm beginning to think that way myself. I'm surprised how I haven't told her about them. Maybe my psyche wants to keep them as a secret sign that everything will work out between us.

On the hundred-yard stretch of water between *Out for Fun* and the unlit neon sign that reads Island Hopper, several gulls float at the end of Sammy and Mary Lou's pier. Along the boardwalk, round tables with thatch umbrellas theme the place. Good thing we've got the inflatable dinghy. I'd hate to be forced to make that swim with my cardio-challenged physique. One of those boats with a fly-fishing platform, a huge outboard engine on back, rests beside the pier.

The back door swings open; a bundle of bouncing brunette curls in the name of Lizzie runs to the end of the pier and tosses handfuls of something to the gulls. They squawk and flutter and peck and fight for a share.

Lizzie brushes her hands together and runs back inside. Barely a minute passes before she trots along the sidewalk at the front of the building, backpack signaling school.

I start for the kitchen when a sonic boom shatters the sublime silence. What a place to locate a naval air station.

In the kitchen, Scotty makes french toast. Bacon sizzles in another pan; coffee dribbles into the decanter. I slip my hands around her waist. "You spoil me, pumpkin."

"My new pet name?"

"Um-hmm." I nuzzle vanilla scented neck, made accessible by a ponytail. The fine hairs at the nape tickle my nose.

She leans back into me. "I hope pumpkin's not a reference to my tummy."

"It just sort of popped out."

"What's that song from the seventies?"

"You like oldies too?"

"What is it? Magic ...?"

"Ah, you mean *Magic Man*, by Heart. That means I'm the man with the magic hands."

"Definitely."

"I see Sammy and Mary Lou like to fish."

"They must've gotten the boat since the last time me and the hubs visited. If I remember correctly, Sammy said something about wanting to guide part time. You should get him to take you out."

"You wouldn't go?"

"I'd rather spend some time with Mary Lou. I'll see if I can find a swimsuit to knock your eyes out when we visit some of those isolated islands."

"Did you see Lizzie feeding the gulls?"

"She's a cutie. Mary Lou emailed me about her birthday party in August, when she turned eleven. I hope I have a cutie like her."

Scotty's statement leaves me numb. I pour coffee and go to the window, but I only see her and a cutie like Lizzie with Scotty's sorry excuse for a husband beside them. No doubt he'll brag to his buddies like he did something special by donating his DNA.

This entire situation—my entire situation—is insane. The love of my life dies in a bizarre accident or suicide, which I've yet to figure out. I can't help but wonder if my mother-in-law's secretive sickness has something to do with the suicide angle. I was suspected of murder by Scotty the suspicious sheriff, only to have her kidnap me and find out she's anything but because she married the king of all jerks. Then I have feelings bordering on love for her, evidenced by my jealousy of her hubs taking on the role of husband and father when the baby's born.

Not insane at all, just crazy. I have the feeling I'll need a psychiatrist before all of this is over.

"You okay?" Scotty's cool hand touches my arm. "I've been asking how many pieces of french toast you want."

"Two's fine."

"Bacon?"

"Whatever."

"Jonathan?"

"Yeah?"

"Please don't ruin this by having feelings you're not sure of. If you fall in love with me, it's got to be the real deal. I won't settle for anything less."

"I'm just in a mood. You know how guys are."

"You've been perfect the entire trip. Don't think I didn't notice how you changed when I said I wanted a cutie like Lizzie. I know we said we'd give it a month to see what happens between us, but expecting a man to raise another man's child is a lot to ask."

"Guy's do it all the time."

"But do they love them like they're their own?"

"I never asked any."

"Could you love my daughter as if she were your own?"

"I haven't thought about it. Honestly, I'd prefer being her dad. I hope that doesn't sound too selfish."

"It doesn't, but I'd expect no less love for my daughter than I'd expect for me. When we anchored yesterday, I thought of the perfect name for her. Can you please turn around and look at me and tell me we'll have a great time the rest of our trip?"

"What name?"

"I'm not counting my oysters before they're shucked."

Smiling, I turn. "What happened to counting your eggs before they hatch?"

"You're in the Keys, Gilligan, get with the program." Scotty gives me a quick kiss. "Let's eat before it gets cold. Then I'll show you how to inflate the dinghy so we can visit Sammy and Mary Lou."

We sit. I take a bite of cinnamon flavored french toast. Scotty gets up for syrup and shakes the bottle at me. "I'd say it'll make you sweeter but you're sweet enough."

"You just want my magic hands to work their magic at your beck and call."

"I wouldn't turn you down."

I sip coffee, crunch bacon, and swallow. "I didn't see any parent pictures in your office. They as bad as the hubs?"

"The exact opposite. I think I got my down-home hospitality — you know, by how I invited you on this trip — from them."

I aim a fork at Scotty. "I still haven't decided whether or not to press charges for kidnapping."

"As we well know, you won't get far with the sheriff."

"Ain't that the truth? Any chance you have magic hands?"

The tip of her pink tongue exits those full lips and pulls back in. "A magic something else too."

"Sounds promising. What about your parents makes you hospitable?"

"I'm sure you noticed the farm stands on your drive to Nags Head."

"Mom and Dad used to stop all the time for peaches." I fork a bite of french toast.

"My folks ran one of those farms when I was a kid. It's a great way to grow up." Scotty pauses for coffee. "Nothing like farm work to learn a work ethic."

"What do they do now?"

"Unlike most married couples, they didn't intend to have children. I snuck in and surprised them."

"Nothing wrong with not having kids."

"They regretted not having more after I came along. Dad spoiled me rotten."

"Like with four-wheel ATVs?"

"I caught you looking at my picture in my office."

"You looked a lot happier muddy than any city girl looks clean."

Scotty shifts. Beneath the table, her sandal plops to the deck, and a cool foot slides up my calf. "You ain't seen nothin' yet."

In the middle of a swallow of coffee, I cough. "Sounds good, Skipper." I lick coffee from my lips. "Are they still farming?"

"I hate to be a downer."

"Did something happen to them?"

"Mom didn't have me until she was forty-three. Since I'm twenty-eight, she's seventy-one. Early onset Alzheimer's landed her in a nursing home in Elizabeth City a few years ago."

"My dad died from—"

"Sorry to interrupt. You told me he died from cirrhosis when I brought you to my office the other day." Scotty eats french toast. "Your mom still around?"

"She remarried a high-powered attorney and lives in Maryland. She's the high maintenance type."

"Are you on good terms?"

"I call, she calls. I visit every other Christmas if they're not out of town visiting his kids by his first wife."

"Do you have brothers or sisters?"

"A younger sister. She lives in Texas. Got married a couple of years ago. They get along great but no kids yet."

"Mom and Dad were great together. I hoped for that with the hubs. You see how that ended up."

I reach over for Scotty's hand. "He's a damn fool. I'd take a four-wheeling country girl who looks like she's been wrestling with the pigs over a high-maintenance city girl any day of the week."

Scotty tips her coffee mug my way. "I'll drink to that, Jonathan."

She sips. I sip. We eat french toast and crunch bacon. I can't think of anything I'd rather do than sit with her and look into those intense green eyes. "Did you always want to be in law enforcement?"

"I went back and forth between that and a wetlands researcher."

"You couldn't ask for two vocations to be so different, Sheriff."

"You never know, I might dump the hubs one day and go to school for something entirely different. Did you always want to sell MRIs?"

"When did I tell you that?"

"You probably don't remember that question because of all the other questions I asked the night after ..."

"You can say it. The night after Andy died."

"When I saw you beside her, I knew you loved her, not to mention how you cried on the way to my office. I hated acting like the big bad sheriff, but I had a job to do."

"That day was more of a blur than anything. I wouldn't want to relive it for anything in the world." I take the last bite of french toast, put two more strips of bacon in my plate, and get up for coffee. "Need a refill?"

"I'm good. Did you have to go to school to sell MRIs?"

"I started doing that after attempting to teach junior high. I admire the dedication of teachers, but I don't have the patience." I sit. "The MRI is a cool machine. You probably know this, but you can look at the thinnest layers of a person with it when you scan them."

"Quite the subtext. I thought about creative writing for a while, but it's a difficult business to break into." Scotty takes her plate to the sink. "We should visit the Hemingway House and Museum. You'll love it."

"The hubs took you?"

"Not a chance. The only books he reads are porn. I went one day while he was fishing. At least he said he was fishing." Scotty palms her breasts. "The supposed guide wore a bikini and had her own built-in life jacket. Double-Ds at least."

"Sounds like a plan."

"Double-Ds or going to Hemingway house?"

"We could always stay here and see what kind of spell those magic hands of yours can cast."

"You instigated that, not me." Scotty takes our plates to the sink. "I'll wash, you dry. Then we'll inflate the dinghy and see what Sammy and Mary Lou are up to."

Chapter 11

Like with her Floridian knowledge of the Florida Keys, Scotty's also a fount of knowledge on inflatable dinghies. I was expecting an oblong doughnut and two plastic oars. In the engine room, when she starts to drag a huge canvas bag that's almost as tall as me from a corner, I stop her. "You shouldn't do that in your condition."

"Sorry. I'm the independent type."

"Uh-huh. Despite finding that extremely sexy, I need to help and you need to let me."

We drag the bag to the ladder and set it upright. I climb the rungs, reach down, and wrestle it to the deck. "This freaking thing is gonna break my back."

Scotty climbs the ladder. "No, sir. That honor is mine before we head home."

"Says the woman who tried to stop my hand from working its magic."

Scotty kicks the bag. "Dump her out. I forgot the air pump and the oars."

"Hey."

About to place her foot on the ladder, she looks up. "What?"

"You didn't say if your dad is still around."

"It's not something I like to talk about." She leads me to the stern, where we lean against the polished mahogany railing. "But if we have any chance at a relationship, I should be open with you about it."

"I like openness in a relationship. At times, Andy could be … I don't know, closed off describes it as well as anything."

"I bet you didn't think that about me when you woke up that hot morning with my naked fat behind beside you."

I bump her shoulder with mine. "How many times do I need to tell you we're overweight instead of fat?"

"I'll compromise by calling it plus-sized. As far as Dad, it happened a week after I married the hubs. I missed him and Mom and drove to the farm for a visit. She sat me down and forced a slice of peach pie alamode on me. I can taste it now, wow."

"You get her recipe?"

"Unfortunately, for my waistline and lack of willpower, yes, I did. The peaches were canned but still great. It was March, Dad was plowing their garden spot. He had this ancient thing with double wheels in front, almost like a tricycle. All we can figure is the wheels hung in a row and turned the tractor over on him."

"Sorry to hear that, Scotty. Sounds like a terrible thing to see."

She slides close, leans her head onto my shoulder. "We heard him scream. He was pinned under one of those huge back tires. He bled from his mouth, so I knew his ribs were crushed. Mom ran inside to call 911. I knelt by Dad. He took my hand and said, 'You know, honey, this looks bad. But I've had a fine life with you and your mama. If it's time for me to go, I'm ready.'"

I can't comment about this. If Andy had been able to tell me anything while she was dying, I don't know how I would've handled it.

Scotty snuggles into my shoulder. "He coughed up blood. I was crying, you can imagine how bad it was."

I hug Scotty close and kiss her hair. "I hate how you had to deal with that."

She looks up at me, green eyes crinkling, dark chocolate wisps of hair at her temples waving in the breeze. "Would you believe he laughed? Then he said if Ted ever did me wrong, he'd come back from the grave and stomp his city-slicker ass all over Dare County."

If ever there's a time to smile, this is it. "Your dad sounds like a guy I could've drank a few beers with."

"He coughed again, kind of let out this little gasp. I'll never forget the last thing he said. 'Honey, like the tides, life's a series of ups and downs. The trick is to not let the downs keep you down. Do whatever you have to … kick, fight, whatever … or completely change your life, but do what it takes to be happy."

"A man I'd be proud to call my father-in-law, Scotty."

She gives me a quick kiss. "There you go, being sweet again. Get that dinghy out while I get the oars and pump. We're burning Florida Keys daylight."

I work the heavy material from the bag. Scotty returns with the pump, sets it on the deck, and goes back for the oars, which she tosses up. I start unrolling the dinghy, which smells like rubber. "The hub's name is Ted?"

She climbs from below. "He hates to be called that. Says he prefers his given name of Thaddeus. He's nothing but a pretentious stuffed shirt with an ego to match." She leans over to help unroll the dinghy. I grab her and roll to the deck, dragging her on top of me. "No stuffed shirts here, pumpkin, just stuffed bellies."

She straddles me, pins me down with those gorgeous eyes. "I could fall in love with you as easy as eating Mom's peach pie."

Her words pin me down too. I've never felt like a schoolboy with his first crush, all goofy and playful. This is exactly how I feel now. I don't know how our trip will end, but I intend to do whatever it takes to not lose her to an idiot husband. I pinch her bra clasp. "Keep looking at me like that, we'll go skinny dipping."

She gets up. "Something to put on the agenda. Let's get this dinghy ready before Sammy and Mary Lou run out on us."

I continue unrolling the dinghy. "You should've called and said we were coming."

"I want to surprise them. Yachts like this are pretty common. That's why I anchored with the name pointing away."

"Mighty sneaky, pumpkin."

Scotty tells me the dinghy has several individual compartments to inflate. She connects the pump's hose to one and presses a button. The pump whirrs; the compartment bulges, puffs, and slowly tightens. The cycle continues until a ten-foot long by four-foot-wide dinghy, including its upturned bow, is ready to launch.

I add the oars. Scotty opens a door on the rear rail at the stern. We work the dinghy out; it plops to the water with a splash. She ties it to a cleat.

BOOM!

I look up. It takes me a few seconds to spot the Navy fighter: a silver speck in the crystal-clear sky. I can barely hear the hollow whisper of its jet engines. "Sheesh. What a freaking noise."

"They hit when you least expect it. You ready?"

"I pat my wallet in my shorts pocket. My treat today. You bought everything so far."

83

Scotty grabs me by the pockets and pulls me close for a kiss. "Uh-huh. You're just dying for a reward from my magic hands."

I answer with a smile. It's her magic tongue I'm more interested in.

We climb into the dinghy. I place the oars in the holders and row. Scotty sits behind me in the bow.

The morning wakes around us: A few piers down, two men in wide-brimmed hats carry fishing gear to a boat. A black pelican sits on a piling, head tucked, long beak down as if its praying, unfazed by the men. Gulls *scree-scree-scree* overhead. Somewhere out of sight, a dog barks.

The air warms and I do too. Sweat trickles down my neck and between my shoulder blades. Scotty nudges my back with the toe of a sandal. "You'll need a shower before I work any magic on you."

"You like salty water, why not salty me?"

"You've got muscles in your back. I bet you'd look great if you worked out."

"All you need to worry about is my magic hands, Skipper. What was in that other bag by the dinghy in the engine room?"

"A double hammock. Great for hanging between two coconut palms and drowsing an afternoon away."

Pulling the oars tightens my shoulders and back. I need to work out, no doubt about it.

We leave *Out for Fun* behind. Spray blows beside us, my dolphin friends returning. Scotty laughs. "Whoa, I've never had them come so close."

I still don't mention how they followed us all the way here. Some secrets are better left unsaid, like my secret of hoping Scotty and I can work things out. I feel that even more because it doesn't bother me to think of her and the hubs in the hammock on one of those isolated islands. After all, I'm with her, and he isn't.

"Row harder with the right oar, Gilligan. We're getting off course."

I do as she asks. Several strokes later we bump the dock. Scotty climbs out and ties a rope to a cleat. At the back door, she knocks. No one answers; she cups her hands on a window and looks inside. I follow her to the front, where she faces me. "Sammy's jeep is gone."

I take her hand. "Sounds like a good time to visit the Hemingway House. Is it close enough to walk?"

"Not too far. There's plenty of sites to see. Fort Zachary Taylor. Key West Aquarium. Audubon House and Tropical Gardens. That pier to the east of Sammy and Mary Lou's place is for fishing."

"Like those on the Outer Banks. Let's start with the Hemingway House and see how it goes."

Scotty leads me along a sidewalk. "Good idea. Sammy and Mary Lou might be back by then."

A half block along, Scotty points to the right. "There's a butterfly conservatory that way."

I squeeze her hand. "You're all the butterfly I need, Skipper."

She returns the squeeze. "Glad to hear it, Gilligan."

Residences line both sides of the street; several rooves gleam black with solar panels. Small trees are scattered here and there, some with normal leaves, some with palm fronds. Cars line both sidewalks. In the growing heat, air moist with humidity, not only does sweat trickle down my neck and shoulder blades, it streams wet lines from my underarms and down my sides.

The aroma of bacon rides the breeze, someone cooking breakfast. Wearing shorts and sunglasses, a young couple walks by, then another, then another. Key West is waking. An orange tram with gold trim—sort of a mini-bus filled with huge windows—drives past us. Few people sit inside. A white lighthouse with a black wrought iron railing and walkway looms up out of the trees. I wonder how old it us. The picket fence ends, replaced by a solid fence, still white but with pickets on top. On the other side of the street, the fence gives way to red brick. Scotty runs me over and through an opening.

Sagging chains connected to black metal posts guide us to the house doors. Scotty stops halfway. "I love how it's square and has a balcony and porches all around."

I admire Hemingway House. "Four arched windows on the bottom and top floors. Is it like that all the way around?"

"All the way. Shuttered for hurricanes."

"Plenty of palm trees everywhere."

"And a garden in back, want to see? We can take a tour inside another time."

"Why not? I'm an outdoorsy type." We stroll by a pool. "How big is that thing?"

"Twenty-four feet wide and sixty-feet long. Ten-feet deep at one end and five-feet deep at the other. The Keys are coral reefs, so it was dug from solid coral. Hemingway wasn't pleased about the price. It was finished in 1938 and cost 20,000 dollars."

I leave Scotty and go to the edge. "Why so much?"

"People got their drinking water from underground cisterns back then. They caught rainwater and stored it in them. It was impossible to catch enough rainwater to fill this thing. They drilled into the salt-water table and installed a pump to fill it."

"Old Ernie wanted to go swimming some kinda bad."

"He loved the ocean and fishing. Have you read *The Old Man and the Sea?*"

"Sorry, that's a classic I need to check out. Where's the garden?"

An elderly couple rounds the corner of the house. He wears tan shorts past his knees, a touristy T with Key West printed on the breast pocket, and boat shoes. His wife has the same T, women's slacks and sandals instead of shorts, and boat shoes. She stops and points. "Would you look at the size of that pool, Herbert?" Her voice is high-pitched and squeaks.

Joining her, Herbert scratches his head. "Why didn't he just swim in the ocean, Agnes? It's only a few blocks away."

Scotty grabs my hand. "Will that be us when were too old to enjoy magic hands and magic tongues?"

I pop her bottom. "I wouldn't know about the tongue part."

"Patience, Jonathan, patience. We've got plenty of time yet."

We continue along the mown yard, grass soft beneath our shoes. The palms thicken, rustle in the breeze. Shrubs surround us, blocking the view of the house. I wave my hand at the amazing colors, sizes, shapes, and varieties of flowers and trees. "Talk about a garden."

Scotty shoves me against a palm and peeks around me. "Do you like surprises?"

"If they're good surprises."

She turns around and presses her bottom against me. "Like this?" I grab her hips; she gyrates them. "Well, well, well, Gilligan. It feels like you like it."

I turn her around for a kiss: long, slow, and deep. She unzips me. "I happen to love salt." She kneels. "As long as it's you I'm tasting."

I don't argue. All I can do is lean back against the coarse bark of the palm and close my eyes. It's my turn to be a hurricane, to feed on moisture and heat.

Palm fronds rustle in the breeze. On the street nearby, traffic murmurs. Somewhere in the garden, amongst the leaves and petals, hummingbird wings whir, dart, and dip.

"Herbert," Agnes squeaks behind us, "do you see what those people are doing?"

"Lucky him," Herbert says. "You ain't done that in I don't know when."

Scotty rolls backward to the grass, holds her sides and cackles like a sea gull. All I can do is laugh with her and zip up. She gets to her feet. "They're gone. I can try again."

"Why ruin a perfectly good memory. It's seared into every gray cell I have now."

"Mine too. Now we can call each other Herbert and Agnes. Let's go see if Sammy and Mary Lou are back."

Chapter 12

About halfway to the bar, Scotty takes her phone from her pocket. "Screw him."

"What?"

"Ted is checking up on me."

"A call? A text?"

"He left a voice message. I had the tone off because I didn't trust him after that first call."

"All he knows is you took the yacht out."

She snatches the phone from her pocket again. "Might as well see what he wants." Her eyes follow the text. She shoves the phone in her pocket. "I really didn't mean that about him checking up on me but that's exactly what he's doing. He knows we always refuel in Savannah and Miami, so he called the diesel place."

Scotty's sandals slap the sidewalk. I lengthen my stride to keep up. "In Savannah?"

"In Miami. The guy told him another guy was with me." Scotty goes to the shade of one of the many palms lining the sidewalk and stops. "I've had the tone off since last night. I just brought the phone out of habit. He must've called while we were asleep."

"Because of the time zone difference in Australia."

"Exactly. I hope I interrupt his fun with whatever woman, or women, he's with." Her nails tap the screen. She puts the phone in her pocket. Not answering. Maybe he's banging a new conquest."

We take maybe a dozen steps along the sidewalk; she stops again. "I put it on vibrate. Wanna bet this is him?" She raises the phone to her ear. "I don't care what that man in Miami said, I'm by myself." She chews her lower lip. Those green eyes dart, enraged emeralds behind narrowed slits. "You what? Look, I'm pregnant with your child, why would I cheat on you?" A pause. "I wish I hadn't called if all it did was make you call Hemingway House and ask the clerk if he saw me with someone." Another pause. "Yes, I like the place and go every time we come. You just lucked out that I was there."

My situation—*our* situation—is getting a lot more serious. Ted better not be the type who doesn't mind hopping on an airliner in the middle of the Australian night and flying all the way to the Keys to catch his wife with another man. At least we'll have roughly twenty-four hours to decide what to do, if and when he does.

"Look, Ted, the guy in Miami saw the cabby helping me with groceries and the clerk at the Hemingway house saw me talking to another tourist. Absolutely nothing is going on." She swipes the phone and shoves it in her pocket. "I don't care if he believes me or not, I'm tired of his lies. Like I said in my office, this has been building for a long time."

Again, sandals slap the sidewalk. Again, I lengthen my stride to keep up. "What's the chance he would fly here to catch us together?"

Scotty stops midstride. "Why? You going to ditch me now?"

"I'm on your side, okay? I just want to know if that's something to worry about."

"He is *not* that type. He's accused me before—all it takes is me glancing at someone. I'm not the cheater, he is. He'll just yell about it at home and that'll be that. His ego's the size of a blue whale. The last thing he wants is his friends thinking he couldn't keep me satisfied."

"Is he the vindictive type?"

"Oh, yeah. If it got out that I was cheating on him, he'd trash my reputation to everyone he knows, from Corolla to Ocracoke and everywhere between. I'm young to be a sheriff. His influence helped me get the job, so he'll use that same influence to ruin me."

Scotty takes off down the sidewalk again. I walk hard to catch up. For someone who claims she wants to see if we have a future, every time the subject of her husband comes up, all she does is act like she's going back to him. The thought hurts and I don't like it. Still, we get along great. The best thing I can do is not push the issue and see what happens with the time we have left. I place my hand on the back of her neck. "Hey, you know I care about you, right?"

"I care about you too. It's just an insane situation, and I don't know how to get out of it."

"Don't forget what your dad said: 'Do whatever you have to … kick, fight, whatever … or completely change your life, but do what it takes to be happy.'"

Scotty slows, slows more, and stops to face me. "When I told Ted that story, it didn't faze him at all. You remember it word for word and use it to give me the best advice Dad ever gave me. You *are* sweet. I wish I had met you a long time ago."

"Then don't give up. We have plenty of time, barring Ted showing up."

"That's true. He didn't like Sammy and Mary Lou, so none of his friends go there."

"No one will see us out on the water either. Let's enjoy ourselves and quit worrying about him."

Warm fingers slip into mine. A smile that makes me smile. "Well, Jonathan, maybe I'll treat you to some magic on one of those isolated islands."

At Sammy and Mary Lou's place, a jeep sits in front. Scotty leads me to a bar inside. No one tends it but it's early. She pops her hand on the bar, oak-grain thick with varnish. "Where's my favorite southern girl and Cajun fisherman?"

A voice screeches surprise from a room through a doorway behind the bar. "Is that my gal pal, Scotty?"

"Sure is, M.L."

"Be right out, hon."

I smile at Scotty. "I think she's happy you're here. Is Scotty your real name? All this time I've been thinking it was something special just for me."

"Sorry to disappoint you, Gilligan."

"Your last name's Scott? As in Scotty Scott?"

"Shut up, Jonathan Smith. What a boring last name. If you didn't have such magic hands, I'd forget you in a heartbeat."

"Who got magic hands?" A wiry man, skin tanned almost to the point of black, deep crow's feet etched into the corners of his eyes, comes in the back door that leads to the pier. He wears baggy cargo shorts and a red tank top. On a strap around his neck, sunglasses hang. Scotty runs over and hugs him. "Hey, Sammy. I see you finally got into the guide business. That's a nice ride tied to the pier."

"Ain't my boat. I give up de idea when Lou take over."

Sammy's gruff voice pronounces "my" like "mooie" and "over" like "ovah." He's definitely Cajun.

"What do you mean?" Scotty says. "I thought being a fishing guide was your thing."

"Ah bought de boat and de rod an' reels an' she bought scuba stuff an' take ovah. She good at it, dough." Sammy winks at me, then faces Scotty. "Well, well, I see you brought dat brudder o' yours dis time. Ain't dat fine."

"Something like that."

"Nice to meet you," I say to Sammy. "What's the chance Mary Lou can take me out? I've always wanted to try fishing the Keys."

"Boy, I'm the brains of this outfit. Ask me instead of Sam." Mary Lou comes around the bar to hug Scotty. She's tanned, but not as deep as Sammy. Wearing zero makeup, a pleated skirt in powder blue that ends at her knees, blonde hair with hints or premature gray at the temples, and no shoes, she steps away from Scotty. "Look atchoo, purty as a pitchure. Who's this brother you brought along??

"I rescued him from a home for wayward guppies."

"He's cute for a brother. You finally kick Ted to the curb like I been tellin' you to do?"

Scotty comes back over and slips her fingers into mine. "We'll see, M.L., we'll see."

"What should I call you?" I ask Mary Lou. "Sammy calls you Lou. Scotty calls you M.L"

"I heard you say you want to go fishin'. Pay me right, you can call me whatever you want."

Scotty sits at the bar. "We saw Lizzie this morning."

Sammy takes a chair at a nearby table. Mary Lou sits beside Scotty. "Growin' like a pelican. Sam says he's gonna teach her to shoot his pistol for when the boys start askin' her out. Y'all want a drink? Sam, fix 'em whatever they want."

Sammy gets up. Scotty waves him back to the chair and pats her tummy. "Not for me. I've got a guppy in the aquarium."

"Do tell," Sammy says. "Do ah ask if de big guppy de little guppy's daddy or not?"

"Stop bein' so nosy," Mary Lou says. "Besides, she'll tell me when I get her alone. How long y'all stayin', Scotty?"

"We're taking it as it comes."

I face Mary Lou. "What kind of classes does a person need to scuba dive?"

"I only take people out for that when they wanna dive shipwrecks. Stick to the reefs, snorkels and fins work fine."

"I've already got those," Scotty says.

"How about Ted?" Mary Lou says.

"How about him what?"

"Where's he at and who's he doin'?"

"He's in Australia—I don't care who he's doing." Scotty loops her elbow into Mary Lou's and pulls her off the stool. "Let's check out your boat for when you lend it to me and Jonathan for snorkeling. *Out for Fun* takes too much water for those shallow reefs."

Mary Lou pulls Scotty to a stop. "Jonathan? Will he get mad if I call him Jonny, like Ted gets mad when I don't call him Thaddeus? How about it, Jonny?"

"Call me whatever, M.L."

M.L. nods at Scotty. "I think you got a winner with Jonny, gal pal."

The ladies leave. Sammy goes behind the bar, fills two iced mugs with draft beer, and sets one on the bar for me. "What de deal is, Jonny?"

I liked Sammy at first. For a split second I *don't* like him, until I realize his tone is the same as a father's tone when he asks his daughter's boyfriend why he's dating her. I sip beer. Except for bits of ice, it goes down smooth. "Long story short, Sammy, we're victims of circumstance."

"You love her? Better or I'll stomp a swamp hole in yo' ass big 'nuff to drive one 'o dem damn jets through that booms 'round heah all de time." Scotty's right about Sammy's Cajun accent: it's thick and amusing. "Time" is "toime."

"I wouldn't blame you if you did, she's a fine woman."

"I knew dat widdout you tellin' me. She been heartbroke by dat damn Ted too damn long. You love her or not?"

Sammy's question is a good one. I swallow beer. "You don't have to worry about me hurting her. We've been through a lot and I know how it feels to hurt."

"Is dat guppy yours?"

I look out the back windows lining the bar wall adjacent to the pier. Mary Lou and Scotty are in deep conversation, evidenced by Mary Lou's waving hands, exactly like a woman telling another woman a man isn't worth loving if he doesn't love your baby when it isn't his.

"Believe it or not, Sammy, I wish her guppy *was* mine."

In the middle of a swallow of beer, Sammy's bushy brows dart up. He sets the mug down. "Well, dat's sayin' sometin'. When you want Lou to take you fishin'?"

"I'll see what Scotty says. We're sort of playing our trip by ear."

"Permit's good eatin'. Fight like de devil, too. You know how ta work a fly rod?"

"Never had the opportunity."

"No matter. Can ketch 'em on spinnin' tackle."

Scotty and Mary Lou come in. Scotty comes over. "You guys getting to know each other?"

"He ain't no fly fisherman," Sammy says. "I spose he'll do."

I pull Scotty into my lap. "We never talked about an agenda."

"They don't exist in the Keys. Let's check out one of those islands we've been talking about tonight. Then we'll come back for some snorkeling tomorrow. M.L.'s going to shut down the bar after, and we'll cook some fresh seafood in her kitchen. That way I can see how much Lizzie has grown."

Scotty and I say our goodbyes. I row the dinghy back to *Out for Fun*, where we secure it to the rear deck. Anchor weighed, we start the generator and the air conditioner in an attempt to dry the sweat dripping down my back.

Steering us away from Island Hopper's pier, Scotty suggests I shower. I say why do that when we're going swimming nude after a grilled steak on whatever isolated island she finds for us to visit.

Chapter 13

Out for Fun cleaves the pea-green ocean aside; water froths white against the bow. Our dolphin friends dart back and forth in front of us: sea-borne children at play, gray backs shining, blowholes spraying when they break the surface, dorsal fins knifing the bow wave's bulge.

Sammy's question about whether or not I love Scotty aggravates me. If I had met her outside of our insane situation, gotten to know her, maybe asked her out for drinks, I'd see her again. Like I remind myself about fat shaming, I'm not in the greatest shape like she's not in the greatest shape.

But that doesn't matter.

A story Dad told me about Mom pops into my memory. He met her in the high school library. Said she was a homely little thing with acne and glasses. Said he asked her about a book she was reading. Said her smile and her excitement at the book told him she was someone worth getting to know.

I feel like I know Scotty already. We've both been through hell but we're surviving. Sure, my hell is bad but I'll heal. Her hell is ongoing. I have no idea how it will end and she doesn't seem to know either.

Doubt is a pain. Whenever I found Andy up in the middle of the night, I doubted her. Whenever she remarked about light and visiting a galaxy, I doubted her. One day—I don't know how—I'll get to the bottom of her strange behavior.

I head to the bridge, where Scotty reads her paperback. "Where's my phone? I'd like to call my father-in-law."

"In the safe under the picture by the window. The one of the humpback whale."

"I take the picture down. "Combination?"

"The lock's broken, have at it."

I retrieve my phone. "I'm glad your fume detector isn't broken. I'd hate to end up grilled like we'll grill those steaks later."

"Jonny, baby, if that alarm goes off and I run out to check those diesel tanks and they blow, you'll be lucky if there's enough of me to cook on my little propane grill."

I take the chair beside her. "Not sure how I feel about 'Jonny.'"

"Just messing with you. I've gotten used to Jonathan."

I go to my room and sit on the bed to dial Stan's number. Just when I realize he might be out on *Hope,* the rings stop.

"Jake, how's it goin'?"

"Not too bad. I have the feeling I'll miss Andy a long time. You and Marie doing okay?"

"I got a nice lady sittin' with her these days. She's got the patience of Job. I'm ashamed to admit, I tried stayin' home a few days and couldn't take bein' around her." Stan pauses like a man weighing his decision to allow me into the eye of his hurricane. "Andy ever say anything to you about Marie?"

"Not a word."

"Knowin' her long as you did, knowin' you never met Marie, your own mother-in-law, that had to come off as strange."

"I don't pry into family business, Stan."

"I respect that, Jake. For what it's worth, I thought you 'an Andy were a good match."

I let the silence slide along the invisible thread of energy connecting Stan and I through our phones. He clears his throat.

"Marie had a cancer scare about two years before you met Andy. Mammogram found a lump, docs took it out, radiation and chemo cleared her up. She went plumb crazy thinkin' she was gonna die anyway. Just when things got back to normal, so I thought, she started shoppin' like she was expectin' World War III. Filled nearly every room in the house with junk. I put most of it in the shed out back but left one room for her so she wouldn't walk an' worry an' wring her hands lookin' for it. I'd find her there in the middle of the night, just sittin' and pawin' that stuff like a pack rat afraid someone's gonna steal it all. Andy ever do anything like that with you?"

Stan's got enough on his plate. I answer the only way I can when a father is grieving his daughter: "Andy was perfect, Stan. You know that like I know that."

"She had her mama's ways at times. She'd get quiet for no reason. Day or so, she'd perk back up. You gone back to work yet? Best thing for a man when he's hurtin'."

"I'm taking some time off. Look, I better go."

"All right. One of these days when the weather's not tryin' to sink *Hope,* we'll do some fishin'."

"Sounds good, talk to you later."

I leave my phone on the bed and go to the bridge. Scotty looks up from the paperback. "How is he?"

I sit. "Have you had any experience with hoarders?"

"I've seen a TV show about them."

I don't want to involve Stan's family in gossip. "Stan says the wife of a friend has a room full of stuff where she goes in the middle of the night."

"The guy won't take her for help?"

I recall Stan saying how he was ashamed of not wanting to stay around Marie. "Stan says the guy's too ashamed."

"Lots of men are ashamed to be seen as weak. Or ashamed what people will think of a family member who's mentally ill. Something's obviously wrong with that guy's wife."

I go to the fridge for a Corona. "How far to our isolated island?"

"Maybe thirty minutes. I've always wanted to spend the night on one of those islands, but no camping is allowed. Where we're going is called Crawfish Key. It's part of the Key West National Wildlife Refuge."

"What about hanging a hammock or building a small fire?"

"We can chance it. Better sleep in our king bed, though."

"Good idea." I put the cold Corona bottle against my forehead. "I'd miss the AC."

"Are our dolphins still with us?"

"What makes them ours?"

"They've stayed with us almost the entire trip. I've never heard of a male and female being on their own in the open ocean."

"They don't mate for life?"

"They live in pods with other males and females. The male does his thing and zips off to find another female. Typical, if you ask me."

I stick the cold bottle to Scotty's thigh; she jerks away. "C'mon," I say, "I wouldn't do you like that."

"How do I know? You'll probably swim back home once you've had me."

I rub her thigh. "You'd miss my magic hands, pumpkin."

"That's true." Scotty points. "See that green dot up ahead? Go get the hammock and grill so we don't waste any time on the yacht when we can lie in the hammock."

"Where's the beach towels?"

"I'll get them after we anchor and change for swimming. We'll set up and come back for the food."

I do everything Scotty asks. On the bridge, we watch the depth finder's jagged line gradually creep upward on the LED screen—as if it's monitoring our hearts and everything we've gone though and are going through. She stops at fifteen feet and lowers the anchor. We're about twenty yards from a picture-perfect beach. Aquamarine wavelets trundle slivers of foam along white sands. Spiraled shells, wet in the sunlight, reflect sparkles and hints of rainbow prisms. Palms lean over the water; fronds wave in the breeze. I imagine their whispering rustle, the wavelets' wash and murmur.

We go to the bow. Two sleek bodies, gray with cream underneath, our dolphin friends crisscross below the surface of the water, green and crystalline.

"They sure look like male and female," Scotty says. "I've never heard or read of a pair leaving a pod."

"How do you know their sex when they're the same length?"

The males are heavier and rounder. This male's dorsal fin notch must be from fighting with another male."

I can't help slipping my hand around Scotty's waist. "Ted better not show up. I'll notch his jaw with a right hook if he does."

"You can have what's left after I get through."

We launch the dinghy and take everything to the beach. Scotty hangs the hammock between two palms. It's midafternoon, too early and too hot for a fire, too far from suppertime to light the grill and cook. Scotty paddles back to *Out for Fun* and returns with my guitar and her paperback. A pen is clipped inside the front cover. She gives me the guitar case. "I think you should serenade me while I read in the hammock."

"Can we both fit in it while I play?"

"One way to find out." She climbs into the tipsy hammock. "If you don't mind your head at my feet, it'll work."

Guitar in hand, I lie in the hammock without tipping us out. Scotty opens the paperback. I rub her calves and play with her toes. Good thing she's not ticklish.

She wears a barely-there bikini, cut high across her hips, cut low into her cleavage, a deep, dark, navy blue. I imagine the taste of smooth skin, vanilla flavored; the gold hoop in her ear lobe between my teeth, my tongue stroking the sensitive pool of skin where her jawline starts, then working my way down her neck and, of course, farther down. I rub her legs, feel the slightest touch of bristling hair on her shins. She slaps my knee. "I distinctly remember asking for a serenade." She takes the pen from the paperback and draws a heart on my knee. "Inspire my creative side, I feel like writing a novel." She draws an arrow through the heart. "About us."

I'm tempted to ask where the story ends but don't. She poises the pen above the paperback's inside cover on the back, and I pull her big toe. "You need a lot more paper than that."

"This is the prologue. Music. Now."

I strum the stings, tune them to pitch, and begin with an A minor chord. Scotty slaps my knee. "Not something sad, something happy. That sounds like a freaking funeral dirge."

"Not a word I expect to hear from a sheriff, Sheriff."

"Maybe Ted will fly over to catch me in bed with you and his plane will crash."

"One problem, pumpkin—we don't want anyone going down with him."

Scotty scribbles in the paperback. I play some chords, fingerpick a made-up tune, and stop. "That do anything for you?"

She clips the pen into the paperback. "Nap time, wannabe lover."

I ease the guitar onto the sand beneath me; it's cheap, who cares? Scotty's toes wiggle. I run a fingernail along the sole of her foot. "Didn't I tell you I'm not ticklish?" she says.

"Can't blame a guy for trying."

Cirrostratus clouds tint the sky a milky, translucent blue. Wavelets swish the sand. In the palms behind us, bird call echoes.

Scotty's breasts rise and fall with the rhythm of sleep, slow and steady. I can't see her green eyes for the sunglasses she lowered from her head when she stopped scribbling in the paperback. Those defined lips twitch and purse. On her straight nose, delicate nostrils flair and relax. A sudden breeze, warm and salty, swirls around us. I smell vanilla lotion.

Out for Fun blocks much of our immediate view. The faint drone of an outboard motor, sounding like an oversize chainsaw on steroids, catches my attention. I wait for it to appear but it passes behind us, silenced by the palms.

The milky blanket of cirrostratus swims by, replaced by cirrocumulus, similar to dandelion puffballs waiting to be blown by a child on a summer afternoon.

Not long after Andy moved in with me on the outskirts of Raleigh, we picnicked at a local park. We fed each other hot dogs and potato chips, chocolate chip cookies and lemonade, then walked a field of wildflowers. She brought a blanket, plucked dandelions and blew the miniature parasols into the air. They fell around us, dotting her like snowflakes. She craned her neck above the stems and leaves and blooms of purple, red, and yellow to look around. Coast clear, she made love to me.

Is she perched above Scotty and I? Reclined on one of those puffball cirrocumuli clouds? Watching and praying and hoping I'll find love again?

Twin dorsal fins cleave the water beside *Out for Fun*. Spray huffs into the air ahead of them. Mates for life in a species where mates for life never happens. Love can surprise those not the least bit ready for it.

At Scotty's temples, brunette wisps waver in the breeze. Am I ready for love after losing love not two weeks ago? Am I ready to face Ted and all his crap? Am I ready, in eight short months, to be a father to his child?

Wrong question in every way possible. If Scotty and I have a future, am I ready to be a father to *her* child? If so, hell will be paid—hell with Ted, hell with my mom, hell with handing Ted's child to him every other weekend and holidays.

I won't have a clue about any of that until Scotty and I decide what to do. I won't have a clue until her baby is born in June either, having been conceived last month, in September.

Despite my emotions concerning this conundrum, including Andy, her death, and now, this triple conundrum of Scotty, her baby, and Ted, I'm the logical sort, which is why I plan ahead, evidenced by my concern.

But I have no plan for any of this.

I stroke the tiny bristles on Scotty's leg. The opportunity of lying in a hammock stretched between two palm trees on an isolated island in the Florida Keys—with a sexy woman who's intelligent and confident and can weather this deal with her husband—is rare. Time to enjoy it by taking a nap.

Chapter 14

We wake to a setting sun, stiff necks, and the urge to pee that sends us scurrying to the palms. When I get back, Scotty lights the propane grill, takes our steaks from the cooler, and places them on paper plates. She gives them to me, along with a container of seasoning from a grocery bag. "Use plenty of that. Meat doesn't taste good without salt."

"Is that the only memory you'll take from our short visit to Hemingway House?"

"One I'll never forget."

From another bag, she takes out tossed salad ingredients and two huge russet potatoes. "How long does it take potatoes to bake in a fire?"

"Quicker to bake them in the microwave on the boat."

"Well, I want them, please. Butter and sour cream that I left on board too. After my baby brings me to parental reality, I'll lose weight if it's the last thing I do."

Those demands met, I row to *Out for Fun* in the dinghy and back for potatoes and other required condiments. "Is her highness satisfied?"

Scotty opens the grill; the steaks sizzle on the grate. "What if I hire you as a pool boy? You can watch my tummy blow up into a belly. Ted probably won't be there for the birth—it'll be just like we were married."

"Sorry. If I can't have you for myself ..." My tone involuntarily lowers.

"I'm teasing, okay?"

"This mess isn't something to tease about."

"I apologize. Can you start the fire? I'll watch the steaks."

I leave for the palms and driftwood. Behind one I watch Scotty. Her ponytail bobs at the nape of her neck while she makes the salads. She wears a sheer cover-up over the bikini; the blue material shows through the white. Despite her teasing, I want her worse than any woman I've ever known. Still, I won't press the issue of sex. I want her to know she's more important, and she is.

I build the fire to about a two-foot circle. Scotty plates our food. We sit on beach towels and eat. She drinks bottled water and I drink Corona. I've never tasted a better steak: medium-rare, juicy, seasoned to perfection. It's difficult to mess up a baked potato, although they are better in an oven. The bite of Corona, bitter and cold, finishes each swallow of food perfectly.

"Can you believe that?"

I look up from my plate. "What?"

"There's a boat about a mile away. I think I see orange and red."

"Coast Guard?"

"Maybe they can't see the fire for the yacht."

"Is it too late to put it out?"

"Leave it, I'll pay the ticket."

I see the boat. Two men stand behind the center console. The motor roars; the bow rises and falls. Red paint decorates the section of white on the hull above the water. One man raises binoculars. The roar of the motor increases.

"They're definitely coming this way."

Scotty takes the sheer cover-up off. "I'll distract them with my boobs."

I spit steak into my palm and laugh. She is too much, ready to take on any situation.

Passing *Out for Fun*, the boat slows and idles to the beach. One of the men takes off sunglasses. "Afternoon. Did you folks know fires aren't allowed on these islands?"

Scotty ducks her head. I get up. "Sorry about that, I'll put it out."

The man leans forward. "Scotty? Is that you?"

She lowers the sunglasses from her head to her eyes and points at her mouth: the universal sign for "I'm eating."

"Where's Ted?"

I kick sand on the fire and go back to the blanket. "I'm Scotty's cousin. She wanted to cruise the Keys and called me to keep her company. She picked me up in Savannah and I took her out to dinner to celebrate her and Ted's news."

"What news is that?"

"They're expecting a baby in June."

Scotty raises the sunglasses. "Sorry, Steve, I didn't recognize you with the sun in my eyes."

"No problem. Look, tell Ted I said congratulations. Just keep the fire small and I'll let it go." The other man cranks the boat and puts it reverse. Steve waves. The boat roars away.

I sit and pick up my plate. "Any chance Ted will call that guy?"

Scotty cups her fingers as if she holds a ball, shakes it, and looks at it. "My Magic Eight-Ball says who knows. Lucky for you I've got a cousin. Unlucky for me she lives in California."

"He could be visiting."

"Really? If we manage to get married, are you gonna be one of *those* husbands?"

"What husband is that?"

"One with selective hearing. I said *she* lives in California."

"You can tell Ted the Coast Guard dude misheard you like I just did, and I'm your female cousin."

"Shut up and eat. Then paddle back for the butter pecan ice cream I forgot."

I do as Scotty asks, taking back all the other stuff except paper bowls and plastic spoons for the ice cream, including my guitar and her paperback. She's kneeling by the fire when I return, having built it up again. I climb from the dinghy with the bag and take it and the blanket to the fire. "Your wish is my demand, your highness."

"Being sweet will get you nowhere, salty man."

"I showered this morning."

"And have been sweating all afternoon. Sit and feed me ice cream before I knight you, knave."

She takes a spoonful. I take a spoonful. "Do you watch those PBS shows like *Downton Abbey?*"

"Don't worry, knave, I won't kill you during sex like Lady Mary did that guy and drag you off somewhere to keep it hidden."

"Just how many people do you and Ted know down here?"

"I hope we've run out. We could visit the aquarium on the other side of Key West from Sammy and Mary Lou's place. We've never been there."

We finish the ice cream. I lie on my side, rest my elbow on the blanket, my head in my hand. Scotty does the same.

To the left of *Out for Fun*, the line of clouds above the horizon burns yellow, orange and, when the sun lowers, the deepest, darkest shade of blood red I've ever seen, shimmering and molten like the crater of a steaming volcano.

The fire bathes the area around us in a circle of wavering light. Embers crackle. Embers pop. Flaming wood collapses in on itself; a shower of sparks rises into the night. The constant breeze dies; palm fronds end their rustle. Those foaming wavelets continue their whispering wash upon the beach like they have for millennia.

Scotty lowers her head to the blanket, and I do too. "How long can we get away with staying here?"

"If I had my way, forever."

"Because of the scenery, right."

"I never get tired of it." She gets up. "But I'm still sticky from the heat. That means a shower and the AC."

Fire out, blanket folded, trash in the bag, we row the dinghy to *Out for Fun*. On the bridge, Scotty flips switches. The generator thrums; the AC purrs. I snap my fingers. "We forgot our skinny dip."

"Plenty of time yet. You shower first. I thought of a few more lines to my novel and want to write them down before I forget them."

"Don't forget the great ending we both deserve."

The bathroom mirror says my five 'o'clock shadow needs shaving. The steak in my teeth says my teeth need brushing and flossing. I give the water heater time to do its job. Shower steaming, I step in and shampoo. Cool air rushes in, the bathroom door opening. Scotty's bare feet patter across the faux marble tiles. The shower door clicks open and clicks closed. "Just in time to rinse your hair, Jonny." I wait; she doesn't rinse my hair. Wet breasts press against my chest. Firm hands run fingernails up and down my back. My reaction is immediate. She rinses my hair, returns the shower to the holder, kisses me, turns around, presses her bottom against me, and I do what men have been doing since the dawn of time.

We finish our showers, towel each other off. She blow-dries her hair and joins me in bed.

In the shower, that sudden and inexplicable offering of herself to me resulted in the speediest sex I've ever experienced. In the huge king-sized bed, our offering of each other to each other results in the slowest, most sensual, hour-long sex I've ever experienced. No inch of skin is left unkissed. No inch of skin is left untouched. No inch of skin is left unexplored. We rest and, like Lady Mary from *Downton Abbey* might say, we venture forth once more.

Scotty sits astride me. She rises and falls like the tide beneath a full moon, like hurricane Dorian's storm surge across the Pamlico Sound, inundating Ocracoke Island in the worst flood in decades with millions of gallons of salt water.

On her pillow, the AC cooled sheets pulled to her chin, she lies on her side. I lie beside her, my back to her front. She slides her hand to my chest. As cliché as it sounds, I've died and gone to Heaven. Our heartbeats slow. My breathing does too. As my last remnant of conscious thought falters, she whispers, "I love you."

This revelation both surprises and puzzles me. Either she thinks I'm asleep or she doesn't. To test her I say nothing. If she shakes me and asks if I heard her, she wants me to return this profound sentiment. If not, she's not ready for my commitment and wants to use our remaining time together to earn it.

She doesn't shake me.

Here I am, on the brink of loving another woman as much—or more—as I loved Andy. The moment must be right. I'll make an excuse to go out alone on Key West for an engagement ring. On the night before we leave, I'll wait until she's almost asleep to whisper "I love you' in her ear. She'll roll over, make love to me again. Ecstatic, we'll cruise back to Manteo with plans of confronting Ted with our demands.

In the distant night a boat roars by. I picture the red and green running lights on the bow, the white running light on the stern. *Out for Fun* rocks gently, more gently, then stills.

Poets and novelists, playwrights and songwriters, have penned many a quote concerning love. In *Sense and Sensibility* by Jane Austen, Marianne Dashwood said: "If but I could but know his heart, everything would become easy." Scotty may be dreaming this sentiment as I think it. Or possibly she's dreaming the one by Emily Bronte in *Wuthering Heights*. I forget the character who said it, but I think the quote is: "Whatever our souls are made of, his and mine are the same." Then again, given Scotty's sense of humor, she may be dreaming the one by Oscar Wilde: "Women are meant to be loved, not to be understood." For myself it's the one by the ancient Chinese philosopher Lao Tzu: "Being deeply loved by someone gives you strength, while loving someone deeply gives you courage."

The night darkens. Stars reflect on the water surrounding us. Somewhere in the world, a meteor blazes across the sky. Somewhere in the world, couples hold each other in bed. Somewhere in the world, a baby wails, having just left the womb. Somewhere in the world, another man gives in to the emotions roiling within his chest, until finally, irrevocably, he realizes beyond all belief, he's in love.

Chapter 15

We lollygag in bed—Scotty's word, not mine—and make love again. Showered once more, dressed in seasonal shorts, T-shirts, and barefoot, a lunch of oatmeal warming our stomachs, we raise anchor and leave Crawfish Key for Key West and our dinner date with Sammy, Mary Lou, and Lizzie.

Scotty's phone doesn't vibrate, a sign that Ted hasn't made any more calls. Our dolphin friends join us again, crisscrossing ahead of the bow.

When Island Hopper's unlit neon sign is a blur in the bridge's windshield, Scotty whips her phone from her shorts pocket and swipes the screen. "Hey, M.L., change of plans ... yeah, it has something to do with Jonny ... great, I knew you'd understand without me even telling you. I still want to have dinner before we leave." She shoves the phone in her pocket and continues toward Island Hopper's pier. "Ready to take the plunge, Jonathan?"

"We're not swimming nude off Sammy and M.L.'s pier, are we?"

"M.L. doesn't know it but she's my maid of honor."

That settles it—Scotty was dreaming the Oscar Wilde quote—"Women are meant to be loved, not to be understood."

"Look, Skipper, no minister will marry anyone already married."

"Do you trust me?"

"If you tell me why I should."

She pulls her T-shirt collar down, exposing a tiny gold cross within her cleavage. "Hypocrite though I may be, attacking you in the shower and in bed—"

"I attacked back."

"Don't interrupt. I felt guilty about it this morning and—"

"You didn't seem to feel guilty when you pinned me against that palm at Hemingway House."

"Stop interrupting."

"I wonder if Herbert got lucky with Agnes? I hear it's great when a woman takes her false teeth out."

Scotty covers her eyes, shakes her head, and peeks between her fingers. She squeaks a giggle. "No doubt about it, I've found my soulmate. My solution to my guilt is simple, Gilligan. We tell a minister we're renewing our vows."

"Cool. Saves me money on an engagement ring."

"Regardless, it'll ease my guilt while we spend the rest of our mornings, afternoons, nights, whenever and wherever, doing what lovers do. Good idea?"

I nudge *Out for Fun's* throttle forward. The diesels rumble. Beneath us, the deck vibrates. "That answer your question?"

Scotty tells me she and Ted visited a church here a few times after they were first married. She came to learn, due to his dalliances, his supposed religious interest was as fake as fake gets. She also tells me how, in her last email from Mary Lou, the minister retired last year, so the new minster won't inform Ted of our nuptial renewal. Yes, it's dishonest. Yes, love makes people do strange things. Still, our hearts are in the right place. The question is, though, when do I tell Scotty I love her? I want to spend every minute of our time left in the Keys in the Keys.

I'm a millionaire but I'm a frugal millionaire—yachts are most definitely *not* on my shopping list—and I want our remaining weeks to sear themselves into our memories.

We drop anchor. Mary Lou runs out in her boat and climbs aboard. "What y'all wearin'? Not shorts and T-shirts I hope."

"Scotty's changing now. Thanks for calling the church and making the appointment."

"Not a problem, Jonny. Tell me this, do you love her or is it the sex?"

"It's the sex." I wink to let M.L. know I'm joking.

"Sam said you told him you care about her. Get this straight—you hurt my gal pal, I'll take it personal."

"You do realize this wedding isn't real."

"It is to her. You can betcha bottom sand dollar on that."

Scotty comes out to the stern. She wears her hair down; it flows like the outgoing tide in Oregon Inlet, brunette instead of sandy blue. Across bare shoulders, spaghetti straps support the yellow sun dress that ends at her knees. A smidgen of liner makes her green eyes pop. Pink lipstick defines those already defined lips; she couldn't be more kissable. Red polish shines on fingernails. Flat-soled sandals reveal the same shade on toenails. The gold cross resides in the beginning of her cleavage. Stunning doesn't define her.

M.L. gets a shopping bag from her boat and gives it to me. "My gal pal got your sizes off your clothes and asked me to pick up a few things. Go see if they fit."

In my bedroom, I dress in tan slacks, a yellow Oxford shirt to match Scotty's sun dress, yellow socks and, since she included no shoes, I slip my boat shoes on. A matching belt from Ted's closet finishes my ensemble.

On the stern, both Scotty and M.L. clap. M.L. makes me turn around. "Not bad, Jonny, not bad at all."

"Tell me about it. Scotty has me working out every night."

Scotty shoves my shoulder. "Shut up and get in the boat. Time to get this ho on the road."

M.L. cracks up laughing. After catching her breath, she says, "Girl, ain't no ho in you but the ho who loves a good man."

Sammy has the jeep running. Lizzie's in school unfortunately—she would've made a great flower girl. We drive along the same street Scotty and I walked on the way to Hemingway House. I whisper in her ear, asking if she wants to honeymoon in the garden, adding I'll stay against that palm regardless of who sees us.

The service is short and sweet. Scotty and I kiss. M.L. cries. Sammy shakes my hand. On the way back to Island Hopper, Scotty tells them we're going to stay on the water three weeks and come back for that dinner on a Saturday so I can meet Lizzie. M.L. says she'll take Scotty and I fishing the following Monday afternoon.

No sooner than we climb aboard *Out for Fun* and crank the generator and the AC, we hit the shower.

And I don't mean to shower.

* * *

Of the twenty-six islands in the Key West National Wildlife Refuge, we repeat our romantic night on Crawfish Key on fourteen islands, snorkel on thirteen, collect shells on six, make love each night, revisit a new palm tree three times, lie on the blanket as the sun sets while I revisit Hurricane Scotty four times, talk endlessly on endless subjects such as natural childbirth, diapers, formula, breastfeeding, various pumps so the dad can assist with feeding at 3 a.m., the merits of backrubs to the mom, the merits of sex as soon as possible after the birth, the idea that finances should be open knowledge between a couple, and the assumption that neither partner should ever be taken for granted.

We run back to Key West for groceries and head out again, for the Dry Tortugas.

Scotty's quite the historian. Fort Jefferson, named for Thomas Jefferson, third president of the United States, was started in 1846 to stand guard over nearby shipping lanes. Composed of over sixteen-million red bricks, it was never considered finished; the construction ended in 1875. The country still managed to arm it with cannon and use it for a prison for Union criminals. Dr. Samuel Mudd, one its most infamous prisoners, who set John Wilkes Booth's broken leg after he shot Abraham Lincoln, was one such prisoner. The island also includes a harbor, where ships could resupply or refit. If a person has ever heard of a prison called "Devil's Island," Fort Jefferson is where the name came from.

All this time, Scotty never whispers I love you in my ear again, and I never tell her I love her. It's implicit in every kiss, in every smile, in every quiet moment, in every touch of our hands as we walk along a beach, when our fingers entwine as if they're tropical vines with one goal in mind: to connect the heartwood of their home trees.

On the fifteenth day, we visit Miami for more groceries and fuel. Ted hasn't called again. Maybe he bought the cousin story. We then set course for the Turks and Caicos Islands. Scotty and Ted have never visited, and I couldn't be happier.

Scotty names the dolphins after Jane Austen's characters in *Pride and Prejudice*: Elizabeth Bennet and Mr. Darcy. She says the male is aloof like Darcy, ashamed of his damaged dorsal like Darcy's ashamed of his bashfulness around strangers, adding how the female is the head of the relationship like Elizabeth is the head of her and Darcy's relationship. I argue that they're equals, both the fictional characters and our dolphin friends. Each supports the other in ways we can't see.

About halfway to our destination, the dolphins are gone one gray morning. Clouds build on the eastern horizon. I remind Scotty it's still hurricane season; she reminds me to shut up. The clouds trundle and roll, grow black and menacing. Wind and waves build. Like Edward Teach, otherwise known as Blackbeard, we batten down the hatches by deflating the dinghy and storing anything capable of taking flight in the engine room. Night falls. Winds reach forty miles an hour with gusts to fifty. Scotty checks for Coast Guard radio reports. One crackles out gale and small craft warnings. I notice the mic hanging from the two-way radio. When she kidnapped me, I could've called for help and didn't even realize it. Kismet, karma, or true love? I'm glad I didn't notice the mic.

Out for Fun is no longer fun. I go to bed seasick. Scotty takes watch until twelve. I wake, puke, rinse the sour taste of bile and partially digested chicken noodle soup and saltines from my mouth, and take a seat in the captain's chair. She tells me it's simple—wake her if the power dies and that's it.

Along with the forward running light, she has the forward flood lights illuminating the deck between the bridge and the bow. Rain curtains sideways. The wipers, slapping back and forth, can't keep up with the downpour. Wind gusts tilt us at an angle. I squeeze the chair's leather armrests. The wind calms. Including my thumbnails, ten half-moon shaped fingernail indentions mar the mahogany-colored leather.

Ham sandwich and coffee in hand, Scotty relieves me at 4 a.m. The smell of mayo churns my gut. I puke again, take the seasickness pills that Scotty offers me with a smile, and return to my bed.

Bleary eyed, crusty eyed, and every eyed in between, I wake to sunshine and calm seas. The diesel engines are quiet, so we're anchored. Scotty's beneath the sheets beside me, nude and inviting. I stroke the curve of her hip; she slaps my hand. "Not before you brush puke smell from your breath."

Yep, we're definitely in love.

Chapter 16

B oat traffic picks up: yachts like ours, sport fishers, charter vessels like Stan's, cruise ships that carry thousands of people, platformed fishing boats like Mary Lou's. In the bulge of our bow wave, the dolphins frolic. We pass a green sea turtle, one flipper missing, probably from a shark attack. We pass a Portuguese Man 'O War's translucent body: a teardrop shaped balloon with twisted tentacles trailing it. Scotty says despite some people saying the best emergency remedy for jellyfish stings—including this monstrosity equipped with an inflated ridge along its top that resembles a sail—is to urinate on the welts, she says it's not true, that the best remedy is to rinse the area with vinegar and soak it in hot water. Although the vision of her behind squatting over me sounds interesting, I'm glad she knows the proper remedy.

On the horizon, sunshine reflects off windows in distant buildings, tropical green behind them. We're east of Cuba and north of Haiti and the Dominican Republic. The heat and humidity say we're closer to the equator than in the Keys and I believe it. Sweat trickles down my shirtless back when I go to the bow for longer than ten minutes. I imagine my arms sizzling like bacon. I imagine the tops of my bare feet turning red like boiling lobsters.

119

Scotty gets on the two-way and asks for directions to a marina that can handle yachts the size of *Out for Fun*. An obliging female voice says to plot Twisted Welk Marina on our GPS. We do so, arrive thirty minutes later, and refuel both the diesel and water tanks. Snug in a slip at eighty-dollars a night, Scotty's baby gets a well-deserved rest. The dolphins remain at sea. Scotty pays the slip owner.

I don a T-shirt and sandals and run a comb through my growing hair. Scotty already wears both. She goes to her room and comes back, ponytail tighter, purse strap slung over her shoulder. The plan is to take a break from the ocean and rent a room for a few nights, enjoy someone else's cooking for a change and experience making love in a different bed, not to mention room service. The guy who fueled the yacht recommended one of the many all-inclusive resorts on the north side of this island. Scotty and I agreed. The guy also recommended a cab. We agreed again.

The cab arrives. We get in, close our eyes, and luxuriate in the AC. A person can only take so much heat, ocean, and humidity.

The thousand-dollar a night room is on the fourth floor. We have a round bed of all things, a double shower with multiple heads on each side, a wet bar, a snack bar, and a balcony overlooking gorgeous white-sand beaches. Scotty pulls the curtain. "Jonathan, I'm about beached out. Let's act like normal people and shower separately. Then we'll shop for normal people clothes and eat supper at a normal people restaurant."

"Look, Skipper, you realize 'normal people' don't spend a thousand dollars a night for a room."

"The hubs earned his money. I don't mind helping him spend it."

"The yacht. You probably have an amazing house on Manteo. He jets all over the world to chase women. He made enough money for all that in real estate?"

"It's possible on the Outer Banks if you stick to it. I admired him for his work ethic, which is the main reason I married him."

"I admire you for yours. Not a lot of women would work if their husbands made his kind of money, much less in law enforcement."

"My farmer parent's background. Some people complain about other people having money, but the majority of millionaires earn every penny. There's not a lot of countries where a person can succeed like that."

Showers done, we visit the resort's adjacent clothing store. I buy a pair each of slacks in navy and gray, a dressy pair of tan shorts, another pair of boat shoes that don't have sand embedded in the insoles, a pack of briefs, and a pair of sandals that don't resemble two strips of salt-encrusted car tires. Scotty buys a sun dress in a floral pattern, a pair of tan women's slacks, a dressy pair of matching shorts, three blouses—one in yellow, one in green, one in a floral pattern—a pack of panties, and tops everything off with a pink silk robe for her and blue one for me.

In another store we stock up on toothbrushes, toothpaste, deodorant: the necessities of smelling human instead of like dead fish after sweating in this sweltering heat.

In the resort lobby, we pass a unisex hair salon, a masseuse, and a gym. This place has it all. An assortment of wigs resides in the hair salon display. Scotty nudges me that way. "Platinum blonde or corn silk yellow? They say blondes have more fun."

I nudge her away from the display. "If I have any more fun with a certain brunette, I'll have a heart attack."

Scotty pats her tummy. "I'm hungry. Let's check out the resort restaurant and see what my baby girl thinks of broiled flounder."

"Not fried?"

"I'm tired of my fat behind."

"I'm not."

"Enough sweet talk. You already get enough of me as it is."

Glass fronted for a view of the pea-green ocean with hardly a wave, filled with round tables covered with red table cloths, including a mahogany bar varnished a rich brown, the restaurant smells of money, grilled steaks, and seafood. My mouth doesn't water; it floods. The greeter seats us at a corner table. Scotty gets up. "Order water with lemon for me, I need to powder my nose."

Taking long, quick strides, she hurries away. I order her water and a rum punch for myself. Several men in high dollar suits courting high dollar women line the bar. One guy has his arms around two women wearing dresses that reveal their backs down to their butts. He kisses one girl. She points to the other. His hand slips inside the other's dress; finger's clench her bottom. The guy's hair, dark and wavy, is gray at the temples. I can't see his face. Unless I miss my guess, he's about to have an interesting evening with those two women.

A woman with long, blonde hair the color of corn silk comes over. She wears a floral sundress like Scotty bought and red lipstick. Sunglasses cover her eyes. High heels make her look tall enough to carry her weight well. She sits. "You look like a man in need of company." Her voice is pitched a notch higher than Scotty's. She leans over; a gold cross falls from her cleavage. "How about it, Gilligan?"

I goggle. She lowers the sunglasses. Familiar green eyes crinkle. "You like?"

"The heels are cool. They'd make you the perfect height for—"

"You didn't have a problem in the shower."

"You were on tiptoe."

"I didn't have a choice, you were lifting me by my hips. See the guy at the bar with the two bimbettes?"

"Isn't that bimbos?"

"That's my name for thirty-year old women who act like teenagers."

"Isn't that cougars?"

"Never mind. Who do you think that guy is?"

"Another friend of Ted's?"

"That's the hubs—Thaddeus Scott himself."

"I take my cell phone out. We should take some pictures for divorce court."

"Put that away."

"Because?"

"He'd find some woman who looks like me and set her up with a guy in bed and take the pictures himself. I told you he's a vindictive bastard."

"Want me to break his nose?"

"He's a third-degree black belt in karate."

"Huh, scratch that idea. My dad left me a Colt 45. I could splatter his brains all over the bimbettes."

"Don't even joke like that."

Our drinks come. We both order broiled flounder, salads, and steamed broccoli. Scotty's as hot as a blonde as she is as a brunette. Ted looks our way a few times: a man on the prowl to make his threesome a foursome. Scotty's disguise works perfectly. If I weren't here, he'd come over for sure.

Our meal arrives. The flounder's like Scotty: firm where I want it, moist where I want it. The salad too, crispy with her sense of humor. The broccoli's broccoli, although it does remind me of the palm fronds over our heads back at Hemingway House. I sip my rum punch. "How old is he?"

"Thirty-nine going on eighteen. Don't raise your eyebrows at me, there's nothing wrong with older men."

"It makes more sense how he made his money—he's been at it a while. Wonder why he's here instead of Australia?"

Scotty forks flounder. "What can I say? He's got bimbettes spread from here to Timbuktu."

"Is that a real place, or is it just a saying?"

"It's in Mali, Gilligan. How can you be so calm with Captain Jerkoff right over there?"

"You're handling it well. Look how fast you came up with your disguise."

"I'm seething inside. The thought of joint custody makes me consider that .45."

"You did say you would share joint custody."

"I was stupid to say that and I don't like to think of myself as stupid. The last thing I want to see is his smirking face every time we exchange the baby every other weekend and holidays, and a week or two in summer. Whatever nanny he hires will be wearing braces and have fake boobs big enough to use for swim floats." In the middle of a sip of rum punch, I cough. Scotty punches my arm. "Think it's funny, don't you?"

"Not at all, but I love your sense of humor."

"Captain Jerkoff hates it. Says I'm sarcastic. I told him how research says sarcasm is a sign of intelligence."

I clink my glass to Scotty's. "I'll drink to that. Do you want to stay a few days or not?"

"I'm not letting him run me away. We'll stay indoors and test that round bed and that huge shower."

I clink the glass again. "Don't forget the room service and the masseuse. Do they make house calls?"

Scotty leans over for a long, luscious, and inviting kiss. "I've got your masseuse in my bra, Jonathan, and you know it."

* * *

Dinner passes without incident. Ted leaves with the bimbettes. In our room we hear moans from behind the wall. Thank goodness it sounds like two voices instead of three. We get in the shower and moan ourselves. I call room service for baby oil and get a massage. Of course, Scotty gets a massage too.

Making love slippery is kind of fun. You have to get toeholds on the sheets, handholds on the headboard, and try not to slide off each other. Scotty dons the high heels and leans over. I'm in perfect bliss. She kicks the heels off, shoves me in bed, and climbs on top. She's soon in bliss as well.

Breakfast involves link sausage, waffles, croissant, strawberry jam, and a carafe of strong coffee. Dessert involves Scotty.

We lounge around watching TV, napping, touching, kissing. Scotty does this thing with her tongue ... does it lower ... even lower ... I close my eyes and reciprocate as soon as she's done.

Supper—our North Carolina upbringing requires we call it supper instead of dinner—consists of two perfectly grilled filet mignons, oven-baked potatoes swimming in butter and sour cream with the crisp peelings coated in sea salt, and more broccoli—gotta have a green. Strawberry shortcake with whipped cream completes the meal. I order extra whipped cream. My mama didn't raise no fools.

In the middle of the night, I turn the lamp on and watch Scotty sleep. She's on her stomach; brunette hair clouds her features. Her lips purse and relax. Mine purse too. If she weren't already pregnant, I might be a daddy by now.

The gold chain loops from her neck. The cross lies face up on the sheet. Scotty surprised me by saying she felt guilty about having sex before having that vow renewal. She's like the gold surface: Faulted with slight scratches. Human. Real. Genuine. Layered. If I didn't feel married to her already, I'd feel guilty about the sex too, but how can I when we've become as close as our dolphin friends, Mr. Darcy and Elizabeth Bennet?

I sniff her hair. Soft and fine, it tickles my nose. Between the smell of the vanilla lotion and the floral aroma of the rinse she uses, she's a tropical garden, lush and natural.

I roll over and place my hand over my heart. Is it skipping? Is it faltering? Does it realize I love her so much it hurts?

Ted's an A-grade idiot. How can he prefer bimbettes over intelligence and humor in a perfect plus-sized package like Scotty? Not to mention how she has no fear if the yacht's fume detector screeches, no fear of the tough and dangerous job of Dare County Sheriff, and no fear of any repercussions of kidnapping me?

I roll over and kiss her cheek. She mumbles unintelligibly. I whisper "I love you" in her ear. Not a twitch, not a murmur.

How will our trip end? Closing my eyes, I shut this thought out of my mind. With a jerk like Ted for a husband, who knows.

Chapter 17

Five days pass. We skulk around the resort but never see Ted or the bimbettes again. Maybe they gave him a heart attack and he's in a morgue somewhere. We're now in the fourth week of our vacation from reality. Scotty wants to cruise back to Key West tomorrow, which is Friday, for our supper with Sammy, Mary Lou, and Lizzie on Saturday.

Because of rain, Thursday morning comes late. It splatters against the window, driven by wind. We're lazy and warm beneath the sheets in the air-conditioned room. I finally get up at nine and go to the bathroom wearing my blue robe. Scotty taps the door. "I'm calling room service for breakfast. Ideas?"

"Are banana pancakes on the menu?"

"Another use for whipped cream besides on me, huh?"

"And on me. How about a North Carolina favorite? Eggs over easy, country ham, grits, and buttermilk biscuits?"

"You realize both our behinds are getting fatter."

I open the door. "Gives me more to squeeze when you're on top, pumpkin."

Scotty shoves by. "Call room service. I need a shower to wake me up."

"Need help with your back?"

Scotty slams the door. "Don't forget the coffee."

127

Yep, just like an old married couple.

Room service says our North Carolina breakfast will be up in thirty minutes. At the window, I pull the curtains aside. We'll have a dreary cruise back to Key West if this rain keeps up.

Scotty comes from the bathroom wearing the pink robe, hair piled and pinned on top of her head. Steam exits the door. "If you shower after breakfast, Jonathan, I'll order those banana pancakes for dessert. You know what happens with the whipped cream."

Someone knocks on the door. "Room service." We're as presentable as always in our robes, so I open the door.

Behind me, Scotty sucks in a hard breath.

Ted stands in the door, flash on his cellphone cycling as he takes pictures. "Well, well, well. Aren't you and your cousin cozy?"

I shove the door; he shoves in. "Damn, Scotty, couldn't you find a man instead this limp noodle?"

"Like you've got room to talk. I saw you with those women at the bar."

"I saw you too. You need a lot better disguise than a blonde wig to fool me." He shakes the phone. "Here's the deal—we get a divorce, you get no alimony. We share joint custody, you get reasonable child support. Take it or leave it." Ted closes the door.

"I've got witnesses who saw you with those women."

Ted aims a thumb my way. "Him? What judge will believe my wife's lover?"

"I'm not as dumb as you think I am. I've had a private investigator build quite the folder on you. A judge will love seeing those pictures of you and the two women and a man in the pool in Italy. It's amazing what a camera with a telephoto lens will magnify. It even made that toothpick with marbles between your legs look big."

Ted's unfazed. "Alimony and child support. I still want joint custody."

"No alimony and no child support. I want full custody."

"Alimony and child support." Ted raises his hand to his mouth like a man who knows what a photograph of him with two women and a man would do to his reputation with his testosterone filled friends in Manteo. "Joint custody, but I expect alternate holidays and a week in the summer."

"Christmas and Thanksgiving are non-negotiable."

"Deal." Ted goes to the door, opens it, and faces me. "How can you stand screwing her fat ass? Oh, keep the damn yacht. I don't want it after your two have done who knows what on it." He slams the door. I drop to the bed.

"That went better than expected."

Scotty joins me. "Tell me about it."

"You think he'll do what he said? The idea of his friends seeing a photo of him with a man shook him."

"I don't trust him. Besides, I bluffed about those photos."

I draw back so I can look her in the eye. "And here I was, thinking you were brilliant enough to actually hire a private detective."

"I did. He took the photos but didn't see anything more than all four of them putting lotion on each other's back. They must've gotten down to business some other time."

"You'll be fine as long as he doesn't ask to see the photos."

"I suppose you're right, it could've been a lot worse."

Someone knocks on the door. A female voice says, "Room service."

I get up. "For what it's worth, I'm glad it's out in the open."

"Me too. Now I can enjoy our North Carolina breakfast."

"*And* that whipped cream." I open the door.

129

* * *

Friday morning dawns clear. The air even has a cool hint to it, along with less humidity. Scotty and I feel like two prisoners released from jail.

When we reach the blue depths off the Turks and Caicos, Mr. Darcy and Elizabeth greet us with crisscrossing sprints in our bow wave. Scotty reminds me to call her Lizzie like in the book. I keep forgetting, I suppose because I think of Lizzie as Sammy and Mary Lou's Lizzie.

Out for Fun performs like a champ. Scotty says her credit card is in her name, but she expects Ted to close the bank account that auto-pays her card, meaning she won't have access to those funds. She also says we have everything we need to get back to Manteo and Pirate's Cove Marina, where she'll stick a For Sale sign in the window, except we'll have to run about ten knots instead of fifteen to conserve fuel. She thinks *Out for Fun* will fetch around a million and a half bucks, which, along with the 200,000 dollars or so she's hidden from Ted, along with my three million from Andy's life insurance policy, will allow us to buy a nice home. We don't discuss where, but I assume it's within driving distance of Manteo to facilitate the custody arrangement with Ted. I might work, might not. I'll be busy changing diapers and making sure Scotty knows how much I love her, including 3 a.m. feedings and back rubs. I smile to myself. She might get some back rubs too, which I know she will.

Although it seems like we're in good shape as far as Ted, Scotty spends a lot of time in the captain's chair with her paperback. Sometimes she reads, sometimes she doesn't. Sometimes I catch her twisting a strand of hair around her finger, eyes blinking as if she's considering a problem to solve.

On the night we should arrive at Key West, I come up behind her and massage her neck. "Mighty tight muscles there, Skipper. What's on your mind?"

"My jerk of a husband."

"Miss him already?"

"You have lost your mind."

"Are you thinking he's too generous by giving you the yacht?"

"Not to mention alimony. I don't trust him one bit. I'd rather cruise through a category five hurricane than see his smirking face when we exchange the baby."

"Have you thought about how he'll influence her?"

"He'll teach her to hate me. When she gets older, I wouldn't put it past him to show her the pictures he took of us in that resort."

"That's pretty scuzzy, even for him."

Scotty swivels the chair, wraps her arms around my waist, and puts her head on my chest. "You'll make a great daddy. I'd do about anything to let you be her daddy 24/7."

"Where's your ideal place to live?"

"I wouldn't mind a place on the sound. It would have to be on stilts for flooding when hurricanes come through."

"You mentioned your parents having a farm, how about that?"

"Oh, wow, that would be Heaven. Raise some chickens. Have a garden. There's nothing like a juicy tomato sandwich with plenty of mayo and salt and pepper to tell you it's summer."

"So says my southern girl. Don't forget the peach pie."

"Or banana pudding. I gain weight just thinking about it."

The radar alarm beeps; a freighter is about a mile away on our left. It smokes past; the alarm ends.

I lean down to kiss Scotty. "Can I entice you to the bedroom?"

"You realize if I weren't already pregnant, I would be by now. Your swimmers are probably doing the backstroke in every nook and cranny I've got."

I take the other chair. "What did you do with your parent's farm?"

I rented it to a couple who said they wanted to turn it into a winery. Last time I looked, not a grape grew anywhere. Looks like they've kept the house up, though."

"How big is it?"

"It's a rambling old thing. Creaking heart-pine floors, stairs too. A huge kitchen and dining room and master bedroom and bathroom upstairs. Dad remodeled it a few years before he died. He really loved Mom."

I kiss her again. It's time. "Like I love you."

She gets up and tucks her face into my chest. Her shoulder's shudder, then stop. She looks up, cheeks wet. "Do you know how long I've wanted to hear that from someone who means it?"

"You deserve it. If you don't know it by now, I think you're amazing."

She reaches into my collar and pulls chest hair. "I knew that before you told me."

"Sure, you're amazing, but you don't know what I'm talking about."

"You could mean a lot of things, especially that thing I do with my tongue."

"It's what you do with it when it involves whipped cream. Before that I just thought of you as a roll in sand. After that, I knew I'd found my bedmate."

Scotty pulls chest hair again. "That's soulmate, Gilligan. Go take that shower so your swimmers can take another high dive into my nooks and crannies."

At dusk, as the sun sizzles into the Gulf of Mexico, all red and shimmering beyond distant ribbons of translucent clouds, we drop anchor a hundred yards off Sammy and Mary Lou's pier. Mr. Darcy and Lizzie glide around us, turning on their sides with one eye focused our way, bottle-nosed teeth grinning as if to say they're glad to see we're as happy as they are. I give them a thumbs up. Life is good.

Scotty calls Mary Lou and says we'll be over at about 4:30 tomorrow afternoon to help cook the seafood that we'll buy in town. Mary Lou's voice gets louder: "Gal pal, that ain't no kinda southern hospitality. "What y'all want? I'll run get it before Lizzie gets home from school."

"Let me ask Jonny." Scotty palms the phone. "Oysters? Shrimp? Clams? Scallops? Fish?"

"Do lobsters live in the Keys?"

"Spiny lobsters. Before M.L. got loud, she said a client caught a limit of permit and gave her some filets."

"Sounds great."

"Which one?"

"One, are you nuts? They *all* sound great."

Scotty tells M.L., who says, "My mama always said you can tell a good man by his appetite. That Jonny's definitely a good man. See y'all later."

Scotty slips the phone in her pocket and comes over to me for a kiss. "Tell me, Gilligan, just *how* will we spend the day until supper time?"

We run to the bedroom, flinging clothes on the way, and do what comes as natural as breathing. Afterward, she lies in the curve of my arm, rubbing my chest. A light sheen of sweat shines on her forehead. I'm pretty much soaked.

The generator chugs beneath us. The AC hums. The faint call of gulls *scree-scree-screeing* seeps through *Out for Fun's* roof.

Scotty props herself on her elbow; brunette strands fall to my face. "I hope you don't mind me asking, but do you miss Andy?"

"I haven't had time to miss her. You know, with you kidnapping me and seducing me."

"I'm serious. Do you?"

"Sometimes."

"Like when?"

"She read too, mostly science fiction. I remember one time the week after she moved in with me. It was March, and we had a cold snap, cold enough to frost. It was a Saturday night. She sat in a rocker by a lamp with her sock feet curled under her. You saw her hair wet. Dry, it sort of puffed out because it was coarse instead of silky like yours. The lamplight made her hair look like a halo around her head. She kept looking at me over the book and smiling. I asked every time what she was smiling about, but she never would say. Then I told her she was my angel, and she got up and took my hand and led me to the bedroom and told me she was going to take me through a portal into another galaxy."

"Remember her outburst in the restaurant?" Scotty asks. "About the chandelier being a portal to another galaxy?"

"What about it?"

"Regardless of her having wine, don't you think that was strange?"

"Maybe. I'll have to go back to my place to sell it and give my notice at work. I might ask some of her friends about her behavior."

"Do you think she had mental problems?"

"Who doesn't to some degree?"

"You have to admit, taking a sunrise swim in October when the water's freezing is a bit strange."

"I'll ask around. She wouldn't have committed suicide, if that's what you mean."

"The way you describe her, she loved you too much to do that."

Silence hangs over us. I'll definitely ask some of Andy's friends if they noticed anything strange about her. Too bad Stan won't tell me more about Marie and her hoarding, which could give me a clue as to whether Andy had similar mannerisms other than that. Mannerisms that meant a mental issue.

I set the alarm on my phone on the nightstand for some well-deserved rest after mine and Scotty's almost constant lovemaking of the past almost four weeks. Her breathing soon settles into the rhythm of sleep. The gold cross rests in the hollow of her throat, reminding me exactly how thankful I am to have met her.

Chapter 18

Scotty and I awake and take separate showers. She piles her blow-dried hair on top of her head and pins it up. The way the necklace's gold chain mingles with the fine hairs at the nape of her neck drives me nuts. I wear tan slacks and the yellow Oxford shirt Mary Lou bought me. New boat shoes make me look less grungy, although my hair's getting long. Scotty wears the yellow sun dress; bare shoulders entice me as much as her neck does. She finishes her ensemble with a new purse—larger for more junk, she says—hanging from her shoulder. The purse came from the resort, where she left the blonde wig in the trash, much to my disappointment. Sandals reveal green nail polish that matches her fingernails. The subtle and sexy aroma of vanilla lotion scents her entire body. I already know what I'm having for dessert tonight.

Mary Lou ferries us to the pier. She smells like oyster brine, says it's from them steaming. We find Sammy in the kitchen and Lizzie at a table in the bar. She jumps up and runs to Scotty, curls bouncing. "You been gone too long, Scooty Poot. What's your brother's name? Mama an' Daddy won't tell me 'cause they like to aggravate me."

Scotty raises her brows at me. Unless I miss my guess—and hers too—Sammy and Mary Lou are using my brother cover because Lizzie knows Scotty's married. I offer Lizzie my hand. "My name's Jonny. I like your name for Scotty. Mind if I call you freckled fart?"

She slaps my hand away. "Not if you want me to like you."

At the bar, sweat beading on his forehead, Sammy wipes it with a dishcloth. "If y'all ready, I'll bring it out."

Scotty and Mary Lou leave to help. Lizzie takes my hand and leads me to a table. "Tell the truth, you're Scotty's boyfriend. I never liked that Ted. He's got mean eyes."

"You're awful smart for a freckled fart, freckled fart. Can it be our secret?"

Lizzie's brown eyes dart toward the bar. Thin framed with a triangle shaped face and a pointy chin, she's as cute as cute can be. She looks back at me. "I like secrets. I got a boyfriend at school. I ain't tellin' Mama an' Daddy 'cause they'll tease me."

"Another secret between you and me, freckled fart."

"You can stop callin' me that, you know. Your hair's kinda curly. Does Scotty like feelin' it?"

"You could say that."

Footsteps tap behind us. Sammy, Mary Lou, and Scotty bring platters of steaming seafood: oysters and clams on the half shell, seared scallops, peeled jumbo shrimp, broiled fish filets, and whole lobsters, deep red, long antennae draped over their backs. Slices of lemon decorate the platter's sides. Sammy goes back for tarter and cocktail sauce. Mary Lou brings Lizzie and Scotty sweet tea with lemon, then fills icy mugs with draft beer for the rest of us. Delicious salty scents rise with the steam, flooding my mouth with saliva. Everyone sits. I reach for a lobster and Scotty slaps my hand. "Mind your manners. I'm saying the blessing."

Lizzie wrinkles her nose at me. "Good idea, Scooty Poot. We gotta keep these men straight."

Mary Lou takes my hand. "Got that right, Lizzie. Us ladies need all the help we can get."

Sammy clears his throat. "Like I got any help cookin' all this food."

Scotty takes my other hand. "I think we should be thankful to be alive and have someone to love. Lots of people can't say that. Bow your head, Jonny, I'm starved."

"Dear Lord, thank you for friends and family. I miss Mom and Dad but I'll see them again one day. Thank you for Jonathan. I never knew a brother could be so sweet." Lizzie giggles. Scotty squeezes my hand. "Sometimes we lose those we love. When we do, I know those loved ones would want life to go on for those they leave behind. We might not understand why they leave—we sure can't explain it—but it happens, so it's best to remember them with love instead of grief. Thank you for this food and for the gift of life inside us. Amen."

"Very nice, gal pal." Mary Lou plops a lobster on my plate. "Dig in, Jonny."

Sammy's already split the tail. I eat succulent pieces of white meat, moist and tender. Scotty loads her plate with shrimp and oysters. Sammy takes a fish filet and several clams. Mary Lou works on a lobster while Lizzie works on shrimp. We feast, washing it down with tea and beer. Satisfied slurps come from Scotty swallowing oysters. Lizzie says how scrumptious the shrimp are, but says they'd be better with melted butter. Sammy says he forgot and leaves for the kitchen. Lizzie keeps downing shrimp regardless. Mary Lou gets up to refill our mugs with beer. Finished with my lobster, I set the empty tail and claws on the platter and get a fish filet, along with several oysters. I wink at Scotty. She winks back like a woman who knows I'm winking because of how some people say oysters are good for the libido.

Tipping my head back to get all the juice from a shell, I hear a cough. Scotty pats Lizzie's back. "You okay, Lizzie?"

No cough. Nothing. Wide-eyed, Lizzie grabs her throat and I'm out of my chair with my clenched fists planted below her diaphragm and squeezing for all I'm worth.

Mary Lou runs over and tries to take her from me. I don't let her. "Sammy!" she screams, "Lizzie's choking!"

Lizzie goes limp in my arms. Scotty beats her back. A piece of shrimp pops from her throat and falls to the table. I set Lizzie in the chair. "Deep breaths, sweety, deep breaths. You're okay, you're okay."

Sammy runs in from the kitchen and kneels beside her. "You okay, baby?"

Tears stream down Lizzie's red cheeks. She nods.

I fall into my chair. My nose runs, my eyes fill. Thank God I didn't lose her—it would be like losing Andy all over again. I cover my face because I know I look like hell crying.

Thin arms circle my neck. Soft curls press my cheek. I hold Lizzie, crying almost as bad as when Andy died. She smells of shampoo and reminds me of a gangly-boned colt running around a pasture on a spring day. Her arms slip from my neck. She snatches a napkin from the holder on the table and wipes my cheeks. "Well, durn, Jonny, the way you carry on, you act like I went off and died."

"You scared the crap out of me, you freckled fart."

She goes to her chair, grabs her plate, and dumps the shrimp in my plate. "You eat 'em. I liked your hug, but not that much."

"Is your tummy sore?" Scotty says.

"He's too flabby to squeeze hard."

Sammy rounds the table and shakes my hand. "You fish for free Monday."

"And any other time," Mary Lou says, sitting in my lap. "If I weren't a married woman and you weren't my gal pal's brother, I'd kiss you sloppy."

I almost break my face grinning. "You guys sure make a brother feel at home."

Everyone takes their seat. Scotty waggles a shrimp at me. "Eat up. Who knows when you'll get another meal like this."

Supper over, dishes washed, everyone sits around the bar area. On the huge flatscreen TV in a corner, football plays. Scotty and Mary Lou go out on the pier and take a seat beneath one of the umbrella-covered tables. Lizzie sits in Sammy's lap, alternately rubbing her eyes and yawning.

Sated with seafood, sipping a cold beer now and then, the murmur of the unwatched football ignored, Scotty and Mary Lou talking, moonlight living on the water in a gleaming, glowing trail, I feel as happy and as satisfied as I've felt in a long time.

Then again, Scotty and I have to go home and deal with Ted soon, and I don't look forward to it one bit. Still, with us as a team, we'll get through it. I even look forward to diaper changes and 3 a.m. feedings.

Scotty comes in. "Ready to row, Jonny?"

We thank Sammy and Mary Lou for supper. They thank us for helping with Lizzie. I tell them she's as sweet as a speckled pup. In Sammy's lap, she wakes enough to flutter a hand our way. "G'night Jonny, g'night, Scooty Poot. See y'all later."

Aboard *Out for Fun*, we get ready for bed and climb in. Neither of us mentions sex—our stomachs are too full. I roll over and nuzzle Scotty's ear. "I love you, Scooty Poot."

"I love you too. You were great with Lizzie. You'll be great with our girl too."

"I haven't thought much about being a fill-in dad. Not seriously, if you know what I mean. After spending time with Lizzie, I know I'll love your baby every bit as much as if she were mine."

"Tell me something I don't know."

"I love your confidence in me."

"I wish I had it in me. I am not looking forward to this thing with Ted."

I kiss Scottie's cheek. "Try not to think about it and get some sleep. You should get plenty of rest since we're taking a break from sex."

"Ain't that the truth, Jonny. 'Night."

Grinning, I turn the lamp off and consider telling Scotty: "You can stop calling me that, you know." Still grinning, I close my eyes. Lizzie's a mess.

* * *

The stinging sensation of my bladder holding three mugs of beer wakes me. When I go back to bed, Scotty's not there. No lights are on in the bridge or the kitchen, but a tiny red dot burns on the bow. I open the door and smell cigarette smoke. At the handrail, Scotty turns. "I guess my secret's out."

"You realize smoking's not good for the baby."

"This is the first one since we left Manteo. I usually do a pack a week, more when Ted's home. I guess it's a stress thing, from worrying about everything we've got to deal with."

I join her at the rail. "You think it'll be that bad?"

"I told you I don't trust him. Whatever it takes, no matter how long I have to fight, no matter what I have to do, I'm not giving up until I get full custody."

"Can't say I blame you. His is *not* daddy material."

141

"And you are." Scotty stubs the cigarette out on the hand rail. "How about we go to church tomorrow?"

"Why not? It's Sunday. Want to ask Lizzie and crew?"

"I'd rather it just be us. Will you be ready to go back to Manteo after Mary Lou takes you fishing Monday?"

"Gotta face the music sometimes, don't we?"

"Unfortunately."

In bed, Scotty burps. "Did any of the food bother you?"

"Gluttony does not become us, Scooty Poot."

"I'll 'scooty poot' you if I have gas with my burps. Go to sleep."

I turn the lamp out. Yep, yet again, just like an old married couple.

* * *

Morning dawns gorgeous and golden. I wake before Scotty and go see if Mr. Darcy and Lizzie are around. The sun is just heaving itself clear of the eastern horizon; I shade my eyes from the glare. At a dock several buildings down, two men with fishing gear climb into a boat similar to Mary Lou's. The outboard sputters and growls as the boat glides away, leaving a feathering wake in the silver water.

Mr. Darcy swims by. I shade my eyes again but can't see Lizzie. "She up and leave you, Mr. Darcy?"

From around the bow, Lizzie's dorsal fin cuts a wake. She swims to Mr. Darcy. I've gotten used to how they open their bottle-nosed snouts and grin, but neither one does. Their eyes, usually intent on either mine or Scotty's every movement, focus on each other instead of me, as if they know a terrible secret and wish they could tell me in human voices instead of with squeaks and chirps what that secret is. Clouds loom in the west,

142

low and roiling, dark and threatening. Maybe Mr. Darcy and Lizzie feel the difference in the pressure drop of a cold front, like dogs sense the impending danger of a coming earthquake.

I go back inside, intent on asking Scotty what she wants for breakfast, but hear the unmistakable heave ... heave ... heave of her throwing up in the bathroom. I go to the cracked door. "Want me to hold your hair?"

Finishing a heave, she looks my way. Beads of sweat pop on her forehead. Strings of damp hair stick to her face. "Happy now?"

"Morning sickness?"

"You said supper didn't bother you."

"I could still hold your hair."

"No woman wants the man she loves to see her puke. Go make coffee."

"But—"

Scotty turns her mouth toward the commode. Her back arches again and again. She groans with each heave, until something splatters in the commode. Makes me nauseous just hearing it.

In the kitchen I get coffee going and open the fridge to consider eggs and bacon. Scotty comes in and plops to a chair at the table. "Almost nine weeks. I thought I was clear of this crap."

"You're lucky. My mom said hers started at four weeks with me and five with my sister. That's about how long we've been keeping busy in the bed."

"You better hope I feel better later, or that bed is going to be for sleeping only."

"Mind if I cook?"

"Do whatever. Just pour me coffee when it's ready."

I take eggs and bacon to the counter by the stove. "Thinking about Lizzie made me think about my sister. She teaches

143

elementary English and hates how some parents aren't parents. She says some of the kids come to school starved for affection, and it breaks her heart."

"That's not happening with us. Ted, on the other hand …"

"Which is another reason you plan to fight him however you can." I fill a mug and take it to the table. "Lisa—that's my sister's name—hated it that Andy died. She met her one year at Christmas and really liked her."

Sipping coffee, Scotty stares off into space, likely thinking about her upcoming custody fight with Ted. At least we'll have until the baby's born next June to get ready, now being mid-November.

The bacon sizzles. I whisk eggs for scrambling, cut a pat of butter in the hot pan, and pour the eggs in. "You still up for church?"

"Everybody needs forgiveness eventually."

"Did you get over feeling guilty about all of our sex?"

"That should be obvious, you idiot."

"Then what do you need to be forgiven for?"

"Anything, everything. My custody fight with Ted, which I assure you, no holds will be barred." Scotty sips coffee. "Do you ever blame yourself for Andy's death?"

"I haven't had time to process it yet. Suicide or an accident, who knows? Like I said, I'll ask her friends if they noticed anything strange about her."

"Do you have any friends outside of her circle?"

"Paul—he suggested I try MRI sales—is one. We work together and go out for a beer and a game of pool once in a while."

"What's he like?"

I stir bubbling eggs. "Decent enough. Standard skirt chaser. Got a man bun, if you're into that kind of thing. He's in better shape than me."

Scotty screws her face into a frown. "Oh, please, I like my men looking like men, not like ponytailed women." She gets up for a plate, covers it with paper towels, and adds bacon from the pan. "I feel a lot better. You might even get lucky this afternoon."

"Just make sure you brush your puke breath with plenty of toothpaste." I plate the eggs, set them on the table, and drop bread in the toaster.

Scotty fills a mug for me, refills hers, and sits. "Who's Andy's closest friend?"

"Sheryl. She's younger. Worked with her at the orthopedic place. Did I tell you what Andy did?"

"My memory's been corrupted by you corrupting me for the last five weeks."

"She was a radiology tech. X-rays, ultrasounds, MRI's, Cat scans." I get up for the toast. "You name it, she could scan with it."

"Too bad ..." Scotty's words trail. She lowers her head.

I swallow the eggs I'm eating. "Too bad what?"

"I was going to say it's too bad doctors can't scan people whose deaths are problematic and figure out what happened."

"You sure seem interested in why Scotty died." I sip coffee.

"As you are. I've always been curious about how the mind works. Too bad I didn't become a shrink so I could've figured me out before I married Ted."

"People do things you'd think they'd never do for all kinds of reasons. If they don't die doing it, all we can do is try to understand why."

"And forgive them too, right? Like you'll forgive Andy if you find something in her background that made her commit suicide."

"Do I have a choice? It's not like I can bring her back from the dead and tell her I forgive her."

"You understand what I mean. That's what matters."

We finish breakfast in silence. To the west, thunder rolls, low and distant, making me feel as if I'm about to enter the eye of a hurricane. I suppose it's all the talk about Andy.

We shower and dress for church—nice clothes instead of shorts and T-shirts—and row to Island Hopper's pier. From the westward cloud bank, still low and dark, a sheet of tattered gray, undulating like a windswept shroud, lowers to the Gulf. The wind freshens. Minutes later I catch the ozone smell of rain. A fat drop splatters my face. More drops rattle to the pier as we climb from the dinghy, then fade to a smattering of individual droplets. Walking along the gray planks, Scotty grabs my arm to stop me. "Look, a rainbow."

Sure enough, beneath those roiling clouds, a perfect rainbow arches over the horizon. "Cool. A sign everything will work out for us."

We hustle along the sidewalk. The clouds break; sunlight streams through them in intense beams, narrow and focused, in what some people call "God Rays."

The church is about half full. The minister wears tattered denims in blue, an untucked red Oxford shirt, leather sandals, and a scruffy goatee. An elderly woman, leathery from the sun, tanned to almost black, plays an organ. The notes drift upward, blend with the sun penetrating the stained-glass windows, fill the church with multicolored warmth. The notes end. The minister opens a Bible, turns a few pages, and closes it.

"I've got little to say today. The sun's coming out and people want to do their thing. I don't blame them, but ..."

His voice carries no fire and brimstone. His arms don't wave like a huge herring gull trying to rise from the beach on its five-foot wingspan.

He raises the Bible. "More than anything, this book is about love. Couples know what I mean when I say forgiveness makes two into one. Sometimes we do things we can't explain" —he gestures to the organ player— "as my wife will be glad to tell you. Still, those things run from serious to not so serious. Even then we might not understand until we look at the fault through the eyes of the person who committed that fault. And I mean, friends, with the eyes of love." He nods to his wife. The quavering organ notes, thick and solemn, fill the church again. People file out. Scotty and I do to.

Our shoes patter the concrete sidewalk. The green smell of palm fronds replaces the ozone small of rain. She slips her fingers into mine. "Do you forgive me?"

"I still might press charges for kidnapping."

"I'll press charges for you keeping my nooks and crannies filled with your swimmers."

"What have you done that needs forgiving?"

"It's what I'll do about Ted and this custody thing."

"Will your Glock come into play?"

"Only if I shoot myself in the head because I'm tired of his constant crap."

We move aside for another couple and continue walking. "Is *Out for Fun* ready for our final cruise back to Manteo?"

"I checked the diesel and water tanks while you showered. Everything's fine."

"Enough groceries to keep your pumpkin looking like a pumpkin?"

"You do realize southern girls are perfectly willing to withhold sex when their man says something stupid. Besides, all our lying around the yacht and eating everything in sight has turned us *both* into pumpkins."

"Maybe we'll catch enough fish with Mary Lou to eat healthy all the way back to Manteo."

"We'll see. Very little about our vacation has been lucky— me headbutting that jackass in Savannah, the guy recognizing us in Miami and telling Ted, Ted catching us in our room at the resort—but I'm willing to believe we can find some luck if we need it."

Chapter 19

I dress in the morning while Scotty finishes in the bathroom. No black cloudbanks mar the crystalline sky, blue with silver toward the western horizon. She doesn't complain of morning sickness; we have coffee and instant oatmeal. Mary Lou has a fishing client at 9 a.m., so Scotty and I lounge around like hound dogs. She's still into that same paperback and suggests I find a fishing magazine in a rack in her room.

Sitting in the chair beside her on the bridge, I open the pages, close them, and visit the bow to see what Mr. Darcy and Lizzie are up to. No dorsal fins cut the water. At the stern, it's the same thing. I shrug and go back inside to read.

Lunch comes. We have turkey sandwiches on whole wheat. I have beer, Scotty has bottled water. Done with both, she goes to her room, comes back with a sheet of paper and a pen, and starts scribbling. I lean to look; she slaps her hand over the paper. "Don't be nosy."

"Writing your will for when Ted drives you to shoot yourself?"

"It's an idea for the next bestselling novel. All I need is a title."

I start to say what, Love, Jake? but don't. I haven't told her my middle name yet and don't see any reason to until we get back to Manteo and get things in somewhat of a semblance of normal. Then she'll have time to get used to calling me Jake instead of Jonathan, if she wants to.

I poke her side. "Does the main character smoke?"

"I love the taste of tobacco, but I'll stop for the baby and me. I want to be around for her as long as I can."

"Don't forget me."

She kisses me. "Yes, and you."

I notice the loaf of bread is still open, the little paper-covered tie beside it. Time to make it official. Past time, really. I twirl the bag closed and tuck the opening beneath the loaf, take the tie and kneel beside Scotty. "Feel like marrying a fatty?"

"How many times do I need to tell you, we're plus sized?" She extends her ring finger. "How romantic."

I twist the tie around her finger. "I can buy a nicer one later."

"Stand up here and kiss me. I might seem high maintenance but I'm not. I'll take the simple things any day of the week over the junk that makes Ted happy."

"Like raising chickens on your parent's farm?"

"Why not?" Scotty grabs my face and plants a great kiss on me. "How's that for an engagement ki—" She grabs her throat and runs from the bridge. I follow her to the bathroom, where she throws the commode seat up and leans over to heave … heave … heave like she intends to throw her guts up, but nothing happens.

I wet a washcloth and press it to her forehead. "Now you know how much I love you."

The heaves pause; she takes a breath. "And how much I love you."

"I assume you aren't going fishing."

"Great assumption." She sits up. "Whew, no sweat that time."

I put the washcloth by the sink. "I guess I'll row on over and have a beer while I wait for Mary Lou."

Scotty stands, slips her arms around me, and kisses me. "I do love you. Little did I know I'd meet my soulmate when I kidnapped him."

I take in the aroma of vanilla lotion. Hair soft and silky presses my cheek. "I know, right? What a crazy world we live in."

We separate. Scotty follows me to the stern. "I'll visit the aquarium when I feel better and wait for you in the bar. Don't let Mary Lou seduce you. We know how romantic it is out on the water."

I shove off and pick up a paddle. "Not a chance, pumpkin. See you later."

The dinghy leaves a feathering wake in the silver water. Scotty waves, turns to wiggle her behind at me, blows me a kiss, and leaves for the bridge.

Yep, we're most definitely in love.

When I'm about halfway to the pier, the notched dorsal fin of Mr. Darcy comes angling toward me. He pauses to look my way, then goes to the side of the dinghy and nudges it around until I point toward *Out for Fun*. I splash him with the paddle. "I'm going fishing, Darcy. Go keep our girls company."

He sticks his head out of the water, squeals and shakes his head. I splash him again and he leaves, dorsal slicing toward the yacht.

Before I start rowing toward Island Hopper again, a sonic boom from one of the Air Force jets shatters the silence. "There oughta be a law," I mumble.

I tie the dinghy to cleats and go inside the bar. A few men sit on stools, making small talk and sipping beers. At the table

151

nearest the TV, a couple sits with mixed drinks, ignoring a commercial about the Keys. Sammy fills a mug from the draft tab and sets it in front of me. "Scotty ain't goin' fishin'?"

"Morning sickness is kicking in. She plans to see the aquarium later. Heard anything from M.L. and her client?"

"Her phone knocked off this morning. She went south lookin' for permit. Thought she'd be back by now. Fish must not be bitin'."

I sip beer. "Is Lizzie chewing her food now?"

"'Bout a hundert times a mouthful. Me an' Lou sure 'preciate what you did. We'd be lost as a gator widdout a swamp if somethin' happened to dat chile."

To keep from grinning at Sammy's thick Cajun accent, I sip beer again. "She's special all right. You and M.L. are special too, adopting her like you did."

Sammy fills a shot glass with rum and downs it. "Here's to love. Be it a little baby, a chile, whatever, there ain't nothin' like love." He tilts his head to one side. "Sounds like Lou comin' in now."

I pick up the faint whine of an outboard engine. Mary Lou passes *Out for Fun* and continues toward the pier. I go out and catch the rope one of her clients throws me. Mary Lou kills the engine. "Tough fishin' today, Jonny. You sure you wanna go?"

"I'm willing if you are."

"Is my gal pal inside with Sammy?"

"Morning sickness has her driving the porcelain yacht."

"Somethin' I ain't sorry I missed."

The two men climb to the pier, rods and tackle in hand. "Sorry, gents," M.L. says. "Go tell Sammy I said to lubricate your sorrows with however many drafts it takes to make you forget about fishin' and remember your wives."

The men thank her and leave for the bar's door. I climb aboard M.L.'s boat. She raises a seat and takes a wide-brimmed straw hat from the compartment beneath it. "Untie us and clamp that to your head and hold on. I'm headin' northeast to see if we can find some doggone fish."

We putter out about twenty-five yards. M.L. lowers the throttle. The outboard whines, the bow rises, we surge forward.

Holding the wheel with both hands, she stands at a center console behind a windshield. I move closer, out of the slipstream buffeting me and the brim of the hat. "Are there more keys out this way?"

"Lotsa coral flats, gotta give it a shot. I hate for you to come back without a nice permit fish for my gal pal to eat tonight. You say the morning sickness got her tossin' her cookies?"

"Nausea right now. She threw up terrible the morning after our dinner together."

"Good lawd, I bet that was a mess. Got your phone? Give 'er a call and see how she's feelin'."

We approach the wake of one of those cigar boats, long and stretched out and running at least sixty. I stick my hand in my cargo short's pocket for my phone.

"Hold on, Jonny! I ain't slowin' down!"

My phone's halfway out when we hit the waves. The bow shoots up and slams down. My phone flies from my hand and goes swimming. I grab the rail around the console before I follow my phone overboard.

"Sorry 'bout that, Jonny. Neither man nor beast nor cell phone waits for me when I'm huntin' fish."

"No problem. I've got my old one at home somewhere to get my contacts from."

We round the western point of Key West. Sparse trees keep me from seeing what's behind them. Clearing those, I see a parking lot and what looks like the walls of a fort. "I lean close to M.L.'s ear. "Scotty didn't say anything about a fort on Key West."

"That's Fort Zachary Taylor. All this water and it's got a doggone moat around most of it."

We continue north in the pea-green sea for at least another thirty minutes by my watch. "How far are you going?"

"There's a spot about ten miles out I'd like to try. No luck there, we'll keep goin'."

The outboard drones, a huge bumblebee on steroids. I sit, nodding as the bow rises rhythmically up and down. Before I know it, warmed by the sun, I'm in a trance. My hand starts to slide off the hat but I wake in time to clamp it down again.

M.L. cackles laughter. "My gal pal been keepin' you up late since you been in the Keys?"

I answer with a nod and a sheepish grin.

"You know she's plumb head over heels in love with you, don't you? You wait until she gets things ironed out with Ted, it'll all work out fine."

I stand close to M.L. again so I won't have to yell over the roar of the outboard. Her voice is as sharp as a filet knife: I can hear her words clear as a ringing bell.

"I'm plumb head over heels in love with her too. As far as I'm concerned, her baby's our baby."

"That's good to know, Jonny. You'll need a hell of a lot of patience where this thing with Ted is gonna take you and her."

M.L. throttles the outboard down. The bow lowers; water gathers at the stern, gurgling and popping with the exhaust that smells of gas and oil, which means it's a two-cycle outboard.

Two rods and reels are in a rack bolted to the inside of the boat lengthwise. M.L. gets one out and gives it to me. "Ever handle a spinning real?"

"I surf fished with my dad as a kid."

"Good. The water here's about two-feet deep. Cast the bucktail jig out and reel-jerk, reel-jerk, and let's see what's here. Start to your left and work to your right." M.L. takes a long pole from the fiberglass floor. "I'll pole us along when you finish that pattern, and you can start over. We'll give it thirty minutes and change that jig from yellow to white. That don't work we'll add a shrimp tail to it and start all over again. That don't work we'll try another spot."

I do as M.L. says. The sun glares off the calm water. Sweat trickles down my spine. M.L. gets bottles of water from a cooler and gives me one. We swallow, pause, swallow, and I cast again. M.L.'s pole rises and falls, evidenced by sound of water dripping into the Gulf.

Two hours pass. We try another spot. Two more hours pass. We try another spot. I get us more water and sit. "It's a good thing women are easier to satisfy than these fish."

M.L. cackles. "Scotty said you got a bigger than average pecker."

"Scotty shouldn't tell everything."

"C'mon, Jonny, you're from the south. You got it, you might as well flaunt it."

I finish the water. The sun touches the horizon. "How far are we from Key West?"

"'Bout an hour, maybe less."

"Will we get there before dark?"

"I got runnin' lights an' a GPS. We'll be all right."

I return to the platform and resume casting. Clouds drifts between us and the sun, huge things, puffy and bloated. They turn blood red. Darkness settles. M.L. stores the pole and the rod. "We might as well—"

BOOM!

"Bless the Air Force's hearts," she says. "They need to move the base where people don't care about peace and quiet and

155

catchin' a durn fish once in a blue moon for all them sonic booms."

The outboard roars; the bow rises. Cooler air dries the sweat on my forehead. Thirty minutes later I sniff. "M.L., you smell smoke?"

"Probably someone on a yacht like y'all's, cookin' with charcoal instead of propane."

The running lights flood the water ahead of us, now black, not pea-green. The closer we get to Key West, the more I smell smoke. It doesn't smell like charcoal; it smells like cloth and rubber. The low shadow of Key West rises before us, lights twinkling in the night. A strange orange glow flickers beyond the lights.

And then, mixed with the glow of that orange light, I see black smoke rising from what can only be the largest yacht anchored exactly where *Out for Fun* is anchored.

M.L. shoves the throttle all the way down; we thrust forward into the night. "Don't you worry, Jonny. Scotty's with Sammy and Lizzie, sure as we standin' here."

The sudden rise in M.L.'s knife-like voice tells me she's not sure about what she just said.

I wish I had my phone. I wish I hadn't gone fishing. I wish Scotty had come with me. I wish all the wishes in the world—until we round the westernmost point on Key West and see *Out for Fun* blazing, Coast Guard ships pumping water on it.

M.L. steers for the pier. I grip the handrail so hard I expect to leave dents in it.

I jump from the boat before M.L. can stop and I roll onto the pier. She hops out behind me. We run inside. Sammy's sitting at a table holding Lizzie. Her arms are around his neck as she softly sobs. Sammy looks up; tears glisten in his eyes. M.L. takes

Lizzie and leaves. I drop into the chair beside Sammy. "Please tell me Scotty isn't … isn't …"

"She was here, Jonny. She went to the aquarium and came back. We was sittin' here talkin' about how much she looked forward to startin' life all over with you when that damn fume alarm squalled. I told her not to go, to give it time to see what it was gonna do. She rowed right out big as she pleases, ain't afraid one bit. I watched her brown hair drop below the deck into the engine room and the damn thing blew. All I could do was run to the phone and call 911."

I look toward what's left of *Out for Fun.* All of Island Hopper's windows facing the pier are cracked, and nothing's left of the yacht but the smoking hull. Scotty had to have gotten out somehow. There's absolutely no way she's dead. A smaller Coast Guard vessel comes from behind *Out for Fun* and heads our way. It's picked Scotty up out of the water and is bringing her to me. I see her brown hair in the running lights glaring down from the framework of poles over the center console.

Sammy and I go out onto the pier. The vessel docks opposite M.L.'s boat. Scotty gets out but something's wrong—she wears a ponytail but it hangs from the opening in the back of a Coast Guard ball cap. I go to her, and she says, "Sir, did you call 911?"

I look out onto the water. "She's still out there. Don't leave her out there. Go find Mr. Darcy and Lizzie. They'll help you find her."

"Ma'am," Sammy says, "I made that call. Did you find … well, did you, you know…"

I look out onto the water again. About fifty yards away, in the glare of the Coast Guard ship's lights illuminating the entire area, Mr. Darcy's notched fin nears something colored a creamy white. He circles it, prods it gently. Lizzie must've been near the yacht when it blew, and she's dead.

"Did you know the person on the yacht?" the Coast Guard woman asks Sammy.

Sammy comes to me, whispers in my ear. "You don't know anything about that yacht or who was on it. Ted will be comin', you understand me? He'll try to pin this on you sure as hell."

The Coast Guard woman faces me. "Did you know the person, sir?"

"I … I, um, I thought it was my sister's yacht, *Hope.* I just got here a few minutes ago and thought it was her. I was supposed to meet her for a beer."

Sammy nudges me toward the bar. "Go on inside. Maybe your sister will be along later."

I do as Sammy says and sit at a table. From the darkened doorway behind the bar, Lizzie still cries.

Sammy and the woman talk. He nods, looks my way, shakes his head. The woman gets in her boat and leaves. Sammy comes in, pours two shots, and drops into the chair beside me. He shoves one of the shot glasses toward me.

"I guess Ted can screw every damned thing in the world now. Probably has a big life insurance policy on Scotty. Hell, he'll screw on the moon if he's a mind to."

I ignore the shot. "She's not dead. We need to go look for her. She's cold, she's sick. Who knows how long she's been treading water? She might have a broken arm or a broken leg, that's all. We'll find her and get her fixed up and we'll get married and have our baby and everything will work out."

Mary Lou comes in and sits beside Sammy. I saw you out the window talkin' to the Coast Guard lady. What'd she say?"

"Scotty's okay," I say. "We need to go find her."

"She's not okay," Sammy says. "That women said they found human remains in the engine room."

M.L. swallows hard; the tendons in her neck bulge and relax. "What did they find?"

"I few teeth, nothin' else."

"She's okay," I say. "We need to go find her."

M.L. gets up, slides her chair around to face me, sits and takes my face in her hands. "Scotty told me about Andy and how much you loved her. She said it broke her heart to see you sittin' on that beach beside her. She said she knew right then and there that you and her were two people who needed each other. She always believed in love, and she could tell you did too by how you cried for Andy."

"She's okay, Mary Lou. Really, she is."

"Jonny, you can't let this break you. My daddy lost a lot of his friends in Vietnam. I see that same empty look in your eyes that I saw in his when he came back."

"Lou," Sammy says, "we got to get him on a bus before Ted gets here. The Coast Guard will be tracing the name on the stern any time now."

"Scotty told me she saw him at that resort. He'll be here in no time."

Sammy slides his chair closer and puts his arm around my shoulders. "Jonny, Scotty wouldn't want you to let Ted make you take the fall for this. He'll do it sure as hell."

I stand. "I'll go look for her. I know y'all can't leave Lizzie, her throat still hurts from getting choked and that's why she's crying."

A wisp of a girl emerges from the darkened doorway. She has brown curls and a triangle shaped chin. Her bare feet patter softly toward me. She takes my hand and pulls, and I kneel in front of her. "Scotty loves you, Jonny, but you need to leave before Ted comes. 'Member how I said he's got mean eyes?" I say nothing. Lizzie presses her hand to my chest. "I saw how you and Scotty looked at each other. Save all that love in your heart. Like Mama said, you can't let this break you."

Lizzie runs to the bar and comes back with Scotty's purse. "Scotty left this. Take it with you."

Still on my knees in the floor, I waver back and forth. I have choices to make and I need to make them now. I can stay and kill Ted when he comes, which will land me in jail for life, or I can go home and grieve when I can. I prefer the latter, because if I grieve now, I don't know how or when it will end.

"C'mon," Sammy says, lifting me by my shoulders. "I'll run you to the bus station."

M.L. gives me a quick hug. Her cheeks are wet and her hair smells of fresh air like Scotty's did after a day on an isolated Keys beach. "You take care now."

Behind the bar a phone rings. M.L. gets it, listens, and hangs up. "That was Ted raisin' hell. Said he's on a plane in thirty minutes, 'headin' this way."

Lizzie pulls me down for a hug. Sammy hustles me out the door. The Jeep tires squeal in reverse and squeal again in forward. He brakes at the bus station, helps me buy a ticket with a credit card from my wallet, and waits until I'm in a seat and watching him through a salt-smeared window.

The last thing I see of Key West is my new friend waving to me from the circle of yellow light that pours from a street lamp over his head.

Chapter 20

In back of the bus, I close my eyes and clutch Scotty's purse to my chest. Maybe, just maybe, if I hold it tight enough, the pressure will support my ribs so my heart won't fling itself to the chewing gum encrusted floor and pump itself empty of every drop of blood in my body.

Car lights flash, pulses of brightness visible behind my eyelids. The faint sound of their slipstreams hiss by. The bus rumbles on through the night. Each time it slows I catch a whiff of diesel exhaust.

Somewhere along the way it stops for a restroom break. The sun rises; the bus stops for a quick breakfast and I stay in my seat. The day passes with the muffled roar of tires on pavement, of the murmurs of passengers boarding and unboarding, of their footsteps thudding the center aisle as they find seats. I keep my eyes lowered so no one will think a glance is an invitation to sit.

I finally use the restroom near Savannah and drink stale coffee in Florence, South Carolina. My back is stiff. My eyes are drained of life from no sleep. In Fayetteville, North Carolina, I rent a car and drive to Manteo, ignoring the landscape. The rental chain takes the car and runs me to the Dare County Sheriff's Department, at what I think is close to five weeks, three

161

days, and twenty hours from when Scotty and I argued in her office. I could easily be wrong.

The person manning the impound lot searches through paperwork, gives it a cursory glance, and hands me the keys to my Camry. He gives the purse hanging from my shoulder more than a cursory glance.

The hotel manager rummages in a back room for my suitcase. Between the time Andy died and when Stan and I spread her ashes, I ran her things to my house near Raleigh. For a second I'm tempted to visit the vacation rental Endless Love and see if Andy's ghost will steal my consciousness like it did before. Instead, I drive to Roanoke Island again, pass the turn to Manteo and the Dare County Sheriff's Department, and connect to 64 West on the other side of the Croatan Sound, for the three hours plus drive to Raleigh.

When I arrive at the end of the five-mile-long Virginia Dare Memorial bridge and pass through the community of Manns Harbor, I start searching the wooded flatlands for Scotty's parent's farm. On one side of the highway runs a blackwater canal. Homes are scarce. On my right the woods abruptly end where they've been clear cut. At a rambling two story house, barn in the back, both set about a hundred yards off the road, I slow and read a sign by the mailbox: Coming Soon, East Lake Winery.

No vehicles, no tractors, no farm implements, no grape vines. Regardless of the sign's claim, its peeling paint and weeds growing around it say no winery is coming here soon, if ever.

I cross the Alligator River and continue to Columbia, where I stop at a convenience store to stretch my legs, my back, and get a large coffee for a boost of caffeine to keep me awake for the last two and a half hours of my drive.

At my subdivision, the mailbox is stuffed. A neighbor catches me before I get inside, silently hands me a plastic garbage bag filled with mail. We've never met. I thank him anyway. In the kitchen I drink tap water. The thermometer that Andy stuck to the outside of the window says thirty-nine degrees and I gawk. That's right, it's late November, when frost is possible at night. That's right, it's night. Did I drive here without lights?

In every room I pull curtains and close shades. Suitcase on my bed, I throw the musty clothes in a corner to wash when I feel like it, which may be never. I go out for Scotty's purse and leave it on the kitchen table. Reminders of her will cut into the soft underbelly of my psyche to the point of considering a butcher's knife across my wrists, Dad's Colt .45 to my temple, or sitting in the Camry with a hose pumping exhaust into the inside, where I take deep breath after deep breath.

I unzip the purse. The paperback is there, a hairbrush with strands of brunette tangled within the bristles, and her wallet. It undoubtedly holds her driver's license and photograph. The microwave clock says 6:15. In the living room, at a corner desk, I power my laptop on, log in, and search for Dare County news.

A link flares in Times New Roman letters: Sheriff Scott Dies in Tragic Yacht Explosion in Key West, Florida. Well Known Real Estate Mogul Thaddeus Scott, Husband of Sheriff Scott, Cannot be Reached for Comment.

No mention of foul play or of him seeing me at that resort. Of course not. To suggest foul play means uncovering me, which would uncover Scotty's story of his pictures with those women and that man as they did whatever around that pool, probably at night when the private investigator was off somewhere eating supper on Scotty's dime. When the PI sees the story of Scotty's death, he'll know the pictures he did take, of them helping each other with suntan lotion, were never worth what she paid for them.

The page continues, I don't click the link. There's no way I can handle Scotty's green eyes looking at me. Laptop closed, I go to the kitchen, zip the purse, and put it on top of the refrigerator.

The thermostat says sixty-two degrees. I leave it there, go to the bathroom for a shower, and crawl in bed. No sleep and no food and next to nothing to drink for well over twenty-four hours weighs on my eyelids like the huge sandbags that were used to stop the encroaching ocean at the beach near the Cape Hatteras Lighthouse before it was moved inland.

Lying there in the dark, I can't understand why I don't cry. I've lost two loves of my life, both I considered soulmates—yes, I now believe in them—in roughly seven weeks. In all the millennia of human existence, what man has suffered as much? This thought doesn't come from ego, or pride, or from any belief in my ability to love more than any other man has ever loved; it comes from the hollow where my heart once beat, where my lungs once expanded and contracted, where Lizzie placed her hand and told me: "Save all that love in your heart. Like Mama said, you can't let this break you."

The wisdom in her soft voice broke me, and I didn't even know it. The tragedy of Mr. Darcy gently nudging Lizzie Bennet's dead body broke me too, and I didn't know it either.

I go to the kitchen and take the novel from Scotty's purse. The sheet of paper she was writing on, saying she was starting a new bestselling novel, is there. Whatever the words, whatever the hope she's penned about us, they'll crack the damn holding my emotions back, and I need to release them or die.

Sitting on the side of the bed, nightstand lamp on, the hush of night all around, I unfold the paper. The words are in verse, as in a song instead of a novel, possibly inspired when I played the guitar for her.

I'm tougher than I look, I'm softer than I sound.
I'd love to find the sweetest man, who can lift me off the ground.
Sail me across the seven seas, and love me all night long,
But I'd settle for the simple things, with them I'd do no wrong.
But I'd settle for the simple things, with him I'd do no wrong.

My hands shake. My eyes sting as if a swarm of jellyfish drifts behind them, looping their tentacles into my optic nerves.

Love me now, please don't wait.
Life's too short to throw away, I need you on my plate.

Unbelievably as it seems, I smile through my grimace of pain. Scotty and her humor, needing me on her plate, referring to our love of food.

Butter pecan doesn't stand a chance, with you here by my side.
But hot peach pie, alamode, might tempt me for a while.
But hot peach pie, alamode, might tempt me for a while.
Until you smile.

Even with her reference to butter pecan ice cream and the peach pie alamode her mom made her eat that time, the thought of me making her smile—after all she'd been through with Ted, after loving me to the point of wanting me to be the real, true, and genuine daddy of her daughter—lets the grimace take hold again. Knowing my tears will smear the ink, knowing I'll crinkle the paper, knowing none of that matters because I'll never forget her words as long as I live, I press my last remnant of her to my face.

Heat and moisture feed the mass of salt water raging from me. The release is so genuine, I bury my face into my pillow and bite the material to keep from waking the neighbors.

Not once but twice I've lost loves. Every shudder of my shoulders, every heavy sob, every exhale that almost makes me heave bile, is evidence to more pain than I believe I can stand.

And then I hear Lizzie's soft voice, a mix of Mary Lou's amusing southern twang and Sammy's French-accented Cajun, telling me to not let this break me.

I'll try my best not to. I don't know if I can.

The tears continue. I hope they're the last I'll cry over both Andy and Scotty. Then I realize I now have the eyes of two hurricanes in which to pilot the hurricane hunter aircraft. What I'll find I have no idea, but I doubt it's something that will bring me happiness instead of grief.

Chapter 21

I awake to light. The bathroom calls. I visit and return to bed. I awake to dark. The phone hanging on the wall in the kitchen rings and I ignore it by rolling over. I awake to light, sip water and return to bed. To stay up admits I'm ready to face the world. I'm not. I awake to twilight. Whether it's dawn or dusk, I don't care. I prove it by not checking the time on the LED alarm clock on the nightstand.

The last time I wake it's 7 a.m. on Sunday morning, time to test my willingness to return to the land of the living instead of remaining in the land of the dead. I read Scotty's song and take a pen from the nightstand drawer to scribble Scotty's Song at the top for a title. The ink isn't as smeared as I thought it would be. I don't smear it further. In the kitchen, I take Scotty's hair brush from her purse and smell the floral aroma of those brunette tangles. No tears sting my eyes. Next is the driver's license photograph. She doesn't smile; no tears sting.

Rambling in the purse for another test, I find her wedding and engagement rings. I think of a project for them and return them until then. Next is a small bottle of vanilla lotion. Tears sting this time but not to the point of crying.

We never ate french toast. The eggs in my fridge are barely in date and the bread on the counter is a month out of date. No mold greens the edges, it'll do. It's then I feel how cold the linoleum is on my bare feet, how cold the air is on my naked body, how goosebumps ridge my arms with hundreds of dots. Thermostat up to sixty-five, I get a robe and slippers and continue with breakfast, including a full carafe of black coffee.

Breakfast done, I ramble in the kitchen junk drawer for my old cell phone and charger. That done I shower again, allowing the hot water to stream over my face and body until I'm shriveled. That done I dress and go to the kitchen for more coffee.

Andy hung a bird feeder from a naked oak limb in the backyard. Strange how it wasn't naked when she hung it back in June. A finch flutters to it, turns its head this way and that, black eyes anxious at the lack of sunflower seeds, and flutters away. A cardinal dressed in blazing scarlet does the same, followed in quick succession by a titmouse, a house sparrow, and a mourning dove, which settles on the frostbitten grass beneath the feeder to strut in a circle, head thrusting forward and back, pink feet bright, downy breast feathers in milky beige flaring in the breeze. Darker wings, sleek and pinioned, fold across its slender tail. No seed litters the grass. It wings upward, cuts through the brightening sky, and fades to a gray bullet against a background of ultramarine blue, similar to the depths between Florida and the Turks and Caicos.

To keep my slippers on, I shuffle through the grass to a metal utility shed for sunflower seed and fill the feeder. My breath forms twin rods of haze exiting my nostrils. Icy air chills my ears. In the kitchen, frost melts on the navy blue of my slippers, turning them nearly black. No birds come; they'll be back.

I sit on the sofa in the living room and thumb the remote. Having not seen TV since leaving home, including my one night with Andy and the trip here to escape Nags Head and to return her luggage, the sight is like something out of a science fiction movie. I turn it off and get up to warm my coffee. The doorbell rings. The one-way peephole reveals Cheryl's blonde hair, straight and long, and her blinking hazel eyes. She holds a bag from a local doughnut shop and two coffees. I suppose she's been driving by to see if I'm home and has this morning. Scotty once said Cheryl had a crush on me. It seems it might be so, not that I'm ready for that anytime soon, if ever. Maybe she called the other day, the first time I woke.

I open the door. Cheryl beams a smile and comes in. "I hope you don't mind me dropping by. I've been wondering where you were. I thought you were coming home sooner than what, five weeks?" She sets the bag and coffees on the coffee table, takes off a pink microfiber jacket, drapes it over the sofa, and sits to cross her legs. Jeans cling to curves. Factory-made rips open the knees. Pink skin shows.

I sit at the opposite end of the sofa. "I appreciate it, but you didn't need to check up on me."

"Nice tan. I promised Andy I would."

"Why would she want you to do that?"

"She worried about you when she went on those trips to train on new equipment for work."

"I thought you went with her."

"Not every time." Cheryl offers me a doughnut and coffee and takes a doughnut for herself. She licks white frosting from her lips and sips coffee. "Eat up while they're warm."

I drop the sticky doughnut in the bag. "Sorry, no taste for sweets right now." Might as well put Cheryl's visit to good use. "Andy never said how long you knew each other."

"We met in school. Went out on a few double dates."

"Did she ever do anything strange?"

"Like what?"

169

"Did she ever act outside of her normal character? Anything like that?"

Cheryl's cheeks turn red. "She told you, didn't she?"

Like Scotty, I once thought about creative writing. I particularly liked the subject of an unreliable character or narrator, one who lied at will to the reader's detriment.

"She did but I didn't mind."

"Good. It wasn't a big thing or anything. We just did it a few times before you two met."

"You know she liked wine. Did it involve that?"

"Oh, yeah, always. One time we did it with marijuana. Have you ever had sex stoned on marijuana? You should try it sometime. Well, you know, if you ever meet someone."

I've just penetrated the outer bands of Andy's hurricane. How many more until I reach the eye wall itself? How many more until the calm of the eye surrounds me?

Cheryl takes another bite of doughnut, swallows, and sips coffee. She puts the cup down and turns to face me, tucking one leg beneath her at the same time. "Are you doing okay? I know how much you and Andy loved each other."

"You and Andy spent a lot of time together, Cheryl." I tone my voice down to let her know I'm serious. "Are you sure you didn't have sex with her after we met?"

Two quick blinks of her hazel eyes followed by a hesitation and another blink tells me she's going to lie. "It was only before you met her. I wouldn't lie about it."

"Did she date much before she met me?"

"Average."

"Did she sleep with them?"

"Average."

"Did you two sleep with any of them at the same time in the same bed?"

170

Cheryl's cheeks redden. "It shouldn't matter, it was before she met you. She always made them use condoms and was on the pill too."

I lean back against the sofa. I've penetrated another outer band of Hurricane Andy. It doesn't please me one bit. "You two went out after work at least two nights a week. Did any guys come on to you?"

"You know guys."

"Did you ever take any of them back to your apartment?"

"You're asking me all this because you think Andy cheated on you and that had something to do with why she died. That's insane. She just had weird ideas about sex and liked to watch and ..."

I don't ask what Cheryl's trailing "and" means. My imagination tells me Andy touched herself, that and she did it with me too. Still, doing that in front of some strange guy or guys ... I'm completely dumbfounded. At least she didn't sleep with any of them; that I couldn't handle. I took our relationship seriously and she said she did too. A betrayal like that, especially if I knew who the guy was, might make even *me* do things I wouldn't normally consider doing.

Cheryl's chin is down; her hands are crossed in her lap. I sip cooling coffee. "Did she ever say anything strange about lights?"

"She read a lot of science fiction back then. She liked the idea of traveling to other galaxies on compressed beams of light. She said a woman's vagina was like that for a man. She had this idea that she was meant for something besides the regular life everyone lives, like working and having kids."

I say nothing. This leads me to believe Andy slept with a lot more men than the few she told me about. If not for her making them use condoms, who knows what diseases she might've gotten and given me. As far as Andy feeling like she was meant for a life other than kids and work, who doesn't feel like we're meant for more on this earth than the humdrum existence of daily living?

"Jake?" Cheryl slides closer. "I'm sorry about Andy, but you need to move on with your life. She always said she wanted the best for you."

My robe is open, one knee visible. Cheryl's eyes dart down and I stand. "My wife died less than two months ago and you—who claim you were her best friend—want to sleep with me in our bed?"

"She knew I liked you. She wouldn't mind."

The perversion of such a statement is beyond amazing. Still, I need more information. In fact, I'm desperate enough to do what I'm going to do.

I open my robe. Cheryl slides over and does what apparently comes naturally. Finished, she closes my robe and ties it, slides to the other end of the sofa. "You had to have needed that. We'll take care of me next time."

I sit. "Are you sure Andy didn't have sex with any guys after she met me? I won't get mad, I just want to know. Maybe she wasn't who I thought she was. You're honest about who you are. Maybe we could date and see what happens. You know, see if we're compatible."

Those hazel eyes blink twice, hesitate, and blink again. "She wouldn't do that to you, Jake."

A thought spins into my mind, like the waterspout Scotty and I saw swirling down from the thunderstorm that day. "Was Paul ever at any of the bars you and Andy went to?"

Cheryl grabs her coffee and downs it in one gulp, as if my question has hit too close to home. She gets up. "I think I left my door unlocked." She rushes out, blonde strands bouncing around her shoulder in a curtain of yellow, and leaves the door open.

I close it, lock it, and dump the coffee cups and doughnuts in the kitchen trash. In my walk-in closet, I dress in jeans and a sweatshirt, put keys and wallet in my pockets, go back to the closet to punch the combination into the quick-access safe bolted to the wall beside the door, and take out Dad's Colt pistol. Just the sight of it will do the job I have in mind. If things go from bad to worse, I'll blow Paul's brains out and claim self-defense.

I put the gun on the Camry's passenger seat, turn the key, and turn it back again. Idiocy, pure idiocy. The .45 secure in the safe again, I call Paul on my recharged phone.

"Jake, how's it goin', bud? You dropped off the face of the earth, didn't you?"

"I needed it. What are you up to?"

"Just waking up. After breakfast and a shower, who knows."

"Mind if I stop by in an hour?"

"Come ahead, see you then."

In the living room, I use the laptop history to bring up the Dare County story again. The link I didn't click before shows Scotty in her sheriff's uniform. She's shiny and bright, happy with a slight smile that means she's pleased with the accomplishment of becoming a woman sheriff at such a young age, despite Ted's influence.

The pain of missing her flares behind my eyes: Afternoons spent on those isolated islands in the hammock, soft breeze serenading us with palm-frond song and soft wavelet whispers. Nights spent in my huge bed doing everything or nothing, quiet talks, kisses and caresses. Mornings spent in *Out for Fun's* kitchen making breakfast, lunch, or supper, between knowing smiles and suggestive glances.

I find I didn't know Andy at all, while I knew Scotty like I know myself. We were the same breath, the same heart, the same soul; we were willing to take on Ted to prove it too. Her strength tells me how to handle Paul: intelligently, rationally, and not in a way that will land me in prison for the rest of my life.

Besides, I still have that project in mind, the one I thought of when I found her rings in her purse, and I can't do that from prison. Also, I'll need some money from that life insurance check. At the laptop again, I log in to my banking website. Good old Mac, he's made arrangements to have the three million dollars transferred to my savings account and every last dime is there, waiting for me to put it to constructive use.

First, I need to deal with Paul, as well as getting more information from him about Andy.

If there is any.

Chapter 22

L ike Cheryl, Paul lives in one of the apartment complexes surrounding Raleigh. Housing is tight here, and I was lucky enough to buy my small starter house—two-bedrooms, a living room, a bathroom, a kitchen—as soon as it came on the market. Frugal by nature, I'd already saved the down payment, which reminds me how I need to move those life insurance funds into some kind of account that will earn me a living if and when I decide to quit work.

Paul opens the door after three knocks. Grungy gym shorts, a gray sweatshirt, and white socks complete his attire. The man bun bounces on the crown of his head as I follow him in. "Kinda cool for shorts, Paul." I move a newspaper and sit on the sofa.

He plops into a recliner. "You doing okay? We've been taking bets at work if you're coming back."

"It depends."

"On?"

"When I feel like it. There's a conflict there I need to clear up."

"You get along great with everyone."

I lean over, set my elbows on my thighs, and look Paul in the eye. "Look, in all honesty I'm having a hard time getting used to Andy's death. One of the guys at one of the bars that she and Cheryl went to told me she was cheating on me."

Zero reaction from Paul. "Damn shame, bro. Did the guy know you?"

"Seems like it."

Paul's hair is as black as his eyes. Unless I miss my guess, they darted off to one side when he asked if the guy knew me. I sit upright. "Seems like you knew him too."

"What bar was it?"

"Corner Place. Out near the medical park."

"Never been there."

"I didn't think so. I have a hard time believing it anyway. You know Andy, she was perfect."

"You were great together." Paul pauses. "I always hoped I'd find someone like her."

I'm tempted to say, *Why, you jerk? So you could cheat with another man's wife like you did with mine?*

"Aside from that," I continue, "I wanted to know if you ever noticed anything strange about her? Like when the regular crowd was out together and I went to the restroom, did she ever say anything strange?"

"About the only thing I recall is her looking at the lights. She was sort of like when a kid's old enough to notice them the first time. Know what I mean?"

Someone knocks on the door. Paul gets up and Cheryl comes in. "Paul, has—" She stops when she sees me. "Oh, hi, Jake."

Paul returns to the recliner. Cheryl sits at the other end of the sofa, knees tight together, purse perched in her lap, manicured nails a rainbow of green, white, and yellow wrapped around the leather strap. "Am I interrupting something?"

"I was asking Paul some of the same questions I asked you. He confirmed everything you said."

176

Paul's black eyes lunge to Cheryl. "What did you tell him?"

I stand. "Doesn't matter, Paul. I now know Andy had issues. I don't blame you for sleeping with her and Cheryl at the same time."

Cheryl springs to her feet. "I didn't tell him that."

"Sure you did," I say. "You're saying it again by coming here to warn him now."

Paul stands. "Look, bro, I'm glad you're not mad. Andy was gorgeous and Cheryl is gorgeous. What man in his right mind would turn them down?"

Smiling, I go to Paul and place my hands on his shoulders. "Friends, right?"

"Always man, Al—"

I grip Paul's shoulders and snap my forehead into his nose. The crunch of cartilage is spectacular. The gout of blood is amazing. The fall to his ass is satisfying. Scotty would be pleased.

I face Cheryl. "What the hell is wrong with you people? You screw or blow everything in sight, taking every chance under the sun with every disease out there, and why? For a few minutes of physical pleasure?"

"Jake, I—"

"Don't even try. I don't know what was going on with Andy but I think she was sick. You're nothing compared to her, she was perfect."

I slam the door behind me. On the way to the Camry, I detour by Paul's Hummer and key the black paint. Should've brought the Colt and blasted those expensive twenty-inch tires.

I pull into my driveway. My phone rings in my pocket. It's Paul. "I saw what you did to my ride, dammit. I want a new paint job."

"Sorry, it was there when I walked by."

"I want my medical bills paid. Cheryl's driving me to the emergency room now."

"I don't know what you're talking about."

"Cheryl's my witness."

"Do you really want it to get out at work how you were screwing my wife and her best friend at the same time?"

"Everyone knew it, Jake. What were you, blind? Hell, Cheryl and me saw her leave the bar with guys plenty of times. Looks didn't matter. Money didn't matter. Age didn't matter. She'd hop on a gear shift if somebody wasn't trying to put it in reverse."

I end the call. Paul's lying. Cheryl's lying. Everybody's lying. Andy was perfect.

At home I wipe blood from my forehead, flush the toilet paper down the commode, close the bedroom door, and fall into bed. The curtains are still pulled. The room is still dark. People like Paul and Cheryl are insane. The world is insane. What happened to love and commitment and everything that goes with it? What happened to morals and values and gratitude and honor and the ability to take pleasure in simple things like the love between soulmates and doing nothing but walking along a beach or lying in a hammock and watching the sun shimmer red and molten as it settles into the darkening waters at dusk?

BAM BAM BAM! "MR. SMITH, THIS IS THE POLICE."

I stay in bed; they bam the door and yell again. I stay in bed; they need a warrant.

They bam the door and yell again. Do they need a warrant? I don't want someone to break in when they take me away to wherever. I get up and open the door. Two officers—one black, one white—grip their pistols at their belts.

"C'mon guys, chill, what's wrong?"

The white officer takes his hand from his pistol. "We got a call forty-five minutes ago that you assaulted a person named Paul Thomas. We talked to him at the ER and confirmed the assault with the woman who drove him there. The doctor confirmed a broken nose."

"Sorry, guys, wasn't me. I've been in bed the last five minutes."

The black officer spins me around, cuffs my wrists, and reads me my Miranda rights. The white officer asks if I need anything. I tell him my wallet and keys are in my pocket and I'd appreciate it if he could lock the door. He does, searches me like a good little officer should, and holds my head down when he puts me in the police cruiser.

They back out of my driveway and I laugh. "C'mon guys, do you big, bad assholes want a lawsuit because you didn't buckle my seat belt?"

They stop; the black officer buckles me in. I ask him if he'd like to go out on a date after all this is over and bring his friend, along with anyone else he'd like to bring. He ignores me. I tell them Andy was perfect.

I tell them that until they take me out and some pencil pusher confiscates my wallet and keys and someone else takes my belt and shoelaces and someone else puts me in a holding cell all by myself.

Someone asks if I want to make my one phone call. I tell him Andy was perfect. He shrugs and leaves. I pee in the corner and shuffle by the stainless-steel commode to take a dump in the other corner and lie on the Lysol smelling bunk and close my eyes and curl into a ball and say Andy was perfect Andy was perfect Andy was perfect.

Chapter 23

They ignore me until I tell them I'm hungry. Someone brings the last thing in the world I want: a chicken salad sandwich on whole wheat, a bag of chips, and a cup of instant coffee. I flush the sandwich. The coffee cup and chip bag clog the commode. They take me out, let someone with a plunger in, and put me back. This person notices the pee and the dump and sends someone with a mop and more Lysol. They take me out, let them in, wait until the corners are spic and span and bitter lemonade with Lysol and put me back again. The bunk accepts what I now remember to call a fetal position. I whisper to my pillow: Andy was perfect Andy was perfect Andy was perfect.

Hallway lights go dark. Out in the blackness, a male voice shouts. I hear the breath of this place; it wheezes through the bars and the painted cinderblocks, wheezes through the trees in the outside world, wheezes in and out my nostrils and hisses in my throat.

What's Scotty doing now? Is she getting *Out for Fun* ready for our cruise to the Florida Keys? Is she taking a shower, all soapy and curvy and feminine? Is she lying in our huge king bed naked, waiting for me to kiss those lips, full and defined?

From somewhere in my head I hear a child's voice: *Like Mama said, you can't let this break you.*

I tell her it's too late. I'm already broken because bad people want me to believe bad things about my wife, who's perfect. I ask the child to bring my wife so she can tell the bad people not to lie about her. The child looks at me with sad eyes. She's thin, with a triangle shaped face, and talks with North Carolina and Louisiana in her voice. The voice drifts away: *You can't let this break you ... you can't let this break you ... you can't let this break you.*

Morning comes with plain oatmeal and fresh coffee, a comb and a toothbrush and paste. Someone watches me while I tend to it all. They then take me to a room with two chairs and a transparent partition that separates the chairs. I sit; a door closes behind me. Beside my head hangs a telephone, its twin on the wall beside the other chair. A door behind the partition opens. A man with a briefcase sits. He points at my phone and places his to his ear. "You don't look well, Jake."

I press the phone harder to my ear. "Do I know you?"

The man's mouth twitches. "It's Mac. They got my number from my card in your wallet."

"They keep saying Andy's bad. We're getting married next month. I wouldn't marry someone who does the things they say she does."

"Do you know what month it is, Jake? What day it is? Do you remember anything about what happened?"

I close my eyes. Wet hair. Sand on red toenails. A cold wet nose against my arm. Scotty saying she loves me.

"Andy's dead. No one can say bad things about her anymore. I was going to shoot him but I didn't want to go to jail. Now I'm here anyway. He deserved a lot more than a broken nose."

181

"Paul will drop the charges if you pay his medical bills and have his Hummer painted. He feels bad about Andy."

"He's a liar."

"I paid what he wanted. We'll settle everything later."

"He's a liar."

"I'm trying to keep you out of jail for another night, Jake. The judge knows about your mental state—they've been videoing you in your cell since they brought you in yesterday. He wants you to voluntarily admit yourself to a mental health facility." The man named Mac runs his fingers through his hair. "After seeing and hearing you, I agree. Where've you been? I haven't heard from you since you called and said you'd be out of town for the near future."

"With friends."

"But where?"

A spark of something brightens behind my eyes, and I lower my head. I was going to kill someone. That's not reasonable. Another spark brightens, words instead of a revelation: *We need a vacation to get our heads on straight.* I raise my head. "When do I go to the facility?"

The man deflates. "At least you'll do that. I'll drive you over now. They'll evaluate you before admitting you. I doubt that's a problem."

The man cradles the phone and knocks on the door behind him. Someone opens it and he leaves. Someone opens the door behind me and takes me to the place where my wallet and keys and belt and shoelaces were taken. The man named Mac waits beside me. With everything either on or in my pockets, I walk with him to a car and get in. He tells me to buckle up and we leave.

He's silent during the drive. I raise my hands to my nose and sniff for gun oil, which isn't there. Did I really plan to shoot someone? That's not like me at all. The satisfying scrape of a key against black paint: that's like me. The crunch of cartilage as I drive my forehead into a liar's nose and the spurt of blood and him falling on his ass: that's like someone I know but I'm not sure who. I look at my hands in my lap. We found a shell on a white beach one day. Splotchy brown outside, spiraled on one end, spiked along the stairstep ridges, creamy white inside the flared opening, rich pink inside: soft and smooth, a lover's defined lips. She called it a queen conch, held it to my ear and said to listen for the ocean, smiled and kissed me. I think I loved this person although I'm married. No, I *was* married.

Another beach: an old man's voice breaking while he talked on his phone. People gathered round me and the woman lying beside me. She was so beautiful. Except for the slits of her eyes with wet hair in them. A fly lit on her cheek and I shooed it away.

A violent boat ride with another man: Skeletons of concrete rose above us. Green waves with frothy crests climbed upward, lifted us upward and slammed us into the trough. The man said something about anyone who cares seeing our backbones and ribs.

The car slows. The man named Mac unbuckles me and takes me through two swinging doors. Did we walk in the sun to get here? Did we breathe fresh air before we smelled the disinfectant sadness of this place?

I'm taken to an office by a woman. She asks how I am today. I answer that I'm not sure. A man sits behind the desk. He's average looking. A pack of cigarettes bulges his shirt pocket. Reading glasses perch on his bald head.

"Mr. Smith, I'm Dr. Robinson. I'm told you're experiencing some confusion." The doctor picks up a pen and sets the point on a pad.

"I'm … I guess muddled is a good word."

"Did you consider shooting someone?"

"Not seriously."

"Did this person do something to upset you?"

"He lied about my wife."

"She died recently, correct?"

"In ... what month is this?"

"November."

"She died last month. Don't you want to know what Paul said?"

"What people say, Mr. Smith, shouldn't make us act irrationally. Words are only words. What matters is the truth of a matter. Have you had any trouble sleeping?"

"No."

"Is your appetite normal?"

"Yes."

"Do you have any medical conditions? High blood pressure? Heart problems? Diabetes?"

"No. Do you have lung cancer yet?"

"Please keep this professional, Mr. Smith."

"I'm just trying to save your life." I lean forward. "I see you wear a wedding band. Do you cheat on your wife?"

"My wife died six months ago in an automobile accident."

"My wife drowned and I don't know why. Have you grieved for your wife yet? I don't think I have."

"It's an important process. I'm working through mine now."

"I'm sorry your wife died. Did you love her?"

"Very much."

A sting hits me behind my eyes. The doctor gives me a tissue and takes one for himself. We sob softly, men who understand the loss of love. All the time I see where some people think we're animals, that we don't have hearts, that we don't have souls, that we're incapable of the same depth of feeling as women. Maybe that's true for some—just like it's true for some women—but those people who judge all by a few couldn't be more wrong.

We drop the tissues in a wastebasket by the desk. The doctor picks up his pad and pen. "If I admit you, what's your long-term goal?"

"To not feel like a nuclear bomb is sitting in my chest waiting to go off. To not feel like I have nothing to live for. To not feel like I won't find another woman to love who won't leave me."

"Do you blame your wife for her death?"

"It was ruled an accident."

"But you think otherwise."

"I don't want to talk about it."

"Do you feel like you might harm yourself or others?"

"I only want to feel normal again."

"How old are you?"

"Twenty-nine."

"Do you know what day it is?"

"No."

"Do you mind a roommate?"

"I'd rather not."

The doctor goes to the door and opens it. The man named Mac comes over. The doctor opens the door wider. "Does Mr. Smith have any family who need to know about his admission?"

Mac sticks his head in the door. "Want me to tell your mom or Lisa, Jake?"

"No." The door starts to close—I jump up and grab it. "Thanks for your help, Mac."

"You got it, buddy. Give me your keys and I'll bring you some clothes tomorrow."

I give Mac my keys and sit. The doctor sits too. "I didn't want to talk about my wife when she died either, but I knew I needed to eventually. It sounds like you don't have any cognitive issues, such as any form of schizophrenia or bipolar disorder. I think you suffer from depression and anxiety concerning the loss of your wife. Were you married long?"

"One day. She drowned the morning after our first honeymoon night. We lived together for about six months. Andy was perfect."

"And what this Paul person said goes against that."

"He's a liar."

"Do you like the outdoors? I took up long distance bicycle riding after my wife died. It helps get my mind on track."

"I like the beach."

"Did you wife drown at the beach?"

"Yes."

"Do you think the beach is good therapy? You might want to stay away from there for a while."

"My wife's death doesn't bother me as much as what Paul said about her."

"People sometimes do things we don't understand and can't explain. Regardless of what Paul says about her, it might've been beyond her control."

"Can I go to my room now?"

"A doctor will be assigned to you. The meal schedules are posted on your room door. We expect all our patients who are able to eat together and attend group therapy together do so." The doctor stands. "With the right attitude, Mr. Smith, you can be home again soon."

"I'd like that."

"Something to look forward to, a fine goal." The doctor makes a phone call and turns his chair. I can't make out what he says. He hangs up, turns back around, and a man in baggy blue pants and a smock opens the door. "How's it goin,' Mr. Smith? I'm Leon. Ready to take a look at your suite?"

Leon's a big bruiser of a black man. Gray tints the tight curls at his temples. He smiles like he likes his job. A wedding band circles his ring finger. He gently takes my arm, leads me through two more double doors, and down a hall floored with white linoleum tiles. Every few steps, paintings—water colors and oils by the layers of color on the thick paper, or the lack of layers—decorate the walls on both sides.

"You married, Leon?"

"You got it."

"How long?"

"My wife says too long."

"I doubt that, you seem like a nice guy."

"She just likes my big pecker is all."

I grin. "Something we have in common."

Leon chuckles. "I think you an' me's gonna get along like rice an' gravy, Mr. Smith."

We pass a large room. Men and women of all ages sit at several tables. Some watch TV. Some talk. Some watch me walk by. One young woman with spiked blonde hair waves. I nod my head.

Down another hall, Leon opens a door. "Here we go, all the amenities of home." He gestures: "Nice bed, nice lamp, nice closet for all your clothes." He drops to a corner chair. "Nice chair for your attending shrink to shrink you from." He taps the center of his broad chest. "That's me."

I sit on the bed. "Yeah?"

"You got it."

"You realize a lot of people would've made assumptions by your North Carolina drawl and lack of annunciation, don't you?"

"Oh, sure, they'd think I clean the toilets round here. I like messin' with folks, 'specially them college professors. Too many folks look at a person's outside before they get to know their inside—that goes for all races too. I'm sorry to hear about your wife. Hard thing to deal with, losin' a loved one. Who's the fella you wanna shoot?"

"My best friend, Paul. Well, he *was* my best friend."

Leon works what must be his six-six frame from the chair and comes over to offer me his huge hand. I take it; it's surprisingly soft. "You give you wife massages, Leon? Your hand sure is soft."

"She buys lotion for 'em. Says I ain't touchin' her unless they're soft." He closes his hand, which engulfs mine. "See how my hand almost covers yours up, Mr. Smith?"

"Call me Jake, I see."

"Pain and heartache can do that to the best of us. Is that how you feel now, all smothered like my hand is smotherin' yours?"

"I guess."

He raises his fingers one at a time. "I'm here to give you your life back like I'm givin' you your hand back—one finger at a time. How does that sound?"

"I'd like that, Leon. I'd like that a lot."

Chapter 24

An orderly brings supper to my room: chicken noodle soup, saltines, ginger ale, and a sleeping pill. Leon let me keep my belt and shoe laces. Said any guy who joked about his pecker size wouldn't dare off himself. I told him I wasn't joking; he busted into a huge grin.

I yawn between sips of soup, nibbles of saltines, and fizzy swallows of ginger ale and forgo the sleeping pill. A shower warms me, makes me sleepier. Brushing my teeth and flossing almost makes me feel human again.

Snug in bed, I curse Paul and Cheryl for taking advantage of Andy like they did. Normal people don't do what Andy did. Then it hits me that I believe what Paul said. Then I *do* want to shoot him, although I know I won't. Breaking his nose was a lot more satisfying; the crunch of cartilage even more so, along with the blood. I doubt even Cheryl will screw him for a good, long while, if ever. His face will swell and turn a dozen shades of blue, followed by sickly yellow. He'll shun every bar in Raleigh—and every girl—for who knows how long. Still, it was good of him to drop the charges against me. Maybe there's a shred of decency in his perverted self yet, not that I'm interested in being friends with him.

I turn the nightstand lamp off and roll over. Beneath the door, a sliver of yellow light illuminates a few blocks of white linoleum. It's possible I hear a yell. It's possible I hear voices. It's possible I hear nothing. I don't want to be here: plans are in the making. Plans that will take a while but I'm willing to put in the work to make them happen.

Like when I was a kid on Christmas Eve, excited to open presents in the morning, excited thoughts scurry through my mind. How will this be? How will that be? How will I look and feel if it works? Better yet, how will I like living in a new home not far from my beloved Outer Banks? I'll make an offer when I get out of here. Then I'll hit the road and give myself a year or so to recover from losing the only two women I could ever love.

* * *

Morning brings Cheerios with banana slices in my room, toast and coffee too. I guess Leon wants to get an idea of how I'll react before I eat with anyone. Morning also brings clean clothes from Mac, who isn't allowed to see me yet. I ask the orderly for any kind of home improvement magazine and get three. One includes an article on how the new types of metal roofing are a lot better than the old stuff. I might need it, might not. It never hurts to learn something new.

The orderly returns at ten a.m. and takes me to the room with the tables and TV. Leon comes in and turns the TV off. The people gathered in the room scatter to sit on a sofa, a loveseat, and two arm chairs, all of which I missed last night. Leon turns one of the chairs from a table backwards and sits. I take another chair and sit beside an armchair, where the girl with the spiked blonde hair looks at me and then looks at Leon. "Who's the new guy and what's he hooked on?"

190

"Look, Sandra," Leon says, "I already told you we don't ask people why they're here. It's up to them to share when they're ready."

"Sorry."

I notice Sandra's needle marks on the insides of her arms, evidence of drug abuse. She offers me her hand. "I'm Sandra, your friendly neighborhood meth freak. And you are?"

I take her hand. "Jake."

She twists my hand palm up. "No needle tracks, Jake, good for you."

On this end of the sofa, a middle-aged woman waves; one eye is bruised. "I'm Lucy. I'm gonna cut my husband's penis off for raping me." She glances at Leon and laughs nervously. "Just kidding, Leon."

Next to Lucy, a guy about my age quirks one eyebrow up. "I told you to super-glue it to his leg in his sleep." He grimaces. "Makes me hurt just to think about it."

"It isn't long enough to glue to his leg."

"People," Leon says, his voice pitched low, "you're here to learn a lot of things about yourselves. One is to learn how hurting someone doesn't solve anything."

The penis gluing guy tosses a hand my way. "I'm Freddy, Jake. I like the highs my bipolar gives me so I can write heavy metal songs for the electric guitar. Therefore, as you might have guessed, I don't take my meds like I should."

I nod at Freddy. "I play acoustic a little."

"Ever write a song?"

"A friend did."

"Any chance I can see it?"

"It's personal."

Beside Freddy, a woman, maybe in her late twenties, average size and weight, with shoulder length brunette hair and an average face, says nothing, and Freddy says, "This is Tammy. She's pretending we're all stupid."

Leon clears is throat. "Someone wants to lose TV and painting privileges, Freddy. No criticizing is allowed. People talk when they're ready to talk."

In the arm chair at the end of the sofa, a black guy, maybe a teenager, with dreadlocks, a tattoo of a cross beneath his right ear, and a wisp of beard on his chin, looks my way. "I'm Jerry, man. You 'bout the normalist person in here. What's wrong with you?"

"Jerry," Leon says, "if you tell Jake why you're here, he might tell you why he's here."

"My mom messed me up." Jerry holds up his wrists, which are bandaged. "Dumb, huh?"

"She did that to you?" I ask.

"I did it to myself. I'm outta here tomorrow. Leon made me see how my worth comes from what I think of me, not what anyone else thinks of me. My uncle in Greensboro is taking me in. Gonna get my GED and go to college and be a shrink like Leon. I had enough of gangs. Love's gotta come from my own heart, not some fool who thinks robbin' and dealin' drugs makes you his brother."

Since everyone's baring their soul except Tammy, I'll bare a little of mine. Besides, the sooner I show Leon I'm ready to get out of here, the sooner I can start my new life. I look at each of them in turn. "You know how you think people are your friends until you find out they're not?"

Everyone but Tammy nods. "Friends sure don't get you hooked on meth," Sandra says.

"What about you, Tammy?" Leon says. She lowers her head. His dark eyes find me. "You mind telling everyone about your wife?"

"I was married twice."

"You didn't tell me that."

"One died but one's alive. We're pregnant and she's divorcing her husband. She's great. We're gonna live on a farm and raise chickens."

Tammy faces me. "Is she divorcing him or is he divorcing her because she slept with you?"

"She's divorcing him because he's a jerk."

"My husband's a jerk too. I knew that when I married him but I did it anyway. I can't believe I was so stupid."

"Do you have any kids? I'm looking forward to being a dad."

Tammy gets up and asks Leon if she can go to her room. Her voice breaks. Leon says she can, then asks if anyone wants to paint. No one does. I go to my room. Leon follows and takes the same chair he did yesterday. "What's this about a second wife?"

I sit on the bed. "I didn't say anything about a second wife."

Nodding, Leon sucks his lower lip until it disappears beneath his upper lip. He points to my nightstand. "You like building things?"

"I'm gonna build a yacht and sail to the Florida Keys with my wife. We'll get back in time to have our baby and move to our farm. It'll be great."

"This is your second wife, right? What's her name?"

"Andy."

"What's your first wife's name?"

"Andy."

Leon does that thing with his lips again. "Did you sleep okay last night?"

"Not bad."

"Eating okay?"

"Chicken noodle soup and crackers isn't much of a meal."

The big black guy pats his stomach. "Me an' you both could lose a few pounds."

193

"What's your name again?"

The black guy sucks his lower lip inside his upper lip. "Leon."

I look around. "Is this a hotel?"

"It's a mental facility, Jake. Do you remember why you're here?"

"My name's Jake? I thought it was Jonathan?"

"When Mac brought your clothes, he told me Jonathan is your first name. Which do you like?"

"Jonathan. That's what my wife calls me. She's great. Did I tell you her name? It's Scotty."

"Nice name." The black guy stands. "You say you're sleeping okay?"

"I'm not tired."

"No sleeping pill tonight, but I'm prescribing something that should help you remember names. Is that okay?"

"You say a guy named Mac brought my clothes? I don't know anyone named Mac."

"He's a good friend of yours."

"Is breakfast coming soon? I'm hungry."

"You want anything special?"

"Chicken salad on whole wheat, chips, and black coffee. That's the first meal my wife and I had. We're pregnant. I'm looking forward to being a dad."

"Okay, sounds good." The black man goes to the door, then faces me. "I'm sending one of those pills with your breakfast too, make sure you take it. I'll check on you this afternoon."

He opens the door, and I say, "That woman who went to her room a minute ago was upset. I wish I knew her name."

"She has a right to be upset. See you later, Jonathan."

I lie on the bed. Someone left three woodworking magazines on my nightstand. I open one to read a page but look around the room instead. Sitting on the side of the bed, I take my shoes and socks off and wiggle my toes in the sand. A few feet away, a huge seashell glitters wet in the afternoon sun. My wife picks it up, holds it to my ear, and tells me to listen to the ocean. Then she kisses me. We walk back to a blanket and make love. Above us, palm fronds whisper in the breeze. Several steps from our feet, tiny waves flecked with foam gurgle like a stream in the Blue Ridge Mountains. I think someone took me there when I was a kid. I'm not sure, but I think a girl was with us. My wife's hair hangs in my face when she leans down to kiss me. She smells of vanilla and sunshine and flowers. Straining for completion I bury my face between her breasts. She sits up, closes her eyes, and cries out three times like a gull hovering over me, calling *scree-scree-scree.*

We lie naked and talk until sundown. I caress the curve of her hips, the rise of her tummy, the swell of her breasts. She's a mountain range. She's the sand dunes on Jockey's Ridge. She's the aquamarine swells of building waves gathering in the Atlantic to roll and thunder beneath Jennette's Pier.

The warm sand beneath my feet shifts and shimmers and dulls. It turns to cold linoleum. How can I remember all that and not names?

It's funny how time slips by. I think I eat that breakfast. I think I take that pill. I think that black guy came and talked to me. I don't remember what he said. A man in baggy white pants and a matching short-sleeved shirt brings me another breakfast. This one's meat loaf, mashed potatoes, and peas. I wash it and another pill down with water. The man comes back for the tray.

I remember to brush and floss. There's no stuff to rub under my arms, so I shower. The water is warm and slick and smooth and my wife and I make love in it standing up. I love how she presses against me. I love how her breasts fill my hands. I love how she leans back and turns her head to kiss me. To say how

195

much I love her is impossible. We share DNA in our baby, a girl who will look like us both but more like my wife. We'll be happier than I could've ever been with my other wife because she's a slut who sleeps with people who say they're my friends when they're just people who want to screw instead of make love.

I towel off and go to bed naked. That lady—I think her name's Tammy—was really upset. She sounded like she was going to cry when I said I was looking forward to being a dad. I'll have to talk to her sometime away from those other people. She knows how important children are, how important being good parents are, how important love is. Maybe her husband is just confused.

I turn the lamp off and wake to hear someone crying. Then I realize my pillow's wet and my eyes hurt and I feel nauseous. My body's trying to tell me something and I don't know what. It's like my brain wants to hide away and hurt—no, it's like my soul wants to hide away and hurt but my heart refuses to let whatever's wrong break me. Didn't somebody tell me that some faraway time ago? I'm sure they did, but those words slide along the edge of my memory until they're completely gone.

In my dreams I see two wives; one's perfect and ones perfecter. I ask myself if perfecter's a word. I answer it is if it works.

The night drags on, an asphalt blackness paving the road to the ozone smell of morning rain. I'd love to be the rain, to runnel along a stream, fill a raging river, discover a deep blue ocean with a single queen conch resting on sandy shores, white and gleaming, my wife offering it to my ear, the slight bulge of her tummy promising new life, the slight smile of her perfect lips offering the promise of perfect love, the light crinkle of her green eyes offering grinning laughter in times of teasing.

I drift away from her.

Into nothing.

Chapter 25

At ten I meet Leon, Sandra, Lucy, Freddy, Tammy, and Jerry in the TV room. Rain thudding on the roof makes everyone look up to see if the world will cave in. Leon pokes and prods but only Jerry talks: his uncle is picking him up today. We separate. I wish Jerry well. Leon leaves. Tammy stays on the sofa. The others leave too, I guess to their rooms. I sit on the sofa and turn to face Tammy. "I can tell you like kids."

A single tear forms silver and slips down her cheek, halting, halting, and quivers on her trembling chin. "I didn't mean that about my husband."

I say nothing.

"I didn't mean to, but he's madder than I ever saw him."

I say nothing.

"Her name was Kim, she … she was one and a half. She had straight black hair and her nose turned up just enough to let us know the boys would be a problem in high school. I didn't mean to."

"You don't have to tell me if you don't want to."

"You understand about children. You understand how precious they are."

"I know I'm looking forward to being a dad."

"My husband was too, that's why he's so mad. I put Kim in the car seat and gave her Mr. Air. That's what she called her stuffed bear because she couldn't say B yet. I turned the air condition on high and had a flat tire a mile from home. I worked through it and managed to put the little spare on. I called work and said I'd be late. I went home and washed my hands and changed panty hose because the others had a run and I went to work and I forgot about Kim and the police came and and and—"

Tammy's face collapses in on itself. She covers it and I take her in my arms and we both cry for her daughter who died in a hot car in the summer because her mom got flustered over a flat tire and forgot all about her without meaning to, which is the last thing in the world any good mom wants to do.

Tammy sobs and heaves and hiccup/cries. If ever a human being felt like an earthquake in another human being's arms, she does. She wets my shirt with tears and snot. She wraps her arms around me like a skydiver would if I were leaning out an airplane door and her chute had failed. I'm sure I'll have fingernail marks in my back.

I smell smoke, thick with rubber and cloth. I grasp a boat's rail while it roars to its destination—an orange glow beyond the flickering lights of a town at night. Somewhere behind a darkened doorway, a young girl softly sobs.

The pain sticks this time, and I cry as hard as Tammy. But like Mary Lou and Lizzie said, I won't let it break me. Life waits, and if I'm lucky, love does too. After all, I'm a hopeless romantic with a plan, regardless of how long it takes.

Tammy and I gradually stop crying. We wipe our noses with tissues from one of the tables and return to the sofa. I pat her hand. "I hope you know what happened to Kim isn't your fault. It was a tragic accident, and that's it."

"That's what the judge said or I'd be charged with involuntary manslaughter. I couldn't talk around anyone else because they don't understand how much a parent loves their child."

"Leon doesn't have children?"

"I think I couldn't talk to him because he expected it. You didn't expect anything, and that means a lot."

"Was it true about your husband divorcing you?"

"Would you blame him? He'll never look at me again without thinking I murdered Kim."

"Did you love each other when you got married?"

"Soulmates. Best friends. We loved to tease and laugh."

"Don't count him out yet, okay? It's understandable how he's upset."

"I hope you're right. I thought about calling him but I'm afraid to."

"How long have you been here?"

"It's been a month since the funeral. He wouldn't even look at me."

"Maybe he needs some time in here."

"Maybe he needs to talk to you."

"I'd rather he talk to Leon."

Tammy shifts on the sofa and sits with her back against me. I put my arms around her. "You realize our therapy group will have a fit if they see us like this."

"Sometimes a woman needs to be held, and this is one of those times. Do you feel like telling me why you were crying as hard as I was?"

"I was seeing a woman who was pregnant with her husband's baby. It was a bad marriage from the start, and she wanted out. I think she had given up until we met, and it all changed."

"Did she go back to him?"

"He saw us together and said he'd give her a divorce. She was fine with that except she didn't want him in the baby's life because he was—and still is—a womanizer from the word go."

Tammy looks back at me. "I can understand that."

I wait for the unsaid question. Tammy looks at me again. "No pressure, but something happened for you to cry like that."

"It didn't work out. I've sort of been in and out of a haze ever since. I'm not doing that anymore."

"You say that like you know it."

"Two of her friends told me to not let her death break me. It was, but not anymore."

Tammy turns in my arms. "I kind of hope my husband doesn't forgive me. You're about the sweetest guy I've ever known, except him when we met."

We get up from the sofa, and I say, "Wonder if we can get Leon to let us out of this joint anytime soon?"

* * *

Being the hopeless romantic that I am, when the Nicholas Sparks novel *The Notebook* came out, I cried like a baby when Allie left Noah. Who didn't think she was going back to Lon, her fiancé, for good? When she came back though, that's the kind of happy ending I like in a poignant love story. Well, that scene in the movie, when they made love after coming in out of a thunderstorm was pretty great too.

I talked Leon into letting me go a week after Tammy's husband came to forgive her. Talk about a happy ending.

Sandra, Lucy, and Freddy threw me a going away party, complete with cupcakes and grape juice for pretend wine. Sandra said Tammy and I inspired her to believe in herself instead of meth. Lucy said she planned to super-glue her husband's penis to his leg the first chance she gets. Then she looked at Leon, laughed, and said, "Screw him. I'm better off without him and that's a fact." Freddy played me a tune he wrote on the electric air guitar. He took his bipolar meds all that week and said it's the right thing to do, regardless of wanting to take a magic spaceship ride on a flying saucer made of a million lights to another astral plain where everyone plays music on the electric air guitar.

At the double doors, where I wait for Mac with my suitcase, Leon pats my shoulder. "Did you know I made everyone leave that day you and Tammy had your breakthrough?"

"With what? Telepathy?"

"After I talked to you in your room the night before, I knew you and Tammy could reach each other because of your love for children. That thing with her daughter was one of the toughest stories I ever heard. Her pain was so deep that only someone else who was looking forward to being a parent could connect to her."

"Were you surprised when I told you about Scotty and her baby dying in an accident?"

"Not surprised as much as sad. Our minds sometimes can't process traumatic events like that. We suppress them until we talk them out or they kill us."

"I'm glad Tammy and I were able to talk them out, Leon."

"Me too. The mind is a wondrous but unknown thing. Doctors like me can't always help, but sometimes we can. Like Freddy and his lithium, bipolar disorder is a chemical problem. Even then, some drugs won't always help." Leon points out the window. "There's Mac. I'm glad you've got a friend like him."

I put the suitcase down and hug Leon. "And a friend like you. Tell your wife she married a good man."

"I tell her that every day." Leon winks. "She doesn't believe it until I whip my big pecker out and shake it at her."

"Hey, whatever works."

Mac comes in. "Hey, bud. Ready to get out of here?"

"In a way, in a way not. Catch you later, Leon."

I put the suitcase in the back seat of my Camry. Mac and I buckle up, and I drive to the exit. "How about you buy me a steak dinner to celebrate my release?"

"You're the one with the three million bucks making you a nice income in that stock portfolio my investor recommended. Is there a steak house in Raleigh that serves caviar and champagne?"

"Dad always said you were a joker. That's why I used you to close on the mortgage for my house."

"I'll settle for a burger."

"You're my kinda lawyer, Mac, a cheap date."

I drive to a steak place anyway, the best place for a great burger. A greeter seats us; we order drafts and the house burgers. I ask for lots of lettuce and a salad, no fries. Mac says, "No fries? You love fries."

I poke my belly flab. "I still do, but I need to lose this."

"Beer doesn't help."

"A man's got to have his one weakness."

The drafts arrive. Mac sips, I sip. "How much do you think my house is worth?"

"With the market the way it is, maybe 200,000. How much do you owe on it?"

"150 or so."

"I'll miss you if you leave town."

"We didn't hang out much."

Mac cracks a grin. "Yeah, but you can afford my fees now."

"And you'll earn some when I sell." I sip beer. "Can I borrow your phone?"

"To apologize to Paul for breaking his nose?"

I hold out my hand. "Ain't happening."

Mac gives me his fancy smartphone. "Why did you do it?"

"Let's just say it's personal and let that be the end of it." I search the internet for real estate listings in Dare County. Beach houses fill the screen. Filtering for farms declutters it, and I scroll.

"Need some help?" Mac says.

"I got it."

He slides close and touches the screen. "Dare County? Are you thinking about living in Nags Head? I thought the area might bother you for a while."

"Only that rental, Endless Love, will. The only way I'll ever go there again is if I'm blindfolded."

I locate the listing. Naturally, Ted is selling it after inheriting it from Scotty. The last thing I want to do is make him richer, but there's no other way to do this. I dial and a woman answers. I make on offer and she balks. I offer ten grand more. She makes an appointment for me to see the house in three days. I tell her I've already seen it and want it as is and give her Mac's number for the closing. She asks my name. I tell her Jake Smith but I want this transaction to be confidential. She has no problem with that, says she'll get the ball rolling, and adds how I should be a happy new homeowner within a month. I give the phone back to Mac. He clips it into the holder on his belt.

"Listen to you, Mr. Big Shot. Money talks."

"The only reason I have that money is because Andy loved me enough to think of my future, so shut the hell up." I clink my beer mug to Mac's. "Please."

The burgers arrive. The waitress asks if I need dressing for the salad. I say plain's fine. She leaves. I take the burger from the bun, wrap it in lettuce, and take a bite. Mac chews and swallows fries. "A burger with no bun and a plain salad instead of fries? I need to take you back to that treatment facility."

I swallow burger. "You're no scarecrow yourself."

"What're your plans besides moving?"

"I'm going to keep my house until I move. I need a base of operations, so to speak."

"To do what exactly?"

"You'll see when you see me again."

"You're being mighty cryptic."

"Like lawyers aren't. Who can read those documents y'all draw up?"

Mac bites his burger. I chew salad. We both sip beer. I let the silence fall for the sake of the meal, which yes, would be a lot better with a bun and fries, but hey, change requires sacrifice.

I pay the tab, drive Mac to my house for his car, and say goodbye. Inside I write a note to stick on the windshield of Paul's Hummer:

Hey, butthead, the next time you kiss Cheryl, if ever, you know, because of the swelling and bruising, just remember how you're tasting my swimmers.

I rip the page from the notepad, ball it up, and drop it in the wastebasket beside my laptop desk. Screw him. Even with dropping the charges, he doesn't deserve a note.

I drive to the nearest Toyota dealership and trade the Camry for a brand new 2019 4-Runner in silver. Got a great deal because it's the end of the year. That's when I realize it's almost Christmas, and I'll have to hang around Raleigh until the weather breaks, which puts my plans somewhat on hold. Next is a treadmill that barely fits in the rear of my new ride, even with the seat folded down. After that is a set of resistance bands. After that is hiking boots and a day pack at a sporting goods store. After that is a bicycle shop for a high-end road/trail bike.

I take everything else home and go back to be fitted to the bike; then it comes home too.

It's now dark and I look my cupboards and fridge over for something with few carbs and fewer calories. That ends up being a can of tuna with some vinegar and hot sauce, a dill pickle, and ice water with lemon. I'm tempted to drink beer but I intend to have only one a day

Two days later, Christmas arrives, cold and clear. I dress appropriately and take the bike out for a spin. All around my neighborhood, kids are doing the same, and they make me think about how fun it would've been to do that with Scotty's girl.

A few hours on the treadmill helps ease the leg burn, but I turn back after two miles. Like with women, pacing myself is a struggle. Resembling Scotty somewhat, Tammy tempted me, but I'd be a jerk like Paul if I had asked her to go to my room that day. Still, I was jerk enough to let Cheryl do what she did. If/when I meet someone, I'll try to do better.

I call Mom and Lisa and wish them Merry Christmas. Both say they hope I'm doing well, code for they hope I'm doing well without Andy.

I think about visiting a bar for New Year's Eve, but don't because I don't feel like being around people and I don't feel like drinking alcohol and I don't feel like seeing people kiss at midnight. In bed early, I read some home improvement magazines from the grocery, along with some outdoors magazines about the best places to bike ride and hike trails. I consider buying a kayak but it's too cold. It's something to consider when I get back to Dare County.

In late December, a bunch of people in Wuhan, China, get sick with something called a corona virus, which is bad news. It turns into a pandemic by March and the U.S. virtually shuts down. Masks are mandated. Even Dare County closes to all visitors. I could drive down since I'm a property owner but I don't. Although I walk the treadmill, ride the bike, stretch the resistance bands, and eat decently — well, except for a glass of red wine or a beer with a petite sirloin now and then — I only lose twenty pounds. Still, it's cool to need size 36 jeans instead of size 38 and to go from a large shirt size to a snug medium. Not that I'm vain, but the mirror beckons me often. My brown hair, sort of curly, covers my ears shy of their lobes, and my beard is about two inches long, more wavy than curly. I keep my mustache trimmed just shy of my upper lip. When things open up a bit, regardless of the virus still infecting people, neighbors I didn't see for weeks do a double take, like I'm a stranger moved in. I wave, they wave. We're glad it's summer. We're glad the grass and trees are green. I'm glad because I buy a bike rack for the 4-Runner and load the bike on it, add my day pack, an insulated water bottle, some low carb snacks, my suitcase crammed with biking and hiking clothes to the 4-Runner's cargo area, and hit the road.

Rarely a day goes by without thoughts of Andy and Scotty. At times I wonder if I'll meet another soulmate: someone to share life's goals, challenges, and children with. Even though my depression made me think I was going to live with Scotty and our girl on her parent's farm I bought, I'd still like to find a southern woman who likes the idea of raising chickens. Most southern women seem to be normal in appearance. Not trying to be judgmental, but I don't know of any normal country girls who dye their hair any color whatsoever, have tattoos, wear studs all around the curves of their ears, one in their nose, one (or more) in their eyebrows, and one in their navel. It must be fun going through a metal detector. Then again, I never got to know one of those women who do all that stuff. What the heck, I might overlook all the metal if I like her enough. I didn't think much of Scotty at first glance—that sure changed in a hurry—and I think that's what made my love for her so intense. Sure, it could've been the emotional high of those weeks in the Keys with her, but when I started loving her as much as I loved Andy, who attracted me immediately, I completely forgot that lack of initial attraction.

Interstate 40 takes me past Hillsborough, Burlington, Greensboro, and Winston-Salem. I stop a time or two for a bathroom, water, and almond break. From Winston-Salem to Wilkesboro, woods, cars, and long-haul trucks accompany me. For obvious reasons, diesel fume smell is not my favorite thing. Rolling hills give way to mountains looming in the distance. Before long I leave I-40. The road is narrower, curvier, and I swear I see my bike's handlebars ahead of me on one particular hairpin turn.

In Todd, North Carolina, along the south fork of the New River, I find the bike trail that meanders through oaks, hickories, maples, and any number of other flora and fauna I can't name. Canoes and kayaks drift along the gurgling river. A man casts a fly rod. A woman does too. Most people, regardless of age, relax completely in the serene setting. Part of that might be because they don't have to wear masks against the corona virus out in nature, away from people.

I chose this trail because it's fairly flat, and I don't want to overdo until I get used to these rides. The internet mentioned Todd Mercantile, a tin-roofed building signed with huge block letters in black. Failing my carb and sugar restricted restrictions, I wear a mask and grab a soda and a huge cinnamon roll and sit in the shade of the porch, lowering the mask between bites and raising it when people walk by. Cars stop, cars go. Bikes stop, bikes go. Shoes shuffle across the wide oak planks. Patrons remark with voices muffled by masks: "We'll be back soon."

"Wait a minute," a middle-aged husband tells his wife, "let's get some more of those cinnamon rolls."

Biking back to the 4-Runner, I'm pleased with the lack of burn in my calves and thighs, trimmer but more defined, not quite up to a bullfrog's standards, thank goodness.

By the time I'm driving again, the sun is setting behind the mountains. Yellow rays penetrate the woods, leaving puzzle piece shadows along the curving asphalt. I'm tired but not, refreshed with clean air and sunshine.

Next stop is Asheville, North Carolina, a hotel, a shower, a quick failure at a fast-food place, and a bed with cool sheets pulled to my chin.

I sleep without dreams. I wake without soreness. For breakfast I fail with a sausage and egg biscuit and coffee with french vanilla creamer. Above her mask, the waitress's eyes grin longer than a waitress should grin. I grin back, maskless. Nothing wrong with being nice.

All summer I repeat these days and nights, eventually tackling trails called Tsali in the Nantahala National Forest and Big Avery Loop in the Pisgah National Forest, where a knee and elbow scraping tumble in a section called Satan's Staircase makes me rethink my readiness for such a venture. Then again, when a ponytailed brunette stops with a first aid kit and a gorgeous smile, I almost forgot the tumble. Conversation leads to how she loves the mountains and hates the beach. Thanking her for the help, I pedal away, cringing at my stinging elbows and knees and how I doubt I'll ever meet another Andy or Scotty. That moment was wonderful for many reasons, one being that neither one of us wore a mask.

Autumn finds me in Virginia, riding the Blue Ridge Parkway in peak season for pumpkin orange, brilliant red, and golden yellow leaves. Mornings come crisp. Some nights I pull over and sleep in the reclined 4-Runner seat. One morning a female ranger, decked out in her brown uniform, taps on my window and tells me it's illegal to camp outside of a designated camping area in the Parkway. I thank her and find an exit to a valley and to a town with a hotel, a shower, and a restaurant with the biggest porterhouse steak and baked potato and draft beer I can find. After all, my pants are 32 and my medium shirt is loose. I freaking deserve it.

Scarfing down juicy beef and buttery potato, followed with icy swallows of the bitter draft I'm not used to, I realize it's been a year since *Out for Fun* took Scotty from me. Then I check my phone and can't believe the date—it's been two years, not one. If she had lived, our baby would be sixteen months old, born last June, walking up a storm, chattering vowels and consonants, a word here, a word there. The thought makes me as sad as when Tammy and I cried in each other's arms at the mental health facility. To my disappointment, I stay this way until Christmas, when I appear unannounced on Mom's doorstep in Maryland.

My hair covers my ears. My beard is a brown facsimile of Santa's beard. Peering at me through the barely open door, Mom doesn't disappoint. "Can I help you?"

"I hope so, ma'am. I'm cold and hungry, and I'm looking for a Christmas hug from my mom."

Wearing a blue dress that falls to her knees, a perm dyed brunette with bright highlights, and flat soled shoes instead of the regular pumps, Mom narrows her mascaraed eyes. "I can assure you, young man, your mother does *not* live here."

I lean against one of the twin wooden columns, painted white, supporting the porch stoop arching over my head. "You do have a son, right?"

"Certainly, I do. He's very sweet and somewhat overweight and keeps his hair trimmed and his face shaved."

Every dark hair in place, Michael, wearing slacks, loafers, and a yellow sweater, opens the door. "Sorry, we don't give money to the homeless." He points behind me. "Did you steal that Toyota?"

I pat his shoulder. "How's it goin', Mikey?" He hates to be called Mikey.

Both his and Mom's eyes narrow because I'm the only person who calls him Mikey. "Jake?" they both say.

"That's me." They let me inside. Mom hugs me. Mikey looks me up and down. "What the hell did you do to yourself? You look like Tom Hanks before he got rescued in that movie."

"*Castaway*, you mean? I don't look that bad."

"Your hair and beard's close. What have you been doing?"

"I've been hiking and biking the mountains in North Carolina and Virginia."

"For two years?" Mom says.

"What did you do in the winter?" Mikey says. "You can't do all that when it snows."

"You can hike when it snows." I sniff coffee. "What's the chance I can get some coffee?"

Mom takes my hand and leads me to the huge kitchen, filled with stainless-steel appliances. "You're just in time for turkey. My, you're so thin. Have you been dieting too?"

"Low carbs, mostly."

"Then you don't want my homemade stuffing and yeast rolls and chocolate pie."

Mikey hands me coffee. "He's not insane, Diane. Are you insane, Jake?"

I sit at the table. "I know you don't mean anything by it, but losing Andy almost made me insane."

Mom bastes the turkey and closes the oven door. "I shouldn't have told you something wasn't right about her. You loved her and I should've kept my big mouth shut."

Mikey sits with coffee. "All that biking and hiking for two years ... what are you doing for money?"

"Some investments are keeping me afloat."

Mom brings silverware to the table. "Are you going back to work now?"

"Pretty soon." I don't say more because I'd rather keep my move to Dare County to myself. It's not like she or Mikey ever comes south.

"Have you met anyone?" Mom says.

"I agree," Mikey says, glancing at Mom. "A good woman makes life better."

I'm a bit ashamed of my previous opinion of Mikey. The big shot attorney obviously loves Mom. "I'll see. Good women don't grow on trees."

Mom pokes me with a fork. "And neither do good men." She leaves and comes back with plates. "Have you talked to Lisa lately? She's expecting in July."

"I'm sure she's happy."

Mom bastes the turkey again. Mikey sips coffee. I take advantage of the silence to compare Lisa's pregnancy timeline to Scotty's. If Scotty hadn't been pregnant when we started making love, and my swimmers did the job swimmers are supposed to do, she would've had my baby in July. Turning away, I bite my lower lip at the stupidity of torturing myself with such a thought. Andy's dead and Scotty's dead; nothing will bring them back. All that's left of them is ashes in the depths ... Andy's in the Atlantic, Scotty's in the Gulf of Mexico.

The delicious meal passes with small talk, some centered on the corona virus. We remark how we hope the world is better prepared if a pandemic strikes again. Mom apologizes for eating at the breakfast nook instead of the dining room. I tell her it's cozier. She shoves first one, then another triangle of chocolate pie toward me. It's amazing how great this food tastes once a person gets used to practically zero carbs. By the living room fireplace, we sip wine in front of oak embers, crackling and glowing. The wine warms my throat and stomach. The fire warms my sock feet.

Following goodnights, we go upstairs: them barehanded, me with my suitcase battered with two years use. Showered and smelling of soap and shampoo and hair rinse, I get in bed beneath patchwork quilts and snuggle the pillow. When Mikey asked what I did during winter because I couldn't ride my bike in the snow, I didn't remember last winter, similar to how I forgot things in the mental health treatment center. Luck led to my answer of hiking. Did I do that or not? I must have—I distinctly recall buying new hiking boots in Charlottesville, Virginia, before I continued north. I turn the pages of my last two years; more blank spots emerge, all centered around experiences with Andy or, in October and November, experiences with Scotty. The mind is a fragile thing: eggshells about to be stepped on, lake ice about to crack, tears quivering on the edges of eyelids. I'll never be able to visit the South Nags Head rental, Endless Love, again, but Andy's sandals I buried beneath that sand fence will haunt me forever, along with the possibility that her mental state concerning lights and portals to other universes and sex with Cheryl and Paul all were a cry for help, like her mom's hoarding is a cry for help.

I go to sleep knowing I won't dwell on it again. In the morning I'll drive to Raleigh and start my new—genuine—life all over again.

Chapter 26

Lucky me, I get 225,000 dollars for my house, pay the mortgage off, and bank 75,000 dollars. After the closing I rent a trailer. Mac helps me load the few pieces of furniture I want to keep, and I drop Andy's clothes off at the Salvation Army. On the 4-Runner's passenger seat, Scotty's purse accompanies me to Dare County and our new/old home.

Two years leave the rusted mailbox dangling from a rotten cedar post on a single bent nail, the hundred-yard driveway muddy and rutted, the paint peeling on the clapboard siding, rows of tin clattering in the wind hissing across the roof, one window shattered, mouse droppings on the dust covered oak floors, a bird nest clinging to a curtain rod, a water stain in the corner ceiling of the largest bedroom upstairs, a moldy stink everywhere, and me completely overwhelmed. Scotty would be pleased regardless, especially because I sold her high-dollar wedding band and engagement ring to partially finance my folly. I can almost hear her laughing.

Furniture wrestled inside, I try the heat pump. Nothing. I check the breakers. Nothing, but—halleluiah—lights. I check the fridge; green mold trails on the inside surface, which is dingy yellow. I check the stove. No halleluiah. A trip to the nearest home improvement store is in order. Since I left Raleigh this morning, I have time. Man cannot eat out when he's (almost) carb free.

As luck would have it, I find a ratty phone book that says Manteo has a store. As luck would *not* have it, the phone doesn't work and the cell signal sucks. I want to verify the store is still there before I make the twenty-minute drive and am tempted to scarf seafood for an early supper.

I order all new appliances at the store; they'll deliver around noon tomorrow. The sales person gives me a card for a recommendation to fix the heat pump. A quick call on my phone ends with the guy saying to buy lots of blankets and quilts because a cold rain is forecast, and he can't make it until next week. I buy that stuff at another store, load the 4-Runner, and search the web for roof repair companies. The guy says he can't do it in the rain; he'll stop by when it clears. Then he calls me to say he already has another job lined up and won't make it until two weeks. I drive back to the appliance store for a 60-inch LED flatscreen TV and chunk it in back of the 4-Runner, go back inside for a DVD player and drive to the library, where a stern-faced woman demands I fill out a library card before I check out several DVDs, one of which is the movie version of Nicholas Spark's *The Notebook*, two of which are the movie versions of Jane Austen's *Sense and Sensibility* and *Pride and Prejudice*. My stomach rumbles for seafood at a different restaurant than the one where I passed out. Some memories are fit to keep; that's not one of them.

The restaurant is another on the causeway. The greeter seats me by a window with a view of the Albemarle Sound. The great sheet of gray water reflects the great sheet of gray cloud pressing down on the horizon. Wind cuts waves. No jet skis or kayaks bob. Winter has come to the Outer Banks, repeating the cycle of tourist and calm, tourist and calm.

I order a broiled seafood platter, no hushpuppies, water with lemon. Customers straggle in. Their jackets smell of salt air and sadness. Or maybe that's just me.

From somewhere behind me a woman's voice lilts low in her throat with laughter. Not quite Scotty's E-string tone, it still reminds me of her. I can't help but look.

Blonde hair to the point of white is streaked with hints of green. I think the term for the style is a pixie cut. Bangs sweep across a high forehead and both ears show. Three golden circles, increasing in size, pierce the left lobe. The right is the same, except studs climb the curve of cartilage. Another ring pierces her right eyebrow. No studs in her straight nose, thank goodness. She wears no makeup and doesn't need any; summer has left her tanned all over, from her toned biceps, forearms and shoulders, to her thighs, calves, and glutes. Imagination suffices when a white blouse and faded denims interfere. Fingernails match the streaks of green in her hair. Beneath the table, toenails match too, revealed by sandals. She can't be more than twenty, all lithe and tight and incredibly sexy despite my aversion to all the hoops and studs. If her tummy is slightly six-packed, what a sight a gold belly button ring would make as I work my way past it with my tongue.

Unfortunately, the guy with her is equally toned. He says something; the woman laughs again. Her teeth are perfectly straight and perfectly white. An afterglow grin reveals how her lower lip quirks down slightly. Fortunately, the waitress comes with my food so I can stop gawking before my neck cramps and the guy wants to beat my butt.

I've eaten half the platter when the young woman leaves, which allows me a view of her behind. Sure, I'm a pervert, but my imagination is on full alert. The jeans cling. The shirt tapers to an impossibly narrow waist. The pixie cut reveals a long neck, muscular and lean. I manage to read a tattoo in cursive at her tapering hairline before she gets too far away: *Freedom.*

Curses ride my subconscious. Does that guy have any idea how lucky he is? Dumb thought: I'm supposed to be immune to dyed hair and studs everywhere in lieu of another southern girl with southern thoughts and a heart filled with gratitude for the simple things in life.

I wonder if I can find one who patches tin rooves, repairs heat pumps, and can throw a mean coat of paint on clapboard siding after she scrapes it?

Bloated from the huge meal, I drive back home and set the LED TV and DVD player up in the living room, light a fire in the fireplace with the cartons, add some half-rotten sticks of oak from the back porch, and settle down on my sofa to watch *The Notebook.*

Rain soon patters the tin roof. A pot from a bottom kitchen cupboard catches the drip in the upstairs bedroom. The metronomic *ding-ding-ding* forces me back up the stairs to slam the door.

When Allie—wet from her and Noah's thunderstorm-halted visit to see the swans, ducks, or whatever they are—strides away from him on his pier, I'm like, OMG, she's as hot as the girl at the restaurant. Then, when they finally make love, which is almost as violent as it is passionate, I turn away because it's been so long since I've made love myself.

I sometimes wonder if women know how special they are in all the ways that they are. Tall, short, thin or not, they have the ability to bring men to their knees with a smile. Bare shoulders and cleavage help—biology 101, the need to procreate—but there's something about a smile.

Andy and Scotty both had great smiles. Andy's was broad and bright. Scotty's was not so broad, and I can't forget her slightly crooked bottom teeth, but when she smiled really big, her lower lip quirked down on the right a smidgeon like the woman at the restaurant, and it drove me insane.

The scene when Allie leaves Noah messes me up terribly, and I dig around in the kitchen cupboards for a paper towel to wipe snot and tears. Being a romantic has its downfalls.

My mattress, box spring, slats, side rails, and head board lean against the living room wall. To avoid the *ding-ding-ding* in the upstairs bedroom, I flop the mattress in front of the fireplace's glowing embers, strip naked, and climb beneath all those quilts and blankets I bought before the haze exiting my mouth snows a blizzard in front of my face.

The list of work harassing my thoughts gives me the epiphany of just why I bought this house: I hope if I fix it up, Scotty will come back to me like Noah hoped Allie would come back to him when he bought and repaired his old manor house. The only difference is—the main difference, that is—Allie was alive and Scotty's dead.

Here I am, thirty-one, lonely, heartbroken from two deaths, living in a house where Scotty's childhood ghost will haunt me the rest of my life, and I never even thought about any of that before I signed the contract to buy this sad old place.

That's life. As the barkers at the North Carolina State Fair say, "Step right up and win the prize. You pays your money, you takes your chances."

Win the prize? It's not a prize to live alone in an old house for fifty or sixty years with the ghost of my soulmate reminding me of what I lost. Then again, what choice do I have? Unless some hapless young maid like the woman at the restaurant comes along.

Chapter 27

Wednesday, the guy flips some kind of switch inside the heat pump to start it. The other guy comes the following Thursday and recommends a new roof. I opt for the new lifetime warranted metal roofing in light gray. In a mood for new, I call another guy for an estimate for vinyl siding in dark gray to offset the roof. Why keep clapboard siding and set myself up for a lifetime of painting every few years? All this time I remove the bird nest, sweep, mop, rent a floor sander, buy urethane, and make the oak planks shine. The library calls through my static-ridden cell signal to ask if I want to renew the DVDs. I do not, so I take them back and revisit the restaurant to see if that musclebound woman with *Freedom* tattooed on her neck happens by.

In a sound side booth, I check the menu. Footsteps patter on the floor and stop beside me. "Are you here to ogle me again?"

I recognize the E-string voice but don't look up. "Just here for a bite."

"My boyfriend can arrange that."

I look up into earth-brown eyes and offer my hand. "Jake."

"Alex." She ignores the hand. "Tonight's special is—"

"You, right?"

Perfect lips purse. "You're in decent shape, but I'd break you like a sea oat stalk."

"Cardio beats muscles. You'd have three orgasms to my one."

At a nearby table, an elderly man clears his throat. Alex looks his way. "Sorry. I dumped him a while back and he doesn't take no for an answer."

"I'm sorry too," I say. "I don't usually say things like that."

"But you're in love with me and can't help stalking me at my job."

"You weren't working the other week."

"I can eat out when I want."

"Where's a good place around here to teach guitar lessons? I'm independently wealthy and need something to do until the weather breaks."

"The YMCA has an opening for someone who teaches guitar. Does yours have the little crank on the end?"

"Yep. It plays *Ring Around the Rosy,* like the ring around the rosy you're giving me."

"Uh-huh. What would you like tonight?"

"A burger no bun. Side salad no dressing. The coldest draft you got. And your phone—"

"Banana pudding to ruin your low carb feast?"

"No."

They make great peach pie alamode here."

"No, just your phone—"

Her brown eyes narrow. "My phone number's off limits. I told you I have a boyfriend."

"And if you didn't?"

"I'd have to test your cardio."

"Your place or mine?"

"On a kayak."

"That sounds kind of awkward."

"It's not, 'cause you and me are not gonna happen. Your burger will be out in a minute."

Alex leaves in a flurry of hip wiggling jeans. The elderly man shakes a finger at me. "She'd kill your skinny ass, boy."

"Yes, sir, no doubt about it."

He watches Alex round the corner and faces me again. "But what a way to go, making love to Tinker Bell from the old Walt Disney movies."

Another waitress brings my draft. The same one brings my food. Alex seems to have traded table assignments. When I make first impressions, I make first impressions.

The new waitress brings my bill. I pay with a credit card and write a note on one of the extra receipts to Alex that I'm usually not such a jerk and will she please let me prove it by taking her fishing on Jennette's Pier. That way she can throw me over if I utter one offensive word, sentence, phrase, or paragraph. Waiting for her to pass near the greeter area, I drop it on the tray she carries when she walks by. Without a pause, she drops it in the wastebasket beside the greeter desk.

* * *

Pier fishing is a unique experience, especially in January. You take a chance on the pier being closed, no fish biting except dogfish—another name for sand sharks—and freezing your, as Dad called it, tookus off.

Having refinished all the downstairs floors by the following weekend, I reward myself with a day of attempting to fish on a blustery Saturday afternoon. Yes, I bought a pair of insulated coveralls, gloves, and a hat with ear muffs. All I need is snow, and I'll be ready to ski the Blue Ridge.

Not dressed in all that stuff yet, I go to a tackle shop and buy a surf rod/spinning reel combo for when the weather warms and I can wade in, a pier rod/spinning reel combo, along with a huge tackle box, a cooler, assorted lures, weights, hooks, swivels and other related paraphernalia—steel leaders are a must for toothy bluefish—including what Dad called a "sand sticker," for holding a surf rod upright in the sand, and a rod mount for the front of the 4-Runner for taking it out on the beach. I consider waders but don't feel like taking a chance on getting knocked down and pulled out by the rough surf. The clerk says if I'm hardcore enough, I could fish the surf in a wetsuit, although no one he knows is that hardcore. I assure him I'm not either, pay, load the 4-Runner, and drive to Jennette's Pier.

Wind gusts buffet me as I walk up the planked incline to the doors. Lining the dunes in scattered clumps, naked sea oat stalks whistle. I must be insane to fish today. The pier is empty—everyone agrees—but I pays my money and I takes my chances.

Then I remember I forgot my insulated clothes and trot back to the 4-Runner. The woman at the counter cuts her eyes at me as I pay. "If you dye all that hair and beard white, you could be Santa." She follows up with a smile to let me know she's joking. I shove the hat and flaps over my ears, work the gloves on, and begin my windblown journey again.

Jennette's is cool because it has covered areas with bench seats for when its windy and rainy. I set up behind one of these areas on the downwind side, and am able to remove my gloves to tie, bait, and cast a bottom rig without the wind beating me to death. Most fisher folks lean a rod against the rail with the tip extending above it just enough to notice the flex in the tip that signals a bite, but not so much as to allow a fish to pull it over. I sit out of the wind, have coffee from an insulated container in the cooler, and wait.

The day is clear and the sun is bright, illuminating the huge swells rolling beachward, each a shade of aquamarine similar to the waters surrounding the Keys. Gusts whistle around the corners of the shelters, and I imagine them to be Andy and Scotty reminding me to remember them. That isn't a problem. Those two will haunt me to the end of time, but happily.

Hope arises in the strangest moments. Whether it's the wind, whether it's the surf, whether it's the realization that Andy's ashes mingle beneath the Atlantic less than a mile from where I sit, with the sand, with the shells, with the endless sea life surrounding her in a watery embrace, I realize she's found her galaxy in which to discover solace from her troubled mind.

Jake?

I don't look up, she's not there.

You have to try for me. You're doing all this to hide from the pain but you can't. Someone's out there for you. Someone who'll love you more than I ever could.

"You're not there, Andy."

You're also doing it because you blame yourself for what I did. Life has a way of turning the tide. Give it time, Jake, give it time.

Her voice fades on the seaward wind. I look east. Someone thrashes across the swells, windsurfing. The sail hides them, but the wet-suited legs shine with salty sheen beneath it. The board rockets over a breaking wave. The rider leans back, drives the board upward in an arc, and I catch a glimpse of a blonde—almost white—pixie-cut hairstyle.

She's too far away to identify, taller than I recall in the restaurant, a statuesque goddess challenging Mother Nature herself. The wind bellies the sail to the point of flexing the graphite mast. The board—a yellow fiberglass knife reflecting sunlight that sparkles in its wake—slices the swells.

I watch until she's a distant spec. How can someone be out here in this environment for the sheer amusement of it? Regardless, I admire her, whoever she is.

Coffee gone, bait gone, cold seeping into the seams of my Santa suit, I pack up and go home.

On the way I consider Alex's flat statement of teaching guitar at the YMCA. I was joking but why not? Unless she was joking. The house repairs should be done in early spring, before the schools of Spanish Mackerel and Bluefish start running, and I don't mind a side job. Heck, I'll volunteer and show Alex, if she ever shows up, how my heart is in the right place.

At home I'm tempted to revisit the causeway and the seafood restaurant where we met, but I remember the extremely cold shoulder she gave me the last time. Instead, I drive the 4-Runner around back, unload all my fishing goodies onto the back porch, and go inside to enjoy my heat pump, my fancy kitchen, a broiled chicken breast, sautéed green beans with garlic, and a glass of white wine in front of the TV and the fireplace, where I watch the *Pride and Prejudice* DVD, having bought it, *Sense and Sensibility*, and *The Notebook*.

I barely get to where Lizzie Bennet and Mr. Darcy meet before I kill the TV.

What I wouldn't give to have Scotty with me. We'd eat and cuddle and remark on the movie and finally, after getting ready for bed, make love endlessly in the night.

Supper done, I add more oak to the fire, turn out the lights, and lie on the sofa.

Wayward gusts of wind moan around the old farmhouse. Leafless shrubs *scratch-scratch-scratch* the clapboard siding that awaits replacement. In the fireplace, embers glow and shimmer like hearts in the night, red and pulsing. A piece of split oak collapses to release a whirlwind of sparks up the chimney.

Andy or Scotty, I can't tell who haunts me the most, whether with windborne words or images of a child running around a farm house, brunette hair in pigtails. Or of a young woman in a new marriage she may already regret, visiting her parents in time to watch her dad die, crushed beneath a tractor tire like life's trials through twin losses of love are crushing me, and like her marriage crushed her, even to the point of death.

I roam the house for a cell signal and call Leon. He assures me I can handle this moment, assures me life will come along with the gift of love when I least expect it. I say I wish I had his positive outlook and he says I already do, unless he needs to visit and bring a bottle of depression pills. We part with a laugh—his is genuine, mine is fake—and I return to the sofa and a fleece throw.

BAM-BAM-BAM

I sit up and blink at my phone on the coffee table. Who the hell's trying to break in at 11:30 p.m.?

BAM-BAM-BAM

I blink again. People usually don't bam the door when they break in. Still, I fetch Dad's .45, turn on the porch lights, and at the window beside the door, goggle at Alex giving me the finger. I show her the .45; she gives me the finger again, followed by her window-muffled voice: "Who the hell are you to buy this house?"

"Who the hell are you to complain about me buying this house?"

She rattles the doorknob. "Let me in so I can beat your ass."

I raise the .45. "Are you as dumb as you look?" I lower the .45. "We can argue or I can make coffee and talk. What'll it be?"

She stomps her feet and rubs her arms, which are not covered. Goosebumps dot her flesh. I stick the .45 in my belt and open the door. "Heat and coffee or freeze and fuss?"

She shoves by and kneels at the fireplace. "My stupid car broke down."

"That doesn't explain your rant about my house."

"I left my jacket in the car like an idiot."

"That *is* pretty dumb."

Alex rubs her hands together over the embers. "Don't you have more wood?"

"On the back porch, wanna get it?"

"So I can freeze again?"

I get wood and drop it beside her. "Help yourself. I'll make coffee."

"Decaf."

"Please?"

"Fine." She gives me the finger again. "Please."

I measure grounds and take a chance. "Such a nasty person for such a fine windsurfer."

"How do you know about that?"

So it *was* her. "I was on Jennette's Pier today. Not trying to blow smoke up your sail, but you were amazing."

"You were actually fishing out in that wind?"

"Bait does better if you soak it until it falls off the hook. Weren't you freezing?"

"The wetsuit and the physical exertion helps."

"Black?"

"Just hot."

I give her a mug and sit on the sofa. She sips, I sip. "About me and this house ..."

"I've wanted it forever but can't afford it."

"Maybe your boyfriend can make an offer? With all the improvements I've done, I'll make a nice profit."

"Says the independently wealthy man."

I cover my knees with a throw and offer her another.

She covers her legs. "I shouldn't be here."

"I didn't make you bang my door."

"I didn't know it was *your* door."

She sips, I sip. The fire does things to her face that should be outlawed: highlights strong cheekbones, dark lashes, thinner lips than Scotty's but still defined.

"I like your tattoo."

She touches the nape of her neck, where I want to kiss, and says nothing.

The fire pops, the embers crackle, the moment is as romantic as romantic gets.

She sips coffee. "I shouldn't be here."

"How bad is your car?"

"You're not married?"

I vow then and there to never mention Andy to her. "I wouldn't have flirted with you if I were."

The fire's glow reveals those perfectly even, perfectly white teeth. She faces me. "Do you ever feel like you've met someone, and something's there when it shouldn't be?"

"We'd never get along."

"Why?"

"I've got your house."

"And I've got a boyfriend waiting for me."

"What can we do to make him go away?" I tap the .45's grip hanging from my belt. "How about it?"

That firelit grin again. "He's not *that* bad."

"He doesn't deserve you."

"Nobody deserves me." She stands. "Can you get a cell signal here? I'll call a tow."

"I can look at your car."

"I'd rather not."

"Because?"

"I don't like owing anyone anything."

"You could buy me dinner."

Her brown eyes brighten for a second, then fade.

"What?" I ask.

"Can you get that cell signal or not?"

"I'll be glad to—"

"I said no, okay?"

"In the kitchen by the stove."

She leaves and makes a call. "They'll pick me up here."

I go to the kitchen and leave my coffee mug beside hers on the counter. "We match."

"Can you stay away from the restaurant?"

"You can't ban me from the pier."

"I won't windsurf there again."

"You're carrying this a bit too far."

"I won't settle for anything less than perfect. You're not perfect."

"Is your boyfriend perfect?"

"No one is perfect."

Then you'll be alone the rest of your life. You're too amazing for that."

"You don't know me."

"You don't know me either. "Sure, I made some stupid comments at the restaurant. That was testosterone talking."

"The need to procreate."

"The need to procreate."

Silence rolls between us on a tide of indecision. Wind moans; embers crackle. My fingers find hers. "No pressure," I whisper. "I just want to get to know you."

Those intense brown eyes find mine. The top of her head comes to my nose. "We'd be perfect dance partners if you wore heels."

"I don't dance." Her coffee scented breath warms my mouth.

"You danced with the wind today. You were—are—amazing."

"I shouldn't be here."

"Then why are you?"

"You won't let me—" She swallows. "You won't let me go."

I release her hand, lean down to touch my nose to hers. "I let you go, Alex."

"I shouldn't be here."

"But you are."

"You would hurt me. I can't do that again."

"I'm not whoever hurt you. Can't we just get to know each other?"

"I'm not—"

Beep-beep. The tow truck's headlights fill the windows. Alex goes to the door, opens it, and I say, "When can I see you again?"

She faces me. "Let fate decide. If we're meant to be, we're meant to be. If not, we're not." She closes the door.

At the window, I watch her run to the truck. "My dear Miss Lizzie Bennet, we're definitely meant to be. You just don't know it yet."

Chapter 28

Spring on the Outer Banks is a spectacle of returning tourists, returning fisher folks, and returning warmth. Well, except for the fact that I haven't seen Alex since the night she stopped by.

Having bought a nice guitar online, I donate my time to teaching at the YMCA in Nags Head. Most students are wannabe rock gods in middle age: two are women, three are men. One woman is a cougar all day long. One of the men might be too, but he likely just loves the guitar that much.

Two students are brothers, ten and twelve. Three are unrelated girls, six, eight, and ten. All the kids call me Papa Clause because of my shaggy appearance and beg me to never cut my beard or hair unless it gets in my eyes, which I do with scissors when needed anyway.

They circle me in chairs on Monday after school. The adults circle me in chairs on Wednesday night. I'm paid in smiles, increased confidence, clean chords, and rhythmic strums that actually sound like music.

I can't shake the feeling of Alex stopping by the Y since she mentioned this to start with. Maybe the guy who broke her heart played guitar and melancholy is keeping her away.

Whoever the jerk is, I'd like to—as us southern boys sometimes say—stomp a mudhole in his ass.

The warmer weather convinces me to wear shorts, T-shirts, and sandals. It also convinces me how house repair instead of bike riding is allowing my middle to grow a smidgeon thicker than I like. When time permits, I stick the bike on its rack and drive the 4-Runner to the Oregon Inlet Fishing Center, where I park and ride the stretch of Highway 12 between there and the causeway intersection. I never see Stan, but *Hope* is gone most days. On the first day I see her at the dock, I notice new outriggers extending upward, a new radar dish on the cabin roof, and a new radio antenna as well. Once I glimpse him in the cabin and consider a conversation but don't. He wouldn't know me with my shaggy appearance, and I don't feel like explaining it. In addition, questions would arise, questions that might lead to my mental health scare. Although I'm not ashamed of it, some people are extremely ashamed of it and the stigma it can carry, especially men with their testosterone-laden chests.

On my rides I sometimes cruise over to Bodie Island Lighthouse and go out on the raised walkways crisscrossing the marsh. Most days are breezy, and the marsh whispers secrets of the millennia it took to form it, countless years of sedimentation, vegetation, blackish brackish water gorging itself on the decaying detritus of each and every life form that calls this place home.

Some days, as the older O'cockers on Ocracoke Island say with their old English brogue, are "slick cam," meaning still, no breeze, heat rising off the marsh, sun baking it and the sweating foreheads, underarms, and backs of strolling tourists.

I've bought a few books on the Outer Banks over the years but have never visited Ocracoke. That's something to remedy eventually.

The bike rides tighten calves and thighs and my rear but do little for my wiry arms, shoulders, and neck. Since Alex's finely tuned body is a mix of Olympic swimmer and Olympic gymnast, I vow to visit the weight and exercise room at the YMCA and see if I can create some six-pack abs like she probably has.

I do so the last weekend in May, after teaching my circle of kids guitar, donning gym shorts, a T-shirt, and sneakers in the men's locker room. The entrance to the gym is in a section of the Y I never visit, down a hallway past the daycare room, lined with windows. Inside, an older woman reads to a girl of about one or two. Brunette curls frame her cheeks. She touches a page and the woman nods. The girl is cuter than cute: an upturned button of a nose, perfect pink bow of a mouth, fine featured even with her remaining baby plumpness. I can't help thinking how Scotty's girl—our girl—might've resembled this girl, how we'd take turns reading to her, how we'd have loved her so much, how she'd be about this age had she and Scotty lived. I leave for the gym, hoping my workout will banish my regrets.

I'm sure weights line one wall, treadmills another, and various equipment is scattered about the huge room, but I see none of it.

Alex's back is to me on the butterfly machine. She wears a tank top soaked with sweat. Beneath the thin material, shoulder blades flex rhythmically. Her torso expands with inhales and exhales. The hair at the nape of her neck, wet and fine, drips sweat across the *Freedom* tattoo. I walk up behind her. "Now I know where you get all your muscles."

"Stalking me, Jake?"

"How do you know it's me?"

"Did you not see that mirrored wall in front of me?"

"I'd say I only have eyes for you, but you'd want me to sing it."

"Are you so old fashioned you only know songs from the past?"

"Billie Holiday, Boyz II Men, Michael Bublé all did it. From the past to the present, great songs stand the test of time. I like the Flamingo's version the best because it's slow and sensual, great for dancing."

"Don't let me keep you from doing whatever it is you came here to do."

I go to the mirrored wall and lean against it to face her. "You never said why you were out my way that night."

"I babysit my sister's daughter sometimes. She's a nurse and works odd hours. Her job, so her husband said, ruined their marriage."

"Do you keep her a lot?"

"Enough to where she calls me mama too."

"Sweet."

"She is." Alex leaves the butterfly machine, grabs a towel off the next one, and wipes sweat from her face. "I'd tell you something but it'd only encourage you."

"You'll dance with me if I sing?"

"I'm stinky and sweaty."

"I happen to love the taste of salt." I lick my lips. "And I mean everywhere."

"Pervert."

"That's what you get for inspiring me. What were you going to tell me?"

"I'm not sure I am."

"Then why mention it?"

"I'm soaking bait until it falls apart."

"Like I did on the pier when I saw you windsurfing. Been kayaking lately?"

"I'm thinking about it."

"You could always drown me if I misbehave. Where do you launch?"

"Different places."

"I see people kayaking in the sound at the causeway."

"Thanks for not harassing me at the restaurant anymore."

"Thanks for mentioning giving guitar lessons here. I enjoy it a lot."

"I just said that for the heck of it."

"Maybe your subconscious wanted to meet me here."

Alex loops the towel around her neck. "Time to go."

"What were you gonna tell me? What might encourage me?"

"I'll tell you if I ever see you again. Do you have a kayak?"

"What do you know about that old house all by itself in the marsh south of the causeway? I've seen it from the windows of those restaurants and I've always wondered why it's there."

"Maybe it's filled with the ghosts of long-lost lovers."

"I might rent a kayak and check it out tomorrow afternoon."

"Too bad, I'll be busy."

"When are you not busy?"

"Never."

I step closer. "You're amazing."

She takes a step away. "You're a wannabe Santa Clause."

"You don't like it? The kids I teach like it."

Alex's defined lips quirk to a partial grin. "All those curls would make a nice hand hold."

"And I'm the pervert."

"And I need to go." She strides away. "Stop looking at my ass."

"Something else amazing."

She waves backwards and goes out the door. I get on the butterfly machine she just left, try three muscle-aching reps, and reduce the weight. Yep, gotta get in a lot better shape before Alex and I make love. Pulled muscles are *not* my thing.

* * *

A dreary rain drizzles Tuesday morning. I console the unlikelihood of kayaking with Alex at the causeway by cooking three eggs over easy, bacon, hash brown potatoes, coffee, and whole wheat toast slathered with grape jelly.

The day drags by. I keep looking out the window and going to my data hot spot by the stove to check the weather radar. On the smartphone screen, green blobs of scattered showers stretch from the Gulf of Mexico to the Outer Banks.

At noon the clouds break. I grab my keys and run to the 4-Runner, but stop halfway out the driveway because a car pulls in and continues toward me. Behind the wheel, a woman with brunette hair waves. The car stops bumper to bumper with the 4-Runner, and Tammy gets out. "Hey, stranger. How's life?"

"Not bad. You look great."

"Thanks. I lost a few pounds and kicked that crappy husband to the curb because he wanted another baby right away to replace Kim and I didn't." She closes the door and comes to the front of the car. "Leon told me you were down this way and how you took up bike riding."

"I didn't tell him my address."

"Do you mind me stopping by? I stayed in Kitty Hawk a few days, thinking I might see you, and remembered seeing a 4-Runner with a bike rack here when I drove down. As luck would have it, here you are."

"I was sort of going somewhere."

"I like your beard and hair."

"How'd you know it was me when you saw me?"

"I didn't until you answered me. It's great seeing you."

"Tammy, I—"

"Have you eaten lunch? I could take you out?"

"I had a big breakfast."

"Are you seeing anyone? I kind of thought you wouldn't … you know, with how you lost your wife. As we know, things like that can affect a person long term."

I look at my shoes. The last thing I want is to hurt Tammy, who's obviously interested in a relationship, but she's no Alex. Still, lying to cover my butt isn't my thing, and I can kayak with Alex another time. "I kind of had a first date lined up."

Raindrops splatter the vehicles. Tammy looks up. "Was it a date outside? Maybe you can cancel?"

"I don't have her number."

"Then she'll know you're not coming. Let's catch up over a cup of coffee."

The rain falls harder. I back the 4-Runner to the house. Tammy follows in her car. Inside, I make coffee while she looks around. "It smells a little like fresh paint. How much work did you do?"

"I refinished the floors and painted the half-bath downstairs."

"Being a guy, you had to have the big TV."

"I need to get one of the satellite services for that and internet."

"I see you've got DVDs." She picks one up. "No porn?"

A mug I'm rinsing clatters into the sink. "Not unless you call Jane Austen movies porn."

She picks up another DVD. "That sex scene in *The Notebook* is close."

"How do you like your coffee?"

Tammy strolls into the kitchen. "Splenda and cream's fine."

"Sorry, no cream." I take a box of Splenda from a cabinet and set it on the counter by the drizzling coffeemaker. She opens the fridge and takes out milk.

We settle on the sofa. Tammy crosses her legs; the pleated skirts she wears slides upward to reveal a smooth thigh. "You sure have lost weight, Jake. Like I said, between that and all your hair and your beard, I wouldn't have recognized you if you hadn't answered me earlier. Even your voice is a little different. It kind of has an edge to it."

"You've lost weight too. If you don't mind me asking, I thought you wanted to work things out with your husband."

"I told you what happened."

"Just wondering if that was all."

"Because I came here looking for you. What an ego."

"No, because you said you and he were soulmates."

Tammy sips coffee. Rain thuds the metal roof. The wind picks up; the greening shrubs brush the window behind the TV. Tammy sips again. "I'm not sure I believe in soulmates anymore."

I say nothing. She can believe whatever she wants. I believe differently.

She thumbs the TV remote, gets up to insert *The Notebook* into the DVD player, and returns to the sofa. "What better thing to do than watch a movie on a rainy afternoon."

Her soft voice lilts sexual innuendo. Either that or the fact I haven't had sex in over two years makes me hear something I don't. She did feel great when we held each other crying, which makes me feel even more perverted now than back then.

We quietly watch the movie. Tammy finishes her coffee. I finish mine. Our mugs sit on the coffee table. During the scene when teenage Noah and Allie are undressing in the old house, Tammy yawns, slides next to me, and leans against my shoulder. I'm tempted to say something but I'm not tempted enough. The warmth of an attractive woman next to me, along with the slight sweetness of perfume on her neck, including her smooth thigh next to my bare thigh due to wearing shorts, is an aphrodisiac beyond aphrodisiacs.

The movie continues. Tammy slides her hand to my chest. The scene where Allie and Noah reunite to make love fills the screen with undressing, kissing, moans, arched backs, and her cry of pleasure at the end.

Tammy swings her leg over mine and sits in my lap. I unbutton her blouse, fingers shaking, and bare her shoulders. The bra is a front closure, which she unclasps. The sight of her breasts in the dim light of the cloudy day is too much to comprehend. She pulls my T-shirt over my head and kisses my neck and chest, slides from my lap to kneel between my legs. All I can do is close my eyes.

I'm a weak jerk and I know it. Tammy might think this means we're a couple and I know it. But if my time with Andy and Scotty taught me anything, I'm a sexual being, and I know that too.

Tammy stands and undresses. I do too. She's much more petite than I remember, more so since she's lost weight. She turns around to sit slowly and carefully in my lap. Again, all I can do is close my eyes.

Allie tells Noah, "Let's do it again."

Tammy's rhythm increases. I ask her to turn around. She does and we kiss. Sweetened coffee flavors her tongue. She leans back and presses down. We're slick with sweat, slick everywhere. I groan. She cries out in little gasps and falls forward, gasping.

Our chests gradually stop heaving. She kisses me, then says, "Sorry about that. Two years without sex made me crazy."

"Same here."

"I hope we didn't leave a stain on your sofa."

"I'll turn the cushion over."

"I bet it's a huge stain."

"I'll get a new sofa."

Tammy kisses me again and dresses. "I'm staying in a hotel with a kitchenette and bought a steak but didn't cook it. You up for supper? It should be room temperature by now, perfect for cooking."

I get up and dress. "Hey, might as well recharge with protein."

Tammy comes back from her car with the steak and a bottle of red wine. "It's still drizzling. Didn't I see lettuce and stuff for salads in your fridge?"

"You read my mind." I take a cast iron pan from the oven and place it on the stove.

The intense aroma of seared beef soon fills the kitchen. We sip wine from the same glass while I make salads. Although guilt twinges me every time she gives me the glass, the thought of the greatest sex I ever had on a sofa—probably because it broke the two-year mark—drives the guilt away.

She takes the salads through an archway, to the small dining room off the kitchen, and comes back to slip her hand into the front of my shorts. "Ready for round two?"

I turn the steak. "You say it's still raining?"

"Enough to keep the pavement wet. I saw a car leave your mailbox."

"I'll get the mail tomorrow."

Supper consists of talk about Tammy's divorce, how she's doing Keto to lose weight, and how she's taking classes to be an RN. I tell her about my bike rides, the other work I and the contractors did on the house, and how I teach guitar at the YMCA.

Dessert for her is more wine in front of the TV. Dessert for me, with a dash of anticipation, is wondering if she'll sit in my lap again. After *The Notebook*, she sticks some action flick I bought from the five-dollar bin at the store in the DVD player, finishes the bottle of wine, and falls asleep cuddled into my shoulder.

Since I can't let her drive because of the wine, I ease her down onto the sofa pillow, cover her with a throw, and go to bed.

The splatter of water against the shower curtain in my bathroom wakes me. The nightstand clock's red LEDs read 11:15. After all our sweating, I should've showered too. The door is halfway open. I roll over and go back to sleep.

The whir of my blow dryer wakes me. Bare feet patter to the bed. There's nothing like the smell and feel of a freshly showered and shampooed woman swinging her leg over yours while saying: "You didn't forget round two, did you?

I roll her over and kiss her. She grabs doubles handfuls of my hair and guides me to where I was about to go anyway. Before I hardly start, she pulls me up again. "I need you, Jake. Please, please, please."

Sofa sex does not compare. Afterward, she giggles. "I bet we soaked all the way through your mattress."

I roll over, taking her with me. "Just making sure we do."

The rain comes again, driving liquid nails on the metal roof above our heads. In the long and lonely night, wind whispers in the oaks, lightning brightens curtains, thunder echoes and rolls. Grass drinks moisture, grows green and lush. Water climbs tree roots to limb and branch; leaves unfurl and blooms bloom. Above the clouds, the moon waits to reveal itself. On the other side of the world, the sun desires to reveal a new day with its first rays gleaming over the Atlantic.

Tammy and I fall asleep. I dream of the soulmate I might've found in Alex. I have no idea what Tammy dreams, but she has strummed the sexual me with the rapid-fire strokes of a Flamenco guitarist's fingernails blurring along the strings with tones both sultry and dark, revealing the power women have over men as weak as myself.

What the morning will bring from her, and what she expects of me in the way of commitment, I have no idea.

I'm sure she'll tell me, and my only hope is that her sexual confidence means she won't be hurt when I tell her she can't stay, that I'm not interested in her except for sex and friends, and that she's special and should find someone who deserves her because I do not.

Chapter 29

The absence of Tammy's hair against my shoulder wakes me. No water sprays the shower curtain. Not that she said anything about cooking breakfast, but no smell of food rises from the kitchen, not even coffee.

The house is quiet and still. No rain. Sun brightens the curtains. I go to the bathroom. Robe on, I go downstairs. Her car is gone. A note written on the back of an envelope she found on the dining room table lies on the spot we left on the sofa cushion.

Jake,

Thank you for last night. You made me realize even more than at the mental health place how special and vital I am as a woman. I still don't believe in soulmates, but knowing how much you loved your wife, I'm sure you're still searching for yours.

Tammy

PS

Don't forget to turn the sofa cushion and your mattress. You wouldn't want that special someone to see those huge spots. Oh, I'm still on the pill, so no worries there, and like I said, I haven't slept with anyone since my husband, so no STD worries either. Don't let it go to your head, but you're great in the sack.

Grinning, I flip the sofa cushion. Upstairs I take the sheets and mattress cover off the bed, revealing not one but two stains on the blue material. Grinning again, I flip the mattress. If I ever manage to bring Alex here, I'd rather make sure last night's evidence is hidden.

Showered and shampooed, I dress, heat coffee in the microwave, have toast, and open the front door to let the crisp morning air freshen the living room. One of the two rocking Adirondack chairs I bought from a hammock place in Nags Head—they're made of recycled plastic milk jugs and won't fade or rot like wood—invites me to sit. The sun rising in the east warms me: an old hound dog with smidgeons of remaining guilt about Tammy muddling my mind. Coffee gone, I load the 4-Runner with my surf fishing equipment and leave for one of the public beach access areas in Nags Head.

At the causeway, a few kayakers paddle, none with white blonde hair with a pixie cut and green streaks. After fishing I'll drive to the Y to see if Alex and I can remake our failed plans.

Today's the first Saturday in June. Beachgoers form groups of every color and every style swimsuit made: teens in bikinis and one-piece suits, kids and moms in the same, toddlers with diapers puffing their swimsuit bottoms, men and boys in swim trunks to their knees. One older guy wears a tiny pair of red Speedos; his beer belly hangs over the front.

I carry my stuff clear of the crowds, jab the sand sticker in place, and set the surf rod in it. Bottom rig attached, hooks baited with a new type of artificial bait that's supposed to mimic shrimp, I wade into the chilly water and cast. The bottom rig's pyramid sinker arcs through the air and splashes into the face of a wave. Now to wait, which consists of tightening the line enough to sense the tap-tap of a biting fish and resting the butt of the rod on my thigh.

From the south, mixed with the screams of swimmers playing in the surf, the soft putter of one of the lifeguards riding a four-wheeler along the beach tells me we're under careful watch. The putter rises in pitch and stops. A whistle blows. I don't look, but apparently some kid needs discipline. The putter starts again, growing louder, and stops behind me. "Catchin' anythang?"

The voice is feminine, high-pitched, and extremely southern.

"No, ma'am. Not nary a bite."

"I'd bite that fine behind of yours if you'd let me."

The rod dips. I jerk it to set the hook and the voice laughs. "That's just a wave doin' that. Then again, men like you prob'ly think they can ketch a girl just by actin' like they want to go on a kayak ride when they spend the afternoon on the sofa having sex with some bimbo."

A hand slaps the back of my head. I turn to face Alex on the four-wheeler. Words escape me worse than at any time in my life. She jabs her raised middle finger at me. "Jerk. I bet she told you I was the mail carrier."

I go up the sandy rise and put the rod in the sand sticker. "You can't see in the window from my mailbox."

"I birdwatch when I kayak and keep binoculars in my car. First, she sits on you backwards. Then you turn her around and she sits facing you. Do either of you have any tonsils left?"

"Exactly how long did you watch?"

"Long enough to know you left a huge stain on the sofa cushion. I see she stayed all night too."

"You came back to check up on me?"

"I waited for you at the causeway. The way you've been hounding me, I knew a little rain wouldn't stop you."

"And you came back this morning?"

"She left at six. How big is the stain on your bed?"

I sit in the sand and look up at her. "She's a friend from back home. That's the first time that happened."

"Couldn't help yourself, huh?"

"Give me a break. It's been over two years since I slept with anyone."

"It's been that long since I slept with anyone either. You don't see me jumping at the first chance I get."

"You've got a boyfriend. As hot as you are, there's no way you're not having sex."

In the surf, a kid yells. Alex looks away for a count of five and looks back. "I meant what I just said about not having sex for two years. As you keep telling me, I *am* amazing. The guy I loved back then taught me that and then up and disappeared on me. I'm not sleeping with anyone until I meet a man who can make me feel like the soulmates we were."

"Believe it or not, I know what you mean." I stand and step close enough to smell the sun screen on Alex's cheeks and nose. The breeze plays with the bangs hanging across her high forehead. Her eyes, the deepest darkest earthen brown indoors, gleam caramel with green hints in the sunlight. "I'm sorry about what you saw. That was sex and nothing else. She doesn't believe in people having soulmates like we do. The last woman I loved like that left me too. All I want is to have that again."

"What disease did the bimbo give you?"

"The last person she was with was her husband two years ago."

"I'm sure your swimmers swam everywhere swimmers can swim."

"She's still on the pill."

"Whatever."

"Look, we can either get passed this or not. For me, I really, genuinely, as much as I possibly can, want to get passed it."

Alex lowers her chin. "I don't know."

"I could drown myself. Then you'd have to save me and give me mouth-to-mouth."

She says nothing. I lift her chin. "Whatever it is between us, whatever this force is that keeps pulling us together, I want to find out what it is."

She jerks her chin from my fingertips. "A farce is more like it. All you want is another trophy wet spot on your sofa."

"It's not that. You're ..." I pause to get my thoughts straight. "You're like the breeze blowing over the marsh at Bodie Island Lighthouse in the spring. Something about you whispers to me like the marsh whispers. Do I want to have sex with you? Not at all. I want to make love to you—all night. I want to live inside you. I want to see if we're better together in life than we can ever be apart."

"You've been watching too many chic flicks."

"I happen to like chic flicks."

"Don't tell me they make you cry."

"Like a baby."

"You're a mental case."

"Only when it comes to you."

"You're good. No, you're *really* good. Do you practice these lines in front of the mirror?"

"Are your panties wet?"

"Don't push your luck."

"One kayak ride and let's see how it goes."

"You forgot about my boyfriend."

"He can't come."

"Tomorrow at nine. I'll have to babysit, but a neighbor helps when I'm busy." Alex cranks the four-wheeler and putters away, waving backwards and shaking her head. I pump my fist three times like a pro-golfer winning with the final putt on the final hole of the final day to win the US Open, the Masters, and all the other major tournaments combined.

Now, if I can just win Alex.

Chapter 30

I get up early to fill an insulated container with coffee, make scrambled egg and bacon sandwiches on whole wheat toast, and pack everything in my daypack, along with sunscreen and a straw hat, wide-brimmed and as corny as corny gets. Hey, corny's better than skin cancer any day of the week.

At the kayak place, I rent what the clerk recommends and wait for Alex, checking my watch every few minutes to make sure she doesn't stand me up like I did her. Not many restaurants along the causeway serve breakfast, so the two-lane highway isn't busy like it is from about 4 p.m. until around eight. If there's one thing visitors come to the Outer Banks for, and I know this from personal experience, it's to eat.

The ever-present gulls wheel and dive into skittering baitfish in the still waters of the sound. A single pelican perches on an ancient pier piling, gray and unused, which may have been the lone remnant from when a hurricane dismantled its wooden structure in the distant or not so distant past. Almost like humankind, the Outer Banks is everchanging: a briny soul that never sleeps, waiting for the next storm to come along and take a windborne bite out of it, similar to how twin deaths have taken a bite out of me, leaving both me and the Outer Banks to hope beyond hope that someone will love us enough to shore us up once again—myself with love, these fragile barrier islands with rebuilding, beach nourishment, and genuine caring for the environment.

To my right, a yellow kayak glides from behind one of the restaurants. The person wears a hat similar to mine, blue instead of straw. The double-ended paddle dips and rises. The bow surges. The stern leaves a feathering wake. Nearing me, Alex pauses to wave. Shoulders flex, biceps bulge, forearm tendons work beneath tanned skin. She's not only amazing, she's magnificent with the discipline it takes to not only acquire her level of physique, but to maintain it. What drives her to such lengths of commitment, I have no idea.

The bow of the kayak comes to a stop beside my rental. Alex looks up from beneath the hat's wide brim. "You rob a scarecrow of that straw hat?"

I take the sunscreen from my pack and slather it on my arms. "Sorry. Should've done this already."

"Amazing. I watch you get laid, you talk me into a trial date, and now you keep me waiting."

"Cool." I put the sun screen away. "I thought this was only a kayak trip, now it's a date." Daypack safe in the bow storage compartment, I ease into the wiggly vessel that has the stability of a canoe and take the paddle from its holder along the side. "You realize I can drown out here like I can in the ocean."

Alex backpaddles the kayak around to point it toward the marsh. "Too bad. I suck at mouth-to-mouth."

"Too bad, my friend left some tonsils for you." I paddle beside Alex and she splashes me.

"I'm still not over seeing that."

"Then why'd you stay long enough to see everything you saw? Got some pervert in you too?"

"Jake?"

249

"Yeah?"

"Do you want to visit that old house or not?"

"Does it have a king-sized bed for after we eat our breakfast I brought?"

"Uh-huh, with a king-sized alligator in it." Alex paddles away and I catch up.

"Don't joke. The wildlife people caught one in a Kitty Hawk canal a few years ago."

I follow her to within fifty yards of the marsh, struggling with ineffective paddle strokes to keep up. She's as much an artist with a double-ended paddle as she is with windsurfing. Each stroke, deep and hard, drives the kayak forward; the feathering wake transforms into an actual V behind her. Sweat beads her hairline, glistens along the *Freedom* tattoo. Muscular back rippling, shoulder blades working, she's a Greek statue, wet with morning dew.

On we go for maybe a half mile, until she takes a hard left toward the marsh and the building. The bow strikes mud. She climbs out and pulls the kayak into the marsh grass, brown and tall. She helps me do the same, saying we're not supposed to go into the building for safety's sake, which is why she's hiding our rides. Daypack in hand, I follow her up the faint impression of a footpath. "You've been here before?"

"Once in a while."

"Can I ask why?"

She doesn't answer.

"I like getting away by myself too. I'm not much of a social animal."

"Right, but get you alone with a bimbo" —she looks over her shoulder at me— "*then* you're an animal."

We arrive at the house, sided in weathered cedar like many older homes in the area. It also sits on pilings to keep it above floods from hurricanes. Alex eases up the creaking steps. "Careful putting your weight in one spot for too long. I haven't been here for a while, and the floor was sagging then." The door squeaks in on rusted hinges. Every window is either cracked or missing, letting in the briny aroma of the marsh. The floor is spongy beneath my feet. "Where can we sit and eat without falling through?"

Alex goes to one of the cracked windows. "Here's not bad. The rain hasn't come in to rot this section of floor."

We sit cross-legged. I give her a sandwich wrapped in foil. "Hope you like scrambled egg and bacon sandwiches."

She unwraps the sandwich. "Isn't it against the law to hate bacon in the south?"

"My feelings exactly." I pour coffee in a mug and set it near her sandaled feet. "Decaf, right?"

"Absolutely." She sips, I sip.

"You babysit, waitress in a restaurant, and ride a four-wheeler to harass people trying to surf fish. Do you have any other aspirations?"

"You mean as in making money ..."

"I hate to say so, but none of those things make a lot of money."

"I wait on rich old men at the restaurant and go home with them after. They pay me a thousand dollars a night and I'm worth every penny."

"A thousand dollars to do what? Change their diapers?"

"I bet your friend needed one after all that bouncing on the sofa."

I tap my coffee mug to hers. "Here's to no more talking about my male indiscretion."

"But it's so much fun." Alex takes a bite of her sandwich and chews.

"How old are you?" I sip coffee.

"Why?"

"You know, college."

"I'm taking some classes online."

"About?"

"Psychology."

"Any particular branch?"

"Disorders that affect the mind, like schizophrenia and bipolar disorder. A friend back home was diagnosed with bipolar disorder, and I found it amazing that lithium made such a difference."

"Where are you from?"

"Elizabeth City."

"What do your parents do?" I take a bite of sandwich.

"Dad died from a heart attack a few years ago. Mom overdosed on sleeping pills a year later. Dad's death tore her up, and I wondered if she did it on purpose or not. She didn't take that many, she took just enough."

"It could've been an accident."

"I told you how that guy hurt me. I can understand how losing someone you love can make you feel like dying." Alex wraps the sandwich, empties the mug, and puts both in my pack. She plays with the buckle on a sandal. The subject of loss is a sore spot for her. I reach over to shake her foot.

"Remember what I told you yesterday, about how I know what you meant about soulmates?"

"What about it?"

"I lost someone I cared about too. We were … it's hard to describe how great we got along."

"What happened?"

I don't want to get into the particulars with Alex. She'll ask more questions that I'll have a hard time answering since they can trace me back to Scotty. "She just up and left. We talked about getting married, having kids. I go to see her one day and she's gone."

"That's what happened with me. This guy … he was … it hurts to think about it. I thought we were perfect for each other. We could lie around all day and talk about nothing or anything. I kind of went a little nuts and started working out after he left."

"I wondered what drove you to work out like you do."

"After the weight started coming off and the muscles started coming on, I realized it was the right thing to do regardless." Alex uncrosses her legs and pulls her knees to her chest. "What's this about being independently wealthy?"

Here I go, time to lie again. "I worked in Greensboro as a bookkeeper. I try to live on the cheap, so I invested in some tech stocks when they first came out. Then, unlike all those people that pulled their money during the corona mess that hit the stock market, I bought low and did great when the market rose again."

"Lucky you. Did you buy my farm outright?"

"I sold my house in Greensboro to finance it."

"What about all the improvements?"

I shake Alex's foot again. "I'm a gigolo on the side. I'd do you for free."

She slaps my hand. "Sorry for being nosy. I really wanted to buy that place one day."

"Any chance your boyfriend would be my best man?"

A grin reveals those even teeth and slight downward quirk of Alex's kissable lower lip. "Oh, so that's how it is," she says. "I'm supposed to dump him and marry you so I can have my farm back."

I slide over to sit by Alex, take her hand, and kiss it. "Sounds like a plan."

"It's not bad."

"I'm sorry about that guy leaving you. I hope he tattooed an L on his forehead for loser."

Alex rubs an L on my forehead with her index finger. "That's you, loser. How do I know you didn't run out on that woman you claim was your soulmate?"

I slide my hand around Alex's waist, pull her close, and kiss her temple. "Because I couldn't hurt her any more than I could hurt you."

"You and your romantic lines."

"Tell me about your tattoo."

"I told my neighbor I wouldn't be gone long." Alex stands. I wrap the rest of my sandwich, swallow cold coffee, and put the mug and sandwich in my pack. "Can I see you again?"

"With romantic lines like yours, do I have a choice?"

"Not a one." I take a few steps on the spongy floor toward the door and stop to turn around. "When can we—" The floor gives way and my foot goes through up to my knee. Pain sears up my shin. "What a dumb move. I think a rusty nail got me."

Alex grabs my arm and helps me out of the hole, eases me to the steps and kneels. "It's a gash but not deep. Can you make it to the kayak? I'd hate to let anyone know we came here."

"It stings more than anything."

"I'm parked by the fishing bridge. We'll load the kayaks on my trailer and take yours back to the rental place and run to my house for first aid. Don't want to let that cut get infected."

"An invite to your place already? Cool."

In the kayaks again, we leave the marsh. I paddle close to Alex. "You know I did that on purpose so we can play doctor."

"You know enemas are good first aid for cuts."

My mouth, which is ready with a comeback for anything besides "enemas," falls open, and Alex says, "How did you like that for a romantic line?"

I close my mouth. "You'll say anything to see my ass."

Alex digs her paddle into the water and pulls ahead. Behind her, I admire each and every muscled stroke. To the south, the Roanoke Sound stretches to the horizon. The sun reflects off the water into my eyes, and I face northward, where the Melvin R. Daniels Bridge's separate walkways along its sides allow people to fish away from traffic.

We load the kayaks, return mine to the rental place, and I follow Alex in the 4-Runner to Roanoke Island. Passing Pirates Cove I wonder if Ted has a new house and a new wife yet, or even if he still lives in the area. Probably does. Gotta keep making the big real estate bucks.

At the intersection, where the Dare County Sheriff's Department is to the right, Alex takes a left. It's hard to believe Scotty's not there, questioning a suspected wife-killer. It's harder to believe she's not still alive instead of being killed in a yacht explosion in the Florida Keys. During the last two years, the memory of hearing *Out for Fun* explode—what I thought was a sonic boom—and seeing the orange glow of fire over the lights of Key West, visits my thoughts less and less. Still, when it does, the effect is the same: I miss Scotty more than ever, and if I dwell on her and the explosion long enough, I easily imagine the orange glow and the smell of burning rubber and cloth. My blow dryer once sucked hair into the intake, and the smell of burning hair made my hands shake, a PTSD legacy from Scotty's death by burning. Lucky for me those episodes never happen in public, or someone might ask why.

Alex continues along the two-lane road—marsh and scattered pines to the left, scattered pines and stunted hardwoods to the right, buildings and businesses few and far between—and enters the community of Wanchese. She takes a right, passes a few streets, and turns into a driveway flanked by live oaks. Their low limbs are trimmed back like amputated arms missing their clawed hands. We park side-by-side in front of a small home up on stilts, like most of those nearby, and meet at the steps. I start up but Alex grabs my arm. "You know how I said a neighbor is watching my niece?"

"Yeah?"

"The neighbor's my boyfriend."

I look at the door and look back. "You mean he's in there? Like *now* in there?"

"Don't you think I'm worth the risk of him kicking your ass?"

"That's a good point, let's go."

Alex grabs my arm. "Confession time."

"You're married."

"He's not my boyfriend. I've been telling you that to discourage you. Since it didn't, I decided to give us a chance." She joins me on my step and gives me a quick kiss. "Sorry about being such a liar."

I kiss her back. "My forgiveness is contingent on the level of your first aid. If my leg rots off, I'll just use you for sex instead of falling hopelessly in love with you."

Inside, Alex goes out a sliding glass door to a covered deck in back, where the "boyfriend" feeds her niece a spoonful of oatmeal. She says something to him; he glances my way and leaves down a set of steps. Alex waves me out. "Greg's a little protective. You still might get your ass kicked if you break my heart. Have a seat so I can introduce you to my cutie pie."

We sit on both sides of Alex's niece; she looks up at me with huge eyes, brown and liquid. She's the little girl I saw at the Y that day.

"Who he, Mama?"

I offer my hand. "I'm Jake."

She spoons oatmeal. "Want some?"

"Jake's already eaten," Alex says. "Wanna tell him your name?"

The headful of brunette curls nods. "I Izzie."

I look at Alex. "Did she say Lizzie?" I hope not. The reminder of Sammy and Mary Lou's Lizzie crying when Mary Lou and I went in the bar to find out what happened to Scotty is hard enough to deal with as it is.

"Izzie. Her name is Isabel."

"I Izzie," Izzie says. "Me no Lizzie." She leans over my knee. "Boo-boo?"

Alex takes Izzie from the chair. "Yep, I need to fix Jake's boo-boo. Grab Izzie's oatmeal, Mr. Boo-boo. She can eat at the coffee table while I clean your boo-boo on the sofa."

At the sofa, when Alex kneels to wipe my cut with a washcloth, Izzie twists her lips into a frown. "Hurt?"

"It will when I get the alcohol," Alex says.

Izzie pats my knee. "It okay, baby."

I split my face with a smile. "You, Izzie, are a mess."

In the middle of spooning oatmeal to her mouth, she plops it to my knee. "You mess."

Alex wipes it off with the washcloth, takes a tube of something she brought from the kitchen, and dabs it on my cut. "I doubt oatmeal works the same as anti-biotic ointment, Izzie."

Izzie rolls her eyes at Alex's statement, then pats my knee again. "Daddy."

Smiling, Alex tilts her head my way. "I think you've won her over. And without any romantic lines."

"Do I look like her dad?"

"Same color hair but not so curly." She stands. "It's kind of hard to put a band aid on such a long scrape. I'll get some gauze and medical tape."

Izzie grabs the TV remote. Alex comes back with the gauze and tape and takes the remote from her. "Greg said you already watched enough TV."

"Come here," I say to Izzie. "Wanna see a trick?"

She comes to me and waits. I close my hand, touch her nose with my knuckles, and poke the tip of my thumb between my curled index and middle fingers. "Gotcha nose, Izzie."

She touches her nose, verifying I'm full of crap, and does the same thing to my nose that I did with hers, showing me the tiny tip of her thumb. "Yo nose."

"I see that. Aren't you smart?"

"Me mart."

Alex sits beside me. "There you go."

"Kiss boo-boo, Mama."

I face Alex. "You heard her, Mama, pucker up."

"She said to kiss your boo-boo, not what you want."

"You didn't mind outside."

"Shut up."

Izzie widens her eyes and smacks Alex's knee. "You bad, Mama."

"I agree," I say, laughing.

"Good grief, now it's two against one." Alex leaves with the gauze and the ointment. "

I follow her down a hall to a bathroom, where she puts the gauze and ointment in a cabinet. "Thanks, doc. I guess I better go."

"You're giving up that easy?"

"Giving up what?"

"Asking me out on another date."

I place my lips next to the row of studs lining the curve of her ear. "How about a real kiss where Izzie can't see?"

"You're as bad as a two-year old."

I pull away and look Alex in the eye. "Is that how old she is?"

"Next month."

"She sure is cute. Calling me daddy was priceless."

"The jerk doesn't see her."

"That sucks. How can a man not love a sweet little girl like Izzie?"

"Don't get too attached. We haven't made that second date yet."

I finger the blonde bangs away from Alex's eyes and forehead and kiss her there, then the tip of her nose, then quickly on her lips. "Have anything in mind?"

"It doesn't involve sex."

"Then you *do* have something in mind."

Izzie's got a play date with Greg's nephew and niece tomorrow. His sister lives across the road. She keeps kids and keeps Izzie when Greg works."

"Your sister sure works a lot."

"She's at a training seminar for that corona virus outbreak for two weeks."

"The country should've closed the borders before it did, but some idiots were against that. What's your idea for our date?"

"I see you have a rod holder on your 4-Runner. Do you have a beach driving permit?"

"You wanna go fishing?"

"Sometime, not tomorrow."

"You don't have to work?"

"I work to supplement the life insurance from my parent's deaths. Gotta make it last, you know?"

"You're frugal, I like that. What are we doing tomorrow?"

"What sites have you not seen on the Outer Banks?"

"I've seen pretty much everything from Hatteras to Corolla."

"Good." Alex's lips twitch, trying to stop a grin. I slip my hand around her back and pull her to me.

"You've got something perverted in mind, sexy lady."

"Maybe, maybe not. Pick me up in the morning at six and you'll see."

"Sunrise sex on the beach?"

"You wish." Alex spins me around and shoves me through the bathroom door. "Out, before the coffee table's covered in oatmeal."

Chapter 31

I stay with Alex and Izzie until around five. Not wanting to invite myself to supper, I leave to run by the grocery in Manteo for a few things. My mistaking Izzie's name for Lizzie makes me think of Ted waiting in every aisle and around every corner. The bastard was so smug, taking pictures of Scotty and me in our room at the resort that day. No doubt he's as smug as he can get now, living it up with who knows how much he made from her life insurance. No doubt he's jetting the world, screwing every woman he can. No doubt, if I ever meet him face-to-face, I'm not sure how it'll affect me or, more importantly, how I'll handle it.

I drive to Jennette's Pier, walk out to the first benches, and lean against the handrail. Weathered and gray, it smells of dried fish and shrimp from people cutting bait for hooks. Scales from one and shells from the other cling to the scarred wood.

Unlike the day I fished, the breeze is gentle and warm, almost silky with its touch across my arms, face, and legs. The waves barely rise and fall on their way to the beach, arriving with hardly a crash against the sand. To the south, cooks in the Outer Banks Pier's restaurant send savory aromas of oceanic cuisine to water my mouth: flounder maybe, or fried oysters, or jumbo green-tailed shrimp, or scallops, sweet and delicate; a hamburger for a kid not into seafood, a steak for someone wanting something different.

Somewhere between the two piers, the oceanfront rental, Endless Love, hosts vacationers unaware of the tragedy not 100 yards from its back deck. I focus on where I think it is, about a quarter mile from the other pier toward me. My hands shake; my breath catches in my throat. The memory of when I pulled Andy from the surf on that October morning makes me turn away. If just looking for that house does this to me, how will I react if I see it again? I don't intend to find out.

Ever.

On the way home, when I leave Manns Harbor, the sun glows golden on the horizon. Its rays burst through distant clouds to fill them with light. Then, a mile from my driveway, the sun burns orange, followed with red, dusky and shimmering, similar to *Out for Fun* burning on the Gulf of Mexico.

Sobs come in a torrent. Brakes catch; tires squeal. I pull onto the shoulder of the road and climb out, stagger to the other side of the 4-Runner and fall to my knees to vomit.

Andy and Scotty, Scotty and Andy—twin ghosts haunting me for whatever reason. Is it possible to love too much? To want them too much? To want to take an October sunrise swim and join them both?

At home I call Leon. We chat about the mundane. His low voice calms me, makes me smile, makes me remember how much he loves his wife, makes me remember how much love I have left to give someone. I cradle the phone and look around the living room. "Who said that?"

I left the front door open, glass up, screen showing in the storm door. A voice rides the breeze, unclear at first and then clear, childish, lilted with North Carolina and Louisiana Cajun: Lizzie's voice.

You can't let this break you … you can't let this break you … you can't let this —

I drop to the sofa. "You're right, Lizzie, I know you are. Are your Mom and Dad doing okay?"

They worry 'bout you, Jonny. Scooty Poot's tryin' to find you and cain't. She done looked all over everwhere. Says it's time to move on without you. Says life's gotta go on for her an' y'alls baby.

"I know, Lizzie. Pray to her for me, okay? Tell her she and our baby need to go to the light. Tell her I'll be there soon."

I'll tell 'em, Jonny. You take care till then, till then, till —

I roll over and smack the buzzing clock — the red LEDs read 5 a.m. — and thud down the stairs.

The smell of the hamburger I bought at the grocery and cooked hangs in the air. The plastic bag that held the romaine lettuce I used for a bun is in the trash, along with the scraps of tomato and onions I sandwiched between the burger and the lettuce. The pan is washed, the dish and silverware too. A clean glass stands upside down in the strainer. I cooked, ate, cleaned, and don't remember a thing. The fridge reveals a six-pack of beer with four missing. That's it, that's what happened. I drank too much and did all that and went to bed and had a crazy dream about Lizzie telling me about Scotty.

Cereal and a banana suffice for breakfast. Dressed and groomed, seatbelted into the 4-Runner, dream all but forgotten, I leave for Alex's place at 5:30. Over the horizon, the hint of clouds, illuminated with smoky ochre highlights, reveals another day. When I thump over the first bridge joint at Manns Harbor, the clouds blaze orange. Halfway over the concrete span, I lower the vizor to block blinding yellow.

Alex. Me. What will today bring for us?

The sun rises on this positive note. Bangs slant over her high forehead. Earthen brown eyes look into mine. I grin like a schoolboy cracking the cover of his junior high yearbook to gawk at his first crush.

What is it about her? Not in a million years did I think a woman with studs in her ear and a tattoo and short hair would attract me this way. Long hair, Scotty's hair—all soft waves flowing over her shoulder and down her back—is my thing. Still, Alex's *Freedom* tattoo is a target for my lips. I could spend all night just kissing her neck: tanned and firm, corded and sensual. Well, maybe half the night. The rest of her deserves my attention as well.

Aside from her gorgeous self and amazing physique, what fool wouldn't admire intelligence and commitment and the work ethic to hold two jobs, including keeping Izzie as much as she does? Like us southern boys say, "My Mama didn't raise no fools," but concerning Alex, I'm well on my way to being a fool over her.

When I pull into her driveway, she comes out and down the steps to the driver side. "Hop out cowboy, this mermaid's driving."

I do as she asks. "Cowboys and mermaids, huh? Do I get to wear spurs when I ride you?"

She throws a day pack in the back and gets in. "So romantic so early." Silence follows us to the intersection to Manteo. We take a right. At the turn to Oregon Inlet, she takes it. "Did you have breakfast? We're in for a long drive."

"I'm good."

She cuts her eyes my way. "How do you like being kidnapped?"

"It depends on where we're going."

She raises her fingers to her lips and pretends to zip them closed.

"Cool," I say, "I prefer my women quiet."

She reaches over and zips my lips closed too.

We climb the Basnight Bridge. Waves crash into the bar. Sunlight glares off the inlet. Alex's tummy shows beneath the cut off shirt she wears. No belly button ring, just firm muscles and tanned skin. My eyes have a mind of their own. Long legs as tanned as her tummy, forearms and biceps too. The faint line of a sports bra over modest breasts, the barest hint of nipples. Blood rushes to my brain; temples thud with heartbeats.

"Alex."

"What?"

I unbuckle the seatbelt and lean over to kiss her studded ear, her ear lobe, her neck, slide my hand between her thighs, which she spreads.

"Jake."

I open my eyes and snap upright in the seat: I was asleep. "You ruined a great dream."

"Does the bulge in your shorts mean it was about me?"

"Naa, it was about my friend."

"I'm not crazy about your friend."

"I think watching us got you off."

"Shut up. We're at Rodanthe and I need to pee. You?"

"I'm good."

Alex parks at a convenient store and comes out minutes later with two coffees and a bag. In the 4-Runner, she puts the coffees in the console and gives me the bag. "Have a sausage biscuit."

I take two wrapped biscuits from the bag. "Two?"

"One's mine." She takes the biscuit from me. "Didn't get enough sleep last night?"

"Not sure." I sip coffee.

"How can you not be sure whether you slept or not?"

"Well, I—"

"Don't even try. Your friend came back, didn't she?"

"I'd turn her down if she did."

Alex sips coffee. "Because ..."

"I promised I wouldn't hurt you."

"You didn't promise."

I look out the window and then look back. "That's how I meant it."

"You're sweet."

"I mean what I say."

Her eyes dart from mine. She gives me her wrapped biscuit. "Unwrap that for me so I can eat and drive. We need to get there before the lines get too long."

We leave Rodanthe, eating and sipping coffee. The only place on Hatteras Island with vehicle lines is the ferry to Ocracoke. I'm touched by her desire to share it with me. History abounds on the Outer Banks, and I've read a few books about Hatteras Island but never about Ocracoke. One interesting tidbit is how German U-boats sank ships at will here in the early days of World War II. I shove that thought from my mind, too similar to *Out for Fun* burning in the night off Key West.

Biscuits and coffees finished, I put the cups and wrappers in the bag and toss it in the rear floor. "Thanks for breakfast."

"No problem."

"Does your tattoo have anything to do with the guy who hurt you?"

"Someone before him."

"Pasts suck."

"That's why it's on the back of my neck, it's always behind me."

"Did he hurt you as much as the other guy?"

"Not my heart."

"Just another jerk?"

"I'd never get a tattoo to commemorate ditching 'just another jerk.'"

"Then may you never get one for me."

A quick smile. "And vice versa, Jake."

First kisses, not those quick pecks like Alex and I shared on her steps yesterday, have engraved themselves into my heart from both Andy and Scotty. When Alex and I share our first real kiss, my sincerest hope is that it blurs those other first kisses to the point of easing the pain and nothing more. First loves should never be erased; they should be remembered fondly, recalled when a new love is within arm's length and you realize she's the spark that lights the way out of all those lonely, dark places in the night, where dreams blur into nightmares of one body lying drowned on a beach while another is reduced to ashes in an instant.

I face the window to finger a tear from one eye. If my heart is ever to be engraved with Alex, it needs to be soon.

We drive through the communities of Waves, Salvo, Avon, and view the black and white candy-striped tower of the Cape Hatteras Lighthouse looming in the distance. Buxton, Frisco, and Hatteras are next, and we stop behind one of the lines waiting for one of the ferries that takes vehicles back and forth between Hatteras and Ocracoke.

Alex shifts the transmission in park but leaves the engine and air conditioning running. "Not too bad, maybe thirty minutes."

"I've always wanted to visit Ocracoke."

"Me too. Now we get to keep this memory if you ever ditch me."

"Not happening, Alex." I unbuckle the seat belt and turn in the seat to face her. "Did your dad name you?"

"Mom did. It was Alexa originally."

"Trimmed it down, huh?"

"Dad did that and I'm glad. I don't want people calling me the same name as that Amazon gadget. Alexa, turn on the heat. Alexa, turn on the AC. Alexa, order pizza."

I grin while Alex frowns and tilts her head side to side with each Alexa sentence. "You're not one for taking orders, huh?"

"That's what the jerk thought he could do."

"What if I said, Alexa, it's time for our first kiss."

"I'd bite your tongue for calling me Alexa."

"Fair enough. Alex, it's time for our first kiss."

"You had that yesterday."

"You know what I mean."

"Patience is a virtue, Jake, and I'm worth the wait." She puts the transmission in drive. "Here we go. Is this your first ferry ride?"

"Sure is."

The 4-Runner jars over the metal ramp. A man waves us to a parking place behind the car in front of us. A waist high railing, thick and painted with black paint, is to my right. "Wanna get out?"

"Let's wait until we leave the dock."

More vehicles park behind us. The last is a huge Cadillac Escalade SUV in gleaming black.

The ferry's engine rumbles beneath us, vibrating my seat and the floorboard. In the side view mirror, the lines of cars waiting for the next ferry draw away. Alex and I get out and weave between the surrounding vehicles until we arrive at the bow. A fence made of yellow webbing stretches across the opening; we must drive off this way at Ocracoke. Her bangs flutter in the wind. Ahead of us lies the unending expanse of the Pamlico Sound. To the east lies the sliver of sand called Ocracoke Island. I face Alex. "How long is Ocracoke?"

"Sixteen miles long from the ferry landing on this end to the village on the other end."

"Isn't there another ferry landing on the other end? I think I saw it on a map one time."

"They go from there to Swan Quarter and Cedar Island." Alex tugs my beard. "Die that black, you could be Edward Teach."

"Blackbeard, you mean."

Alex closes her eyes. Her chest rises and falls with a deep breath. She opens her eyes. "I love the Outer Banks for the beaches, but I love the history too. From Ocracoke to Manteo to Corolla, it's loaded with stuff like shipwrecks and the Lost Colony and the wild Spanish Mustangs. There's a small herd on Ocracoke. Back before cars, the locals tamed them to ride and plow their gardens."

"You sure know a lot about Ocracoke."

"I've read a few books."

I lean against the rail. Ocracoke grows larger. Someone behind me shoves by. A man and a woman stand beside Alex, and I clench my fists. The man is Scotty's widower, Ted. The woman, a Barbie doll blonde, tall and slim, wearing a huge diamond ring and matching wedding band, must be his new trophy wife. Ted lights a cigarette. Wind blows smoke toward Alex and she twists her lips into a frown. "Why do some people think they can light a stinking cigarette with other people around? I can't stand the things."

I go to Ted and tap his back. "Think you can put that out? It's bothering my wife."

Ted turns. "Then tell her to go somewhere else."

"We were here first. *You* go somewhere else."

I'm tempted to headbutt the bastard. Instead, I take Alex's hand. "It's a shame they let egotistical jerks with no

269

consideration for others on these ferries. Let's find a spot where this one isn't."

We go to the ferry's center, where we climb stairs to an air-conditioned sightseeing tower. "Be right back," Alex says. "Gotta lose that coffee."

She returns. "We better get to your ride so we'll be ready to offload."

In the 4-Runner again, we wait. The ferry docks bow first and we drive forward. I glance in the passenger side mirror. The black Escalade isn't moving. Ted gets out and kneels by what must be a flat tire. "Ain't that a shame," I say. "Mr. Jerkface has a flat."

Alex grins my way. "I saw him get out of his Caddy. Good thing too, I'd hate to let the air out of someone else's tire."

"You did that?"

"I didn't need to pee, I needed to deflate an asshole."

"Aren't you a bad girl? I think I'm in love."

Alex steers us onto a two-lane road and accelerates. "From what I saw of your so-called friend at your place, you're into bad girls."

"Jealous?"

"I can be bad too."

"Promises, promises."

"Shut up and enjoy the scenery. We'll have an early lunch and see some sites and beat all the cars back to the ferry."

"Do you have plans for me at your place?"

"You have yet to sing me that song."

I take one of her hands from the steering wheel and kiss it. "Vanilla?"

"I'm trying a new sunscreen."

Holding Alex's palm to my mouth as if it were a microphone, I hum the tune to *I Only Have Eyes for You*. She jerks her hand away. "That's not singing."

"That's solo singing, as in so low you can't hear it."

"Pure country boy, huh? Corny jokes and all."

"Who even picks and grins while playing the guitar."

"Right. Wheat straw between your teeth at the same time too, I bet." She points to a sign on the side of the road. "There's the wild horse corral but I don't see any."

"Some stallion's probably got one of the mares in a compromising position."

Alex cuts her brown eyes my way. "A position you'd like to get me in."

"You'd buck me off."

"Because?"

"I'm sort of well endowed."

"Yeah, right, like a sea horse. An eensy weensy itty-bitty sea horse."

"My friend didn't complain."

"Well, if and when that happens with me—that's a huge if, in case you get any ideas—it's been more than two years since I've had sex, so I'll buck for sure."

"In a good way or bad way?" I point at my crotch. "You know, with me being well endowed and all."

"You are so full of yourself."

"Only because I'd like to fill *you* with myself."

Alex steers into a roadside restaurant. "A burger is the only thing I want to fill myself with right now."

"I pictured you for a hot dog girl. Want fries with that?"

"Fries and no hot dog, Mr. Sexual Innuendo."

Since it's early, and few people are eating, we get our food fast. I forgo lettuce for a bun, add ketchup, and dive in. Alex fingers ketchup from the corner of my mouth. "You're as bad as Izzie."

"I noticed Greg was sort of quiet when I came over."

"Did you see the scars on his arms?"

"No."

"He has them on his chest too. They're burns from a car accident a year ago."

"Was he quiet because he's depressed from it?" I drink water with lemon.

"What do you know about bipolar disorder?"

I remember Jerry at the mental health place. "A guy back home has it. He didn't like taking his meds. Said they kept him from being creative."

"Did anything set his bipolar off?"

"He never said."

"It's dormant in some people until they suffer some kind of trauma. Greg's accident set his off. He was a mess until he started taking lithium."

"That's what the guy back home takes." I start to ask if Greg's okay, but Alex wouldn't trust him with Izzie if he weren't.

She swirls a fry in ketchup. "That guy with the Escalade … any chance you've seen his picture in the Outer Banks real estate advertisements in those magazines most of the stores have in their lobbies?"

"You mean the ones they put out for tourists?"

"He's a big real estate guy. Lots of cash. His wife died in some kind of boat accident in the Florida Keys in November of 2019."

I pause to concoct a lie. "I wasn't around then."

"She was the sheriff. I saw them in the restaurant a few times. She was nice enough but he was a real jerk." Alex eats the fry and sips water.

Her dredging up of the past—my past—isn't the least bit expected. "At least she got away from him," I say. "If he's as bad as you say and we saw, she's better off in Heaven."

"Maybe she has a tattoo like mine on her neck. To be free from a jerk like him is good reason to get one."

I take a bite of burger, much better because of the toasted bun, and wash it down with water. "You never told me about your tattoo. Well, about the guy who hurt you."

"Another time, okay? This day is about us."

I clink my glass to hers. "I like the sound of that. How about tonight?"

A smooth foot rubs my calf. "We'll see, Jake, we'll see."

We finish lunch and hop in the 4-Runner. Alex drives to Ocracoke Village, turns down a backroad, and I say, "If you're looking for a place to park so we can fool around, we could've stayed at your place."

"I'm looking for something I've always wanted to see. I told you how I like history."

"And?"

"We went right by the sign."

"I was too busy thinking about your foot rubbing my leg to notice a sign. In fact, Alexa, any time I'm with you, I hardly see anything else."

"Watch that Alexa crap if you ever want that kiss." White headstones come into view. She parks. "I've seen pictures of it in some of those books. It's near this cemetery, but we have to walk to it."

I meet Alex at the front of the 4-Runner. "What are we looking for?"

She takes my hand and leads me between headstones, through the cool shade of live oak trees. We walk too fast to read the engravings. On the older stones, weathered and pitted, lichen etches gray veins through names and dates. "That," she says, pointing toward a white picket fence ahead, "is what I want to see—the British Cemetery."

"Why are British people buried here?"

At the fence she points again, this time toward a plaque attached to a post. Behind it, within the area surrounded by the picket fence, four headstones stand, stark white in the shade of more trees around the fence. I read the plaque:

These gravesites contain the bodies of four British seamen.
Their ship, the armed Trawler HMS Bedfordshire, was on loan to our Navy
by Great Britain to help protect our shores during the early days of World War II.
On May 11, 1942, the Bedfordshire was torpedoed and sunk by a German sub.
All hands were lost and these four were the only bodies recovered.

Sweat pops on my forehead; my knees weaken. I don't read the last sentence, something about the Coast Guard taking care of the graves.

BOOM!

I look into the sky for the jet that made the sonic boom. No. The last time I heard that was when Scotty—

My knees shake. I stumble away, flames flaring in my vision—flames that incinerated the love of my life—and grab the coarse bark of an oak to throw up.

Alex comes over and rubs my back while I heave. Minced globs of chewed hamburger and french fries spew from my mouth, mixed with the full glass of water with acidic lemon. I have to lie about this by telling her it's something I ate at home and not PTSD from someone's death haunting me. At least I have my head on straight enough to realize that instead of thinking it's a bizarre dream where I'm not sure if I slept or not. One thing for sure, this crap needs to stop before it ruins any chance I have with Alex. I stand and wipe my mouth.

"Whew, sorry about that. I think it was something I ate last night."

"You feel better?" The concern and caring in her brown eyes and endearing voice makes me smile.

"Not just anyone would rub a guy's back while he throws his guts up."

She rubs my arm. "In case you haven't noticed, I'm not just anyone."

"I noticed that the first day I met you."

Alex palms my cheek. "I'd kiss you if it weren't for your puke breath. Ready to go?"

"Not if you want to read that other plaque about the ship."

"I read it while you read the other one. It's a list of all the men who died on the Bedfordshire. Imagine those men so far from home. They came all the way here to help us because we didn't have the ships to protect our coast after Pearl Harbor. That's what I call honor and sacrifice."

"You like those old-fashioned values?"

"I sure do. Under my pixie cut, studs, tattoo, and green streaks in my hair, I'm an old-fashioned country girl straight from the south."

I pat my chest a few times. "Be still my beating heart. I thought I was falling in love and now I know I am."

"Right. Let's get you in the air conditioning where it's cool. I've got plans for you later and don't want to get home late."

In the 4-Runner, I buckle my seatbelt. "As long as your plans don't include a hamburger and fries."

Chapter 32

After a long wait for the ferry, where we stay in the cool AC, then the drive to Hatteras, I ask Alex to stop so I can get a ginger ale to rinse the yuck from my mouth and drink the rest to ease my stomach, which isn't queasy at all. I hate lying, but that's all I can do. Meeting Ted was bad enough; the last thing I want to think about is ships exploding with Scotty on them.

We continue north along Highway 12. Sand stands in huge piles along the ocean side shoulder, pushed into place by bulldozers and front-end loaders after the last nor'easter. Some people say the Outer Banks won't last much longer because of global warming. Such a death sentence for such an amazing place saddens me. All I can do is enjoy it as much as possible with the time I have left on this earth, preferably with Alex.

By the dashboard clock, we arrive at her place roughly two hours later, at 2 p.m. Inside, I flop on the sofa and kick my sandals off. "Mind if I make myself at home, Alexa?"

She goes to the kitchen and comes back with two beers. "Shut up if you want one of these and a kiss."

"I'm too pooped to pucker." I sniff my funky underarms. "Mind if I use your shower?"

"So you can tempt me to shower with you?"

"I knew we were on the same wave length." I take the beer.

Alex lowers the bottle and licks her lips. "Shower all you want." She drinks again. "Without me. Everything's in there you'll need—shampoo, soap, washcloth, towel. You can even shave your legs if you want."

I get up and drink the beer in one long pull. "Whoa, icy. Be back in a few."

In the shower, I vow to shove my stupid thoughts, dreams, nightmares, whatever, about Scotty out of my head. Alex makes me the happiest and most satisfied I've been since Scotty, and I need to concentrate on her before I mess things up.

My clothes are too funky to wear again. I slip her pink robe on and go to the living room to turn around. "Whatcha think?"

"Not bad." She goes to the bathroom and comes back with my clothes. "I'll wash these so you can put them back on. I'd like a shower too, and I'll need my robe."

I untie the belt. "Want it back now?"

"Don't even go there, pervert. I saw your underwear in your clothes." She goes to a washer, throws the clothes in, and starts the cycle. "Extra clean for extra stinky."

"Sorry about leaving my stuff in the bathroom. I was gonna get them."

"Darn right you were. You're not trying me out for housewife material. Any man I marry's gonna do his fair share of the daily duties."

"You just wanna marry me for my house. Then you'll divorce me and sweet talk the judge into letting you keep it."

"You figured me out. I'm getting that shower."

I walk around the living room. Interesting observation: no family photos, not even of a sister, although photos of Izzie are scattered on a table by a window. A couple were beneath magnets on the fridge door, one as a newborn. There are no photos of Alex by herself either, just a few selfies with Izzie on the beach.

I go down the hall and tap on the bathroom door. "Got enough hot water?"

"What?"

"Can I join you?"

"What?"

I go back to the sofa. Can't blame a guy for trying.

Wrapped in a towel tucked in at her cleavage, Alex comes in, hair dripping. "What did you want?"

I look up at her. "That should be obvious after I threw my lunch up."

"I have plans for supper. It's early yet."

I yawn. "Mind if I take a nap in your robe until then? You can put on some clothes."

"I can dry my hair in a towel." Alex's feet patter down the hall. I go to her bedroom, take off the robe, and climb between the sheets, cool from the AC. Her pillow smells of flowers, probably from hair conditioner when she showers before bed. Afternoon sun casts oak limb shadows on white curtains. I yawn again, in need of more sleep than I got last night.

It's interesting how time passes in that magical place between dreams and sleep, how daydreams darken to night things, like wishes of someone waking you with the soft fingertips brushing your forehead, of warm lips kissing your cheek.

"When you said you wanted a nap, I assumed you meant on the sofa."

I stretch. "Best nap I've head in two years."

Alex lifts the sheet. "Where's my robe?"

"On your dresser." I slide over. "How about a snuggle?"

"My towel isn't enough deterrent."

"Time for some trust, pumpkin."

Alex blinks, blinks again. "A new pet name?"

"It's just sort of popped out." I raise the sheets. "Please?"

"Time for trust, huh?"

"Why not?"

"And you won't try to romance me out of my towel?"

"Not even if you want me to."

Alex climbs in, pulls the covers up, and snuggles into my shoulder. "Isn't this nice?"

"I hope you like tents."

"Camping's okay, why?"

"My tent pole is gonna make a tent with you naked against me."

"Nothing naked is touching you except my legs."

"Yeah, but—"

"I thought I could trust you." She props on elbow and looks me in the eye. "You did say you'd never hurt me."

"If I hurt you, I'd be hurting Izzie. That'll never happen."

"There you go, being sweet again."

"I'd like kids one day—a girl first, then a boy. Take Izzie for example, she already calls me daddy."

"She only called you that once."

"She'd be easy to love." It's my turn to raise on elbow and look Alex in the eye. "Let's promise not to hurt each other. Forgiveness is easy when you care about someone, but honesty should keep people from hurting each other to start with."

"Honesty?" She tilts her head to one side. "Are you lying to me about something and you want to get it off your chest?"

I kiss her forehead, nose, and follow with a kiss to her lips, light and quick. "Something great is happening between us and I don't want anything to mess it up. When were you gonna tell me Izzie's your daughter?"

Alex's lips part for a count of three. "Why do you say that?"

"No family photos anywhere but of her. I realize you might have some photo albums around with your parents in them, but since your sister's still alive, and since you have plenty of photos of her, and—"

Alex places her fingers over my mouth. "And since I never told you my sister's name ..."

I move her fingers. "Thanks for reminding me. So why tell me Izzie's your pretend sister's daughter?"

"You tell me. You *did* figure it out."

"One reason might be because you didn't think a guy would want a woman with a built-in family. Another could be because you only want a sexual relationship and nothing else. The last reason is you were gonna tell me when you knew you could trust me enough to forgive you for lying about Izzie."

"Which one do you want it to be?"

I roll over onto Alex and pin her arms beside her head. "My mama didn't raise fools, pumpkin. All I want is sex."

Alex wiggles her hips. "Your tent pole collapsed."

"A few kisses would raise it again."

Alex's expression softens; the muscles in her tense body relax beneath me. "It's too soon, okay?"

I roll over. "I'm just teasing. Have I earned your trust?"

"Close your eyes and you'll see."

I do as requested; the bed shakes. "Open your eyes," she says.

I do that too. Alex stands beside me, wrapped in the robe again. "You're just about perfect, Jake, but I want a man who's as good in the kitchen as he is in bed. How are you at shucking oysters?"

"I never tried."

"You're gonna try tonight." She slips panties and shorts on, strategically doing so to keep me from seeing those curvy attractions I strain to see, and grabs a sports bra and a blouse. "Take your nap. I'm running over to a seafood market for a steamer bucket to cook here. We'll pig out on oysters, shrimp, crabs, corn on the cob, and whatever else catches my appetite."

I don't mention my vomiting episode at the British cemetery. Besides, since it was brought on by my emotions instead of bad food, the steamer bucket sounds great. "What about Izzie? I'd like to get to know her better. You know, being her daddy and all."

"You're really amping up the sweetness factor. Her play date is also a sleepover."

I get out of the bed. "You, pumpkin, assume a lot."

"You don't want to sleep with me?"

"I'm not stupid."

"To sleep, nothing else. I'm not ready for a sexual relationship."

"You could relate with yourself while I watch."

Alex's mouth falls open. I hold my hands up. "Just kidding, I'd love sleeping with you and nothing else. Want some money for the steamer bucket?"

"I got it. You made my day by forgiving me about Izzie."

By the time Alex gets back, I'm dressed in my clean clothes. She sets the bucket on the stove. Steam soon jets from beneath the lid, sending out the aromatic aromas of crabs, corn, and whatever else is inside. She also bought more beer. I put four bottles in the freezer.

A great day on the Outer Banks, a great supper planned with this great woman, and nothing in the way but my stupid dreams and throwing up at the cemetery. That crap's gonna stop if it's the last thing I do. And if I'm really, really, lucky, love will settle its fickle finger on both our hearts before the night is over.

On the table on the deck, Alex spreads sheets of newspapers, drains the steamer bucket in the sink, and pours the contents on the papers. I get us a beer apiece and a stack of napkins. She gets two oyster knives and two shell crackers she bought with the beer.

Crab shells pile the paper. Alex says she forgot something and comes back with melted butter and cocktail sauce. We chew bits of succulent crab meat: sweet, juicy, and buttery. We pop oyster shells open and eat them with their briny liquid or dip them in spicy cocktail sauce. Every other bite or so is washed down with beer; bits of ice float in the bottles. Every other bite or so includes buttered and salted corn on the cob, along with baby red skin potatoes, tender and earthy. I go for the other two bottles of beer and sit again. "This is amazing."

Alex works an oyster knife into a shell. "I know, right? It's like devouring the entire Outer Banks in one sitting." The shell pops open. "Except for the oysters. We're not known for those."

I dip a shrimp in butter. "We're known for green-tailed shrimp, that's for sure."

"I really like being with you, Jake. You're …"

"Sexy?"

"Yes, but …"

"Funny?"

"That too, but …"

"You think I'd make a great daddy for Izzie?"

"Surprisingly so, after not knowing you hardly any time at all, yes."

"I'm sure teaching the kids at the Y helps."

"I'm not explaining myself very well." Alex slurps the oyster from its shell.

I swallow beer, wincing at the icy hit on my teeth and down my throat. "I know what it is—we're like two old shoes, broken in and comfortable with each other."

Grinning, Alex waggles a finger at me. "Exactly. That and it feels like we've been together before. Know what I mean?"

"Hey, I wouldn't wear just any woman's pink bath robe."

"And I wouldn't hop in bed with just any naked man either." Alex drinks beer. "Let's finish eating, cold seafood sucks. Then we can find an old movie on TV and snuggle on the sofa."

Stuffed with supper and beer, we gather shells and empty corn cobs for the trash, wash our hands in the sink, and go to the sofa. Alex thumbs the remote and channel surfs. "As much as I pay for cable, you'd think something worth a flip is on."

I take the remote and turn the TV off. "Is the guy who hurt you Izzie's dad?"

"Yes."

"I'll never understand how some dads don't love their kids."

"He didn't know about her."

"Why did he leave?"

Alex leans her head on my shoulder. "I didn't give him a choice."

"Is that all?"

"It hurts to think about it. I regretted it and tried to find him." She sits up, wipes a tear from her cheek. "Would you believe I was so stupid as to not get his cell number? I did online searches through those people finder sites. I even went to his hometown and asked around, a total waste of time."

"You wanted him back ..."

"I looked until I had Izzie. Life moves on, you know?"

Those earthen brown eyes draw me in. I kiss those blonde, almost white bangs slanted across her forehead, finger several green strands, and look into her eyes again. "What's your idea of a perfect life?"

283

"It's corny."

"Find and keep a soulmate, right?"

"And enjoy the simple things. Like I said, I'm a country girl at heart. Give me a farm and a garden, even some chickens, I could be happy."

"It's better shared. That's my ideal too."

"I don't want to sound like a broken record, but you *are* sweet."

I let the moment bloom between us: two molecules of emotion in a sea of curiosity as to which one of us will say those words first—those words every human can't wait to hear—but only if it comes straight from the heart.

"Jake, I—"

"I know it's too soon. Today was only our first date."

"How much time do we give ourselves?"

"It's not something to rush."

"Then why do I get the feeling you're ready?"

"We're two old shoes, remember?"

Alex turns, leans against me, and pulls my hands around her. "You make me feel safe."

I laugh. "You? The muscle-bound wind surfer slash kayaker slash weightlifter? I make *you* feel safe?"

"Shut up."

"And let's not forget the woman who let the air out of that guy's tire on the ferry."

"He deserved it. He never loved his wife."

"You say that like you knew her."

"What kind of relationship did they have if she was in the Florida Keys without him?"

The reminder of Scotty keeps me from commenting.

"I told you how Izzie's dad had brown hair but not so curly."

"And?"

"You remind me of him in other ways."

"How so?"

"Your eyes and your voice."

"Your voice is similar to the woman I told you about. Other than that, that's it."

"How is it similar?"

"Kind of low. I haven't heard her in over two years, so that's all I remember. She smoked too, so that could've been it."

"Yuck. I think we know my opinion on cigarettes from that jerk on the ferry."

I nuzzle the nape of Alex's neck. "I like your vanilla sunscreen."

"That's some lotion I'm trying." She turns in my arms. Earthen brown eyes find mine. "Want to take me and Izzie to the beach Saturday?"

"You're working the rest of the week?"

"Six hours every day lifeguarding."

"What about late afternoon?"

"One of the waitresses is out sick, so I'm working at the restaurant every night. I'll use that excuse to beg off Saturday, and you'll get your fill of us both."

"As disappointed as I am to not spend any time with you and Izzie until Saturday, I admire your work ethic."

"Like I admire you teaching the kids guitar." Alex takes my hand and kisses the palm. "Where have you been all my life, old shoe?"

"I could ask you the same."

Alex stretches those tanned legs, muscular and toned, out on the sofa. The shorts she wears ride high on her thighs, smooth and shining in the lamplight. The shirt is another cutoff. My hand rests on her slightly six-packed abs, where I rub a teasing circle around her navel. She leans her head against my chest. My finger works lower, to the waistband of her shorts, and slips beneath the snap. Alex puts her hand on my hand. "I'm not ready for sex, but ..."

I unsnap her shorts. Heat and moisture, moisture and heat. Hurricane Scotty is now Hurricane Alex, and I think Scotty would approve.

Almost immediately, Alex cries out. I have never wanted a woman more in my life. She lifts my head, pulls me to her for a kiss. "That, sir, was amazing."

I grin hugely. "Ready to get married?"

She grins back. "Don't tempt me."

We return to our former position on the sofa, her back against my front, my arms around her, our hands clasped at her flat tummy.

Isn't life amazing, for two old shoes who fit together as great as Alex and I do to find each other?

Absolutely.

Alex admits she wanted sex but isn't on the pill. I admit to not having condoms. We both admit we should behave the rest of the night and go to bed, me in boxers and her in a sleep shirt. Part of her reason, she admits, for how she wants to wait for sex, is because the last time she went to church was after Izzie was conceived, and guilt about our antics on the sofa nags her somewhat. I say I understand and I do, that the last time I went to church was a while back too. Of course, that was with Scotty, and I'm glad I can think about her without the same stress I experienced at the British Cemetery.

Alex and I kiss and say goodnight. She snuggles up to me— hand on my chest, head on my shoulder—like we've been together for years. Life can't get any better. As far as sex again, she's worth whatever wait it takes, even if that wait is marriage. Again, since my mama didn't raise no fools, the best thing is to take things slow and easy and let Alex make any suggestions about more sleepovers, sexless or not.

* * *

We wake to the sound of her phone alarm. She tells me to sleep until breakfast is ready. I do until she shakes my shoulder. "Daddy sleep."

I open my eyes; Izzie grins. "Daddy wake."

Behind her, Alex pats Izzie's head. "I tried to get her to tickle you instead of shaking your shoulder."

"Smart girl, Izzie. Your mama's trying to get you in trouble."

Izzie points to her chest. "Me 'mart, Daddy."

I look up at Alex, tears in my eyes. "And you call me sweet."

She sits beside me. "Aw, don't cry. I had no idea you were so tender hearted."

"It's just—" I wipe my nose. "It's just that I have everything right here in this room I ever wanted, you know?"

Izzie runs to the dresser for a tissue and comes back to shove it under my nose. "Blow, Daddy. Got boogie."

My tears turn to laughter. I grab Izzie in a bear hug. "If you aren't the sweetest little girl in the world, I don't know who is."

Alex takes Izzie from me. "Let Daddy get dressed so we can eat and I can go to work."

Alex closes the door. "Eat, Daddy!" Lizzie yells with her little girl's voice, high-pitched and insistent.

Grinning like a maniac I get dressed. This is the most I've ever been bossed around by two females in my life.

And I like it.

A lot.

287

Chapter 33

Wednesday, Alex calls between lifeguarding and waitressing jobs to remind me about us taking Izzie to the beach Saturday. I visit a kite store in Nags Head and find one I think Izzie will like: a green sea turtle. The two-line stunt kites tempt me, but I'd hate to take someone's head off. Being June, the beaches are crowded, and having never flown one of those things—the videos in the store looked fun—that could happen.

I also choose the sea turtle to see if the memory of the sea turtle with a flipper missing—the one I saw with Scotty on *Out for Fun*—will cause me any anxiety like my memory of the yacht burning caused me at the British Cemetery. It does not, but the bottlenose dolphin kite bugged the heck out of me. The vision of Mr. Darcy gently nudging Lizzie Bennet's lifeless body will haunt me forever.

Thursday, Alex calls between jobs again and puts Izzie on the phone. She babbles about TV and cartoons and a friend named Jimmy and a friend named Nora, calling me daddy at the end of every sentence. Alex takes the phone to tell me Jimmy and Nora are Greg's sister's kids. In the background, Izzie yells, "We play, Daddy!" and my heart continues to melt.

Izzie comes down with a sniffle Friday. I promise to take her and Alex to the beach when she's well. Saturday afternoon, when I call to check on Izzie, her sniffles are miraculously cured. Alex asks if she and Izzie can pick up a pizza and bring it to my place for supper, and I say "Yes, absolutely."

Around three I run to the grocery for beer and a bottle each of white and red wine—one of them should go with pizza—along with the makings for tossed salads. Back home I make fresh-squeezed lemonade for Izzie—none of that powdered junk for my girl—and clean the counters, sweep the wood floors, and mop the linoleum in the kitchen and bathrooms.

Alex and Izzie arrive at five sharp. Brunette ringlets bouncing, Izzie runs to me with a stuffed starfish toy named Susie clutched in one hand. I pick her up for a hug and put her down to help Alex with not one, but two pizza boxes. "Whoa, we're gonna carb out tonight."

"I didn't know what you like. I got one supreme and one veggie."

"Both are great." In the kitchen, I open the fridge. "Beer? Wine? I got red and white?"

"Red with pepperoni, why not?"

I pour wine and lemonade, grab a beer for me, and we all go to the dining room table, where plates, silverware, and plenty of napkins wait.

Alex opens a box to reveal mounds of cheese, mushrooms, green peppers, black olives, tomatoes, and pepperoni. The scent of melted cheese and tomato sauce doesn't make my mouth water, it makes it flood. Izzie stands in her chair and points at the pizza. "Don't want 'roni, Mama."

Alex opens the other box. "That's another reason I got the veggie—the pepperonis are too spicy for her."

Plates filled, I take a cheesy bite, and Izzie waggles a finger at me. "No, Daddy."

I chew, swallow, and face Alex. "What'd I do wrong?"

"Show Daddy, Izzie."

"Izzie puts her hands together and bows her head. "Bless Mama ... bless Daddy ... bless Izzie. No bless 'roni, amen."

I tousle her curls. "You, Izzie, are a mess."

"I 'mart. Pizza, pease."

Alex cuts a slice into bite-size pieces and gives them to Izzie. "I'm glad the people didn't turn this place into a winery."

"Ready to move in?" I take another bite of pizza.

"The idea of fresh vegetables from our own garden is tempting."

"How big a garden?"

"One big enough to work with one of those reverse-tine tillers. Not too big, though. I'm not into canning."

"I could get a tractor."

About to bite a slice of pizza, Alex stops. "When I was asking around about this place, one of the realtors said the man who used to own it died when a tractor rolled over on him. A tractor sounds like bad luck."

"It must. Your face went white."

"They also told me his daughter found him. Just thinking about that ..."

I take Alex's hand. "That doesn't mean it would happen to me."

"No tractor, Jake." Her voice rises a notch.

"Just a lawn sized one, that's all. No need to get upset."

"Can we just eat?"

Izzie eyes Alex and then me. "Bad, Daddy."

"I guess you're right, Izzie."

We eat in silence. The pizza doesn't taste the same as when we were happy. Izzie spills lemonade and Alex snaps at her. I wipe the table with napkins. Everyone loses their appetite. Izzie goes to the sofa and sits with her toy starfish.

Off and on all day, the North Carolina heat and humidity has been building, evidenced by the mountains of cumulonimbus clouds filling the sky, glowing white with the sun behind them. Their foothills grow dark and roiling. In the distance, lightning illuminates a patch of darkness.

I wash dishes, Alex dries. Except for the clink of silverware on the sink, quiet envelopes us.

Dishes done, she sits by Izzie and apologizes for snapping at her. Izzie says nothing.

I go to the window that overlooks the old garden spot, where the faint rise of old rows and the twist of grass-covered soil marks the place where Scotty's dad died so long ago.

Footsteps patter on the wood floor; arms encircle me. "I'm sorry, Jake."

Her breath warms my ear. I want to raise her hand and kiss it but don't. We've crossed a line I didn't see coming, a line that tells me something's wrong between us. That day Izzie made me cry, when Alex said she didn't know I was so tenderhearted, returns. Yes, I'm tenderhearted. A man who vomits and cries to the point of near hysterics when he loses his wife is tenderhearted. A man who vomits at the picture in his mind of a yacht and the second love of his life burning is tenderhearted. A man who passes out when he returns to the rental house where he and his wife spent only one honeymoon night together is tenderhearted.

The storm hits. Wind whips the trees. Lightning flashes, thunder crashes, rain pounds the tin roof, then stops.

"Is Izzie afraid of storms?"

"She asleep on the sofa. She's a lot stronger than me."

I sense more in this statement than I hear in Alex's low voice. "You really loved her dad, didn't you?"

291

Alex takes her arms from around me and moves a few steps away. "Jake, I ..."

"He's been gone two years, Alex. He's never coming back."

"Never's a long time, Jake."

"You're gonna wait for him the rest of your life while I'm here right now?"

"Part of me feels that way."

"At least you're telling me now, before Izzie and I get attached to each other." I get the leftover pizza from the fridge and shove it at Alex. "You want this place, you can have it. I'll rent it to you for fifty damn dollars a month and move to who the hell knows where. I can't fall in love with someone again and have them rip my heart out. I almost didn't survive the last time, no way I'll survive this time."

Alex doesn't take the pizza. "Didn't you hear me say *part* of me wants to do that? If you could have the chance to start over with whatever woman hurt you, wouldn't you take that chance?"

"Thanks for the warning. Here I am, ready to practically propose, and you tell me even if you fall in love with me, you'd go running back to Izzie's dad regardless of how much he hurt you."

"You're not listening, I said only part of me thinks that way. Yes, if he came back, it'd tear me up inside." Alex pauses. "But he's not here and you are." She takes the pizza, puts it in the fridge, and comes back. "I'm scared, okay?"

"Who isn't when it comes to relationships?"

"We've only known each other a few weeks and it scares me to think I love you already."

"That's not a bad thing."

"I want to make sure it's love instead of what it could be."

"Like what?"

"Wishing for a dad for Izzie. Wishing for someone to talk to. Wishing for someone to do nothing with, or anything."

Alex saying she thinks she might love me already gives me hope. Sure, a glimmer of hope, but I'll take hope any way I can get it.

I grab her hips and pull her to me. "Don't forget wishing for someone to fool around with on your sofa."

A smile appears with those white teeth, even and perfect. "You were amazing."

"Glad to hear it." I kiss a streak of green hair slanted across her forehead. "How do we overcome all our angst concerning your past?"

"It's my angst, not yours."

If only that were true, with the ghosts of Andy and Scotty hovering at the edge of my consciousness to reveal themselves when I allow it. "Be that as it may, ideas?"

Wrinkles furrow Alex's brow. "I'm willing to take a chance on getting hurt if you are."

"You mean keep seeing each other? What happens if Izzie's dad comes back, you just up and leave? That ain't happening."

"I don't know what I'll feel for him until I see him."

"That's not the least bit fair to either me or Izzie."

"It is what it is."

Lightning strikes. Thunder rattles every window in the house. Izzie doesn't stir. The rain returns in inconsistent taps on the window, following with windblown sheets of water that runnel along the panes. Take this chance or not? Three strikes, you're out, Gilligan. Might as well drive to Endless Love, dig Andy's sandals from their sandy grave, and hang them along with mine on the fence and follow her and Scotty into the sunrise one October morning if Alex and I don't work out.

Alex holds me, rests her head on my shoulder. "Please give me a chance, Jake."

"I want to, but ..."

She pulls away and grabs her neck. "Look, a million I love yous are right here in my throat, just waiting to come out."

"Then let them."

"I think I will ... in time."

My first inclination is to ask how much more, but the possibility of hearing Alex say she loves me a million times stops me. "You know those small propane grills people use to tailgate with?"

"They use a cylinder that screws on the side, why?"

"When's your next day off from both jobs?"

"If you have interesting plans, I'll get someone to fill in for me. Does it involve my sleeping princess on the sofa?"

"You know it does. Call me when you know what day you want to take off. I'll pick you and Izzie up the next morning."

"I don't get to know what we're doing?"

"It'll be a surprise."

Alex grabs my belt and pulls me to her. "Like the surprise you gave me on my sofa?"

"Good thing Izzie wasn't around."

"I like surprises. I might have one for you sometime soon."

I wrap my arms around Alex's narrow waist and nuzzle her neck, sweet with vanilla lotion. "Like what? Getting on the pill so my swimmers can swim in your ocean?"

"Well, I guess I *was* sort of tropical that night."

I let her go; she pulls me back. "What's wrong? Got a bulge in your boxers?"

"If anyone should know."

Alex turns around and presses her bottom against me. "How about now?"

I turn her around. "Stop that."

She goes to the sofa and sits by Izzie. "Come over here and listen to the rain while I think about my surprise for you."

I do as she says. "Good thing your shirt covers your tummy. We know what happens when it doesn't."

"Hush and listen, Jake, hush and listen." She settles against me, warm and firm. Even with the thought of some jackass coming back to take her away from me, I'm happy again. A fight, a battle, a war—none of those describe what he'll get from me if that happens.

The storm fades, leaving the gentle murmur of rain in the darkness gathering around us, along with its ozone aroma. Izzie's breaths are soft. Alex's breaths grow soft too, as sleep takes her. No lamps are on. Headlights pass on the road every few minutes.

To have this moment is a miracle.

A miracle I never thought I'd have again.

I can only wonder what the next days, weeks, and even months will bring for Alex, Izzie, and I.

Chapter 34

Alex calls Sunday night to tell me she's free from both jobs on Monday. I drive to the local home improvement store and buy one of those portable propane grills and two tanks. Monday around ten a.m., I get a beach driving permit at the Nags Head Town Hall and drive to the tackle shop for another surf rod combo for Alex. Not wanting Izzie to feel left out, the purchase includes a kid's rod and reel combo that's pretty much a toy. Hot dogs, condiments, bottles of water, milk for Izzie, ice, and tossed salad fixings go in a cooler. Chips, buns, and chocolate chip cookies go in a bag. The cookies are for anyone with a sweet tooth.

At Alex's place, Izzie runs out with her toy starfish, yelling, "Car seat, Daddy! Car seat!" It isn't hot yet in the shade of the oaks; I melt regardless. Alex brings the car seat out. I strap it and Izzie in. Alex comes back with her day pack, which, she says, holds both adult and children's sunscreen and the blue hat she wore the day we went kayaking. Since, as I always say, my mama didn't raise no fools, my corny straw hat's in the back with everything else.

We head south at the intersection of 158 and Highway 12, toward Oregon Inlet, and Alex looks my way. "I always wanted to drive out on the beach at Oregon Inlet and surf fish and have a picnic."

"How do you know that's where we're going?"

"How can you forget we're like two old shoes already, Jake?"

An "Uh-oh" squeaks behind us.

"What?" Alex asks Izzie.

"No shoes, Mama."

"Your sandals are in the bag, okay?"

"Tank you, Mama."

"You're very welcome, Izzie."

"Daddy?"

I look at Izzie's reflection in the rear-view mirror. "What's up?"

"Daddy?"

"Yes?"

"Daddy?"

"Yes, ma'am."

Izzie points at Alex. "Kiss Mama."

I glance at Alex. "Did you tell her to say that?"

"No, but it's a good idea."

I look at Izzie again. "I never noticed she has green eyes, not brown like yours."

"My mom's DNA, I guess." Alex kisses my cheek. "Satisfied, Izzie?"

"On his yips, Mama."

Alex and I both laugh: two old shoes with their tongues flapping at the curly haired mess in the back seat.

I enter the beach access ramp on the north side of the inlet, stop to lower the tire pressure to avoid getting stuck in the sand, and drive through dunes until we reach the surf. Sunlight sparkles on the aquamarine Atlantic. Waves roll and crash. Along the section of sand that stays wet from the wave's rise and fall, leaving a sheen of glimmering moisture pockmarked with bubbles that form miniature geysers, we pass sanderlings in their search for a meal. Izzie says, "Birds, Mama!" and squeals with laughter when they run toward the retreating foam, backward-kneed legs a blur, pencil thin beaks probing the sand like miniature feathered jackhammers, only to run and flutter away from the next wave as if they're afraid to get their three-toed feet wet. Here and there, four-wheel-drive vehicles parked with multiple surf rods extending from front bumpers identify hard-core fishers of whatever species is biting. In June it's speckled sea trout and flounder, both worthy fare on any table.

Roughly halfway between the Basnight Bridge and the bar, where Stan and I crossed three years ago come this October to spread Andy's ashes, I park with the rear bumper facing Oregon Inlet. Gratitude fills me. The occasion carries no hint of tragedy, and the weather—clear skies, an airliner contrail here and there, enough wind to keep one fairly comfortable—is perfect.

Alex releases a squirming Izzie from her car seat. I open the 4-Runner's rear door. We both unload everything, stick two sand stickers beside the beach towels Alex has laid out, and add the surf rods. Izzie takes her toy rod before I can show her how to press the button and cast and runs to the water, wet diaper bulging beneath her yellow one-piece swimsuit. Alex calls her back, changes her diaper on one of the towels, slathers sunscreen on her, and plops a child's wide-brimmed straw hat on her head. "Look," she says, pointing at me, "you've got a hat like daddy."

Izzie drops the toy rod, takes the hat off, and studies it. "Little hat. Daddy big head." She puts the hat back on, picks up the rod, and runs on a circle. "Daddy big head, Daddy big head, Daddy big head."

Alex takes her T-shirt off to reveal a skimpy bikini top in lime green to match the streaks in her hair and the polish on her finger and toe nails. Pervert that I am, I can't stop looking at her tanned six-pack abs. The breeze feathers blond bangs across her forehead. Stunning doesn't do her justice. She comes over with a bottle of sunscreen. "Take your shirt off, Daddy. Time for lotion."

I pull my T-shirt off. "Do I get to do you?"

"My back and nothing else. Can't have you fishing with a bulge in your boxers."

I turn around. Cold sunscreen hits my back, followed by warm hands rubbing firmly. "You'd be an excellent masseuse, young lady." I glance over my shoulder. "You know I'd be a great one too, right?"

"We already covered that on my sofa that night."

"Not quite the same thing."

She gives me the bottle. "Do your front and your legs before you do my back."

"I'll do my legs, you do my front."

"Have it your way." Alex squirts a streak of cold sunscreen across my chest, which makes me cringe.

"You do realize I get to do the same thing to you."

She rubs my chest. "We need to get your pecs in shape, Gilligan."

Scotty's name for me while we were in the Keys surprises me. "You like that old show?"

"Izzie loves the reruns."

I grab Alex and rub my stomach on hers. Instead of shoving me away like I expect, she wraps her arms around me for a kiss: long, deep, and intense.

Something whacks my behind. "Fish, Daddy." I scoop Izzie up and blow a raspberry on her plump belly. She drops the toy rod and squeals laughter in my ear.

I put her down. "Geez, police sirens got nothing on you, you little squealer."

Alex rubs sunscreen on her chest and stomach. "That's what I said the last time she did that." She gives me the sunscreen. "Do my back so we can see who catches the first fish."

With bottom rigs baited with shrimp on one hook and cut mullet on the other, we cast the pyramid weights into the water, reel the lines tight, and return the rods to the sand stickers. Izzie comes over and I show her how to cast the plastic weight on her toy rod, which she does at the water's edge between Alex and I.

We stand for a moment. Alex brings the beach towels over. We lie down to watch for the telltale pull on a rod tip that marks a fish taking the bait. Izzie comes over and plops down between us. "I tired."

"I'm hot," Alex says, fanning her face. "We'll have to bring a beach umbrella next time."

"When's your birthday? I'll get you one."

"You did that on my sofa. And very nicely, I might add."

Izzie eyes us both in turn, and I say, "We need to watch what we say, Mama."

"True. Izzie, can you get us a bottle of water from the cooler?" Alex watches her scurry away. "Her birthday's next month. I'm inviting Greg and his sister and her husband and Jimmy and Nora."

"What about me, pumpkin?"

"Who do you think is gonna cook the hot dogs and hamburgers?"

"Do I get a reward after?"

"I'm still working on that surprise I told you about."

I look back at Izzie, tugging at the cooler lid. "Is sex involved?"

"You get to cook some more."

"I heated you up on the sofa. How long before I get my surprise?"

"I'm thinking October is the best time for it."

I get up from the beach towel. "Sounds interesting. Let me help Izzie with the cooler." Although I have no idea what Alex's surprise is, if it includes me cooking, maybe it involves a sleepover with breakfast, which I'll enjoy even more if something happens at night besides sleeping.

On the towel again, cold water cooling our throats, I ask Alex if she and Izzie would like to look for shells while I watch the rods. Izzie hops up and grabs Alex's hand. "C'mon, Mama."

I wait until they're absorbed in searching the sand for shells, then go to my bait cooler for a whole mullet, tie a hook in place of the plastic weight on Izzie's toy rod, hook the mullet to it, cast it into the water, and yell for Izzie to come get her rod before a fish pulls it in.

She comes running, losing her hat in the process, brunette curls bouncing, and takes the rod from me to crank the reel. Eyes narrowed, she grunts, "Uh, Daddy. It too big."

"Reel him in, sweetie, you got him."

The mullet, as long as my hand, breaks the surface. She keeps reeling until it hangs in the air at the end of the rod and looks around at Alex. "Look, Mama!"

"I see, I see. You caught the first fish, baby!"

My cheeks ache from grinning, and they ache again on more days like this.

The following weekend, we catch enough fish to have at home that night. The next Monday, when nothing bites, I teach Izzie how to fly the green sea turtle kite. Two weekends later, she waits until all the invitees finish singing Happy Birthday before she blows out the two candles—with more spit than air.

Filled with hot dogs, burgers, and beer, the party goers leave. Izzie falls asleep in the floor in front of the TV. Alex and I snuggle and kiss on the sofa. To say I'm happy is the biggest understatement of my life.

We repeat these wonderful times at my place when her work schedule allows, sometimes with Greg or his sister babysitting. Snuggles and kisses turn into partially clothed touching and Alex in my lap with nothing but panties and a sports bra on, wiggling her hips and moaning. I remark on her willpower. She says I have no idea how much willpower she has. I say I know by how hard she grinds against a certain excited something of mine.

The first week of October, on a Saturday afternoon around four, she comes over by herself, says Izzie's with Greg's sister, and plops onto the sofa. "Remember that October surprise I have for you?"

"You're gonna undress and wrap a big red bow around your waist?"

"You'll like that it involves a blindfold."

I sit beside her. "I hope you brought one."

"It also involves you calling your guitar students and telling them you need to cancel this coming week."

I make the calls. "Now what?"

"Go upstairs and pack a suitcase and your bathroom stuff for a week. My stuff's in my car. Make sure to pack sandals."

"Are we eloping to Hawaii?"

Alex swings her leg over and sits in my lap. "We'll see." We kiss. My hands slide between her shirt and her back to rub smooth skin, warm and muscular, and fine shoulder blades. She hops up. "No, sir. Pack that suitcase so I can blindfold you. Then you'll see what your surprise is."

I get up. "A week on Ocracoke?"

"Don't even try."

"A week in your bed?"

She points toward the stairs. "Now!"

What man doesn't love surprises, especially when they involve a gorgeous woman who wants to blindfold him. I do as I'm ordered and go back downstairs. Waiting by the sofa, she pulls a bandana from her pocket, folds it a few times, and twirls a hand in the air. "Turn around like a good boy."

I put the suitcase down and turn. "Should I get the surf rods?"

She places the bandana over my eyes and snugs a knot. "Are they in the barn?"

"Them and the cooler and the tackle."

"Good idea. We'll definitely fish to keep you from attacking me every time I turn around."

"Well, it's too cold to swim, that's for sure."

Alex takes my hand and leads me to her car, which is a lot lower than my 4-Runner, and pushes my head down as I get in. "Off to jail with you, pervert."

"No handcuffs?"

She clicks my seatbelt; the door slams. The trunk lock clicks. The car shimmies when she loads my suitcase. Minutes later she returns to open the back door. "I should take your 4-Runner to fit the rods and tackle box and cooler."

"We still can."

"The cooler and tackle box fits on the seat fine. Good thing the rods are two-piece. I can break them down and shove the ends between us."

Graphite clatters; she shoves the rods against my arm on the console. The back door slams, followed by the driver door and her seat belt clicking. "I hope you show the proper appreciation for all my efforts this coming week."

"I will if you brought baby oil for a massage."

The engine turns over. "My mama didn't raise no fools, Jake."

At the end of my driveway, we take what feels like a left, evidenced by centrifugal force swinging me to the right. "Ah, we're headed toward Manteo."

"And?"

"Just an observation."

"No more observations until I take the blindfold off, jailbird."

"Yes, ma'am. Don't forget the handcuffs when I give you that massage. I want to be in complete control."

Alex says nothing. I concentrate on the drive to feel where she's taking me. Cars pass to our left with slipstream swishes of air. Here and there an eighteen wheeler's tires rumble by; their slipstreams shudder the car. Counting the seconds to determine the minutes frustrates me and I quit. The car tires thump over the first joint of what can only be the Virginia Dare Bridge, connecting Manns Harbor to Roanoke Island. More thumps follow, at least five minute's worth, before the road quiets across Roanoke Island.

Alex brakes us to a stop at what I think is the intersection to Manteo. "Any guesses yet?"

"You could take a right to your house for a quick roll on your sofa."

"I knew better than to ask."

We accelerate. More thumps of a bridge resonate beneath the tires, what must be the Washington Baum Bridge to the causeway. The thumps end. Before long the smell of frying seafood comes through the car vents, signaling us passing the causeway restaurants. Alex brakes. I shift to the left with her right turn. We're headed down Highway 12, either to Rodanthe, Waves, Salvo, Avon, Buxton, Hatteras, or Ocracoke.

But am I right? She doesn't accelerate as usual. We can't be going more than thirty-five. The tires don't sing like they would otherwise.

I try counting seconds again until I get frustrated. "I have to admit, you've got me fooled bigtime."

"Good. That means it'll be surprise bigtime."

Maybe another minute passes. We slow and turn left, ease along quietly, and enter some kind of shade. "We're here, Jake."

"I can tell. It's darker beneath this blindfold."

"Sit tight while I unload our stuff. Be back in a minute."

Doors open, rods clatter, doors close. All is quiet. The trunk opens and closes. More quiet. My door opens. Alex takes me by the arm. "Out, jailbird." Like at my place, she puts her hand on my head to get me out of the car without bumping my noggin. She walks me along slowly and stops. "Lift your foot for the steps. There's a rail to your left to hold if you need it."

Weathered wood, cracked and warm from sunlight, meets my palm. My guess is we're going to stay at a beach house in Nags Head somewhere. My foot finds flat floor. A door squeaks open. "One more step and you get to see your surprise."

I take a step. Air-conditioned coolness floods my body. Alex tugs at the knot in the bandana. "I guarantee you're gonna love this place. I've always wanted to stay at an oceanfront rental for a week. Now I get to do it with you."

She takes the blindfold off, leaving me as completely speechless as at any moment in my entire life.

We're standing in the beach house that Andy rented for our honeymoon.

The one and only—Endless Love.

Chapter 35

Pine floors, juniper paneling that extends to high ceilings, an open-plan house with the kitchen to the right, TV and living room to the left, and the sofa where Andy and I kissed before she went to the bedroom for the lace nightgown—each memory jars me to the core.

My knees buckle. I go to the sofa and manage to sit instead of drop. "Whew, climbing the steps blindfolded made me dizzy."

Alex sits beside me. "Do you like my surprise? I think it's great."

I cover my eyes so she won't see the pain in them. "Sorry, I'm kinda overwhelmed. This is the nicest thing anyone has ever done for me."

"Aw, don't cry." She puts her arm around my shoulders. "You're such a sweetheart."

If the next week here doesn't kill me, nothing will. Still, I have to suffer through it. I don't intend to dredge up my tragic past and ruin any chance Alex and I have of a permanent relationship. Gritting my teeth, I uncover my eyes to take in her brown eyes. "Seriously, this is great." I kiss her. "And you're great too."

She goes to the kitchen. "See the bags? I paid for early check-in and bought groceries for the week." She opens the fridge. "Eggs, milk, water. Maybe we can catch supper in the surf for a couple of nights. We can still go out some if you want. You didn't see it, but there's a propane grill under the house where I parked. We can buy a nice steak too."

To my right, the back door, glass paned, gives me a view of the deck where Andy and I made love, our bodies damp with mist from the rougher than average surf that night. The deck is between the master bedroom and the breakfast nook, blocking any view from the rentals on either side of us.

Alex goes to the door. "Lots of privacy for fooling around under the stars at night."

It's all I can do to speak through the nausea filling my throat. "I thought—" I swallow. "I thought you weren't ready for sex."

She comes over and sits beside me. "I visited a gynecologist last week. I do feel guilty about it to an extent, but the pill will let us do all those things you've been wanting to do since we met." A leg covered in faded denim swings over my lap. "I want to drive any memories of that so-called friend of yours as far away from you as possible. Wanna start now?"

I close my eyes and see Scotty's green eyes. If she were here instead of Alex, I might be able to deal with all this. That includes the memories of Andy and her sandals, which I buried beside the fence she hung them on before she made her final walk to the ocean.

Alex digs her fingers into my ribs. "Open your eyes and stop thinking about that friend of yours before I pack all this stuff and leave you here."

I do as she asks. She rewards me with a bright smile from her even teeth. What I wouldn't give to see Scotty's smile, with her slightly crooked bottom teeth. Alex gets up. "Let's take a walk on the beach."

307

"You don't get enough of the beach on that four-wheeler when you're watching swimmers?"

"That's different, that's work. We could sit on the deck if you want. I never get tired of listening to the waves."

I take my phone from my pocket to check the time. If we go out to eat, that's an hour or so I don't have to feel like Andy's and Scotty's ghosts are trying to drag me into the Atlantic. I also might need to call Leon to help get me through the week. "My phone's dead and I forgot my charger."

"Who were you gonna call?"

"I was checking the time to see if it's too early for supper. I'd like to go out for a steak if it's okay."

"And two glasses of red wine to go with it. Just enough so the alcohol doesn't affect what happens when we get back tonight."

We change clothes. Alex comes from the bedroom in a yellow, knee-length skirt, a white blouse, and black high-heels. The blouse's V-neck reveals modest cleavage. I go into the bedroom and come out in tan slacks, a turtleneck shirt, black and snug, and loafers.

"Don't we look great?" she asks, fingering her hair out of her eyes.

"You do. With this beard almost to my chest, I look like a reject from the homeless bin."

She goes to the bedroom, returns with a brush, and runs it through my unruly curls. "You could use a trim after we leave next Saturday. Until then I intend to use your hair for a handhold as often as you'll let me." She finishes my hair and turns me around. "I hope my surprise gives you an idea of how much I care about you."

"It does." My voice comes out flat and unconvincing.

"Is that all?"

"I guess I'm overwhelmed."

"Uh-huh, like you said while ago." She gives me a quick kiss. "The major overwhelming comes after supper. Let's go."

No sooner than we leave the driveway, my nausea eases. How I'm going to get through a week of dealing with Endless Love, I have no idea. One step at a time is all I can do, starting with Alex's plans for later. Pretending she's Scotty is worth a shot, as much as I hate doing it. Still, pretending she's Andy is out of the question, especially with those sandals buried beside the fence.

Supper passes quietly. I even enjoy a rib eye, baked potato, and salad. Alex and I make small talk about unimportant subjects over wine. From time to time I catch her watching me as if I'm a science experiment, and I wonder if it's because of my reaction to her dual surprises of an oceanfront rental for a week and her birth-control revelation.

The restaurant's pretty nice: a band plays soft jazz on a stage in front of a dance floor. Alex comes from the lady's room and asks if I'd like to hum *I Only Have Eyes for You* in her ear, that the management might throw us out if I sing. What can a guy do but acquiesce to such a request by a gorgeous woman leaning over him with the V-neck of her blouse open to reveal such a sexy body?

We join on the sparsely crowded dance floor—her arms around my neck, my hands at the small of her back—both of us swaying to the sound of mellow electric guitar, husky alto saxophone, and the rhythmic thump of an upright bass. At a time like this, a kiss is as natural and expected as the tides, and I take full advantage of this location—not Endless Love—to kiss Alex. Her lips are soft, warm, and smooth with sheer lip balm that tastes like peaches. Tongues dart and touch. Bodies press together. I end the kiss. "We better stop before I have trouble walking back to the table without everyone eyeing my crotch."

Alex grabs my butt and pulls me against her. "Is that your way of saying you're ready to leave and see how many stains we can make in that huge king-size bed at the rental?"

"Well ..."

"I bet we can make more than you and your friend made in *your* bed."

"Are you ever gonna stop bringing that up?"

"I will when I prove I'm better than she is at all the things she did to you on your sofa." Alex leads me to our table, sits, and takes a credit card from her purse. "My treat, Jake. This is a night you'll never forget."

At the rental, when we park, and the motion detecting driveway lights, including lights that illuminate the walkway under the house, come on, the fence where Andy's sandals are buried brightens into view. Cursing under my breath, I despise my phone and its dead battery. That call to Leon might get me through the night, if not the rest of them.

Inside, I ramble through grocery bags. "Got any baking soda I can mix with water? I don't feel so hot after all that food."

From behind me, Alex slips her hands around my waist. "Baking soda? Why do you think I would bring that?"

"No reason."

"We don't have to do anything tonight if you don't feel like it."

I turn in her arms. "You're the best, you know that?"

"I just don't like seeing you feel bad, like that day at the British Cemetery on Ocracoke. Talk about sick."

"I'm not that bad now. Maybe it'll pass later."

"I brought baby oil for your massage."

"That means lying on my stomach."

"Oh, yeah, I didn't think about that. Want to find something on TV?"

I go to the fridge for a bottle of water. "Good idea. Between that and sipping cold water, maybe I'll get better before bedtime."

We go to the sofa. Alex thumbs the remote. I drink water. She finds some old black-and-white movie I'm not familiar with. I put the water bottle on the coffee table and yawn, which has its intended effect of causing Alex to yawn. "Wow, I've had a long day," she says. "I think I'll get ready for bed."

She goes to the bedroom for a nighty that shimmers like black silk in the hall lights. The bathroom door clicks as it closes. She still plans to show me how much she cares about me and I can't let that happen. Sprawling on the sofa, I close my eyes. Water runs in the bathroom. An electric toothbrush hums. Water runs again. The bathroom door clicks open and Alex pads barefoot toward the sofa. "Jake, c'mon to bed. Jake?" The TV goes silent. She clicks the lamp off. Good thing she didn't shake my shoulder. The bedroom door clicks closed.

Of all the oceanfront rentals in Nags Head and South Nags Head, why did Alex pick this one? And that's not including all those in Kitty Hawk and Kill Devil Hills. Cool from the AC taking the heat off the house from the warm day, I go to one of the other bedrooms for a blanket and return to the sofa to cover myself.

Outside the doors leading to the deck, waves crash with dull regularity: nature's liquid metronome timed to the beat of my heart. About a mile away, Andy's ashes lie at the bottom of the Atlantic. Much farther away, roughly 1100 miles by bus and rental car, Scotty's ashes lie at the bottom of the Gulf of Mexico. Two loves lost within five weeks of each other, and I'm the person who lost them. What it'll take to get over both, I have no idea. Even a third love asleep in the nearby bedroom, who likely cares about me to the point of admitting she loves me soon, can't help.

And I mean at all.

Despite the anguish of my situation muddling my thoughts, or maybe it's because the stress of my situation exhausts me mentally, the warm blanket soon has me yawning for real. Like oak leaves fluttering along the Blue Ridge Parkway in fall, all red and orange and spicy scented, I fall into a chasm of shades of color: blonde and brunette hair soft within my hands; into sensations: kisses and shuddering orgasms; into sounds: moans and whimpers of release; into silence: Scotty and I wrapped within each other's arms in as real and as genuine a love as any man can experience once—let alone twice—and never—not ever—three times.

No man is that blessed.

Jake.

I don't open my eyes to the voice. It's an illusion, a doppelganger, a fake.

We need to talk, Jake. It's time to face the music. You pays your money, you takes your chances. Time to finish this, Jake.

I've been expecting this ever since I found Andy in that freezing October surf three years ago. In the kitchen I check the magnetic calendar I saw earlier on the fridge. What are the chances?

Three years ago tomorrow.

You pays your money, you takes your chances.

That's right, Jake. Come talk it over before the sun comes up, all crimson and shimmering and gorgeous above the ocean's aquamarine swells ... above the ocean's aquamarine swells ... above the ocean's aquamarine swells ...

I follow his voice to the bathroom on the other end of the house. He's considerate, wanting to talk it over away from Alex, who's asleep and dreaming in the dark, possibly dreaming of the life that she and Izzie want to share with me, the life that simply cannot be because it's time I finish paying for what I've done and not done.

My loafers whisper along the heart-pine floors. A night light glows in the hall. Somewhere in the dark, the central air conditioning unit hums soft and low: a funeral dirge to remind me of what's to come.

In a bathroom for another bedroom, when I click the light on, nonother than Jonathan Smith—alias Jake Smith—stares back. He's about thirty pounds overweight: puffy cheeks, thick around the middle. His hair is cut close; his face is cleanshaven.

He raises a finger to point at me. "You can't let two people die and not pay the price, Jake."

"I know."

"That's good, Jake, that's good. No need to fight it, right?"

"No need to fight it."

"That's right, you could've saved them and you didn't. Now another woman loves you, and you can't let her death be on your conscience. We got that clear, right, Jake?"

"Can I write and tell her why?"

"Just let her know where you're going like Andy let you know where she was going with her footprints."

"I really am in love with Alex. All I want is to be with her and be a dad to Izzie. You know, to make up for not being able to be a dad to Scotty's girl."

"Water under Basnight Bridge, Jake, water under Basnight Bridge." My plus-sized reflection tilts his head to one side. "No backing out, okay?"

"I could—"

"Nope, you gotta be a man about this so Alex can get back the man she lost. That's who she wants, Jake, not you. Besides, Izzie needs a real dad, not you. You know that, right?"

"I know that."

"You got our plan straight in our heads?"

"Yes."

"Good, Jake, good. Set the alarm on your watch for 6:30, right when it starts getting light. Gotta time it right, you know."

I set my alarm. "I know."

"Good, Jake, good. Now go on back to the sofa and get some sleep." Jonathan holds his hand up as if he wants a high five. I touch my hand to the mirror. When I lower it he's gone.

On the sofa again, I start to pull the blanket to my chin but get up and dig through kitchen drawers for a pen or pencil and a piece of paper instead. Jonathan's right about a lot of things, but he's not right about me telling Alex what I need to tell her.

A pen and pad are in the third drawer. I click the pen.

Dear Alex,
More than anything I want to be with you and Izzie, but there are too many things in my past I wish I could undo and can't. As much as I love you and Izzie, I'm afraid those things will damage you like they've damaged me, and that's the last thing I want. If you ever find Izzie's dad, and if he still loves you, don't let the memory of me get in the way. You can't let this break you like my past has broken me.
Love, Jake.

I read the note, short and sweet, and nod, satisfied. No need to write more: get it over and done with, for both mine and Alex's sakes.

On the sofa again, I fold the note, leave it on the coffee table, and close my eyes to wait for my watch alarm.

I'll be home soon. And if I'm lucky, as well as blessed, I can tell Andy and Scotty how sorry I am for letting them down.

Chapter 36

When my watch alarm beeps, I'm still awake. Rubbing my bleary eyes, I get up and go to the glass-paned doors leading to the deck. A thin line of dusky ochre—bloody clouds illuminated by the sun rising beneath them—spans the eastern horizon. No wind disturbs the sea oats scattered in clumps along the crests of the sand dunes. No gulls wing either north or south in their dawn search for a morsel of some sea creature to break their fast. No sanderlings scurry back and forth in the foam feathering upon the rise of the beach, where I sat three years ago, beside my dead wife.

My greatest desire at this moment—even greater than my desire to end my pitiful excuse for a life—is to go to the bedroom and watch Alex sleep.

I'd turn the lamp on and kiss those blonde bangs sweeping across her high forehead. I'd smile as those defined lips purse with dreams. I'd cry at the thought of tears streaming from those beautiful earthen-brown eyes, with hints of sea green. What secrets do her eyes hold? Secrets from the time she loved another man to the point of waiting for him so long? Secrets from whatever drove her to exercise to the point of shaping her body into a mix of Olympic swimmer grace and Olympic gymnast muscle mass?

Cold air greets me on the deck. Two steps down, beside a picnic table—weathered gray from the constant exposure of salt mist—is where Andy spread a blanket on the deck for us to make love for the first time at this rental. I continue to the walkway leading toward the Atlantic, stop at the steps that descend to the mound of wind-blown sand that partially covers them, and turn around. No lights brighten the bedroom. Alex is still asleep, blissfully unaware of what she'll find when she wakes.

I go down the steps and dig into the sand at the fence, find Andy's gritty sandals, and hang them and my loafers side by side by shoving the toes over the narrow strips of wood. Alex won't know what this final tribute to Andy means but I will, and that's what matters. My wife of one night and I spent those short hours in love as much as the six months we lived together, when she suggested moving in one spring day as we kissed on a blanket in a field of wildflowers.

This memory wells tears I'd hoped wouldn't. I leave footprints behind me on my way to the surf and into the rising globe of the sun, all golden and shimmering within the ribbons of clouds hanging above the horizon.

My sock feet meet the sheen of wet sand, wetted by a departing wave, which leaves foam like white lace on Andy's nightgown that night. Now, up to my knees ... now, up to my thighs ... now, up to my waist. I'm thankful for the ocean's calm: no sand is violently sucked from beneath my feet to topple me over. I can take my time dying, and the gentle pull of current and outgoing tide will ease me down beside Andy, where we'll spend eternity together.

"Jake!"

I continue walking, water to my chest.

"Jake! What are you doing!" Water splashes behind me; someone grabs my arm and jerks me around. Her eyes are the most intense shade of emerald green I've ever seen. Scotty's come to see me off. "I'm sorry," I say. "I hope you know how much I love you."

"What's wrong with you, Jake? What are you doing?"

"It's time."

"You said you'd never hurt me. If you do this I'll die."

"You're already dead."

She wraps her arms around me and holds me tight. "Please come to the house so we can talk. I don't understand what's wrong."

"The sun's rising. I can't wait too long."

She pulls away to look into my eyes. "There's more sunrises, okay?" She takes my hand and leads me to the beach, over the slight rise, up the dune, to the steps and the deck. We take turns rinsing sand from our feet with a water hose and go inside. Scotty undresses me, sits me on a sofa, and wraps towels around me. "I need to change, be right back." Bare feet pad to the bedroom; she returns in a robe and sits beside me. "Want some coffee to warm us up?"

"I'm all right if you are."

She leans against me, places her head on my shoulder, and slips a hand around my waist. "I don't understand what's wrong. Don't you know I love you?"

"I love you too."

"Why were your shoes beside those sandals on the fence?"

I close my eyes. Did I ever tell Scotty about Andy leaving her sandals on the fence that morning?

"Jake."

I open my eyes.

Scotty's green eyes meet mine. "Do you remember the guy on the ferry whose wife died when the yacht exploded in the Florida Keys?"

"He was a jerk."

"Do you remember how I flattened his tire?"

"That was you? I thought that was Alex?"

"Who do you think I am?"

"You're someone I love."

Scotty turns my face toward her, pauses to stare, and covers my beard with one hand and my forehead with her other hand. "Is it really ... I can't ... I can't believe ..." She gets up from the sofa, stares at me again, and sits again. "I'm about to explode with questions but that doesn't matter—what matters is you." Her chest expands with a deep breath. "I never asked your last name, what is it?"

"Smith."

"Okay, we're getting somewhere. Is Jake your first or your middle name?"

"It's my middle name. My first name is Jonathan."

"Really?"

"Yeah, why?"

"I need to tell you about the woman who died on that yacht."

"I know all about it."

"Not from my point of view. First, I want to tell you why I rented this house. A man and his wife got married in 2019 and spent only one night here before he found her drowned in the surf the next morning. Rumor has it that he was so devastated by her death, he was crying and had just thrown up when an elderly man walking a dog found him and called 911. I rented this house because I wanted another couple who loves each other as much as we do to stay here. It's silly, but I hope that man somehow understands how important love is, and how he

318

can find love again if he only lets it into his heart." Scotty gets up. "I'm making coffee before I freeze."

I follow her. "I miss your green eyes."

"What about Alex's brown eyes? Did you like those?"

"Alex is great."

Scotty measures coffee into the maker. "How about Izzie?"

"I like it when she calls me daddy."

"Do you know where we are? I understand if you don't. I've been taking some psychology classes online, and I think I know what's going on."

"Alex brought me here. Do you know where she is?"

"I'll tell you in a minute. Let me get the suitcases from the bedroom and bring them in here so we can change."

Scotty comes back, opens one suitcase, and slips jeans and a sweatshirt on. She must've been working out in Heaven: she's in great shape. I take jeans and a sweater from the other suitcase and put them on. Scotty puts on socks from her suitcase, gets socks from the other suitcase, and slips them on my feet. She pours coffee and we sit on the sofa.

"Back to my story. Rumor has it that the man whose wife died got drunk a week later, and the woman, whose husband is a jerk, took him with her to the Florida Keys."

I don't understand why Scotty's telling me things she knows, but I'll play along. Otherwise she might not let me go to meet her and Andy in the sunrise tomorrow.

"What happened then?"

"You met her husband on the ferry. You saw how he is."

In the middle of sipping coffee, I swallow. "He's a jerk."

"Let's be blunt, okay? He's an asshole."

"And?"

"The woman and man whose wife died fell in love on their trip to the Keys. The wanted to come back and get married, but she knew her asshole husband would make their lives miserable. She was also afraid of how he would influence her baby, and she couldn't let that happen."

"That makes sense."

"You realize she was prepared to do anything to keep that from happening, right?"

"She was a mom. That's what moms do."

"Can you forgive her for what she did? She only did it because she was desperate."

"I can ..." I close my eyes and shake my head. Something's not ... something's not right at all. Scotty's fingertips touch my face. No, that's not right either—Scotty's dead. I open my eyes. "Alex? Where've you been?"

"I've been loving you, Jake."

"Why are your eyes green?"

The faintest of smiles barely quirks her lower lip downward. "I wear contact lenses." She kisses my cheek. "I stayed with Sammy and Mary Lou for a year. She cut and dyed my hair the night you left. Ted didn't even come by—all he did was call and tell Sammy he'd talked to the Coast Guard. I wanted to slap myself for not getting your phone number. Then I wanted to throw myself off Basnight Bridge when I couldn't find you in Raleigh. All every receptionist at every MRI sales office said was former employees' names were confidential. When Ted told me at that resort how I needed a better disguise to fool him, he was right. I went back to Sammy and Mary Lou's and started swimming and dieting. That helped but it wasn't enough. I pierced my ear like it is now, pierced my eyebrow too. I knew that would help with my disguise. Do you have any idea how much I missed you and wanted to find you? You're the guy I've been waiting for all this time. I did all that and rented a house near Manteo because I knew you'd come back eventually."

"I didn't know you wore contacts."

"You still don't get it, do you?"

"I get you're Alex and you love me."

She gets up and paces the floor. "You have post-traumatic stress disorder because of Andy's and Scotty's deaths and you were going to drown yourself." She stops to face me. "I need you to snap out of it once and for all, so I'll just say it."

She kneels between my knees and looks into my eyes. "I'm not Alex, Jonathan, I'm Scotty. Sammy and Mary Lou helped me fake my death so I could get away from Ted. We knew it would devastate you but I thought I could find you."

She shakes her head slowly. "I'm sure you're wondering why Sammy said I went down into the engine room and how the Coast Guard said they found my teeth. I took the teeth from that skull in my office. I taped the test button for the fume alarm down when I went to the yacht, not before, and Sammy lied about it to help me. There's a drain valve on the diesel tank and I opened it. Then I climbed to the deck and threw a book of lit matches in a corner of the engine room to give me time to run to the bow and dive off."

Don't believe her, Jake. It's just a story to stop you from joining Andy and Scotty in the ocean. C'mon now, time to get up and get to the beach before the sun gets too high.

Something about the old Jake sounds off. I can't explain it, he just sounds off. I focus on Alex's green—I thought Alex had brown eyes. This is crazy ... I'm crazy. Then again, maybe not. I focus on Alex's green eyes again, taking them in, trying to see inside her. I can't. Regardless, I can ask her something that might help. "Why did you kidnap me? You didn't need me to fake your death."

"I already told you how it made me feel to see you so upset about losing your wife. I've always wanted a man to love me for me and not some trophy wife like Ted married me for. It tore me up to let you think I was dead. It tore me up to let Lizzie

J. Willis Sanders

think that too, but I needed her to be genuinely upset so you'd leave before Ted got there. Sammy was right when he said Ted would blame the explosion on you if he could. Lucky for us he didn't come over, and you were on a bus if he did."

Alex gets up from her knees and sits on the sofa beside me. "I'm sorry I hurt you, but I was even more desperate after we fell in love." She takes the studs from her right ear, including the one in her eyebrow, and drops them to the coffee table. Then she sweeps her bangs back and puffs up her cheeks. "Well, who am I?"

C'mon, Jake. You pays your money, you takes your—

Something brightens inside my skull—a flare of light, a hint of vanilla, a pair of incandescent green eyes, a smile with its slightly quirked lower lip—and it all silences the old Jake's voice.

I slowly raise my palm to one tanned cheek, rub a slow circle there, long to kiss there. She asked me to forgive her and I already have.

"You're the woman who made me forget everything about the Hemingway Museum, except the garden and a certain palm tree."

"I'm glad you remember something, even if it's just that."

I'm tempted to cry, but happiness—pure and soul-cleansing—shoves the pain away. "Do you remember the words to that song you wrote?"

"Did you—" The catch in Scotty's voice tells me she's almost ready to cry too, but a gorgeous smile tells me she's happy like I am—too happy to allow regret to ruin our reunion. Tears wet her eyes. She takes my hand from her cheek and kisses the palm. "Did you finish my song for me?"

I go to the kitchen for the pad and pen, and she says, "You scared me to death with that note you left on the coffee table. I dropped it on the beach and that's where it'll stay."

On the sofa again, I give her the pad. "You first. If you remember your song after three years, I should be able to come up with something."

Scotty writes, and I marvel at how calm we are. Most anyone who went through what we went through would be crying and who knows what all, but I'm beginning to think how, when two people who love each other as much as we do are apart—but still alive—something deep down inside us knows we'll be together again one day. She pauses, and I nudge her with my elbow. "What's wrong, Skipper? Can't remember it?"

"I'll 'Skipper' you, Gilligan. Shut up and let me concentrate."

"Hey, at least it's not a headbutt."

"It will be if you keep talking." She continues to write, brow furrowing, forehead wrinkling, and gives me the pad. "There you go, smart ass, your turn."

I read what Scotty wrote. "I love the line about you needing a man who can lift you off the ground. Good thing you lost that flabby butt, huh?"

"You didn't mind it when I backed up to you in the shower."

"I like the lines about banana pudding and peach pie alamode."

"The line about peach pie is to honor Mom."

I put the pad on the coffee table and lean over to write. "I'm lucky, all I need to write is one verse. You already wrote a verse and a chorus."

Scotty smacks the back of my head. "Hurry up, Gilligan. I've got something else to tell you."

Despite dying to know what Scotty means, I work out a verse, add her chorus after it, and hold the pad where we both can read it.

I'm tougher than I look, I'm softer than I sound
I'd love to find the sweetest man, who can lift me off the ground
Sail me across the seven seas, and love me all night long
But I'd settle for the simple things, with them I'd do no wrong
But I'd settle for the simple things, with him I'd do no wrong
Love me now, please don't wait
Life's too short to throw away, I need you on my plate
Butter pecan doesn't stand a chance, with you here by my side
But hot peach pie, alamode, might tempt me for a while.
But hot peach pie, alamode, might tempt me for a while.
Until you smile.
I'm just a southern girl, with salt down in my soul
Tryin' to find the sweetest man, who'll treat me like pure gold
Hold me close, hold me long,
Kisses in the morning light, talk till the breath of dawn
Kisses in the morning light, talk till the breath of dawn
Love me now, please don't wait
Life's too short to throw away, I need you on my plate
Butter pecan doesn't stand a chance, with you here by my side
But hot peach pie, alamode, might tempt me for a while.
But hot peach pie, alamode, might tempt me for a while.
Until you smile.

"'A southern girl with salt down in her soul.' Great job, Gilligan. You can sing it when we get married. Izzie will make a great flower girl."

I drop the pad and pen on the coffee table. "What else are you gonna tell me?"

"By now you realize Izzie was born in the Keys, while I stayed with Sammy and Mary Lou and exercised and dieted my

324

behind off. Being a former sheriff, and knowing where to find the criminal element, has its perks. I found a guy to help me with new ID and a birth certificate. That's how I came to be Alex Hannah."

"You never told me your last name either. I guess we'll have to use Alex Hannah the rest of our lives so Ted will leave us alone."

"Alex Smith when we get married."

"Was Lizzie upset when she found out you faked your death?"

"She didn't call me Scooty Poot for a week."

"Your purse is on top of my fridge."

"I wanted you to have that for when you got down about my death. You know, because of the cross necklace."

"I sold your rings to help buy my house."

"Can you imagine how I felt when your hairy self came to the door of *my* house that night?"

"Now it'll be *our* house."

"Do you mind calling me Alex?"

"Not if you don't mind calling me Jake. That's what everyone calls me, but you pissed me off that day in your office so bad, all you were gonna get was Jonathan. What else are you gonna tell me?"

"I'm hungry. Want to go out or eat in?"

"In, so you can tell me whatever it is you're gonna tell me."

We go to the kitchen. Alex/Scotty—this is really weird, but I'll get used to it—takes eggs and bacon from the fridge.

"I like my body a lot more like this," she says, putting them on the counter, "but I thought we'd eat whatever this week." She places a pan on the stove. "Did my death make you lose weight and go Santa Claus on me?"

"It was something I found out about Andy."

"Your tone says it wasn't good."

"She was sleeping around on me. The worst thing of all is she was doing it with my best friend and her best friend."

"A threesome with your best friends?"

"With other people too." I get a knife from a drawer and open the bacon. "I went a little crazy and thought about shooting my friend." I laugh. Alex pauses from cracking eggs into a bowl.

"What's so funny?" she says.

"I broke his nose with a head butt instead of shooting him. The bones *do* crunch."

"Beats the heck out of going to prison for shooting someone. How did you lose the weight?"

"Well, I was arrested for head butting the guy. I don't remember some of it, but I remember taking a dump and a pee in my holding cell. My attorney came and said the judge wanted me to voluntarily go to a mental health facility. Paul—he's the guy I head butted—dropped the charges because I paid his medical bills and to have his car painted after I keyed it."

"What happened in the medical facility?"

"You won't like one aspect of it."

Whipping the eggs in a bowl, Alex stops. "Don't tell me that's where you met your sex buddy?"

"Believe it or not, if it wasn't for her, I might still be in that place. Leon—he's the doctor who was treating the group I was in—left us alone one day because I mentioned how I wanted to be a dad, and how what was wrong with her was because of a child." I put another pan on the stove. "She accidentally left her daughter in a car seat in a hot car."

Alex faces me. "Don't tell me her daughter ..."

"Afraid so. Tammy—that's her name—broke down after she told me about her daughter. I broke down too, from the memory of your yacht burning."

Alex slips her arms around me. "I wouldn't have faked my death if there were any other way to get away from Ted. You know that, right?"

"I understand. The night before, I could tell you were really thinking about something."

"Uh-huh, enough to smoke a cigarette. That was the last one."

Eggs and bacon done, we reheat our coffee and go to the breakfast nook overlooking the beach. Alex tells me how she hadn't seen Ted until that day on the ferry to Ocracoke, and it proved her disguise was a lot better than the one she tried at the resort that day. I tell her about my bike riding expeditions in North Carolina and Virginia, including my Christmas with Mom and Mikey. We talk about getting married and decide not to make a big deal over it, just to invite Greg and his sister and her husband and their kids, Jimmy and Nora.

Between bites of eggs, bacon, and swallows of coffee, I glance around, realizing I'm now comfortable being in Endless Love.

"Jake?"

"Yeah?"

"I remember seeing Andy's sandals on the fence when I answered the 911 call that day. When I saw your loafers on the fence and you in the water while ago, I had no idea you were her husband. I thought you might've heard about what happened here and decided to kill yourself because of the woman you said you loved in your past."

"Now you know that woman was you."

"And I'm glad she is."

We take our dishes to the sink. Alex runs water and adds soap. "I'll wash, you dry. We might as well get used to it, right?"

I look through the cabinets for a dish towel. "Sounds good to me, the soon to be Mrs. Smith."

Alex cuts off the water. "I wanted us to have breakfast and calm all our emotions before I tell you this."

"I hope it's something good."

"Remember how I thought I was a month pregnant with Ted's baby when we met?"

"What do you mean 'thought?' How can that be something you just think?"

"I missed my period and thought I was pregnant."

"You didn't get one of those home pregnancy tests?"

"I didn't see the need."

"But you had Izzie."

"If Izzie was born in June, she would've been Ted's. When was her birthday and what does that tell you?"

I do the math in my head. If Scotty wasn't pregnant while we were going at it on our Florida Keys vacation, and since Izzie was born a month later in July, that means …

My mouth falls open and Alex laughs. "Ladies and gentlemen, I do believe the light bulb has gone off." She holds her hand to my mouth as if she has a microphone. "Tell me, Mr. Smith, how does it feel to be a daddy, Daddy?"

"She's really …? Izzie's really …?"

"Sorry, ladies and gentlemen, Daddy's speechless." Alex lowers the pretend microphone.

"Wait a minute. If Izzie's mine, you didn't need to make yourself over to hide from Ted. We could've taken a DNA test and come back here and told him to take a flying leap off a short pier."

Alex pats my knee. "I'm the wannabe writer, remember? Where's the plot hole in all that?"

"There aren't any if Izzie's mine."

"Do you think we could waltz back here and tell Ted about Izzie after I blew up his yacht and faked my death? Not only would he file charges and want me to pay for his yacht, law enforcement would file charges against me for faking my death."

"Huh." I shake my head. "Thanks for closing my plot hole."

After everything Scotty and Jonathan—now Alex and I— have gone through, the news that Izzie is my daughter makes me realize how important family is.

"I believe you, but my mom won't like any explanation I tell her."

Alex lowers her head. "I didn't think about that. It wouldn't sound good for you to sleep with another woman less than a month after Andy ... well, you know."

"It's no biggy. I'll tell her I adopted Izzie because her dad is a scuzzball. It's not like I see her much anyway."

"Do you think she'll like me?"

"Does it matter?"

"Maybe I'll leave the ear and eyebrow studs at home and dye my hair all blonde instead of streaked green. I didn't like doing all that stuff anyway, but I had to do what I had to do."

I pull Alex to me. Her warmth in my arms is as amazing as anything I've ever experienced. Well, except for the fact that I'm a dad.

"Jonathan?"

"What happened to Jake?"

"I have to get used to it. Remember what I told you about Greg and his bipolar disorder?"

I nod. "You said it started after a car accident."

"Did Andy ever have an accident? Or maybe a medical scare?"

"You think she could've had bipolar disorder like Greg?"

"Want more coffee? I don't mind washing two more mugs and I'd rather sit."

I get two mugs and fill them. We go back to the breakfast nook. "Does your theory have anything to do with those psychology classes you're taking?"

"Part of the reason I started taking them was because I wanted to see if Andy's behavior could be explained. I saw how upset you were about her death, and I wanted to know if it was an accident or not." Alex pauses to sip coffee. I do too.

"What did you find out?"

"Bipolar disorder can be inherited. Does Andy's mom have any kind of mental problems?"

In the middle of a sip of coffee, I lower the mug. "Damn."

"What?"

"I feel for Stan."

"Why?"

"You know how some men are with medical stuff. Marie—that's Andy's mom—is a hoarder. Stan also told me how he catches her up in the middle of the night, in the one room where he lets her keep the stuff."

"Not sleeping is one of the symptoms of bipolar disorder. Did Andy do anything like that?"

"I'd find her awake in the middle of the night at times. The next day she'd talk a lot more about lights and galaxies, like she did that night at the restaurant."

"Not getting enough sleep makes bipolar disorder worse. Before Greg was diagnosed, I found him on my deck a few times at night."

I sip coffee again. How will Stan feel when he learns Marie could've been treated and lived normally for however long she's been sick? If I'm lucky—and I'm running a great streak of luck at the moment, having reunited with Scotty and found out I'm a dad—he'll be too happy about Marie getting better than to blame himself.

Drinking coffee, Alex lowers the mug. "When you said you feel for Stan, do you mean because he'll blame himself for what happened to Andy?"

"I mean he might blame himself for not getting his wife any help. I hope not. I blamed myself for Andy's death without any reason why. Is sleeping with multiple people a symptom of bipolar disorder too?"

"It varies from person to person, but it sometimes is."

"I can't believe this. If I had known Andy's sleeping with other people was a symptom of bipolar disorder, I could've helped her get treatment. That and all those other symptoms too."

"You're not the only person in the world who didn't know about bipolar disorder until a loved one was diagnosed."

"I just wish I knew about it before Andy drowned herself."

"I know you do. What's important now is telling Stan so Marie can see a doctor and get the help she needs."

As much as Andy's death weighs on my shoulders, Alex is right. "I'll tell him as soon as I can."

Alex takes our coffee mugs to the kitchen sink, empties and refills them. "Our coffee got cold."

She comes back to the breakfast nook. "When Andy died, I looked all over this house for a suicide note. As troubled as she was, and as much as you loved her, I still think she loved you."

"But you didn't find a note."

"I didn't know where to look then."

"You know where to look now?"

"Remember when you told me how the chandelier in the restaurant fascinated her? When she told you it was a portal to another galaxy?"

"What does that have to do with her leaving a note?"

"People with bipolar disorder sometimes feel like they have a special purpose in life. If Andy thought she could enter another galaxy through a light, that might be why she drowned herself by walking toward the sunrise." Alex flips the switch for the light over the breakfast nook table. "I wouldn't be surprised if she left you a note in one of the lights."

We study the fixture, a bunch of enclosed globes no bigger than a light bulb. No note is visible. Alex flips the switch off and starts toward the kitchen. "Hey," I say.

She stops. "What?"

"You don't have a sister. Why were you out my way that night?"

"I'd get a notion to drive by my parents farm once in a while."

"Was Izzie with you?"

"She was with Greg."

"How did you keep all your lies straight?"

"The car was okay too. It cranked right up when the tow guy came. I batted my eyelashes at him and he went on home without pay like a good boy."

"Wrapped him around your pinky, huh?"

"Just like I did you on *Out for Fun*. Little did I know I'd fall in love with you." Alex goes to the kitchen. "These lights are the same as the breakfast nook and the ones over the dining room table."

"Wanna split up and check all the lights in the house?"

"Let's check the bedroom first. I used the nightstand lamp last night, but the fixture over the bed is one of those old styles that looks like a flying saucer."

I follow Alex to the hall. "You sure came up with a good disguise for Ted."

"My bottom teeth were the worst. Had to wear braces for a year." In the bedroom, Alex flips the light switch and points at the fixture hanging from the ceiling. "My past as a sheriff is paying off, there's your note."

The shadow of what looks like a folded piece of paper blocks part of the light in the fixture. "She must've done that while I was in the bathroom, getting ready for bed."

Alex climbs on the bed, takes the paper from inside the fixture, and sits on the covers. "Do you want me to read it first in case it upsets you?"

I sit beside her. "That might be a good idea."

She reads. The tendons in her neck tighten with a hard swallow. "She really loved you, Jake. It's so sad how mental illnesses like bipolar disorder can ruin lives without the person or the people around them even knowing they have it."

"Which is why I need to tell Stan about Marie as soon as possible." I take the note from Alex.

Dear Jake,

My fingers shake; my eyes fill. I look at Alex. "I don't know if I can do this."

She kisses my cheek. "You need closure, Jake. This will help."

"You are so amazing. If someone said it wouldn't bother me for a woman I love to fake her death and not tell me about it, I'd tell them they had lost their mind."

"I tried to find you as hard as I knew how. I didn't decide to fake my death until that night you caught me smoking, and I completely forgot about not having your phone number."

"Hey, we're together now and that's what matters." I return to Andy's note.

Dear Jake,

You know I have trouble sleeping and last night was the same. My mind fills with thought after thought when that happens, but tonight all I can do is watch you while you sleep. Loving you is the best thing in my life, Jake, and it always will be.

I can't say what, but I've done things I'm ashamed of, things no woman should do when she loves a man as much as I love you. If you knew what I did, I think you'd forgive me because I know something's wrong with me. Then there's times when I feel like I rule the world, when everything shines like when the sun rises over the ocean. I can feel that happening now, and it's time I follow the portal of light to my new galaxy. In some way or another, whether it's with the memory of your smile or the memory of us making love, you'll always be with me. Please don't let this break you. You have a huge heart, and there's someone else out there to share it with until we're together again.
Love always and forever,
Andy

Like when I read Scotty's song, I press the note into my eyes and cry. Yes, Andy was the love of my life, and even better than that, she knew it. Now, with her blessing, I have another love of my life in Scotty ... well, in Alex. And we have a daughter to love too. Andy would be pleased.

Alex rubs my back. "See? I told you she loved you."

I lower the wet paper from my eyes and fold it. I'll never read it again, but I'll have it put in my suit coat pocket when death finally takes me.

Alex takes the paper and puts it on the nightstand. "Are you okay? You have such a tender heart."

I manage a weak smile. "I'm getting married to the second love of my life and I'm a daddy too. What does that tell you?"

"Good. Monday we'll go to the Dare County Register of Deeds Office and get the marriage license, and ..."

"*And* what? You've got the same devious look in your gorgeous green eyes that you had when you got in the shower naked."

"Like I did on *Out for Fun,* right? When you couldn't stop looking at my flabby behind in the mirror while you were shaving, right?"

"Exactly."

"I propose we get the license and find a minister and get married. Then we'll go get Izzie and come back here for the rest of the week."

"Not a bad idea. Izzie already thinks I'm her daddy."

"You will be after were married. We can tell Greg and everyone else next weekend."

I get up from the bed and look at my watch. "Do you mind if we go see Stan? I'd like to tell him so he can make plans to help Marie as soon as possible."

Alex stands. "Don't forget your loafers on the fence."

I leave for the fence, take my loafers and Andy's sandals off the narrow strips of wood, and go to the deck to rinse the sand off my feet. At the door, I start to go inside for a towel to dry my feet but sit at the picnic table instead. Inside, at the kitchen sink, Alex is washing the coffee mugs we left when we talked about the possibility of Andy having bipolar disorder. I face the beach.

Three years ago today I lost Andy. In my wildest dreams I never thought I'd be back here now, as happy as I've ever been.

And a daddy too.

The midmorning sun glares onto the beach, brightening the sand. Here and there a beachcomber stops to study a shell. If they like it, they pocket it and continue on their way. If not, they search for some other bit of curiosity: a treasure to take home from the Outer Banks.

A flock of sanderlings flutters across the waves from the south and darts to the rise where the surf spreads a blanket of white lace on the sand, leaving a wet sheen shining in the sunlight.

The beach is a never-ending miracle of life and death. Here Andy died and here I was born, delivered by Alex, delivered further by the promise of fatherhood.

Monday, before we get married, I'll run to a florist for some flowers for our flower girl, Izzie. I'll get some daisies too, and Alex and I can put them in her hair. She'll look up at us, green eyes wide and questioning, and I'll tell her how much I love her and her mama. Alex will explain how we're getting married, and how she'll always have a daddy, night and day and every minute in between, especially when it's time to talk about boys and learning to drive. Now that I think about it, Izzie looks like me with all those brown curls, and she looks like Alex, with the way her lower lips quirks downward when she grins. I smile at the thought.

After the ceremony, I'll have Alex drive to the farm house so I can charge my phone and call Stan to see if Marie's gotten a doctor appointment yet. The news that Marie could've gotten better a lot sooner will hurt, but Stan's made of stern stuff: the brine of the Atlantic, the heart of a working man, the soul of a father and of a husband. Yes, he might shed a tear when we tell him this afternoon, and yes, I might have to explain how I blamed myself for Andy's death while shedding a tear also, but if I know Stan, and I do, he'll say that's the last thing Andy would want.

I'll ask him to phone me when Marie's better. The saddest part of this is how he'll have to tell her about Andy, and I'll make sure to wait until she works through her grief before I ask Alex if we can invite them over for supper one night.

Regardless of how long it takes for her to get better—six months, a year, or more—when we're done eating, maybe having peach pie alamode on a picnic table in the back yard in the shade of the oaks—home-made ice cream, naturally—I'll tell them how Izzie needs a fill-in grandma and grandpa close by: a grandma for hugs and cookies and a grandpa to teach her how to fish and read the tides.

Especially the tides of life.

Maybe by then I can tell them how Izzie has a brother or a sister on the way, one who needs those lessons as much as she does.

And maybe, just maybe, we can take Izzie to see her other grandma, Scotty's mom, who's a short drive away in Elizabeth City. I don't know how far the grip of Alzheimer's has taken her from her daughter, but I hope some glint of recognition will spark within her eyes when she realizes her family has grown by not only Izzie, but by me, her son-in-law.

The beach is a never-ending miracle of life and death. Humans are grains of sand, the detritus of time rolling on wave after wave. If everyone is as blessed as Alex and I, we cling to one another with love, and that's all each of us—in our human frailty—can hope for.

The mind is both a blessing and a curse. Neurons and synapses communicate in a symphony of complicated simplicity that no scientist has yet to unravel. Artists and musical geniuses named Rembrandt and DaVinci, Mozart and Bach, have populated our world for hundreds of years, sharing their gifts, yet some of the most gifted individuals are virtual unknowns, savants born either blind or mentally challenged, but who can teach themselves to play a piano to the point of recreating a song after hearing it once, or who can perform complicated mathematical problems by identifying numbers with colors, or who can— I stop because this intriguing list is endless.

But then we have people like Andy, Marie, Greg, and Freddy, the electric guitar player I met at the mental health facility, and others all around us. They spend long nights mulling over their existence in their search for significance until a diagnosis and treatment sets them free.

Stan either experienced shame or weakness or both from his inability to cope with Marie's illness, along with the fear of the unknown. He's not the only individual to do that, who has done that, or who will do that, and he's not the least bit alone in his failure. And to think, all that might help someone with bipolar disorder is a medicine called lithium.

I'm no doctor and don't claim to be—I'm sure some cases of bipolar disorder, like all illnesses, require more complicated treatments—but Alex's knowledge has left me with two important facts: mental illness is not something to be ashamed of, and it's a misunderstood illness that needs understanding. I'm a firsthand witness to those facts.

Alex joins me at the picnic table; the warmth of her at my side is a comfort in the cool October air. My loafers and Andy's sandals sit on the weathered boards. Alex touches each but says nothing.

I've never been sure about much of anything in my life, but I'm sure about Alex. She's thinking how lucky we are to have found each other—not once but twice. She's thinking how sad it is that Andy lost her life to such a treatable illness and, most importantly of all, she's wondering how, in all the beaches of all the world, from the Outer Banks, to the Florida Keys, to the Turks and Caicos, did she and I—two miniscule grains of sand amongst all the other miniscule grains of sand—manage to find each other on a cold October morning three years ago?

She kisses me, takes my hand, and leads me to the bedroom, where we will attempt to answer that question physically and emotionally, if not scientifically.

Dear Andy,

Thank you for the blessing you gave me in your letter those three short years ago. You knew me better than I knew myself, and you knew I'm one of those men who exists to find his soulmate: two grains of sand on a beach, two sea oat stalks whistling in the wind, two people living as one until they're twin stars, always and forever, twinkling over a seaward sky.

See you soon,
Love, Jake.

Book Club Questions

1. What did you like best about this book?

2. What did you like least about this book?

3. What other books did this one remind you of?

4. Which characters did you like best?

5. Which characters did you like least?

6. If this book were a movie, who would you choose to play the characters?

7. What other books by this author have you read? How did they compare to this book?

8. What feelings did this book evoke in you?

9. If you got the chance to ask the author of this book one question, what would it be?

10. Which character in the book would you most like to meet?

11. What do you think of the book's title? How does it relate to the book's contents? What other title might you choose?

12. What do you think the author's purpose was in writing this book? What ideas was he or she trying to get across?

13. How original and unique was this book?

14. Did this book seem realistic?

15. How well do you think the author built the world in the book?

16. Did the characters seem believable to you? Did they remind you of anyone?

17. What did you already know about this book's subject before you read this book?

18. What new things did you learn?

19. What questions do you still have?

20. Were you happy with the ending?

Please enjoy the first chapter from *The Coincidence of Hope,* coming in the spring of 2022.

Visitors

The Ardennes American Cemetery
Neuville-en-Condroz, Belgium
December 6, 2011

Surrounding Joe Matthan, hundreds of white crosses fill the vast cemetery. Beyond them, in front of a backdrop of leafless trees, each bone-gray in the dawn, an American flag hangs from its pole. The sun rises. Through the trees its light slashes the crosses with crimson, followed by orange, followed by yellow. Each cross is a reminder to humanity of the offerings beneath them, many forgotten. The sun climbs. The shimmering globe bursts above the trees. Frost sparkles on the brown grass. Here and there, patches of snow glitter with rainbow hues. Another day is born. Another day to live. Another day to die. The stone crosses now reflect the light, white and crisp, and Joe is on the way to find his own grave.

For decades it's the same thing: wake up inside a body not his, muscles not his, bones not his. Even the brain isn't his, nor the touch, nor the vision or hearing, nor the taste or smell, although he experiences them all. He is a ghost, a spirit, an essence without a body. He has no idea why, yet this is his existence. Each host either eats breakfast or doesn't, dresses or doesn't, or puts on a robe and stares in a mirror or out a window. Sometimes they don't get up. Sometimes they cry. Sometimes they smile. Sometimes they marry. Sometimes they divorce. Of all the things they might do, most vary. Some go to work and some don't. Some kiss a significant other and some don't. Some wake their kids for school and some don't. Joe prefers the hosts in a happy marriage. Kids are a plus.

He hates how it doesn't always happen that way.

A few days ago, when his last host, a fifty-eight-year-old plumber—he loved putting a model train around the Christmas tree for his grandkids—died from colon cancer, he found himself within the body of a young man dressing in a United States Army uniform. This morning the young man is looking for Joe's headstone in the Ardennes American Cemetery in Belgium. The memorial center's chaplain said some people are coming to see Private Matthan's grave for the first time, and it's the young man's job to attend them during the visit. Although Joe is excited to see who's coming, he's afraid to see his own grave. Death isn't fun, but living this way isn't fun either. He's gotten tired of it over the years, although bored is a better word.

Within the multitude of white crosses—5,329 to be exact, 792 of them unnamed— the young man searches. His breath plumes. Sunlight melts the frost, and the droplets dapple his black shoes. The air is fresh and clean. The intense aroma reminds Joe of a snowstorm back home. The young man's musky anti-perspirant does not.

He turns, takes a few more steps, and stops at a cross to lean closer.

Joseph S. Matthan

PFC, 106th Infantry Div., Nebraska

Dec. 17, 1944

Joe nods his phantom head. *That's me all right. I wonder why I wasn't shipped back home? It's not like my injuries were that bad.*

Nodding as if acknowledging either the location of the grave or the sacrifice, the young man stands.

It's then that Joe sees a freshly dug hole, small and rectangular, in his grave. The young man scratches his head as if he doesn't know anything about it. The chaplain didn't mention it, so it must be a mystery. He and Joe see something in their peripheral vision, and the young man turns.

In the distance, leaving the huge memorial building constructed of gleaming marble, three figures enter the morning sun. One, an elderly woman, walks slow and a bit stooped over. The second, a middle-aged man with blond hair, carries what resembles a small chest made of dark wood, wrapped in clear plastic. The last is the uniformed Army chaplain.

The three people come closer. The elderly woman's face grows clearer, along with the face of the blond man.

Then, like the exploding grenade that ended Joe's dreams of life and love so long ago, the ghostly remains of his heart bursts with astonishment as he recognizes exactly who these two people are.

About the Author

J. Willis Sanders lives in southern Virginia, with his wife and several stringed musical instruments.

With several novels published and more on the way, he enjoys crafting intriguing characters with equally intriguing conflicts to overcome. He also loves the natural world and, more often than not, his stories include those settings. Most also utilize intense love relationships and layered themes.

His first novel (not this one, but he plans to publish it) is a ghostly World War II era historical that takes place mostly in the midwestern United States, which utilizes some little-known facts about German POW camps there at that time. It's the first of a three-book series, in which characters from the first book continue their lives.

Although he loves history, he has written several contemporary novels as well, and some include interesting paranormal twists, both with and without religious themes.

He also loves the Outer Banks of North Carolina, and has published three novels within different time frames based on the area, what he calls his Outer Banks of North Carolina Series.

Another genre he enjoys is thriller novels, so he is launching a series with a main female character named Reid Stone.

Other hobbies include reading (of course), vegetable gardening, playing music with friends, and songwriting, some of which are in a few of his novels.

To follow the author's work, please visit any of the following:

https://jwillissanders.wixsite.com/writer

https://www.facebook.com/J-Willis-Sanders-874367072622901

https://www.amazon.com/J-Willis-Sanders/e/B092RZG6MC?ref_=dbs_p_ebk_r00_abau_000000

Readers: to help those considering a purchase, please consider leaving a review on Amazon.com, Goodreads.com, or wherever you purchased this book.
Thank you.

CPSIA information can be obtained
at www.ICGtesting.com
Printed in the USA
LVHW100721140622
721182LV00002B/104

9 781954 763159